RUNEFANG

THE MIGHTY PROVINCE of Wissenland comes under attack from an undead horde, led by a seemingly indestructible wight lord whose deathless forces vanquish all who oppose them. The fate of the state lies in the balance and as the Imperial troops are pushed remorselessly back, the elector count and his advisors come up with a desperate plan. They must find the missing Solland runefang, for with this legendary weapon they will surely win the day. Baron von Rabwald and a small force of men head into the mountains to seek the sword, unaware that a rival band of warriors dogs their steps. Can Rabwald and his men find the runefang and emerge from the mountains alive, let alone get the sword back in time to turn the tide of battle?

Runefang is an explosive tale of fantasy adventure from C.L. Werner, author of the Witch Hunter novels.

A WARHAMMER NOVEL

RUNEFANG

C. L. WERNER

For Helmer, who always reminds me how not to end a book.

A BLACK LIBRARY PUBLICATION

First published in Great Britain in 2008 by
BL Publishing,
Games Workshop Ltd.,
Willow Road, Nottingham,
NG7 2WS, UK

10 9 8 7 6 5 4 3 2 1

Cover illustration by Ralph Horsley
Map by Nuala Kinrade.

A CIP record for this book is available from the British Library.

ISBN 13: 978 1 84416 548 3
ISBN 10: 1 84416 548 5

Distributed in the US by Simon & Schuster
1230 Avenue of the Americas, New York, NY 10020.

See the Black Library on the Internet at
www.blacklibrary.com

Find out more about Games Workshop
and the world of Warhammer at
www.games-workshop.com

THIS IS A DARK age, a bloody age, an age of daemons and of sorcery. It is an age of battle and death, and of the world's ending. Amidst all of the fire, flame and fury it is a time, too, of mighty heroes, of bold deeds and great courage.

AT THE HEART of the Old World sprawls the Empire, the largest and most powerful of the human realms. Known for its engineers, sorcerers, traders and soldiers, it is a land of great mountains, mighty rivers, dark forests and vast cities. It is a land riven by uncertainty, as three pretenders all vye for control of the Imperial throne.

BUT THESE ARE far from civilised times. Across the length and breadth of the Old World, from the knightly palaces of Bretonnia to ice-bound Kislev in the far north, come rumblings of war. In the towering Worlds Edge Mountains, the orc tribes are gathering for another assault. Bandits and renegades harry the wild southern lands of the Border Princes. There are rumours of rat-things, the skaven, emerging from the sewers and swamps across the land. And from the northern wildernesses there is the ever-present threat of Chaos, of daemons and beastmen corrupted by the foul powers of the Dark Gods. As the time of battle draws ever near, the Empire needs heroes like never before.

PROLOGUE

In that time, the lands of Sigmar were sore beset by wicked-
ness and malice. For the sake of greed, men turned their
swords against sovereign and son. For the sake of glory, men
bowed before false crowns and false blood. For the sake of
power, men forgot their Lord Sigmar and sought to unmake
that which He had forged in courage, in valour and in
might. Three thrones were raised, to slake the hubris of
usurpers, and men forgot which was their rightful liege. The
land was without master. The country became a domain of
wolves and goblins. The city became the lair of pestilence and
blight. The Empire was slain, not by the fang of the lion
without, but by the gnawing of the worm within. Brother for-
got brother and men turned their faces from the sun.

While petty lords built petty crowns and named themselves
emperor of all, while ragged armies fought ragged wars and
called slaughter glory, ancient evils stirred in the black places
they had been driven into. Evil revelled in the unseeing lust

of men, for by such folly would it know its hour. Even as the lords squabbled over their titles and honours, even as the barons made sport of war, old enemies crept back from the shadows, to test the mettle of the broken land.

With fire and steel, the Great Beast descended from the mountains, driving all before him. Ironclaw his teaming horde named him, and upon him the powers of Old Night smiled. Numberless was the host he led, a swarming mass of snarling horror come from the wastes to reclaim the land that man had squandered. Slinking goblin, raging orc and mighty troll, all flocked to serve the Ironclaw. Like a storm, his host crashed down upon the places of men, and none could stand before him.

Across Averland and the Moot he came, killing all who would not flee. The fields became ash and the pastures were as mire beneath the boots of the Ironclaw. Cities fell to rubble until not even their name survived them. Towns were left as open graves, the butchered dead choking their streets. The howl of orc and wolf praised the darkness where once men sang prayers to the gods.

Into the west the Ironclaw marched, following the smell of man's fear. The country emptied before him. Men forsook their homes in their despair and abandoned all they had built. The fury of the Ironclaw was great, to find that the strength of men was so weak. In his rage, he unleashed the worst of his brood, giving them liberty to raze the land and work what havoc they would. No bird nor beast nor tree nor field did the orcs spare, leaving the land a barren desolation.

The Ironclaw turned his host north, and the city of Nuln burned. He turned his horde against Sigismund and the pretender's army was scattered to the winds. Still, the Ironclaw searched, trying to find the strength that had banished the orcs to waste and cavern. In Pfeildorf, the terrified masses took shelter, trying to hide from the beast that ravaged the land.

Our lord, Count Eldred, ruler of Solland by right of blood and birth, could have fled before the Ironclaw, to cower in the north as other lords had done, but Count Eldred would not abandon his land, would not leave his people behind to be slaughtered. With the sword bestowed upon his house by the hand of Mighty Sigmar, the noble Runefang of Solland, he would stand before the Ironclaw and defy him.

The orcs brought siege to Pfeildorf and for weeks the cruel weapons of the goblins rained death upon those within its walls. Time and again, those within were forced to the battlements to turn the orcs back. Time and again, the Ironclaw was repulsed, his warriors slinking away to lick their wounds. Always, more came, for their numbers were without number, and always did the numbers of the men of Pfeildorf dwindle.

At last, it became known that the walls could be held no longer. Men gave voice to the gods in that moment, ambition, glory and greed forgotten in the hour of their doom. Count Eldred saluted Lord Sigmar, praising him with the runefang held high. Then he turned his horse and rode to the gate of the city to await the coming of the Ironclaw. Only his closest knights rode with him, to meet their deaths with their sovereign, those who had sworn their oaths upon the runefang's cold steel.

The great rams of the orcs crashed against the steel-banded doors. Again and again, the rams pounded against the gates, until the walls shuddered. Some dared hope the gods had remembered them and that the gates would hold, but the spite of men was not so easily washed away and the hour of the beast had come. With a great crack, the gates fell open and the foul howls of orcs echoed through the city.

A great green-skinned beast with bear's strength and boar's tusks was first to enter the city. Beneath his horned helm was a face scarred with cruelty, malice and wrath; the mark of such evil that Count Eldred knew he gazed upon the warlord:

*that which the orcs named Gorbad and which men named
Ironclaw. The count did not falter before the monster's fiery
eyes and did not flinch as the very weight of the Ironclaw
made flagstones crack beneath his feet. Count Eldred
remembered his oaths to land and people; he remembered the
legacy handed down to him by Lord Sigmar.*

*Count Eldred drew the runefang from his scabbard and
made ready to face the Ironclaw, and his knights felt shame
that their courage was so small beside that of their lord. Even
the Ironclaw hesitated, raising his brutish axe in respect to
this man who had the strength to stand against him.*

*Of that great battle, no man can speak, for all who stood
with Count Eldred shared his doom. The gods had decreed
that the hour of the beast was not past, that there was yet
wickedness within the hearts of men that must be scoured
with flame and steel. Pfeildorf was cast into ruin by the Ironclaw and its people were put to the sword, but the Ironclaw
knew that he had found the echo of that strength which had
driven his kind into hole and hollow. He bore away with him
the runefang, the blade of the only man who had the courage
to face him. It became a token of his victory, a symbol of his
might, a reminder to his horde why he was their master, a
warning to himself that there was yet strength in the blood
of men.*

*When at last the Ironclaw was driven from the lands of
men, hounded back into the wastes, he bore with him still
Count Eldred's runefang. From all the plunder of half the
Empire, this alone did the Ironclaw value, for in the runefang did he sense the power of men, the power forever denied
to the beasts of the dark.*

– From the Saga of the Southern Sword

CHAPTER ONE

ARMIN VON STARKBERG strode from his tent, nodding to the page who held the flap for him. The page was a young, dark-haired boy, perhaps only a few winters younger than Armin had been when he'd earned the spurs of a knight. The thought gave him pause. Would that be the legacy of this battle? A host of squires and pages given their spurs, not because of some act of valour, but simply to fill out the ranks of a depleted order? Armin clenched his hand into the sign of the goddess Myrmidia to ward away the ugly image. The man who rode to war with his head full of doubt and defeat only brought his fears to fruition.

The knight stood just outside his pavilion, letting the breeze brush along his closely-cropped skull, feeling the unseen fingers of the wind tease across his patrician features. Eyes as blue as the waters of the Reik studied the cluster of tents that surrounded his, a field of black and red pavilions that swarmed in every direction, blotting out the larger camp that surrounded them. As he watched, each tent disgorged its occupant. Tall and broad of shoulder, their faces weathered by years of strict drill and discipline, their quality tested in a dozen campaigns across the province, these were the pride of Count Eberfeld's army, the razored edge of Wissenland's sword. Armin felt his chest swell as he looked on them, their red armour shining like rubies in the fading light of day, their surcoats as dark as the descending night. Upon the breast of each surcoat, picked out in golden thread, was the image of a sword.

That was who they were, Armin reflected. That was the legacy, the heritage that rested upon their shoulders and within their souls. For the sons of the Solland, the scarred frontier of Wissenland, there was no greater honour than to wear the red armour and the black surcoat, to be admitted into the almost sacred ranks of the Order of the Southern Sword. The knights could trace their history back to the very founding of Solland, and they had been there to the very end, when the orcs had come with fire and steel to lay waste to the province and slaughter its last lord, the Count Eldred. The order had endured their realm's destruction, transferring their loyalty to the lords of Wissenland when that province absorbed the ruined carcass of Solland into its domains.

An older knight, his dark hair peppered with lines of silver and a nest of crows' feet stretching from his eyes, approached Armin. The veteran dropped to one knee as he reached the younger warrior, setting his helmet on the ground beside him. Armin nodded and motioned for the knight to rise. Of the three marshals who commanded the order, it was old Eugen Grosschopp whose council he valued and trusted the most. As the youngest hochmeister in the history of the order, Armin often felt the weight of tradition and precedent working against him. In another order, perhaps it would not have mattered, but the Order of the Southern Sword was fanatical about its traditions, even maintaining the archaic title of hochmeister for its leader where other knightly orders had adopted the convention of placing Grand Masters at their heads.

There were some within the ranks who still resented Hochmeister Mannstein's appointment of one so young to be his successor. Even on the eve of battle, Armin had heard such rumblings within the pavilions of his warriors. Marshal Eugen was not one of them. He valued the hochmeister for his abilities on the battlefield, his fitness to lead and his bravery in combat. Eugen didn't care a goblin's backside about how many years a man had under his belt, or how many titles he bore before or after his name.

'Your report, marshal,' Armin said, addressing the older knight. Eugen set his helm beneath his arm as he stood, fixing the hochmeister with his dark eyes.

'The men await your pleasure, my lord,' Eugen said. Armin looked past the marshal and watched as, across the camp, squires in the livery of the order led massive warhorses towards each tent. Powerful, majestic destriers, the smallest seventeen hands high, the steeds of the Southern Swords were the finest in Wissenland, perhaps the finest in the Empire. Tradition held that there was a bit of Bretonnian courser in the pedigree of the order's destriers. Armin did not know. He did not think that anything but the grace of the gods could produce such magnificent animals. They carried the heavy steel barding that covered nearly their entire bodies as though born into the metal skins. They would show little more strain even with an armoured rider astride their back. The quality of any body of cavalry was decided by the kind of horses that carried the riders into war, and by the kind of men who rode their steeds into the fray. It made Armin proud to know that even beside such destriers, the Knights of the Southern Sword were not found wanting.

'Count Eberfeld has given us the centre,' Armin reminded his marshal. 'Ours is the position of honour. All eyes will be upon us. Remind the men that it is not their honour that will be judged today, but the honour of the order.'

'They know the oaths they have sworn,' Eugen replied. 'No knight of the Southern Sword has ever forsaken his duty.'

Armin watched as the knights mounted the small wooden ladders their squires placed before them and lifted their red-armoured forms into the saddles of their steeds. Like statues, the destriers stood silently waiting for the jostling bulks of their riders to settle into the leather stirrups and wood-framed seats.

'You have heard the rumours circulating through the camp?' Armin asked by way of broaching the subject. He knew that Eugen would not be so remiss in his duties as to fail to become familiar with the mood among the common soldiers in Count Eberfeld's army.

'Spook stories and old wives' tales,' Eugen sneered. 'Even our squires are too stout to be troubled by such gossip!'

Armin nodded his head, but he had his doubts. The reports that had come back from General Hock's scouts were troubling. Since the first attack had been reported, seven towns and villages had been razed, not so much as a dog left alive within the smouldering ruins. If the perpetrators had been beastmen or orcs, or even a free company turned brigand, Armin would never have questioned the valour of his men, but the things that were despoiling Wissenland were none of these, at least, not any more. The walking dead, abominations from beyond the grave, that was what was menacing the people of Wissenland. Against any mortal thing, the courage of the Knights of the Southern Sword was beyond question, but faced by these deathless horrors the courage of even the bravest man might falter. Even the most stalwart heart might know doubt.

The supernatural was nothing new in the long history of the order, but the menace Wissenland now faced was very different from the shambling mobs of decaying corpses called up by the curse of a witch or the malice of a vampire. These things marched with purpose, with some dread simulacrum of discipline. By night, they marched in ordered ranks, crushing anything too slow or too stubborn to flee from their path. By day, they rested within fortified encampments.

Armin felt a chill run down his spine as he recalled the deserted camp he had seen, the earthen berms and deep trenches, the palisade of sharpened logs and the cunning arrangement of gates within the defences to allow the occupants swift egress from any of the four sides of the fortification. General Hock had balked at the prospect of laying siege to one of these encampments, for how could one starve into submission a foe who was already dead? Worse, the best soldiers in the assembled Wissenland force, the three knightly orders that had answered Count Eberfeld's call to arms, would be squandered in such an engagement. The power of the knight was the cavalry charge, which was impossible to execute against an immobile fort.

So it was that they had marched ahead of the undead host, anticipating its ghastly movement across the land. By day, the dead camped, but by night they marched. General Hock intended to bring his army smashing against the lifeless legion while they were strung out along the narrow road, which they had been following since the destruction of the village of Dobrin, before they reached the town of Heufurth.

The Order of the Southern Sword would spearhead that attack. Watching his knights slowly form ranks on the parade ground just below his pavilion, Armin knew that he could ask for no finer warriors. They would play the part they had been given, and all the horrors of Khemri would not hold them back. Armin quietened his fears. Young or old, he was their hochmeister and they would look to him to lead the way.

Armin drew a deep breath, holding the air within him for a long moment before letting it out through his teeth. Eugen gave him a curious look.

'It is good,' Armin told him.

'What is good?' the marshal replied, not understanding.

Armin looked down at his men, at three hundred of the best cavalry known to man. They had fought in many battles, in many lands. From the Siege of Averheim to crushing the orc warhost of Uhrghul, the knights had never faltered. They had upheld their oaths to Wissenland and done their duty to their adopted liege and lord. This time was different, however. This time they were fighting for something more.

The hochmeister turned his head and smiled at Eugen. 'It is good to feel the air of Solland in my lungs again. Now, let's to our horses and show Count Eberfeld how hard the sons of the Solland fight for their own!'

THE KNIGHTS OF the Southern Sword formed ranks, steel-tipped lances standing rigid and proud in their sheaths, their black pennants fluttering sombrely. Eugen sat to Armin's left, his company of knights given the honour of leading the charge by their hochmeister. To his right, was Johannis Roth, the hero of the Battle of Meissen, where the tide had finally turned against Warlord Uhrghul Skullcracker. In recognition of his bravery, Johannis had been given the duty of bearing the order's standard into battle.

Armin felt the bittersweet pang of nostalgia and loss as he looked upon it, a tattered length of singed fabric, its scarlet field splotched with blood stains and pitted with ragged tears. Yet the standard held a respect that was beyond the rich finery of a nobleman's banner. It had been part of a tapestry that had adorned the halls of the Counts of Solland, one of the few things that had been recovered from the ruins of Pfeildorf after the horde of the Ironclaw had ransacked it in the aftermath of the Battle of Solland's Crown. There was power in the threadbare tapestry, an echo of the glory and strength that had been Solland, a strength the men who fought beneath it could feel flowing through their limbs, infusing their hearts with an iron resolve.

Beyond the ranks of his knights, Armin could see the rest of Count Eberfeld's heavy cavalry forming up: the Geschberg Guard, their massive warhammers slung from the horns of their saddles, their features hidden behind the extravagantly horned great helms they wore; the Sablebacks, their ranks filled with the nobility of

Wissenland, the polished steel of their armour gleaming with a blue hue beneath the rising moon, their fur cloaks billowing about the hindquarters of their massive coursers. To the other side of Armin's knights were the Kreutzhofen Spears, commoner cavalry maintained by the merchant guilds, mounted on swift-footed rounseys, and armoured in stiff brigandines of canvas and steel, their slender weapons a pale echo of the enormous lances carried by the knights.

Armin turned in his saddle, glancing over the heads of the knights behind him, watching as the count's infantry trudged into position, fixing every company in his mind. A battle was decided not only upon knowing where the enemy was, but where your allies were as well. He could see the halberdiers from Grunwald and the spearmen from Beroun. There were the grimy archers that had mustered in the Sol Valley and marched to answer the count's call to war. He could see the swarthy crossbowmen who had marched down from Kreutzhofen alongside the cavalry, their felt hats and elaborate uniforms betraying a touch of the Tilean about them, and the Brotherhood of Schwerstetten, a regiment of mercenaries drawn down from the Reikland border by the smell of war, their ranks sporting men from a dozen lands and weapons from a dozen more, their hawk-eyed Captain Valdner studying the battlefield with a tactician's eye.

Beside the mercenaries were Baron Ernst von Rabwald's men-at-arms, a mixed force of halberdiers and crossbowmen, the mounted baron looming above his soldiers as he conferred with his officers.

The last group to move into position was one that did much to bolster Armin's confidence: a gang of stocky, broad-shouldered dwarfs pushing a trio of wide-mouthed cannons into place upon a small hillock. Armin did not know what strange paths led the dwarfs to be employed in Count Eberfeld's army, what curious circumstances had drawn them down from the Black Mountains, but their fire-belching artillery was a welcome sight. At the Siege of Averheim, Armin had been on the receiving end of dwarf cannons and so he had a first–hand grasp of the terrific impact they could have on any battle. It would be nice to have the formidable guns as allies rather than foes this time.

Upon another hill, the sapphire banner of Wissenland fluttered above a golden pavilion. Even from a distance, Armin could make out the hulking figure of General Hock leaning over his map-strewn table. Count Eberfeld would not be far away, surrounded by his advisors and guards, monitoring every turn in the battle, wishing every moment that he was riding with his Sablebacks rather than conferring with strategists and trying to decipher Hock's maps.

The battlefield showed General Hock's eye for an advantage. The count's army occupied the high ground, giving the Wissenland commanders an unobstructed view of the pastureland that straddled the Heufurth road. Beyond the pastures were thick stretches of forest. Hock's scouts had been watching the hideous army for days, reporting on their movements. The lifeless warriors displayed a rigid, slavish adherence to maintaining their ordered ranks. They favoured open ground where their files could maintain formation, going to great lengths to avoid broken ground and obstructions. Indeed, when such elements proved unavoidable, the entire army seemed to undergo a sort of fit as it slowly adjusted to the change in its regimen. Like puppets dancing on strings, the dead army wasn't terribly good at accepting sudden adjustments in its performance.

With the forests forming a distinct limit to the battlefield, Hock intended to exploit it to the fullest. They would funnel the dead army into a killing ground from which there would be no escape. There was always a mind guiding such hideous monsters, an inhuman intellect that stirred them from their graves and set them upon the living. Necromancer, vampire or warlock, Count Eberfeld was determined that whatever force had gathered the abominable army would not slip back into the black shadows of night. The cavalry would bear the brunt of the attack, smashing through the centre of the enemy formations. The breach the knights created would be exploited by the infantry following behind. Like a butcher's cleaver, the cavalry would cut its way through the enemy, breaking its lines and re-forming ranks on the far side of the disintegrated formations of the lifeless warriors. The horsemen would form a wall, blocking any chance for the enemy to retreat back down the road. The infantry would press against the disordered ruin the knights left behind, pushing it towards the wall of cavalry and the knights' waiting swords.

Armin smiled as he recalled the plan. It was the same strategy Hock had used against the beastmen of Thugok Festerhorn when the brutish warherds had menaced Steingart. The slaughter of the mutants had been so decisive that Count Eberfeld had promoted Hock to the rank of general. If it served him half as well today, there would be titles and lands in the general's future.

Night strengthened its hold on the land, the last rays of the dying sun a distant memory. The warm autumn breeze grew cold, biting at the face it had earlier caressed. The horses of the cavalry companies whinnied and stamped their hooves, protesting at the prolonged exposure to the cooling darkness. Among the infantry there aroused a surly murmur that their officers never could quite silence completely. Even some of Armin's knights grumbled under their breath when they thought the marshals were not listening. Armin knew it was only nerves, the jitters that shivered through any army as it waited to do battle. In many ways, combat was never so hard on a soldier as waiting for the fight to begin.

An excited tremor ran through the army as a pair of riders appeared on the Heufurth road, but the excitement abated when it became obvious that the men were alone. As they rode past the line of knights, Armin saw that the men wore scruffy leather hauberks, brambles and dust clinging to their beards. More of General Hock's scouts, riding back to report to their commander. The wild-eyed look on each scout's face, the way he lashed his steed with savage disregard, told Armin that whatever news they brought, it was of great import. Had the army of the dead turned from the Heufurth road? Was it no longer marching relentlessly towards the battlefield that Hock had so carefully chosen?

Armin's fears for the disposition of the enemy were silenced by the flag that rose to replace the sapphire banner above Count Eberfeld's golden pavilion. It was a silver pennant and upon it were two symbols: the fang of Ulric and the spear of Myrmidia, the god and goddess of war and conflict. With the battle flag raised, every man in the army knew that the wait would soon be over.

As Armin looked back from the count's pavilion and the raising of the battle flag, he witnessed a sinister change crawling across the far side of the road. Where the path passed around the bend of the forest, a thick mist had appeared, almost glowing as the moonlight shone upon it. Another murmur passed through the ranks of the Wissenlanders as they watched the eerie fog billow out from beyond the trees. Horses stamped and snorted, but this time it was not idleness that disturbed them. Armin could feel a new chill to the air, a clammy coldness that was not the natural cool of night.

Silence descended once more, and this time it took no officers to enforce it. Every man in the Wissenland host watched tensely as the glowing fog continued to roll down the road, billowing out to stretch from the forested slopes to the east to the thick woods on the west. It spread across the pastures, like some ethereal tide, washing remorselessly forwards, drawing nearer to the waiting soldiers and knights.

Dimly, at first, a sound rolled out from the fog. It took Armin a moment to identify it, but at length he decided it was the rattle of armoured bodies marching on the hard-packed earth of the road. No other sound accompanied it: not the snorting of draft animals, not the shouts of officers, not even the cough of a marcher choking on the dust of the trail, but only the rattle of jostling armour. Like all Wissenlanders, Armin was a pious man, but his prayers were normally voiced to Taal and Rhya, Myrmidia and Shallya. Now, only one god pulled at his devotion, the one who was all but forgotten in this age of strife. With his hand, he made the sign of Sigmar Heldenhammer, the first emperor, the man-god who had driven the black lord of the undead from the lands of the Empire and who had preserved civilisation against all the horrors of Old Night.

Shapes appeared within the fog, spindle-thin and moving with a ghastly precision that sent a fresh thrill of anxiety quivering through Armin's belly. The knight realised that no mortal host moved like that. The shapes might be mirror images of one another, for all the difference there was in their motions. They were not many, staggered out in a long line. Armin could see some that appeared to be mounted, though upon such lean, scrawny steeds that the knight could not grasp how the animals could support their riders. Then, through the opacity of the mist, Armin found his answer, instantly repenting his curiosity. He had expected horror, he had heard the tales of the nature of the foe the count had called upon them to fight, but there was no way a man, however disciplined, could prepare himself for the flesh and blood reality behind the horror.

No, not flesh and blood: only bones. The rider he saw through the fog was nothing more than a skeleton, its body absolutely picked clean of skin, meat and muscle. Upon its skull, it wore a strange, high-peaked helmet, stained almost black with decay. Around its waist, it wore a chain belt from which was suspended a quiver that slapped against its thigh bone. The horse beneath it was likewise stripped bare, an equine apparition, as removed from the trappings of the mortal coil as its repulsive rider, the last sorry remnants of tack and harness hanging in rotten strips from its skull.

There were dozens of the silent, skeletal riders, their fleshless steeds moving in a grotesquely slow manner, as through straining to cross a greater distance than the mortal terrain Armin's eyes could see. Beyond them marched small clutches of infantry. Devoid of the strange helmets of the riders, the infantry sported grimy bands of iron and bronze around the crowns of their skulls. Strips of festering leather hung from their midsections, pathetic reminders of the armour they had worn in life. Each of the infantry carried a quiver like the horsemen's, but much larger. Armin could see large shafts protruding from the decaying quivers, another shaft gripped firmly in each skeleton's right hand. The knight was perplexed by the strange weapons. They were too big to be arrows, too short to be spears and certainly lacking any kind of edge, Armin could not decide precisely what the things were meant to be.

For what felt like an eternity, the Wissenlanders watched the ghastly army march, spellbound by the unreal horror of that silent legion. Then the silence was shattered with a resounding boom from the hill. Fire and smoke belched from the mouth of a cannon. In rapid succession, the dwarfs fired the other guns. Havoc smashed into the spindly shapes marching through the mist, as the deadly salvo bore home. Against a fortification, the dwarfs would use huge balls of iron to batter down walls of stone, but against less formidable targets they had turned to fiendish innovation. It had been called 'chain-shot' during the Siege of Averheim, a pair of fist-sized balls of pig-iron fired from a cannon, a length of chain fixing the two spheres together. When blasted out of a cannon, the iron spheres spun end-over-end, the chain hurtling along with them. The effect of the chain-shot smashing into a company of knights was hideous, the chain slashing through the legs of horses and men like a farmer's scythe through a field of wheat.

Now, the chain-shot worked its awful potency against the undead warriors. Armin could see scores of them drop as the cannon-fire slashed through them, spilling them in jumbles of shattered bone and crumbling armour. Infantry or horseman, the chain-shot took its gruesome toll, leaving inhuman corpses and equine carcasses littered across pasture and path. Yet still no cry went up from the enemy ranks. The dead that had been struck down fell in silence, giving no voice to the violence of their destruction. Only the rolling echoes from the cannons gave testament that the Wissenlanders had indeed struck the first blow.

The colour faded from Armin's face as he saw some of the toppled skeletons rise once more, to crawl towards the count's army, leaving their dismembered legs behind. The sight was one that threatened to unman every soldier present, driving home the horror they faced. Men who had looked death in the eye many times, who had struggled against the inhuman barbarity of orcs and the abominable cruelty of beastmen, felt the icy touch of fear clawing at their hearts. This was something more than death, something obscene and vile beyond description. Where other men found terror in this realisation, Armin found determination.

'Men of Wissenland!' Armin roared, his voice carrying like the boom of the dwarf guns. 'Do these wraiths unman you? Do they fill your hearts with fear? Think how much greater the fear will be when it is your wives and daughters who cower before them!' The hochmeister drew his sword, the blade singing with a metallic rasp as it cleared the scabbard. 'Strike, you dogs! Strike and send these wretches back to their tombs! For Count Eberfeld! For Wissenland! For the ghosts of Solland, strike these wretches down!'

The hochmeister set his spurs into the flank of his destrier and with a surge of motion, the massive animal was rushing towards the mist. Armin's ears filled with the thunder of hooves as his knights galloped with him. Around them, the remaining cavalry was charging forwards, weapons at the ready, war cries filling the air. Behind them, the infantry surged forwards, to cover the flanks and rush into the holes the knights would create in the enemy line. The voices of Armin's knights lifted in song as they charged, the bittersweet ballad called 'The Lament of Solland'.

Ahead of them, the ragged clusters of walking dead reacted to the charging knights with slow, precise deliberation. The infantry, those that had been left whole in the aftermath of the cannon-fire, crooked their arms back with an eerie unison of motion, the strange short, fat-bodied spears clutched in their bony claws. Still maintaining their hideous silence, the skeletons sent their javelins hurtling across the field towards the onrushing cavalry.

The iron missiles crashed against the thick steel armour of Armin's knights and the heavy barding of the destriers, their pointed tips blunting against the armour and glancing harmlessly into the dirt. Against the lightly armoured Kreutzhofen horsemen, however, some of the iron pila struck home, stabbing into unprotected flesh, ruining shields as the cumbersome iron shafts became embedded in the wood. More troubling to the knights were the mounted archers, firing their compact bows with a cold, emotionless precision. More than a few steeds were brought down, bronze-tipped arrows sticking from throat and eye. In the rush of the charge, the thrown riders were smashed beneath the hooves of their comrades.

The charging knights lowered their lances as the hochmeister's voice rang out. Like the fangs of some great beast, they were thrust at the silent, deadly foe. A promise of death cast in steel and carved from oak, the men who bore them intended to visit, in full, their capacity to ruin.

Even as the knights smashed through them, the skeletal peltasts and undead horsemen continued their missile fire. Armin saw that they were nothing more than skirmishers, ranging out ahead of the main army, which he observed as a stretch of shadow slowly crawling out through the mist. Where mortal skirmishers would have broken and scattered before the cavalry could reach them, the peltasts held their ground, hurling pila until the very moment when their brittle bones were shattered beneath the charge. They made a sickening contrast to the men and greenskins that Armin had ridden down in his time, barely jostling his steed as the huge destrier smashed through them, breaking apart like bundles of sticks as his lance found its targets.

Soon they were beyond the skirmishers, rushing towards the main enemy formation. Armin saw that there was little visual unity to the skeletal warriors they quickly closed upon. They carried a riotous mixture of weapons, from rusty old swords to worm-eaten scythes and blunted wood axes. He saw the squat shapes of dwarfs, the horned skulls of beastmen and the hulking bones of orcs mixed among the ranks of those skeletons that had once belonged to men. Whatever their shapes, however, and whatever the weapons gripped in their withered talons, they moved as one.

As the charge bore down on the undead host, Armin saw that they did not present a single battleline. There were holes in the formation, curious gaps in their defence. The hochmeister felt a tinge of alarm as he saw the strange deployment, but it was much too late to turn back the attack. The Knights of the Southern Sword smashed into the skeleton warriors with a thunderous impact, hurling shattered bones into the air, grinding skulls beneath hooves and impaling rotten ribcages on lances.

Then they were through, their charge carrying them past the massed ranks of the undead. The sudden absence of foes was almost more shocking than the initial impact of the attack. Armin saw a second line of undead warriors, as curiously arranged as the first, with pockets and gaps between the units. These differed from the motley rabble of the front line, however. Each of these skeletons was encased in a rusty iron breastplate and wore a heavy iron helm with flaring cheekguards.

Enormous rectangular shields, which Armin could liken only to Tilean pavises, were held against their bodies as they marched. Armin noted at once the arrangement of these better-armed skeletons. They were positioned in such a way that they approximated the gaps left in the first line. Before Armin could make sense of the observation, the knights were past the second line and crashing against a third. Armoured like the second line, these were arranged in the gaps left between the units of the second rank, approximating the positions of the front line. It was like the arrangement of squares on a chessboard, though how deep the pattern might continue, Armin did not want to consider.

The charge had lost much of its impetus after its brutal passage through the front ranks. Smashing into the shield wall presented by the third line, many of the horsemen floundered, unable to punch through the undead warriors. Only the Knights of the Southern Sword had the power to smash their way through the third line, battering their way through ironclad husks of men fifteen deep. When they had won clear, Armin risked a look back, watching as the survivors of the charge silently and steadily re-formed their ranks, ignoring the broken carcasses of their fallen. A chill went up Armin's spine as he realised that the first line would be doing the same. Indeed, by straining, he could see the second line merging with the first, forming a single uninterrupted front, like a gate being slammed shut behind the knights.

Armin bellowed a command to his men, urging them to awareness of their danger. Then he saw it: a fourth line of skeletons, their ranks staggered in the chequerboard fashion of the others. They were yet more heavily armoured, their scrawny frames draped in scales of bronze and iron, their skulls encased in rounded helms with skirts of chain and horsehair plumes. They bore thick round shields of iron, if anything more massive than the rectangles carried by the middle ranks. Immense spears with barbed tips projected out from over the rims of their shields.

With the same eerie unison, the armoured skeletons turned towards Armin's knights, the only cavalry that had won clear of the third rank. Relentlessly, they converged upon the knights, striving to pin them with their backs to the quickly re-forming third line. Armin's bellowed commands became desperate shouts, urging his men to wheel their steeds into the swiftly narrowing gap between the units of the fourth line. There was no thought of challenging the massed ranks of the armoured spearmen. Grossly outnumbered and with the momentum of their attack already lost, Armin had no delusions about how his knights would fare against that field of spears. They had to drive through the fourth line before they could close ranks and cut off their chance for escape. The knights heard their hochmeister's orders, spurring their warhorses to follow his lead. The rearmost riders were cut down as the undead units converged, pulled from their saddles by the barbed spears, the bellies of their destriers slashed open by the corroded polearms.

The tattered standard fluttered forlornly above the riders as they plunged through the gap. Lances were cast aside and swords drawn, as the knights slashed at the skeletons that closed upon them. Armin's ears filled with the shrieks of horses and the cries of men as they died upon the ancient spears of the revenants. Still they drove onwards, steel flashing through the mist, shattering mouldering bones with every strike. Armin thought they would never win clear, Then, suddenly his warhorse plunged into open pasture, grinding the helm of one last wight beneath its hooves. Johannis Roth smashed his way to Armin's side. Then Eugen joined him with a few dozen others. Behind them, the ranks of the fourth line became a solid wall of bloodied bronze and grinning bone. For an instant, Armin felt the urge to turn his men around, to charge back into the enemy with their silent, mocking smiles, but such mad thoughts died quickly. Armin felt as though his entire body shrivelled with the magnitude of his despair. Through the mists, he could see thin, shadowy shapes.

They had won through the fourth line only to find a fifth. Horsehair plumes and barbed spears slowly resolved, as the shadows marched out of the fog.

THE CROAKING OF CROWS was a ghastly din that scratched relentlessly at Armin's mind. The morning sun was a smouldering crimson flame on the horizon, like a pool of molten blood. A crow landed on Armin's shoulder, stabbing its beak cruelly into his cheek. Armin growled at the carrion eater, struggling to crawl away from its vile attentions. The black bird cawed angrily and hopped off its creeping perch, choosing to fasten onto the arm that the hochmeister left behind him.

Loss of blood caused sparks to dance before Armin's eyes. His brain felt numb, unable to focus on the horrible things his eyes tried to fill it with. He could not summon any sense of intimacy for the broken, mangled things that were strewn all around him, the carcasses and corpses of his knights. Dark blood bubbled up from some ruptured organ, spraying from Armin's red-stained teeth. He flopped down on his back, blinking as the gory spittle dripped down into his eyes. He had just blinked away his own gore when his gaze set upon the figure standing with its back to the rising sun, the rays turning its bronze spear into a shaft of fire, its plumed helm casting dark shadows over its skeletal face. One of its comrades stood beside it, one of the walking damned. Armin idly wondered if they were the ones that had slain him. He wondered if there was even enough life left within their bony husks to know any sense of accomplishment from killing the hochmeister of the Order of the Southern Sword.

The numb detachment that befuddled Armin's mind was burned away as an icy chill swept through him. The blood that still clung to his veins grew cold and his eyes grew wide in terror. The croaking of the crows was drowned out by the thunder of his failing heart. The scream that tried to rip from his throat froze in paralysed lungs.

A shape loomed between the two skeletons, glaring down at Armin. Beneath the shadow of its hood, the knight could see amber witch-lights glowing in the sockets of a leering skull. He had the impression of an armoured body encased in black scales, of iron-clad claws closed around a bladed staff, of a ragged crimson cloak that billowed around the apparition, moved by no earthly wind. The thing stared at him for a time, and Armin could feel his soul shrivelling with each passing breath. Somehow, even as he felt his spirit being devoured, Armin understood that he was already dead. In the last moment of clarity, Armin von Starkberg felt the true measure of terror.

After a time, the apparition turned away from the dead knight, leaving the crows to their repast.

CHAPTER TWO

THE SMALL DIRT streets of Koeblitz had been churned into a froth of mud by the arrival of Count Eberfeld's army. Every stable, granary and storehouse in the town had been commandeered by General Hock, every house, hovel and business transformed into a bivouac for the ragged survivors of the ill-fated battle. The rustic peasantry of Wissenland was wary enough of soldiers at the best of times, but the air of despondency that clung to Eberfeld's men was a contagion that soon spread to the farmers and tradesmen of Koeblitz, infecting them with the same raw fear they saw lurking in the eyes of the soldiers. As he prowled through the mire that slithered between the sagging, half-timbered buildings of Koeblitz, Baron Ernst von Rabwald could count on one hand the number of civilians he saw haunting the streets, the rest keeping behind shuttered windows and locked doors, anxiously waiting for the return of normality to their dull little lives.

The baron cut an incongruous figure as he marched down the muddy lanes. He was tall and possessed of a lean, panther's build, wearing a silver-chased breast-plate upon which was stamped the raven of his demesne, the barony of Rabwald. An azure cape flowed from his broad shoulders, the coat-of-arms of Rabwald woven into the garment with cloth of gold. The gloves that clothed his hands were of softest doeskin, matched rubies gleaming from each knuckle. One hand rested easily upon the golden hilt of the longsword that hung from his belt, the other scratched at the faint trace of stubble that marked his proud, aristocratic face.

Baron Ernst von Rabwald was accustomed to having his hair shorn and his face shaved every morning by his valet. Again and again, his mind turned to the petty annoyance of this break in his daily ritual, despite all the other concerns that crowded his thoughts.

Ernst watched as a small group of dismounted horse-men from Kreutzhofen wearily made their way down the lane. The Kreutzhofen Spears had suffered hideous losses in the battle, second only to those suffered by the Knights of the Southern Sword. These men had braved the belly of the beast, and had been spat out from the very mouth of the monster. Ernst watched the tired men slowly trudge through the mire, their hauberks filthy with blood and grime, their faces pinched and pale with fatigue. They had fought well, these horsemen, but at the end of the day they were still commoners. Ernst's path did not waver as the soldiers marched towards him. He met their weary eyes for an instant, and then the soldiers made way for the nobleman, passing to either side of the baron as they continued down the street. Even in the aftermath of battle there were pro-prieties to be observed. Noble did not give ground to peasant. That was the kind of man Ernst had been raised to be.

Ernst continued to march past the mud-brick hovels that swarmed around the outskirts of Koeblitz, past the pig wallows and chicken coops that seemed to litter every inch of ground the townsfolk had not delineated as road. There was urgency in his step, an immediacy that was absent in the dejected, defeated countenances of the soldiers who watched him pass by from whatever hasty bivouac they had appropriated from the people of Koeblitz. Some huddled in the shadows of lean-tos, warming their hands over tiny campfires and trying to keep rust from their blades. Others watched him from the doorways of timber-framed houses, their shoulders draped in furs and blankets provided by their reluctant hosts.

Ernst did not appreciate the sullen gleam in the eyes of some of those who watched him, the envy and spite that a nobleman saw far too often. So long as it remained in the eye and did not slip onto the tongue, a noble was well advised to ignore such petty insurrection. He knew that most of the resentment grew from a belief that the nobility did not share in the same trials and hardships of their people. He could have ridden with the Sablebacks, his position and family entitled him to such prestigious company, yet he had decided to fight alongside the commoners who had followed him from Rabwald. It was a decision he had always made and would always make. Obligations and duties, as well as honours and privileges, went with the title of Baron von Rabwald. That was also the kind of man he had been raised to be.

In the baron's wake, stalking after him as faithfully as his shadow, was a brutish hulk of humanity. A suit of chainmail struggled to contain swollen arms and muscled chest, the battered steel breastplate a shabby echo of the silvered armour worn by the baron. A conical spangenhelm framed a grisly countenance of smashed features and jagged scars, frosty blue eyes set above a great gash of a frown. The warrior carried an enormous sword across his powerful shoulder, the blade rippling like a steel lightning bolt, the leather grip wrapped in wire to prevent the weapon from slipping through fingers dampened by sweat and blood. A riot of black tassels dangled from the haft of the sword while a grinning steel skull formed its pommel. It was a weapon as ugly and intimidating as the man who bore it.

Max Kessler was a name spoken of in guarded whispers in the north of Wissenland, where custom and circumstance might bring a man into the demesne of Rabwald. The hulking warrior was one of the deadliest swordsmen in the region, a man who had walked away from more duels than were easily counted. The black tassels that were looped through the sockets of the sword's pommel each denoted a man whose life had ended on that blade. For many years, Kessler had served as the baron's champion, acting as his master's proxy against all those who challenged his authority. By long tradition, any man could challenge any ruling of law by demanding trial by combat. Only the suicidal and the desperate continued to do so in Rabwald.

Ernst found his champion's presence reassuring. There were few men he trusted so well as Max Kessler, and none he counted upon so fully. Even in the face of the walking dead, Kessler had not wavered, plying his giant sword with the same brutal deliberation as he did against any mortal foe. Few men had such nerve. If he was honest, Ernst would admit that even he had felt his determination falter as the undead had closed upon them. There was no better man to have watching his back.

Ernst paused, staring at the mud beneath his boots as a sudden surge of melancholy swept through him. He hoped it would not come to that. He hoped he could make them see reason. The count's decision sat ill with him, offending his sense of honour and chivalry. He knew his first duty was to the count and Wissenland, whatever his private concerns, however much the count's order smacked of treachery.

'Is something wrong, my lord?' Kessler's voice was a deep growl, like the snarl of a bear. Ernst turned and stared at the scarred swordsman.

'When we get there, let me do the talking,' Ernst told him. He scratched at the irritating stubble on his face. 'If things go badly, try not to kill anyone,' he added.

'SHALLYA'S MERCY! CAN'T you stop that caterwauling!' The Kreutzhofener's outburst was punctuated by a violent downward motion of his hand, the little wafer-thin strips of bone slapping angrily against the frayed cavalry blanket stretched across the ground. Theodo grinned at the sullen soldier.

'I take it you yield?' Theodo asked, rubbing salt into the wound. The soldier glared back at him, and then smashed his fist against the backs of the cards he had folded onto the blanket. A few of the other men, gathered around the blanket, snickered at the Kreutzhofener's discomfort. A crimson flush blossomed in the faces of others, their eyes growing harder as some of the Kreutzhofener's anger fed into their own.

Theodo Hobshollow leaned back, grinning his pearly smile, one thumb plucking at the breast of his striped vest, the other tapping the edges of the cards gripped firmly in his hand. There was something infuriatingly childlike about the little gambler, from his plump ruddy cheeks to his curly brown mop of hair, something that made the soldiers quick to forget the predatory gleam in his tiny eyes and the smug twist in his smile. It was easy to underestimate so slight a creature. The halfling barely rose to the waist of the smallest of his fellow gamblers. Indeed, he had required the appropriation of a hay bale to sit on, simply to stare the soldiers in the eye without wrenching his neck. He sat there, swinging his bare, hairy feet, his fat little hands wrapped around his cards with all the attentiveness of a miser clinging to his last shilling.

The game had been suggested to the soldiers shortly after their arrival in Koeblitz and they had thought to make an easy mark of the halfling. As General Hock's cook, Theodo could be expected to have a purse as fat as the paunch that strained against his belt and disfigured his broadcloth breeches. A site had been chosen, a spot where they could conduct their games without any undue attention from officers and nobles. The grimy little yard that was squashed between some of the mud-brick hovels that squatted just beyond the township proper seemed an ideal choice when the halfling suggested it: isolated and far too squalid to be threatened by any wandering captains. Now the soldiers were regretting that decision.

'Who can concentrate with that racket going on?' the Kreutzhofener bellowed, waving his fist in the direction of the din that was grinding on his nerves. The other soldiers followed the sweep of the Kreutzhofener's hand. Theodo kept staring at the cards lying flat against the blanket.

The gamblers were not the only denizens of the muddy little yard. It was not the occupants of the hovels who bedevilled them, for they had retreated into their homes with positively indecent haste as soon as the men had entered the yard. No, it was the chickens in the wicker coops and the pigs in their slatted sties that were causing the commotion that was grating on the Kreutzhofener's nerves. Of course, it was difficult to fault the animals, not with that gigantic… thing looming over their cages, noisily smacking its lips.

If Theodo did not rise much higher than the waist of the shortest of the soldiers, the tallest of them was similarly dwarfed by the personage who caused the swine such fright. Immense was a word used far too liberally to truly convey the enormity of the mammoth shape, or to illustrate the timid awe it evoked.

Iron-shod boots as big as beer barrels supported legs as thick as tree trunks, wrapped in leggings that might have started life as tent canvas. The thick belt that circled the brute's enormous gut had a dented shield for a buckle, the crude scabbard that hung from it appeared to have been stitched from the hides of a dozen wolves, the hilt of the gargantuan sword it contained resembling nothing so much as a wagon yoke. A ragged girdle of tarnished bronze, which looked as though it had been ripped from the carcass of a cannon, circled the monster's waist above his belt, a crude bestial face scratched into the metal.

A deeply stained shirt of sailcloth failed miserably in its efforts to contain the gargantuan mass of corded muscles that rippled through the brute's chest and arms, the rugged garment mended with scores of broad leather patches. A thick, stump-like neck rose from the yard-wide shoulders, supporting a craggy boulder of a head. The rounded steel helmet that covered that head was as big as a cart wheel, its rim fringed in fur, a serrated crest running along its top like the spiny back of some reptile.

The face beneath that helm was as monolithic as a mountain. A thick, low brow shadowed small, dull eyes. A crushed, blunted nose crouched above the immense gash of his mouth, like a craggy stone perched above a gaping canyon. Yellow, tusk-like teeth protruded past the leathery lips, the smallest bigger than a man's thumb. The stamp of raw, primordial strength was written in every inch of the figure's imposing frame, written in words that even the feeblest slackwit could not fail to understand. Even the most raging madman had enough sense to give an ogre a wide berth.

This ogre's name was Ghrum and his current interest was cramming a joint of exceedingly fresh pork into his cavernous maw, an activity that the remaining pigs did not seem particularly pleased with. The only one who did not seem tortured by their incessant squealing was the ogre himself.

'Tell that animal to stop antagonising the swine!' the Kreutzhofener snapped. Theodo simply smiled at him, enjoying the hint of fear that intruded upon the man's anger.

'Why don't you go ask him?' the halfling suggested. For a moment, the Kreutzhofener's face turned a most pleasant shade of green. Theodo paused, waiting for any of the soldiers to move. He wheezed a theatrical sigh. 'Well, then, on to more important things. I notice that you've laid down your hand, Karl. Would it be fair to interpret that as yielding? That is how a player abandons the fray when they play Sword and Drake in Nuln.'

The Kreutzhofener scowled at the halfling, glanced at the blanket, and then scowled again. 'Take it you pox-ridden toad!' The soldier rose and pushed his way through his comrades. Theodo watched him leave, a look of shock and hurt pulling at his cherubic face.

'How unfriendly,' Theodo whined. The halfling clapped his little hands together and an avaricious gleam filled his eyes. 'That makes me the winner! Would somebody be kind enough to hand me Karl's boots?'

'You've been winning an awful lot, burrow rat,' one of the other soldiers spat. Theodo sighed again.

'It's not my fault if you fellows can't concentrate on what you're doing,' he objected. 'Sword and Drake is not so much a game of chance as a contest of skill, a test of nerves.' Theodo spread his arms in an apologetic shrug.

The soldier's expression turned livid. 'Why you miserable little maggot!' He took a pace forwards, his hand clenched into a fist. Theodo scrambled up onto his hay bale, cringing away from the furious man. A brief sneer of triumph flickered on the soldier's grizzled countenance, and then his eyes grew wide with horror as realisation of what he was doing overcame the emotion commanding his body. Before he could react, the soldier felt giant fingers close around his shoulder with all the tenderness of a wolftrap. His feet kicked weakly as he was lifted into the air.

'You sit! Be nice! No cheat!' Each of the truncated sentences was spoken in a grinding bellow that pounded against the soldier's ears like a kettledrum. He crashed against the ground as his captor released him, none-too-gently. The ogre glowered at him for a moment, and then stuffed the head of the hog he had been eating into his massive maw, cracking the skull with one noisy bite.

Theodo smoothed his vest and recovered his grin, sitting back down on his hay bale perch with all the dignity of a king upon his throne. He waved at Ghrum, and the ogre slowly lumbered back to his place by the pigsty. The halfling smiled at the soldier who had threatened him, enjoying the way the man's body continued to shake like a leaf after his experience.

'Could someone fetch Brueller a blanket? He seems to have caught a chill,' Theodo said, his voice loud enough to reach the other gamblers. A few notes of nervous laughter answered the halfling's jest. The trembling soldier glared back at Theodo.

'Sometime I'll catch you when your damn monster ain't around,' Brueller promised, darkly, his voice low.

Theodo assumed a pained expression. 'Ghrum is only here to keep the game honest,' he protested, 'to make sure no big people try to take advantage of a poor little cook from the Moot. Surely you have nothing against fair play and honesty?' The last question was a bit distorted by Theodo's efforts to keep from laughing as he said it.

Brueller continued to glare at Theodo, but he pushed a few silver crowns onto the blanket all the same. Men were so terribly predictable, something that had allowed Theodo to prosper quite well indeed since his forced emigration from his homeland. One could always depend on the tall folk's arrogance and greed.

THE MARE AND Mule was the largest of Koeblitz's three taverns, a rambling two-storey structure that loomed on the outskirts of the town. In better times, the tavern had served as a way-stop for the coach lines that plied the roads between Wissenburg and Averheim. Now, however, few travelled that brigand-haunted route. The bitter relations between the provinces of Averland and Wissenland had broken into full-out fighting far too many times in the recent past to allow open trade between their capital cities. The maintenance of the road had been allowed to slide. The wardens who had once patrolled it and kept it free from the attentions of highwaymen and goblins had been posted to less neglected regions. With the demise of the road, the fortunes of those who depended upon it for their livelihood had fallen.

The Mare and Mule was only one of many businesses that wallowed in the mire of fading custom. The plaster walls displayed jagged cracks and patches discoloured by the attentions of sun and rain. The wood shingle roof was visibly decaying, the splintered shingles ravaged by summer heat and winter snow. The stone wall that surrounded the tavern's courtyard was pitted with holes where mortar and rock had succumbed to the elements, and the courtyard was overgrown with weeds and strewn with the refuse of better days. The only coach that resided within the yard was a crumbling wreck pushed against a sagging wall to help support it.

On an ordinary day, the Mare and Mule would play host only to a rabble of farmers and tradesmen, those too poor or too apathetic about the quality of their ale to patronise the other drinking halls in Koeblitz. However, with Count Eberfeld's army bivouacked in the town, times were anything but ordinary, and the dilapidated tavern was playing host to the remains of the Brotherhood of Schwerstetten. The great hall of the tavern echoed with the sullen curses and angry boasts of the grizzled mercenaries, who had requisitioned the establishment for their billet and appropriated its cheap, watery fare as recompense for grievances suffered in the battle, and grievances suffered since.

Captain Valdner watched his men nurse their grudges, the treacle-like ale they poured down their gullets scarcely strong enough to slur their tongues, much less make them forget their hurts. Few of these were physical, since the hideous enemy they had confronted at the crossroads hadn't fought like a mortal foe, but had hacked and stabbed any wounded soldier until the last spark of life had fled from his carcass before seeking out a new enemy to strike down. Valdner grimly accepted that it had been this single-mindedness on the part of the undead horrors that had allowed any of them to escape at all, leaving their dying comrades to occupy the skeletal warriors while the other mercenaries fled.

It was an ugly memory, one that Valdner was certain would disturb him for many a night to come, the cries of abandoned men as the skeletons chopped them to bits, haunting his dreams. That was a hurt each of his men carried inside him, the guilt and shame of leaving friends to die while they saved their own skins. Even those who understood Valdner's decision, understood that by lingering they would only have been killed, but even those who appreciated his tactical judgement could not rout the self-loathing that clawed at their hearts.

There was a more practical reason for their ugly humour, too. A mercenary company was only as profitable as its reputation and, rightly or wrongly, that reputation was measured by the success of its last venture. Their part in the defeat suffered by the Wissenlanders would not ennoble them to prospective employers, and it would drive down the price they could command. It would also be difficult to replace the losses they had suffered. Certainly, it was no great task to round out the ranks with a gaggle of brick-headed farm louts with delusions of fame and fortune, but to attract genuine professionals who knew what they were doing was another matter entirely. Valdner did not look forward to that prospect. He had entered Count Eberfeld's employ with nearly three score hardened fighters: swordsmen from the Reikland, axemen from Middenland, halberdiers from Ostermark, marines from Marienburg, kossars from Nordland. Now, his command numbered a little over twenty. Even the pragmatic observation that the survivors would enjoy a larger share of the count's gold did little to improve their spirits.

Valdner stared hard at the scarred oak table he sat at, his thin, delicate hands tracing the network of knife marks gouged into the wood. Perhaps if they saw some of the count's gold it would help matters along. The promise of gold could lead a man far, but the feel of gold in his hands, the smell of it in his nose, the shine of it in his eyes, that was a power that even the gods envied.

The mercenary captain looked up as two of his men approached the table. He nodded in greeting to them as they sat down. One was a tall Nordlander, his elaborate moustache teased into blond tusks that bisected his cheeks. He wore a tattered brigandine, the armour patched a dozen times over, and a heavy fur coat that all but swept the floor behind him as he walked. A big bearskin hat was smashed down about his ears, the black fur making a stark contrast to his pale complexion and ruddy cheeks. A big axe nestled in a loop on his belt, a pair of small daggers sheltering in sheathes stitched into the breast of his armour. The other man was short, almost plump, dressed in a leather hauberk and an extravagant grey cloak with silver buttons. A leather hat with a ridiculously wide brim perched atop the Reiklander's head, casting his features in shadow. Eelskin gloves covered the man's hands. Valdner was not surprised to find that one of them rested on the pommel of the slender steel blade that swung from his belt, while the other fiercely clutched the tiny silver hammer that hung from a chain around his neck.

'Raban,' Valdner said, addressing the axeman. The Nordlander took a seat at the table, slamming the leather flagon he held against the tabletop, sloshing its contents across the wood. He released the flagon and shook the damp from his fingers. The swordsman made no move to sit, standing to the side of the table between Valdner and Raban, instead.

'Captain,' Raban responded. The axeman took a pull from his flagon, letting it crash back to the table with similar results as before. He sucked beads of ale from his moustache and smiled at Valdner.

'He said he'd talk to the count about our money,' Valdner told the axeman. Raban shrugged his shoulders. Valdner felt fire sear through his veins at the Nordlander's doubtful air. 'I've had dealings with Baron von Rabwald before. He is a man of his word, a man of honour and breeding. I trust him to honour his agreement with us.'

'If you say so,' Raban muttered, dipping his finger in the dregs of ale collecting in the pitted surface of the table, 'but I haven't met a nob yet who didn't value gold more than his word.'

'I trust Baron von Rabwald,' Valdner said, a warning note in his voice.

'You can't trust any of these Wissenlanders,' sneered the cloaked swordsman. 'Filthy heathen scavengers all of them! Spitting on the sovereignty of Altdorf! Placing other gods above Lord Sigmar!' The Reiklander clenched the silver icon tighter, the eelskin creaking with the force of his gesture.

'You're working yourself up again, Anselm,' Valdner said. 'You know the rules of the Brotherhood. So long as there is gold, we play no favourites either with Emperors or with gods.'

'That's just the point, captain,' interjected Raban, licking ale from his finger. 'So far there hasn't been any gold, just a lot of talk and promises, and a lot of our men lying dead on the battlefield.'

Valdner leaned back in his chair, his hand slowly moving to the dagger in his belt. He cast a suspicious glance across the tavern, relaxing only slightly when he found the rest of his men still engaged with their libations. He turned his gaze back to Raban, staring into the Nordlander's cold eyes. 'You think I've dealt false with you?' Valdner asked, measuring every word for the right mixture of disbelief and challenge.

'Not you, captain, them Wissenlanders,' Raban replied, shaking his head. 'I've got a good sense for when somebody is trying to do me wrong. Right now, it's telling me that this baron isn't going to give us enough to plant our dead, allowing them bone-bags left anything to bury when they got through.'

'I trust Baron von Rabwald,' Valdner repeated. 'He wouldn't go back on his word, not with me.'

'These Wissenlanders are all heathens,' Anselm cautioned, his words coming out in a hiss. 'That is why the ground spits up its dead, to visit the just wrath of Sigmar upon these–'

'Enough!' Valdner growled, slamming his hand against the table. 'What would you have me do? Walk away from what is owed us? Stick a knife in Baron von Rabwald? Slit General Hock's throat? Why stop there? Why don't we just call Count Eberfeld a thief and a liar? I'm certain that will get us our gold!' The outburst caused Raban to tilt his head downward, keeping his eyes from meeting those of his captain. Anselm fidgeted nervously, his thumb rubbing the chain around his neck as it always did when he was anxious.

'Any time either of you wants to be captain, just let me know,' Valdner said, challenging the two mercenaries. 'When the baron gets here we'll get our pay.'

'And then we clear out,' Raban was quick to add. There was a trace of fear in his voice, a fear that was in all of the men. It was the main reason they were so eager to get their pay. None of them relished the prospect of fighting the undead a second time. Once they had their pay, Count Eberfeld would lose his hold over them. They could leave Wissenland to its fate with never a backward glance. At least, most of them wouldn't look back.

'If that is what everyone still wants to do,' Valdner said. 'As soon as the baron returns we can gather up our gear and put this place behind us.'

LIKE MANY OF the settlements of Wissenland, the town of Koeblitz was surrounded by fields. Foolish indeed was the community that did not attempt to provide for its own needs. Even big cities like Nuln sometimes suffered for growing too big to feed its populace, depending on the ever-capricious fates to deliver sustenance from abroad for the growling bellies of its people.

Koeblitz was not too large to feed its own, and a maze of wheat fields ringed the town to its west and north, filling the landscape with tall golden stalks for miles, before succumbing to the encroaching forest and marsh. The peasants of Koeblitz depended on their fields for their livelihood and were as attentive to them as any shepherd with his flock. Day or night, rain or shine, it was a rare thing not to find some of the farmers prowling their fields, nervously watching for any trace of weevil or blight.

The three men who prowled the fields this day, however, were neither farmers nor any other inhabitant of Koeblitz. The ragged tunics of hide and leather that they wore had been tanned from the hides of deer and wisent from the forests far to the south. The yellowtinted wood that formed the slender bows each man bore was from the pines of the Black Mountains. Each man had the rugged stamp of the wild frontier about him. The face of each was anxious, eyes scanning the rows of wheat with a scrutiny more intense even than that of the farmers. The men moved with cautious, furtive steps, slipping into the uncomfortable role of hunted instead of hunter. With every second step, one of the bowmen would glance over his shoulder, watching the timber walls of Koeblitz for any sign that they had been seen.

It was not until they had won free from the concealment of the wheat that the three men realised they had been discovered. Several fields had been left fallow, allowing the soil to recover for a season before more seed was sown. The fallow fields offered no cover for the fugitives, leaving them bare before the eyes of any sentinel patrolling the walls of the town. It was not, however, from behind that their challenge came.

A slender, long-armed man stood at the edge of the nearest open field. He wore black leather breeches and tunic, steel bow guards binding his forearms. A slim sword hung from his belt and he held a longbow in his gloved hands. A brown felt hat rested on the archer's head of steel-grey hair, the white eagle feather tucked in its band shivering in the breeze. The face beneath the hat was not unlike the rugged countenances of the men emerging from the wheat rows, a hard lean face with the cold gleam of the predator in the eye and the stamp of wild desolation in the leathery skin.

The three fugitives froze when they saw the archer standing before them. They looked around, hastily, but found that the bowman was alone. The observation did little to ease their anxiety. They knew the man they faced.

'Go back,' the bowman told them, his voice full of command. For a moment, the three hunters seemed to consider the prospect, and then one of them, a sandy-haired man with a scar over his eye, stepped forward.

'It's no good, Ekdahl,' he said, a quiver of nervousness in his words, 'we've made up our minds. We're not going to throw our lives away fighting the count's wars.'

Ekdahl's intense stare burrowed into the hunter's eyes. 'You didn't think it was the count's war when you marched with me from the Sol Valley. You didn't think it was the count's war when those things came down from the Black Mountains and slaughtered every living thing in Bernbruck.'

'They're heading north now, away from the mountains,' one of the other men said. Ekdahl looked over at him and shook his head.

'That makes it proper to abandon the rest of the province to these devils?' he demanded. 'That gives you the right to renounce the oaths of service you have sworn to the count?'

'You go too far calling us cowards, Ekdahl!' protested the third fugitive, fingering the wood-axe thrust beneath his belt.

'I don't call you cowards,' Ekdahl said, his voice like the snarl of a wolf. 'I call you deserters.' The word lingered in the air after he said it, stinging the three Sollanders like a lash. Some of their bravado drained out of them, but not their desire to escape. The hunter with the axe pulled the weapon from his belt. The others produced knife and dagger from their boots. Ekdahl did not move a muscle, but kept his chilly gaze trained on them.

'We don't want to kill you, Ekdahl,' the sandy-haired deserter said. 'Give us your word you won't give alarm until after we're gone.' The last was spoken more as plea than a demand. These were desperate men, but they had not yet allowed themselves to become so desperate as to countenance murder.

Ekdahl nodded his head sadly. 'Be on your way then,' he told them. 'I won't move from this spot until you're well away in the trees.' He raised a gloved hand and pointed at the looming edge of the forest, some three hundred yards away. The three fugitives stared at him suspiciously for a moment, and then turned and hurried across the fallow fields. Ekdahl watched them run, cold deliberation turning his heart to steel, his nerves to iron. He had brought these men up from the south to serve Count Eberfeld. He was responsible for them, both in glory and in disgrace.

The deserters were a hundred yards away. Ekdahl calmly, slowly, nocked an arrow to his bow. Straightening, he pulled his arm back, letting the tension on the bow string gather. He squinted down the length of the arrow, watching the little fleeing figures. He drew a final breath, and then released the arrow. His target crumpled into the dirt and stayed there. He could faintly hear the other two shouting, giving voice to their fear and rage. Ekdahl dismissed their cries, thinking only of the dishonour they had brought upon him.

Another arrow was nocked and Ekdahl sighted along the shaft. He let his targets run, let them feel the fear that roared through their veins. The arrow was loosed, and a second body crumpled in the dirt, a feathered shaft sprouting from its back.

Ekdahl could see the last deserter look back, terror on his face. The archer folded his arms around his bow, resting the tip of the weapon on the ground. The fugitive turned and fled, drawing on every speck of strength and energy in his body. Ahead of him, the dark shadows of the forest beckoned, tormenting with its promise of sanctuary.

Ekdahl watched the third man run, observing his desperate flight with the cold deliberation of the true predator. He waited, eyes fixed on the dwindling figure in the distance: two hundred yards, three hundred yards. The trees were almost within his reach, their branches stretching out to him, welcoming him to safety and refuge. The deserter's flagging pace quickened as one last reserve of strength fired his frame, the vitality that only realised hope could bestow.

In one fluid motion, Ekdahl raised his longbow, nocked an arrow and sent the missile flying. So swift did he strike, any who watched him would have thought the archer had fired wildly, for surely no man could take aim and let fly with such speed. Across the fields, at a distance of nearly three hundred and twenty yards, a running shape fell, dropping into the shadow of the forest.

Ekdahl gave no further thought to the three bodies strewn across the field. He did not pause to bask in that last display of stunning marksmanship. The bowman slung his weapon over his shoulder and turned. With long, unhurried strides, he entered the rows of wheat that the deserters had so recently quitted, making his way back to Koeblitz and the leader the dead men had betrayed, the leader that Ekdahl had sworn to serve.

BARON VON RABWALD sighed as he approached the crumbling walls that ringed the Mare and Mule and its small courtyard, a bitter taste in his mouth. His depressed stare took in the handful of mercenaries sprawled in the courtyard, basking in the clean air and warm sun like lizards, bottles of cheap Reikland wine and jacks of even cheaper ale clasped in their grimy fists. He looked away from the sleeping sell-swords and glanced at the stern-faced crossbowmen, who patrolled the outside of the wall, the arms of their leather jerkins and the brims of their steel kettlehelms sporting the black sash of Kreutzhofen.

General Hock had given strict orders that his men were not to patronise the three taverns of Koeblitz, wanting to keep the survivors of his army fit for a swift rendezvous with the force that Count Eberfeld's viceroy was mustering at Wissenburg. The order had gone down poorly with the regular soldiers, but it had gone even worse with Captain Valdner's mercenaries. A compromise had been reached, allowing the sellswords to bivouac at the Mare and Mule, an establishment that was far enough from the billets of the rest of the army to avoid any undue problems. To ensure that the regular

Wissenland regiments followed his policy, however, General Hock had insisted on posting a guard on the tavern. Ernst wondered if it had occurred to Captain Valdner that the men the general had prowling outside the walls were not there so much to keep soldiers out, as to keep the mercenaries in.

Ernst fingered the heavy silver pectoral that hung around his neck, tracing the embossed coat of arms. He sighed again. There was no way out, no way he could satisfy both his word to Valdner and his duty to Count Eberfeld. If only the captain weren't so stubborn! If only he would change his mind about leaving! Ernst would be able to exact some concessions from Count Eberfeld if Valdner agreed to stay and fight.

There was nothing else for it. Ernst nodded grimly to the sergeant posted at the courtyard gate. The sergeant returned his look and hurried off to carry out pre-arranged orders. Ernst marched past the remaining guards, Max Kessler's brawny mass prowling after him. A few of the mercenaries in the courtyard looked up as the nobleman passed, one or two even muttering ugly oaths under their breath. One look at the baron's formidable champion was enough to still such contemptuous whispers. Even sell-swords found Kessler's reputation imposing.

The interior of the tavern was a decaying shambles, the rotting husk of better days. The timbers that lined the soot-stained plaster walls displayed jagged scars where scroll-work and ornamentation had been pried loose and sold off. The tables were a motley collection of raw timber, log benches providing most of the seating, the few remaining chairs a mismatched collection that more properly belonged on a refuse heap. Niches in the wooden pillars that lined the hall might once have held brass-caged lanterns. Now they played host to cracked clay pots in which foul-smelling candles of pig fat smouldered. The long bar was scarred from long use, warped by water damage and pitted by termites, the wall behind it sporting a great blank space where once a mirror of polished glass had hung.

The mercenaries had the run of the establishment. The elderly proprietor of the tavern had long ago given up attempting to restrain his guests, instead keeping to his room on the floor above to wait out the storm. Perhaps his raucous guests might feel some pity for their host and leave a few coins to pay for their custom, perhaps they wouldn't. Fate had dealt so poorly with him that the tavern keeper no longer cared overmuch which way the winds blew.

Ernst wrinkled his nose at the stench of unwashed humanity and cheap alcohol that filled the tavern. There were more catcalls from the sell-swords, some of the men inside so lost in drink that they did not care overmuch about Kessler's presence, or else failed to recognise the warrior with the greatsword resting across his shoulders. Ernst ignored the surly jeers that struck at him from the shadows, training his attention on the table where he saw Captain Valdner sitting. There were two other sell-swords with him, a rakish fellow wearing an almost shapeless leather hat and another with the stamp of the savage north about him. The nobleman took a deep breath and strode over to the mercenary leader.

Valdner did not meet the baron's gaze as he approached. The moustached northerner glared at Ernst with almost murderous contempt, maintaining his hostile display even when Kessler glowered back at him. The way he sneered back at Kessler, the baron got the impression that the northerner knew Kessler's reputation well, and would like nothing more than to put it to the test. Unlike most such bravos, Ernst considered that the ill-favoured mercenary might pose a serious challenge to his champion.

'Captain Valdner,' the baron said, his words intruding upon the tense silence, 'I would speak with you.' The mercenary commander looked up, as though noticing his guest for the first time. He caught the eye of the mercenary trying to stare down Kessler, gesturing with his head for the northerner to move. The axeman glared one last time at the two Wissenlanders, and then abandoned his seat, taking up a position behind Valdner's chair. The swordsman with the hat moved to a spot at the other side of Valdner. Ernst took over the abandoned chair, Kessler standing behind him.

'To what do I owe this honour, Herr Baron?' Valdner asked, sipping absently from his jack of ale. 'Should I be so bold as to believe the count has seen fit to settle his debt with my men?'

'I have brought your complaint before his excellency,' Ernst said, the words heavy on his tongue. 'He wants you to reconsider your decision to leave his service.'

A snarled oath escaped the moustached axeman, punctuated by the blob of spit he sent flying to the floor. Valdner raised his hand to still the stream of obscenities erupting from the northerner.

'You will forgive Raban,' Valdner said. 'Courtly manners are in short supply in his homeland. However, the sentiment he expresses is not as foreign as his manners. I've had a taste of the count's service. It has cost me near two-thirds of my command. I have no intention of squandering the rest of my men fighting monsters.'

'The count will make it worthwhile to stay,' Ernst promised. A thin smile stretched across Valdner's face as he shook his head.

'The dead find it difficult to spend gold, however rich the purse,' he pointed out. Valdner looked aside to Raban on his left and Anselm on his right. He shook his head again. 'No, Herr Baron, I have made my choice. I want what is owed my men and then we shall be on our way.'

Ernst's expression grew grimmer. 'Forget the count for a moment. Think of the people. Think of all the towns and villages that lie exposed to those monsters. Think of all the lives that are in peril, of the women and children who will be slaughtered by these fiends if we don't stop them. I'm not asking you to fight for the count, I'm asking you to fight for Wissenland.'

Captain Valdner shook his head again. 'None of my men have ties with this land. You ask them to risk their lives for strangers, for ground that is no more than dirt to them. They've already paid a heavy price, standing against these deathless horrors. I won't ask them to pay any more.'

Ernst stared into Valdner's eyes, feeling the tinge of pain in his voice as he spoke. He saw the way the officer looked aside at the mercenaries around him. 'Can we speak alone, captain?'

Valdner tapped his finger against the tabletop, considering the nobleman's request. At length, he nodded. 'Anselm, Raban, leave us,' he said. With suspicious looks at the baron, the two mercenaries slowly filed away. Kessler kept his eyes on them as the two men prowled towards the bar. The mercenary captain watched Kessler, waiting for him to follow the example set by his own men. Ernst caught Valdner's stare. With a nod of his head, the baron motioned for his guard to likewise depart.

'Your men are behind this, aren't they Bruno?' the baron asked frankly. Colour flushed through Valdner's features.

'It is *my* decision, Ernst,' he said.

Ernst leaned back in his seat, shaking his head in disbelief. 'No, it isn't. You wouldn't abandon your home. You wouldn't slink off like some damned coward–'

'Coward?' Valdner growled, slamming his drink against the table. 'You've a fine tongue today Ernst! My men might not be the count's Sablebacks or the Emperor's Reiksguard, but there's more valour in any one of them than–'

'Than a baron?' An icy chill seemed to accompany the question. Some of the colour faded from Valdner's face.

'I didn't say that. Look, if it were a mortal foe, if the count asked us to fight Averlanders or orcs, I'm sure my men could be persuaded to fight, but this is different, these things aren't mortal. I can't ask my men to die for nothing.'

'Not for nothing,' the baron persisted, 'for Wissenland.'

'I've already told you. To my men, that is nothing. They left that sort of sentiment behind when they took up the road of the sell-sword. They left any sense of loyalty behind when they saw their homes burned, their families butchered and their villages despoiled. The only thing most of them have left is greed. The lure of gold–'

'Count Eberfeld won't pay,' Ernst interrupted. Captain Valdner scowled as he heard the words, for all that he had expected to hear them. 'He needs every crown to hire more men to fight the scourge. He won't spend a groat on men who intend to leave.'

Valdner was silent for a long moment. 'Thank you, Ernst. I'll adjust my plans accordingly.' The baron reached across the table and closed a firm grip around Valdner's hand.

'Don't do anything stupid,' Ernst hissed.

'They are my men,' Valdner replied, trying to pull away. The baron laughed cruelly.

'They're scum, Bruno, killers and brigands from half the Empire, vermin who would knife their own kinsmen if they saw a profit in it!'

'They are my men,' Valdner repeated. 'I am responsible for them. A man doesn't abandon his responsibilities when it is convenient. I was raised to understand honour. Let me keep that much dignity.'

Ernst released the mercenary's arm, a sad look in his eyes. 'I could engage you to protect my lands, the demesne of Rabwald. That would free up more of my own men. The count might agree to that. I'd trust you to keep your ruffians in line.'

Captain Valdner grinned and shook his head. 'I'm sure that would please the baroness no end,' he laughed. 'How is the old witch, by the way?'

'She's well,' Ernst replied, his voice strained.

'Sorry to hear it,' Valdner said, reaching down for his ale.

'She's my mother, Bruno,' the baron reminded him. Valdner laughed as he threw back his head and bolted the rest of his ale.

'She's not mine, thank all the gods!' The sound of raised voices in the courtyard broke into the mercenary's grim humour. He could hear the clomp of armoured men rushing through the gate. Valdner started to his feet, reaching for his sword, staring in disbelief at the baron. Kessler's immense blade stabbed across the length of the table, hovering inches from the captain's neck. Valdner's blade froze halfway from its scabbard.

Soldiers in the livery of Kreutzhofen and Rabwald came trooping into the tavern, crossbows levelled, swords at the ready. Some of the mercenaries sprang to their feet, ready for a fight. Their courage wilted before the menace of the crossbows, however, realising that they would be struck down long before they reached any of their foes. A barrel-chested figure encased in resplendent platemail stalked past the crossbowmen, a thick-bladed sabre clenched in his gloved hand. The bald-headed officer glared at the surprised sell-swords through the misted glass of his monocle, a pitiless expression of contempt pulling at the flabby jowls of his face.

'You did say the count wouldn't pay,' Valdner growled, slamming his sword back into its scabbard. Ernst rose from the table, trying to keep the guilt from his face. He turned and strode towards the armoured officer.

'I was told I would have time to change their mind,' he reprimanded the officer. General Hock's stern expression didn't alter.

'These scum have used up all their chances,' the general growled. 'Why his excellency allowed a fine nobleman like you to plead with these animals, I'll never understand. All of that is over now.' He looked away from the baron, his eyes canvassing the mercenaries, their hands clutching at their weapons. He gave a short, grunting chuckle.

'All right you vermin!' General Hock bellowed. 'I want every sword, spear and bludgeon piled up on the floor! Right here!' He gestured with his sabre at a spot in the middle of the room. 'One at a time, single file.' He sneered as he saw their hesitancy, as he watched the hate in their eyes smoulder. General Hock glanced aside at the crossbowmen. A flick of his hand had them raise their weapons to fire. With oaths and curses, the mercenaries began to file towards the centre of the room, depositing their weapons on the floor.

'I want everything!' General Hock roared. 'I catch a man holding back so much as a dagger, I'll have him quartered! You scum don't want to fight, fine. We'll give your arms to somebody that does!'

The general's abuse grated on the restraint of the mercenaries, goading them with barbs of humiliation. The indignity was too much for Raban. With a roar, the Nordlander drew his axe. Before he could take a step towards General Hock, however, he was slammed to the ground, steel smashing into his back. Raban twisted his neck, staring up at the man who had struck him. His ferocity struggled against the pain dulling his senses and he started to lift himself from the floor. Kessler drove the pommel of his greatsword into Raban's skull, knocking him back down. The axe dropped from the mercenary's fingers and before he could reach for it again, the tip of Kessler's sword sent it sliding across the tavern.

'I'll kill you for that!' Raban snarled. Kessler nodded his mangled face, accepting the Nordlander's challenge.

'Another tassel for my sword,' the Wissenlander said, and then gestured with his blade at the ring of crossbowmen. 'Some other time, though, when the arena is less prejudiced.'

The other mercenaries continued to file past the pile of weapons, dropping their arms with murderous scowls at General Hock and Baron von Rabwald.

'You might have left them some dignity,' Ernst told the general. The officer laughed.

'Leave this swine with swords and a grudge? They'd turn brigand in a heartbeat, looting the whole province while we were busy fighting the battles they want no part in.' General Hock removed his monocle, cleaning it with a perfumed handkerchief. 'No, it's much better this way. Without weapons there is only so much mischief they can get up to, and that easily dealt with,' he promised, locking eyes with the last man approaching the pile.

Captain Valdner glared back at him, and then shifted his gaze to the nobleman. With a quick move, Valdner brought the flat of his sword smashing down against his armoured knee, snapping the blade. Valdner tossed the broken sword at the feet of the two men and marched back across the tavern to join the other mercenaries.

'Insolent dog!' General Hock snarled. He started to stalk after the departing Valdner, but the baron held him back.

'Let him go,' Ernst said, a bitter sadness in his voice. 'Just let him go.'

CHAPTER THREE

THE ATMOSPHERE INSIDE Count Eberfeld's command tent was heavy with tension, subduing the effect of the warm carpets that covered the ground, the vibrant tapestries that concealed the canvas walls and the richness of the mahogany furniture. Even the taste of the heady Tilean wine being served from crystal decanters was lessened by the brooding intensity of the men gathered around the long table at the centre of the tent. Fear, guilt and despair mingled to form an angry, sullen humour that infected every man present.

'We should have prevailed easily if those damn peasants had held our flank!' growled Baron von Schwalb, the bearded giant who had commanded the Sablebacks during the ill-fated battle. The nobleman's white cloak was still stained with blood, one arm crushed against his breast where a sling of leather and wood held it firm. He glared across the table where the commanders of the commoner regiments stood. If he thought either his title or his anger would cow men who had so recently escaped the talons of the walking dead, then von Schwalb was greatly mistaken.

'Maybe your lordship should have considered restraining his men,' spat Captain Gunther Meitz, leader of the Kreutzhofen crossbows. He was a stocky, bull of a man, with forearms grossly swollen by years of working the cumbersome mechanism of his weaponry. 'If my men had been allowed to get into position before you and your nobs went galloping off to–'

'My men were following the plan laid down by General Hock and his excellency!' von Schwalb exploded, pounding his fist against the table. To the baron's left stood the thin, armoured figure of Andres von Weidinger, acting feldmeister of the Geschberg Guard after his predecessor had been dragged from his horse by the bony claws of the undead. The knight's haggard face was livid with a barely contained rage.

'If any are guilty of an excess of zeal, it is our brethren of the Southern Sword,' von Weidinger said, glaring at Marshal Eugen. Like von Weidinger, Eugen had assumed acting command of his knights after the death of his own commander. Unlike the Geschberg Guard, however, Eugen only had five men left to call his own.

The old Sollander's eyes were like chips of ice as he stared back at von Weidinger and the other knight felt much of his bluster melt beneath that frosty gaze. When he spoke, Eugen's voice was a tired, scratchy growl. 'Dare you say the Order of the Southern Sword did not do its part?' the knight challenged. 'We have left most of our comrades lying on the field of battle. Many died trying to fight their way free from the midst of the enemy while your men were busy scattering into the forests.'

Eugen turned his cold eyes on the other officers in the room. 'Perhaps if any of you had an ounce of their valour we would not be vexing ourselves trying to place blame for defeat, but toasting our victory instead.'

The accusing barb had Baron von Schwalb on his feet, one hand dropping to the dagger fastened to his belt. 'You dare call me a coward! You presume to tell us how our courage is not equal to that rabble of beggar knights that upstart popinjay Armin led to the slaughter!'

The ice melted in Eugen's eyes, his hands closing into fists. 'Draw your steel, baron, and everyone here will see the quality of your blood.'

The threat had scarcely been spoken when a loud crash drew all eyes from the enraged men. Shards of shattered crystal skittered across the dark surface of the table, those nearest the head of the table spattered with wine as a decanter was dashed against the unyielding wood. The man who had smashed the decanter stood before the table, glowering at those arrayed around it. He was a tall, stately man, dressed in leather riding breeches, a fine ruffled silk shirt and stiff black boots that rose almost to his knees. A gold medallion hung around his neck and upon his fingers he wore jewelled rings that further announced the many positions and titles he claimed. It was, however, the sword he wore, the broad-bladed weapon with the finely engraved golden hilt, the clawed pommel inset with gemstones, that proclaimed the highest title he bore: Count of Wissenland and Protector of Solland.

Count Eberfeld stared at his officers, locking eyes with each one until he felt them bend before his distemper. He held the stare of Baron von Schwalb longest, but at last even that fiery disposition bowed to the count's will. Count Eberfeld waited until von Schwalb was seated before settling back into the gilded throne-like chair at the head of the table.

'I will hear no more of this,' Count Eberfeld said, his stern tones stretching into every corner of the command tent. Pitched within the garden of the burgomeister of Koeblitz, the tent offered a more familiar and spacious setting for the count's military headquarters than the gaggle of rooms he had commandeered within the bur-gomeister's manor. It helped to impress upon his officers that despite their defeat in battle, things had not changed. They were still at war and he was still in com-mand. During the long war with Averland, Count Eberfeld had seen his father use custom, tradition and the familiar to bolster the flagging spirits of his troops in the aftermath of one defeat or another. Nothing seemed to stifle doubt and dissension quite like the sta-tus quo.

'This bickering avails us nothing,' Count Eberfeld con-tinued. 'It can only breed ill-feeling and bad blood between your commands at a time when we most need to be united in purpose and spirit.' The count leaned forward in his chair, holding out the medallion that marked him as commander of the armies of Wis-senland. 'If you would place blame for our defeat,' he said, tapping a jewelled finger against the medallion, 'then it lies with me.'

The statement brought shouts of denial from the gathered officers and noblemen. They might be pre-pared to point the finger at one another, but not a man among them was ready to cast blame on his ruler and sovereign. General Hock's reaction was typical of the sentiment that filled the babble within the tent.

'Nay, your excellency,' the general protested, his long moustache trembling with the volume of his protest. 'It is I who am at fault! It was my plan that brought ruin to your army, my strategy that was not equal to the task! Do not blame yourself, excellency! I assume the responsibility and would offer my resignation from my position.' The declaration brought silence to the room, nobleman and soldier alike staring at the grizzled general in disbelief. General Hock had been the field commander of Wissenland's army for as long as many of them could remember, a carry-over from the time of Count Eberfeld's father.

The count shook his head. 'No, old friend, I will not accept it. I am not some Marienburg merchant-prince who replaces his captains the first time they fail. Nor will I allow you to take the blame for our defeat. I could have contested any part of your strategy when you presented it to me. I could have, but I did not.' The count shifted his gaze from General Hock and glanced along the table. 'I did not because, like the general, I saw no flaw in the trap he had prepared for our enemy. Like all of you, I underestimated the nature of the foe we faced. I dismissed them as a rabble of shambling monsters that could never stand before discipline and force of arms.'

'Our armies have faced the walking dead before,' protested Ernst from his seat near the count. 'In my grandfather's time, a necromancer despoiled the graves of Oberaltgaeu and marched upon the town. The re-animants were soon put down, with few casualties among Rabwald's soldiers.'

Count Eberfeld nodded. 'True enough, Herr Baron,' he said. 'The history of our land is filled with such accounts, unholy curses and obscene magics that caused the dead to rise from their tombs and prey upon the living.' A haunted quality seeped into the count's words and there was a troubled light in his eyes. 'This is different, different from anything passed down to us from our grandfathers or even their grandfathers. Did you not feel it? A hideous power, a damnable force surrounding that infernal army.'

'The fog,' whispered von Weidinger.

'Not the fog,' Count Eberfeld corrected him, 'but rather that which commanded the mists, the profane power that coursed through the entire hideous host. More than some witch's curse, more than some necromancer's foul sorcery, even from my position on the hill, I could feel it, like the breath of Old Night itself!' The ruler of Wissenland suppressed a shudder, falling silent as he banished the fear that had slowly seeped back into his mind. When he had composed himself, his words were once again spoken with authority and command.

'We underestimated our enemy. We expected some shambling host of mindless monsters, or else a legion guided by the black will of a necromancer, steeped in the dark art but unversed in the ways of war. For our hubris, for our ignorance of our enemy, we have left many good men on the battlefield. We will not make the same mistake again, gentlemen. I will not allow it.' Count Eberfeld motioned to one of his retainers, who bowed and quickly dashed from the command tent.

'Where do we go, I ask you, my lords and captains? Where do we go to learn the ways of the damned and the dead?' The count let the question linger in the air. He did not expect anyone to answer him. A grim smile pulled at his face as he saw a tawny-haired retainer slip into the tent. The footman held the flap aside, allowing three figures robed in black to enter. 'I will tell you. When you would know the ways of the dead, you must seek out those who minister to the dead.'

As the count spoke, the others in the room began to notice the three sinister apparitions that the footman had conducted into their midst. Each wore a garment of coarse black cloth, a raven embroidered upon the breast. The foremost of them was a crook-backed old man, his head as barren of hair as the pit of a peach, his nose as hooked as the beak of a vulture. A tall, slender figure walked behind the old man, cloaked in black, a sombre hood drawn high over the head and concealing any hint of the face beneath. Last of all strode a massive brute, an enormous broadsword hanging from the belt he wore over his vestment. The outline of armoured breastplate and greaves could be seen beneath the vestment and his hands were encased in gauntlets of blackened steel. The warrior's face was also hidden, concealed behind the dark confines of the great helm he wore.

'Priests of Morr!' The shocked whisper hissed across the room, many of the assembled leaders making the signs of Shallya and Ulric as they hastily averted their gaze from the sinister servants of the god of death.

'Your excellency!' shouted the outraged Petr Grebel, high priest of the cult of Myrmidia in Wissenland. The old cleric's bony hand was closed tightly around a protective amulet, his bearded face contorted into a scowl of disapproval. 'It is unseemly for these ill-omened–'

Count Eberfeld interrupted the war-priest's protest. 'They are here at my invitation,' the count told him. 'No man leaves this world without passing into the dominion of Morr. Who better to tell us the wisdom of the dead than those who serve the god and are privy to his dark secrets?'

The vulture-faced priest bowed to Count Eberfeld, and then turned and bowed to the others assembled in the tent. He waved his withered claw and the hooded figure came over and joined him. The black-garbed warrior remained standing beside the tapestried wall, arms folded across his chest.

'His excellency sent a petition for aid to my temple,' the old priest said, his voice like the rustle of cobwebs. 'I and my brethren considered his request long into the night, seeking guidance from the Father of Dreams and the Long Sleep.'

'And what wisdom did the god bestow upon you, Father Vadian?' Count Eberfeld asked, eagerness in his tone.

The old priest gestured once more to the hooded figure beside him. 'The wisdom I bring here to you,' Vadian answered, 'the words of the Crone of Morr.'

A hush came over the room, a silence so perfect that even the breeze that tugged at the tent seemed a howling maelstrom. Not a man in the room had failed to hear tales about the Crone of Morr. Some said she was a witch, others a handmaiden to the powers of Old Night. There were many who said she was the bride of Morr, that any living man who dared touch her cold pale flesh would be struck dead by the god's terrible wrath. It was agreed by all that she had strange and awful powers, that she could call spirits back from the Gardens of Morr, that she could converse with shades and ghosts.

Sometimes, in the extremes of despair and loss, a grieving family would petition the priests of Morr, ask them to have the crone call back the soul of the departed that they might speak with them one last time. Her abode, it was whispered, was a cave deep in the side of Barren Hill, a shunned and lifeless place where even weeds failed to take root. The frightful templars of

Morr, the dread Black Guard, watched over her, though whether as guards or captors few could agree.

Now this legend, this enigma stood before them. Her soft voice whispered past the heavy folds of her hood. The voice might have been described as alluring, even beautiful, but none of the men gathered around the table would have called it so. There was something within her words, something beyond sound and speech, something that evoked a chill in the air and caused the skin to crawl. Even the light seemed repulsed by her voice, and long shadows began to fill the tent.

'Woe to Wissenland!' the crone cried out. 'Doom is come to the sons of Merogens! Ancient hate walks the land once more, making steel from rust, changing dust back to bone. Zahaak has returned, he who was called Zahaak the Usurper in life, he who was named Zahaak the Worm, Zahaak Carrion-caller in death and beyond death. From the dust of ages he returns to slay the living, raise the dead and bring low the realm of the Merogens. A conqueror, a general, a king, slave of the Unspeakable One, now he will visit the desolation he brought to his homeland to the grey hills of the Merogens. Woe to Wissenland, know your destroyer and despair!'

The crone slumped forwards against the table, officers scattering before her. Like a weary moth, her hooded head sagged down onto the wood as her knees slowly buckled beneath her. Gradually, the light began to reassert itself, the crawling chill dissipating from the air.

It was Baron von Rabwald who broke the long silence that followed the crone's whispered words. 'Well... that was... informative,' he muttered, forcing something midway between a laugh and a shudder from his throat.

'I would say considerably less,' Grebel observed. The cleric stabbed a finger at the still reeling medium. 'The quality of your divinations is lacking, witch. Or are we supposed to be awed by the cheap mummery of a withered hag and the credulous gravediggers who give her succour? "Zahaak the Usurper, Zahaak the Worm"? What good is your pronouncement, witch? What is this "Zahaak"? What good does it serve us, this useless knowledge? Has any here heard the name before?'

'The name is known to me,' a gruff voice answered Grebel's tirade. Sitting near the end of the table, smoking a clay pipe stuffed with pungent weed, many gathered at the table had almost forgotten the presence of Skanir Durgrund, captain of the dwarf artillery that Count Eberfeld had engaged to supplement his forces. The dwarf's grey beard was long and plaited, his hair escaping from beneath the smoke-blackened leather cap he wore in a wild, unruly cascade. His stocky, powerful build was girded in a shirt of metal scales no larger than coins, meshed together in interlocking rows that rendered the armour more durable than steel plate. A monstrous hammer, its peen tipped in engraved silver, its gromril head sporting the visages of warrior ancestors, rested against the side of Skanir's chair. Even in the presence of Count Eberfeld, none had presumed to ask the dwarf to relinquish his weapon. One look at the hard, craggy face, one glance into the stony, flint-like eyes and few would be reckless enough to maintain the idea.

Skanir waited, the clay pipe smouldering in his leathery hand, letting the full attention of all within the room fix firmly upon him. He was a dwarf of few words and was little inclined to repeat himself for those who did not attend them carefully.

'The name of Zahaak would be well known to the men of the Empire were it not for the sacrifices of my people. It is only by the blood of my ancestors and my kin that the black name of Zahaak is not still cursed by the people of Sigmar.'

'But who is he?' asked Count Eberfeld. 'What is he?'

Skanir knocked the bowl of his pipe against the steel-nailed heel of his boot, and then restored the extinguished pipe to its place on his belt. Impossibly, his stern features became even harder as he continued. 'Zahaak is a monster born from the fear and ambition of vanished men, a thing of obscene mage-craft and sorcery. Your witch gives him many titles, but among my people he is known as the Sword of Nagashizzar.'

Cold fingers clutched at the hearts of every man in the tent as they heard the dwarf invoke the haunted fortress of the dead. If the name of Zahaak had passed from the memories of men, that of the thing he served had not. Even millenna after his destruction by the man-god Sigmar, men still trembled in fear when they considered the ancient terror that had been Nagash the Black, the first necromancer. The priests of Morr made the sign of their grim deity as Skanir spoke, invoking the protection of their god against the shadow of the father of the undead.

'Many are the debts against Zahaak recorded in the Great Book of Grudges,' Skanir said. 'Many times did he lead the armies of Nagashizzar against the strongholds of my people, laying siege to Ekrund, Karak Azgal, Karak Azul and even the iron doors of Karak Eight Peaks with his deathless legions. Always we beat his armies back. Always they came again, filling the burial vaults with our butchered dead. Against our strongholds, Zahaak's armies wrought a terrible toll, against the nations of men who dwelt on the plains, the destruction was more terrible still. He had been a king among them, for a time, but when the crown he had stolen was taken from him in turn, Zahaak looked to the lord of Nagashizzar for sanctuary: sanctuary and the one thing more important to him than his own life, vengeance! He returned for that vengeance, a fleshless wight leading a legion of skeleton warriors. Against those who had been his own blood, Zahaak gave neither mercy nor pity and the land was scoured of his race. From the oldest grey-beard to the youngest babe-in-arms, none escaped him.'

'One of the Dark Lords of Nagash,' hissed von Weidinger, turning fearful eyes towards Count Eberfeld. 'This thing is one of the Dark Lords of Nagash!' he repeated. 'It was a test of even Lord Sigmar's divine powers to drive those monsters into the dust! What chance do we have against them!'

Count Eberfeld shook his head. 'I do not know what our chances are, I only know that we must stand and we must fight. I will not see my lands despoiled, my people slaughtered by this gravesend vermin! Run if you like, baron. I will give your lands to those with the spine to defend them, those who are fit to be called men!'

The count's reprimand brought Baron von Weidinger's head low, the commander of the Sablebacks fixing his eyes on the tabletop and kept them there while indignation and shame slowly drained from his face. Count Eberfeld had already dismissed von Weidinger's frightened outburst, returning his attention instead to Skanir.

'You say that your people defeated Zahaak, Captain Durgrund,' the count said. 'Can you tell us how?'

'The Lord of Nagashizzar stirred from his blasphemies and marched against the lands of men to kill your Lord Sigmar and wipe his seed from the earth,' Skanir replied. 'He moved his legions through Black Fire Pass, into the south of your Empire. But Zahaak did not march with him. Zahaak was sent to take the longer road, marching along the mountains, to fall upon the Empire from the west. Then Sigmar would be caught between two mighty hordes of deathless warriors and the ruin of the man-god would be complete. The Black One's plot depended upon Zahaak's swift passage through the mountains. The ice and snow would not bother those without flesh to feel it. Craggy heights are no barrier to those who will not tire from the climb. The barren rocks are of little concern to those without bellies to fill. Only one barrier threatened Zahaak's march, those who already called the mountains home. Zahaak trusted that terror of his legion would keep my ancestors cowering behind the stone walls of their strongholds. In this, he trusted too greatly.

'Word was sent through the Underway and, from all the kingdoms of the dwarfs, warriors came. Oaths had been sworn to the people of Sigmar and they would be kept. In every valley, on every hill and crag, we gave battle to Zahaak's legions, grinding them away like flint upon steel. The mountains themselves aided us, denying Zahaak the open ground to assemble his armies and bring the full weight of their strength against us. By the dozens and the hundreds, we destroyed them, until, at last, in a place which is still called Drung-a-Uzkul, Zahaak Kinslayer fell beneath our hammers. His legion broke without him and the western attack never appeared. Sigmar was free to march against the Black One and the lands of men were kept safe.'

'But now this wight, this Zahaak, has returned,' General Hock said. 'Perhaps your ancestors were not as successful in destroying him as you claim.' A dangerous quality shone in Skanir's eyes as he listened to the general.

'They say strange lights shine once more in the towers of Nagashizzar,' the dwarf replied, his voice a deep growl. 'They say that the Black One stalks the halls of his fortress once more. Perhaps your Sigmar was not as successful at vanquishing him as your priests claim.'

'The undead are an abomination in the sight of Morr,' Father Vadian said, interposing himself between the glowering general and the surly dwarf. 'There is no peace for such unholy creatures. Their spirits are forever denied passage into the Gardens of Morr and the rest that is the reward of the righteous. They are condemned to wander the earth forever, without form or substance, tormented and abhorred.'

The old priest raised one of his talon-like fingers. 'It is not unheard of that such damned souls can regain physical form, however. They can infest the bodies of those who practise the black arts, possessing the flesh of a living vessel. At certain times, when the powers of the profane are at their strongest, when Morrsleib is at its fullest and fell winds blow from the north, the bones of the accursed can rise once more with blasphemous mockery of life. If this Zahaak was indeed a minion of he whose name it is obscenity to speak, then the black powers of his master would have been strong in him. Even if Captain Durgrund's ancestors did slay him, who can say how long a grave may hold such a creature.'

'The question remains,' Ernst said, looking from priest to dwarf, 'how do we, as mortal men, destroy something empowered by such ancient evil?'

'You must seek out the stone fang.' The words were spoken in a hoarse whisper. The Crone of Morr had risen from her stupor, leaning against the powerful body of the Black Guardsman for support. Her voice seemed drained, withered, lacking in vitality. Gone was the ethereal energy that had coloured her earlier speech, the icy chill that had drawn light and warmth from the room. It was the voice of a woman now, not the voice of an oracle.

The crone shivered against the armour of her guard, cringing away from the attention her words had drawn to her. Almost, it seemed, she would not explain her cryptic statement, but finally the soft whisper spoke again from behind the heavy folds of her hood. 'Many nights have I consulted the spirits of the dead, seeking to divine the nature of this evil that persecutes our land. From them, I learned that Zahaak has been destroyed before. Long ago, the dwarfs crafted a weapon against him, something they called Zonbinzahn. It was this the king of Karag Dar used in his final battle to destroy the wight and return him to his grave.' The woman bowed her head as she finished speaking, turning her face aside from the expectant visages of the men seated at the table.

'So we must find this weapon to destroy the wight?' Ernst asked the woman. She did not look at him, but simply nodded her head. 'How do we do that? What manner of weapon is this Zonbinzahn?' He addressed this last question not to the crone, but to Skanir. The dwarf shrugged his shoulders.

'The name is not known to me,' he said, 'but much of the lore of Karag Dar was lost when the stronghold was overrun by grobi centuries ago. It translates as "Sun-in-Tooth", if that has any meaning.'

The dwarf's words caused Marshal Eugen to rise to his feet, a look that was equal parts awe and disbelief on his face. The knight rounded the table, walking closer to the seated dwarf. 'You are sure that is what it means? "Sun-Tooth"?'

'I should know how to speak my own language, man-ling,' Skanir growled back. The comment brought a few chuckles from around the table.

Eugen paid the laughter less attention than he did the dwarf's ill-humour. He faced Count Eberfeld. 'The Sun-Tooth!' the knight exclaimed. Still his enthusiasm met with only quizzical looks. 'Grudge Settler!' he elaborated. 'The Sword of Solland, the land of the sun! It was called "Sun-Fang" in the old ballads. "Sun-Tooth" and "Sun-Fang"! Don't you see, the lost runefang of Count Eldred!'

The knight's statement summoned a chorus of arguments and protests around the table. Count Eberfeld kept silent, staring at the jewelled hilt of the sword he wore, the Runefang of Wissenland. His fingers stroked the cold metal, feeling the ages seep into the skin, feeling the long history of the sword flow into him. The echoes of forgotten battles rang in his ears, and the smell of old blood stung his nose. When he closed his eyes, he fancied that he could see the long line of his ancestors, battered and bloody in their armour, fists clenched firmly around the runefang's hilt. There was a watchful, expectant quality in their eyes as they looked back at him, like spectral judges waiting to test his soul.

With an effort, Count Eberfeld pulled himself from the illusion. He opened his eyes and the din of battle faded from his ears, the smell of blood vanished from his nose. He heard General Hock's deep voice booming above the babble of argument. 'We don't even know that the weapon the witch describes *is* the runefang! She has not said so, nor has the dwarf offered any support to your claim!'

'Is it possible, Captain Durgrund?' Eugen asked the dwarf. 'Could Zonbinzahn be the lost runefang?'

The dwarf looked uncomfortable with the question. 'Maybe,' he decided at last. 'The witch did say a stone fang, which could mean a steel sword. Iron is brother to stone, and steel is its son. If stone can have fangs, then most certainly they would be swords.'

'Then you do think it could be the runefang?' Count Eberfeld asked, a quiet intensity in his voice.

'It is possible. Alaric the Mad did help the warriors of Karag Dar during the campaign against Zahaak. He might have bestowed one of the swords crafted for your Sigmar on the king of Karag Dar, since the blade was to be used to defend the lands of men more than the halls of dwarfs. It could be just like the knight here says.'

Count Eberfeld digested Skanir's words, nodding as he considered them. At last he reached his decision. Rising, he drew his sword from its ivory scabbard. The weapon glistened in the sunlight filtering through the canvas of the tent, seeming to almost glow with a steely blue light. He kissed the cool steel of the blade, and then set the weapon reverently on the top of the table.

'The matter is decided then,' he told his officers. 'We must gather our strength and ride against this horror once more. This time with me in the vanguard.'

An expression of horror filled General Hock's face. The old soldier grabbed the count's arm, the strength of his grip rumpling the soft fabric of the sleeves. 'My lord, you can't risk yourself! Think of your people! They cannot endure without their sovereign!'

'I fear if we do not destroy Zahaak, I won't have any people left to rule,' Count Eberfeld admonished him, pulling away from the general's grip.

'But if you failed, excellency,' Grebel warned, 'think of what it would mean. The sword of Wissenland would be lost with you! The very sovereignty of our land would be challenged. Averland and the Reik already gaze upon Wissenland with covetous eyes. The loss of the runefang would weaken our legitimacy. Would you have Wissenland absorbed by other lands, have it vanish the way of Solland?'

'There is a more practical consideration,' Skanir said, drawing the count's attention back to him. 'If the witch is indeed speaking of the runefang that was given to Solland, and if it was indeed used to destroy Zahaak, then the runes Alaric placed upon it might be very different from those on your sword. The spirit of each blade is its own.'

'You mean that our runefang might not be able to kill Zahaak?' Ernst asked. The dwarf nodded his head grimly.

'Then there is nothing else for it,' Count Eberfeld concluded. 'We must find the Solland Runefang.'

'How can we do that?' scoffed Baron von Schwalb. 'The sword was stolen by the orcs when they killed Count Eldred and sacked Pfeildorf! It hasn't been seen by human eyes for centuries!'

'Maybe not,' Skanir agreed, 'but quite a few dwarfs have seen it. After the Ironclaw's defeat at Grunburg, the sword passed into the hands of one of his lieutenants, a warlord called Gordreg Throatripper. The orc was killed after he tried to lay siege to Karak Hirn. His body was carried off by his warriors and entombed somewhere in the Black Mountains.' The dwarf spat on the ground, his words turning bitter. 'It's the custom of the filthy grobi to break into the war-crypts of my people and bury the carcasses of their vile warlords in them.'

'So the Sword of Solland could still be lying in some orc's tomb?' Eugen asked, uncertain whether the prospect was disgusting or exciting. The indignity of spending centuries with the rotting bones of an orc was hardly the sort of fate the runefang deserved.

'Why not have the witch tell us!' Captain Meitz suggested. 'Her spooks and spectres should surely be able to spot it easily!'

The Crone of Morr pressed still closer to the hulking Black Guardsman. 'It doesn't work that way,' she said, her voice small and weak. 'One must be careful what one asks the spirits. You never know what else might be listening.' She suppressed a shudder. 'I would not dare consult them here, not so close to *him*!'

'But you could ask them to guide you, at least if you were further away,' said Ernst. 'Further away from Zahaak's army?' The woman gave the faintest nod of her head.

Skanir laughed, straightening in his chair. 'Let the witch guide you all she wants. If the grobi put Gordreg in one of our crypts, then you'll need a dwarf to find it for you. Otherwise you'll be scratching around canyons and caves for years, and even then you might never find it.'

'Does that mean you are offering your services as guide, Captain Durgrund?' Count Eberfeld asked. Skanir stroked his beard for a moment, and then nodded.

'If you're set on this treasure hunt, a dwarf is the last person who'd call the idea ridiculous,' Skanir said. 'Finding lost treasure is in our blood. Yes, I'll go. I can leave my uncle in command of the cannon. My fee is five hundred gold crowns and half of whatever other treasure the orcs buried with Gordreg.'

Skanir's price brought roars of protest from every quarter, but the count brushed them aside. 'Done,' he said. He had no intention of wasting time haggling with a dwarf over his fee, something that was commonly measured in days rather than hours. Besides, he had seen a fair sampling of dwarf stonework when he'd visited Karak Norn years ago. If dwarfs had a mind to hide something, then it tended to remain hidden. Without Skanir's knowledge of dwarf engineering they might never find the crypt.

'And who leads this wild goose chase?' grumbled von Schwalb. Count Eberfeld stared across the table at the man he had already chosen for the job.

'I think Baron von Rabwald would be the best choice, don't you?' Count Eberfeld asked, enjoying the grimace that flickered across von Schwalb's features. 'He has proven himself a tireless and loyal servant of Wissenland and a most capable commander in the field. I don't think there is anyone I would trust more.'

Ernst felt his face grow flush as the count heaped praise on him. 'Excellency, I must respectfully decline. My place is with my men.'

Count Eberfeld waved aside Ernst's protest. 'I was planning on dismissing your men, baron. Send them back to guard against any move by the enemy towards Rabwald.'

'Are you certain they can be spared?' The count had offered the best bait he could to tempt Ernst: an honourable way to spare his men the horror of fighting Zahaak's army again. The baron did not fear to do so, but he did not want to see his men cut down in hopeless battle. They could return to their homes, prepare Rabwald's defences, and maybe make a decent fight of it should Zahaak's legion press deep enough into Wissenland to threaten the barony.

'I am having new units mustered in the north,' Count Eberfeld replied. 'There will be plenty of fresh troops to replace yours. Naturally, you'll be given a small command to lead, enough soldiers to provide protection, but not so many that the enemy will notice.'

'I'll handpick the best men from each regiment to accompany the baron,' General Hock offered.

'Your excellency, general, I would also offer the services of my order,' said Marshal Eugen. 'Recovering the Runefang of Solland would be the greatest glory our order could ever hope to claim. Indeed, after our losses, perhaps it is the only glory still left to us. Please, my lord, accept the humble services of my men in this. Allow us this final honour. Five knights can mean little to your army, but we may count for much to the baron and his expedition.'

Count Eberfeld shook his head. 'The decision is not mine to make, marshal.' The knight turned bowing before von Rabwald's chair. The baron reached forwards, grabbing his shoulder.

'It will be an honour to have such renowned warriors as the Knights of the Southern Sword riding at my side,' he said. There were actually tears in Eugen's eyes as the old veteran looked up at the baron.

Count Eberfeld replaced his runefang in its ivory scabbard. 'It is settled then. General Hock will visit each of your regiments and draw men and provisions for the baron's expedition. I expect every man at this table to give the general complete assistance. Time is of the essence, gentlemen. We cannot count upon Zahaak's legion to remain encamped upon the battlefield for long, and when those fiends start marching again, Wissenland will bleed.'

CHAPTER FOUR

'IDIOT,' THE HAGGARD-faced halfling muttered under his breath for what must have been the hundredth time in the last thirty minutes. The ruddy glow of schnapps burned beneath his cheeks, not the cheap ale the village taps had to offer, but rather a sampling of the private (and illegal) stock that he kept hidden in the oversized cart that served as his mobile kitchen. A bit too large a sampling. His head felt as if a pair of weasels were racing around inside his skull. He'd been a bit too flush with his winnings of the night before and the resultant celebration had been a bit excessive. Fine and well, but when he had awakened from his stupor he found that a very important personage was no longer standing guard over his tiny kitchen wagon. If the alcohol hadn't sickened him, the surge of fear he felt when he found Ghrum gone certainly would have. Tiny hands clenched into impotent fists, trembling as a surge of anger coursed through his body.

'Theodo Hobshollow,' he snarled under his breath, 'if you had half a brain you'd be a menace.' The halfling kicked angrily at a small stone lying in the street, cursing still more lividly as his hairy foot discovered the moist stickiness of a dog turd rather than the rigid substance of stone. Theodo rolled his eyes skyward as he wiped the filth from his foot. The streets were bustling with soldiers and townsfolk hurrying to outfit the small expedition that Baron von Rabwald was detaching from the main body of the count's army. Some of them laughed as they saw his distress, others simply pushed their way past him, brushing him aside with that air of superiority and arrogance that Theodo so despised in the tall folk.

The halfling's eyes narrowed as he noticed two men slithering their way through the crowd. They were trying to be stealthy, but failing quite miserably at it. The intense, sullen look on their faces gave away any possibility that the men weren't about some sinister business. Somebody was clearly in a great deal of trouble, Theodo realised as the men continued to squirm their way through the crowd. Then his keen eyes widened with shock as he recognised one of those faces. It was Brueller, one of the less gracious rubes he'd suckered into his crooked card game the previous night!

Oh yes, someone was most certainly in a lot of trouble. Unfortunately, it looked like that someone was named Theodo Hobshollow. The halfling felt a lump grow in his throat as he spotted the ugly-looking sword hanging from Brueller's belt.

Theodo darted into the street traffic like a rabbit scrambling into undergrowth, slipping his tiny body between armoured knights and dirty crossbowmen with the nimbleness of a fox. From the corner of his eye, he could see the two soldiers react to his sudden movement, pushing and shoving their way through the crowd, but what progress they were making was far too little and far too slow. Every step seemed to increase the smouldering anger on the faces of the men. A shiver tingled up Theodo's spine as he considered what they would do to him.

Still, they'd need to catch him first, and as the halfling darted and dodged his way between legs, putting ever increasing distance between him and his pursuers, he didn't think that was going to be very likely. With his small size, the two men wouldn't even be able to see him through the press of bodies he was weaving his way through. Just to make sure the men remained off his trail, Theodo turned around, darting back across the road, and started to return back up the street from the other side, doubling back on his route. The two soldiers would be busy chasing after him in the direction they had seen him run off in, and the harder they tried to catch up with him, the more distance they would put between them and their quarry.

At least that was how it should have worked, but just as Theodo began to feel pleased with himself, he spotted another familiar face stalking in his direction, another of his late gaming companions. There weren't two soldiers after him, there were three. The halfling smiled nervously as the soldier stomped nearer, shoving pedestrians from his path, his hand closing around the hilt of the sword sheathed at his side. Theodo's eyes darted from side to side, looking for some avenue of escape. Looking back the way he had come, he could see the first two soldiers turning around, probably having caught sight of their comrade. No escape in that direction, he considered. Looking to the other side of the street, he saw the clutter of refuse and buzzing flies that marked the black mouth of an alleyway. Hardly an inviting proposition, but there was an old saying in the Moot, 'any burrow in a storm'. Theodo could scramble down the alley, race out the other end and lose himself on the next street.

A good plan, Theodo thought, but sadly reality was at odds with him again. As the halfling ran into the shadowy, narrow alleyway, his bare feet squishing through stinking garbage and mucky slime, he found himself staring at the grimy face of a brick wall not thirty feet from the mouth of the alley, closing it entirely. The term 'dead end' flared up in Theodo's mind and he rolled his eyes as he considered how appropriate the term was.

'There he is,' a voice snarled from behind him. Theodo turned to see the shadowy silhouettes of the three soldiers filling the neck of the alley. 'Mr Lucky,' Brueller added, ripping his sword from its scabbard, his comrades following his lead.

'Let's see just how lucky you really are,' the man growled as he began to slowly make his way down the alley, murder burning in his eyes.

Theodo watched as the men began to stalk towards him. The halfling reached for the dagger he wore on his belt, and then cursed anew as his hand closed over empty space. He'd left it behind in the kitchen! He'd been so furious at Ghrum for wandering off, so desperate to find the ogre that he'd completely forgotten it! Theodo lowered his gaze, looking around him for anything he might use as a weapon. His hands came up with a jagged length of wood. Brueller stopped advancing, a look of fear crossing his harsh features. He took a step back, raising his hands in a placating gesture. Theodo felt a swell of pride as he saw his enemy retreat

before his fierce defiance. It came as a crushing blow to
his ego when he realised that the man's fright was far
too theatrical to be genuine.

'Oh no,' Brueller chuckled. 'He's got a stick!' The
man's comrades laughed evilly at his jest. 'I'd better be
careful or I might get hurt!'

Theodo felt his face grow bright with embarrassment
as the men continued to laugh at him. Wasn't whatever
they had in mind nasty enough, did they really need to
mock him as well.

'I should tell you,' Theodo growled through clenched
teeth, 'that when I used to cook the soup for the guards'
mess, I always made it a point to clean my feet in the
bowl first.' The eyes of all three of his foemen glared
down at the halfling's hairy, grimy, muck-encrusted feet.

'You filthy sow-nuzzling piglet!' roared Brueller. He
rushed forwards, his rage overcoming any semblance of
caution or training. The sword gripped in his gloved
hand flashed downwards, directed in a stroke that
should have cleaved the halfling from collar to groin.

Theodo had learned long ago that there was one good
thing about being smaller than men. Men were used to
fighting folk much closer to their own size, and, of
course, there was the little matter of speed to take into
consideration. Most men tended to discount that as
well. Since a halfling resembled a chubby six-year old,
men often thought of them as such, ungainly and inde-
cisive. Theodo ducked past Brueller's blade, slipping
inside his guard as the man overextended. A jagged
scrap of wood smacked into the soldier's groin.

'Bad day to forget your codpiece,' Theodo chided
Brueller. The sword had fallen from his stunned fingers
and he had dropped to the filthy cobbles, shuddering as
red pain coursed through his body. 'You'll be pissing

splinters for weeks,' Theodo added. The other two soldiers stepped forwards. The halfling considered the broken remains of his improvised club, and then looked at the steel swords clenched in his enemies' hands. There was no doubt about it, he had certainly overplayed this hand, and been left holding the jester.

'I'm gonna shove that stick right up your arse,' declared one of the soldiers, a scowling brute with a livid white scar running down his cheek. Theodo's attention fixed upon the man for an instant, and then he was springing away from the lunge of Scar's companion. A bluff, get his attention in one direction while the real action is taking place behind his back. Theodo was too old a scoundrel at the card table to fall for that. The other soldier, a red-haired scoundrel with the bulbous wreck of a nose that had been broken once too often, recovered from his failed attack, scowling at the halfling.

Red-hair announced his intention with an almost bestial growl, swiping at Theodo with a stroke that should have sent the halfling's head dancing down the alleyway if it had connected. As it was, he could feel the cold breeze of the blade's passing as he dodged beyond its reach. The sword swept past him, slashing into the pile of garbage heaped against the wall of the alleyway, sparks dancing in the thick shadow.

Thick shadow? It had been dingy, grimy and loathsome in this little pest hole when Theodo had scrambled into it, but he couldn't say it had been quite so dark. He looked past the glowering, would-be murderers. A smug smile flashed on Theodo's face and there was a swagger in his movement as he stepped back, casting aside his club and hooking his thumbs in the pockets of his vest. The two soldiers took a menacing step towards the halfling, and then all the colour drained from their faces. There was only one reason Theodo would be smiling like that.

The men turned as one, overcome with horror as they saw the immense shape that completely filled the mouth of the alleyway, the source of the sudden shadow that had overwhelmed the dingy light. The ogre's hostile gaze canvassed them, his tiny eyes glaring into the gloom. Theodo's attackers were as still as statues, even the man writhing on the cobblestones had grown silent, the terrifying sight of the hulking monster overcame even the pain throbbing between his legs. The moment grew, stretching the silence into an almost tangible thing.

Fear still paralysed Red-hair when Ghrum lurched towards him. An enormous arm reached forwards, a gigantic hand grizzled with scars and calluses closing around the blade of his sword. There was a dull, crumpling noise, and when Ghrum opened his hand again, Red-hair's sword had been curled as neatly as a horseshoe. The soldier's eyes grew still wider, and with a shriek he threw down the useless weapon and turned to flee the alleyway. The ogre lashed out instinctively, swatting Red-hair with the back of his immense, hairy hand. Red-hair was thrown across the alley as though he'd been launched from a catapult. Theodo closed his eyes as the sickening sound of the man's impact cracked through the air. Red-hair's body wilted against the wall, trickles of dust tumbling down from where his impact had damaged the bricks.

Scar dropped his weapon and backed away, blubbering like a baby. Ghrum's monstrous face showed his annoyance. Ogres didn't have any real concept of pity and they certainly didn't respect cowardice. Ghrum stomped after the retreating soldier, looming over him like an angry mountain. The man was sobbing now, digging through his pockets for coins, bits of food, anything he thought the ogre might accept to let him live. Ghrum just glowered down at Scar. He lowered a fist, holding it in front of the man's face. With a quick motion, one mammoth finger snapped out, smacking into Scar's forehead like a cudgel. The soldier's eyes rolled back in his head and he collapsed into a stagnant heap of garbage.

Theodo hurried to the fallen man, checking that the ogre hadn't hit him too hard, and also being sure to retrieve the silver he had tried to bribe Ghrum with. Scar was alive, but he'd have a nice dent in his face when he woke up. Red-hair was alive too, but it didn't take a surgeon to realise that there were some broken bones among the twisted wreckage crumpled against the wall. With an almost dainty touch, Theodo relieved the moaning soldier of the gold arm band he wore. Then he turned and glared up at the huge shape filling the alley.

'And just where did you get off to, eh?' Theodo snapped. Ghrum lowered his eyes, a gesture that didn't really work too well with someone as small as Theodo.

'They was gettin' rid of the bad horses,' the ogre explained. Theodo rolled his eyes as he saw the entire flank of a stallion tucked into Ghrum's belt. Several of the horses injured during the battle had to be destroyed and it had become common practice among General Hock's cavalry to give the carcasses to Ghrum, the best way they knew to ensure some frugal officer didn't get the idea to put them in *their* cook pots.

'So while you are out stuffing that gigantic gut of yours, you leave me to get knifed like a dog!' Theodo exploded. 'Is there anything approaching a brain in that misshapen head of yours?'

'Ghrum sorry,' the ogre answered sheepishly. 'Ghrum not do anything good,' he added with a touch of despondency. Theodo shook his head, rolling his eyes. For all his immense size and strength, the ogre was as thin-skinned as a maiden-child.

Theodo sighed. 'Just don't do it again, okay.' As frustrating as Ghrum could be at times, the halfling simply couldn't find it in him to stay mad at the lummox, even over so serious a breach of common sense as the current predicament. The ogre nodded, but his expression was still downcast. Theodo patted the ogre's tree-like leg. 'Let's get back to the kitchen and we'll see about simmering that old horse leg you've got there. I still have some of those nice Drakwald spices you like stashed away.' That bit of news dispelled the ogre's funk and he lumbered after the halfling.

Theodo paused at the mouth of the alley, looking down at the still-reeling figure of Brueller. 'See you get a surgeon down here for your friends,' he advised, 'and I wouldn't suggest trying this sort of thing again. Next time my friend here won't be so restrained.'

Brueller glared back at the halfling. 'This isn't over you muck-sucking–'

Theodo looked up at Ghrum. The ogre reached down, grabbing Brueller's arm. With a quick tug he popped it from the socket. The soldier's howling scream was almost deafening.

'Worrying about that arm should slow you down,' Theodo commented, marching out into the street, Ghrum following in his wake. 'Trust me, it's going to hurt twice as much going back in as it did coming out.'

* * *

FEW PLACES IN Koeblitz were quite as active as the guild-hall where Ernst had billeted his soldiers. The men hurriedly packed their gear, an energy in their actions that was absent from the rest of the camp. These men weren't making ready for another brutal foray against the undead, and that was what set them apart from their fellows. They were out of the fight and on their way to hearth and home where the cold, lifeless legions of Zahaak would plague them only in memories and dreams.

They were not cowards, these men their baron had led down from the green fields of the north. Against any normal foe, they would have protested being dismissed in so summary a fashion. Zahaak, however, was no natural foe, but a thing of death and darkness. Many felt it was hopeless to try to stand against such an enemy, a thing already dead yet imbued with a cruel, profane vitality. No man wanted to sell his life on the impossible, to bleed his last for a cause that was already lost. Worse, it was whispered through the camp that those who fell in battle against Zahaak's legion rose again to join it. Myth or truth, the prospect was enough to chill the hardiest soul.

No, he did not hold the anxious enthusiasm of his men against them as they shouldered their crossbows and halberds. They had fought well in battle, as well as any man could against such terrible power. They had earned their reprieve, earned it with the blood of the kin they had left behind on the battlefield. Even so, Ernst felt a sickness in his heart as he watched his men form ranks, as he listened to their surviving officers bark orders. Part of him wished he was going with them, back to the deep forests and rolling hills of their home. Part of him wished that they were coming with him, these old comrades in arms, but he knew that Rabwald needed them more than their baron did. If the enemy found its way to the barony, Rabwald would need every man to defend it.

Some of the soldiers had offered to stay with their baron in a show of loyalty that had moved the nobleman deeply. He had turned them all away, and when he saw the flash of relief on the faces of his men when he did so, he knew that he had made the right choice. Let them return to their homes and their families. Let them use whatever time they had as best they could. Who could say how late the hour had grown for Wissenland? If the count could not stop Zahaak's legion, then all their hopes rested on the prophecies of a witch.

The soldiers of Rabwald snapped to attention at a command from their sergeant. The men turned and faced the baron, snapping their heels and saluting their ruler with all the precision and dignity of an elector count's royal guard. Only the tears rolling down the faces of many of them spoiled the effect. They wanted to return to their homes with all their hearts, but that fact couldn't keep them from feeling that they were abandoning their baron, couldn't keep tiny knives of guilt from stabbing at their conscience. Ernst returned their salute, standing as still as a statue while he watched his troops march from the guildhall. A sense of aloneness coursed through him. It was a ridiculous feeling to entertain while standing in the middle of Count Eberfeld's army, but he felt it just the same as the last of his soldiers tramped past the double-doors of the hall.

A shadow moved against the plaster wall of the guildhall, drawing Ernst's lingering gaze away from the open doors. He smiled when he saw the figure advancing towards him, the shadows doing little to hide the brutish, mangled face that stared back at him. Kessler strode to his baron's side, offering him a little silver flask. The baron accepted the flask and let the stinging warmth of the brandy slide down his throat. Kessler upended the flask as it was returned to him, taking a long pull. He coughed and wiped the fiery residue from his lips with his sleeve.

'You should be a bit more careful,' Ernst reprimanded his champion.

Max Kessler smiled back at him, that crooked, broken smile that told of a jaw broken too many times to retain its symmetry. 'Not used to a nobleman's brew,' he said. 'Bit too fine for my tastes.'

'You can still leave with them, you know,' the baron reminded Kessler. The swordsman grunted and shook his head.

'Them you can send away,' he said. 'Me, I'm staying. There aren't any warm beds to entice me back to Rabwald, no crops waiting for me to tend them. My place is here, with my baron.'

Ernst recovered the flask from Kessler and took another sip of the rich Estalian brandy. 'It could be nothing more than a fool's errand. We've only the words of a witch to go by, after all. All of us might be doing nothing more than chasing shadows while all of the real fighting is happening back here.'

Kessler's broken smile broadened. 'If it's a fool's errand then you should have at least one fool along for the ride,' he said. 'That way you'll have somebody to blame if we wind up chasing our tails.'

GREY SMOKE FILLED the small shrine, billowing around the polished marble archway that opened onto a bare stone wall. The doorway was a symbol, a talisman of the gate that no mortal could cross, the bridge between the land of the living and the gardens of the dead. A small fire smouldered in the depression of the stone altar that stood before the doorway to nowhere, acrid fumes rising from the dried twigs and raven bones the priests of Morr had cast into the flames. The priests stood in a silent circle around the altar, letting the smoke billow around them. Sometimes their gaunt shadows vanished completely within the fumes, as though shrouded in fog. Sometimes the smoke seemed to shrink away from them, almost like a living thing, repulsed by their morbid mantles of black.

Carlinda stood well away from the altar and the smoke. The rituals of the priests were different from those that she practised, for all that they were bound upon the same purpose. Father Vadian had explained it to her once, likening the difference as being that between a man and a fish: a man must learn to swim, must think about how to swim, must concentrate his body and mind to swim, but a fish simply *does*.

It was the same way with her 'gift'. The priests had to train their minds and souls, had to spend years learning the proper rites and prayers to do what Carlinda was able to do simply by opening her mind to the power. It frightened her, and she knew that it frightened the priests. The voices frightened her, the whispers that were always there, scratching at her brain, trying to force their way in; the little grey shapes that flickered at the corner of her vision, vanishing whenever she tried to focus upon them. Father Vadian had explained it to her, saying that it was the breath of Morr, swirling around her like a veil, filling her with his sombre energies. The wall between the realm of the living and the realm of the dead was thin around her, allowing Carlinda to cross that inviolate barrier, to see into the gardens of the dead, enabling other things to see into the world of the living.

Carlinda felt a flutter of fear pass through her and she pulled the coarse black robe she wore more tightly around her. She had been warned that without control, her 'gift' would destroy her, that the breath of Morr would consume her, that things from beyond might infest her body and send her soul shrieking into the darkness. She had tried so desperately to learn that control, but she knew it was still beyond her. The priests learned control before they were ever allowed even the slightest invocation of Morr's dark power. She, a simple widow from a simple village, had such power that even the scions of the temple held her in reverence and fear. Perhaps that made it too late to learn to control it. Perhaps it was already too strong to control.

Even if Father Vadian had not asked her, she would have held back from partaking in the ritual. She wondered if the priest felt it too, that overwhelming sense of threat clawing at the edge of awareness, like a wolf prowling just beyond a campfire. In Count Eberfeld's tent, as she called upon the ancient spirits, it had taken all of her will to keep that *other* from sensing her, to keep it from invading her mind. Now, as Vadian and the other priests called upon Morr for guidance, as they sought wisdom from the departed dead, Carlinda could feel the unseen menace hovering all around them. She felt another tremor of fear. Father Vadian was right to exclude her.

The priests began their low, muffled chant, folding their hands before them and bowing their hooded heads. The smoke billowing from the altar grew brighter, fading into an ashy hue. It swirled above the priests, contorting into a spiral that danced above their heads. The chanting increased in tempo and speed, the motions of the smoke responding in kind. As the voices of the priests grew louder, the volume of grey haze above them swelled, becoming a foggy cloud that seemed to push back the ceiling of the shrine to accommodate it.

Carlinda watched as the cloud began to split, figures beginning to form within the haze. Father Vadian had broken away from the chanting, his voice ringing out loud above the chants of his acolytes. The figures began to take on distinct forms, the outlines of heads and shoulders becoming clear. At the periphery of the cloud, Carlinda saw three tiny shapes form, three little things with huge, infant heads and stumpy infant arms.

With a gasp, Carlinda looked away, a burning hurt searing her from the inside. At once the chanting became muffled, as though something was trying to smother the sounds. Father Vadian's voice became a shout, yet this too was being smothered. Horror displaced the old pain that stabbed at Carlinda, her eyes wide with terror. She'd allowed her control to slip and, without fully realising it, she'd opened herself to that trio of tiny wraiths, those pitiable things that were forever reaching out for her. But there was something else reaching out for her now, something much more powerful.

The smoke above the priests had grown dark, like a noxious fume. The figures that had been forming in the haze vanished, scattered before the onrushing wave of force that rushed into the vacuum. The ashen hue blackened until it was darker than the night. The swirling smoke collapsed upon itself, converging into a mass of shadow. Carlinda could see a shape mustering within that shadow, could see the smoke forming the outline of an immense skull. Nests of worms squirmed within the sockets of that fleshless face, writhing with something too unclean to be called life. The chants of the priests turned to muted cries of terror, and they scrambled away from the altar.

Hurriedly, Carlinda concentrated on closing off the cord of power that had allowed the thing to find her. She concentrated, her pulse roaring like thunder, her soul cowering within its fleshy shell. She tried to close her mind to the morbid energies of Morr's breath. The hideous skull turned in the air above the altar, shifting its maggot-filled sockets in every direction, looking, searching. Sweat beaded on Carlinda's brow and dripped down her spine. Her breast heaved with the rapid, desperate breaths she gasped down into her lungs. I will not think his name, she told herself. I will not think his name. I will not think his name.

Zahaak, the Worm.

The shadowy apparition spun around the altar, glaring full into Carlinda's face. The rictus grin of the sending seemed to laugh at her feeble efforts to deny it. Maggots dripped down from the sockets of the skull, writhing tendrils of black evil. Like great eels, they slithered across the shrine towards her. Carlinda watched the worms crawl towards her, unable to move, unable even to scream. She had to concentrate, had to keep her mind closed to the energies swirling around her. If she opened up to them now, if she opened up to them here, then the thing in the shadow would rush in, would fill her and would discover all that she knew.

The shadow maggots continued to writhe across the shrine, flopping with loathsome undulations. Carlinda felt her resolve falter as she imagined those slimy, ropy bodies twining around her legs. Her flesh crawled in anticipation of their cold, clammy touch. The death's head grin of the sending seemed to gloat at her weakness. *Soon*, it said to her, *you will belong to me.*

From Carlinda's left, an armoured figure forced itself towards the spectral worms. The Black Guardsman held his sword in both hands, straining to cut his way through the invisible force that strove to hold him back. Carlinda tore her eyes from the templar, refusing to be distracted by his efforts. She forced herself to stare into the sneering visage of the sending, forced herself to watch the endless stream of maggots dripping from its eyes.

Every movement strained his muscles, every step was a burning agony in his flesh, yet the templar struggled onwards. It was like fighting against a powerful current, a current that bit and clawed as it swept past. The Black Guardsman ground his teeth against the pain. There was room in his mind for only one thing: the stream of worms crawling towards the Crone of Morr. He would stop those shadowy maggots from reaching her, or he would die in the attempt. Victory or death, the only choices a Black Guardsman could ever accept.

The worms were slithering nearer to Carlinda, their oozing shapes causing the grass to wither beneath them. Perhaps the sending had intended to break Carlinda's concentration so that it could rush into her body, using the worms only as a means to distract her. Now, however, the worms moved with a new urgency, an awful new sense of purpose about them. The stink of unclean death filled the shrine, gagging those who drew its filth into their lungs.

Carlinda's gaze wavered, and she stared down at the ground where the worms were nearly upon her. A few more feet and the first would touch her, would place its slimy coils around her. She forced her eyes shut.

The templar reached the worm just as it reared back to launch itself at the woman. His thick-bladed sword lashed out, cutting through the current of force that strove to hold him back, chopping through the shadowy essence of the worm. The thing faded like mist as the knight's sword caught it, leaving no sign of its existence except the withered grass left in its wake. The templar felt the current draw back and he leapt forwards, placing his body between the carpet of black maggots and Carlinda.

In that instant, there was a tremendous flash of cold, icy light. The smell of death was vanquished, and the horde of worms vanished as though they had never been. The sending and the smoke it had inhabited were gone, only a thin wisp rising from the clutter of twigs and bones lying strewn across the altar. Father Vadian clutched one arm to his chest, the sleeve of his robe still smoking from where he had swept his arm through the ritual fire, breaking the awful spell.

The old priest turned to Carlinda, striding towards her as the other priests slowly filtered back into the profaned shrine. The oracle looked back at him, studying the grim intensity on his face.

'The enemy is more powerful than we dreaded,' Vadian said. 'To profane a rite of Morr, in a place sacred to the god of death...' He suppressed the panic that was edging his words. 'He already knows of you. How much more might he also know?' The priest shook his head. 'You should not go with them when they leave tomorrow.'

Carlinda took a hesitant, ungainly step towards the priest. The templar caught her before she could fall. 'I must go,' she rasped, her voice hoarse from her exertions. 'They are going because of what the spirits have told me. Whatever happens to them, it will be my responsibility.'

'What if this happens again?' Vadian demanded, his voice hard but without cruelty.

'I will stay closed to the breath of Morr,' she answered. 'Not until we are far from here will I call out to the spirits again.'

'Who can say how far is far enough against something with that kind of power?' Father Vadian frowned when he saw that his words were not weakening the woman's resolve. He glanced away from her, looking instead into the iron mask of the templar.

'Sergeant-acolyte Kant will accompany you,' Father Vadian said. 'If the enemy is able to profane the sacred rites of Morr, at least it respects steel blessed in Morr's name.'

THE BARN THAT had been commandeered by the archers from the Sol Valley was a rambling, half-timbered structure leaning precariously against a motley array of wooden struts and beams. Cows and mules had been turned out from the building, forced to shelter in the field behind the farmer's house, but their animal reek lingered on, soaked into the walls of the barn. More polished soldiers would have found the billet untenable, but the rough woodsmen and hunters from the Solland were used to far worse conditions. So long as there was a roof over their heads and soft straw under their backs, they were content.

General Hock wrinkled his nose at the stench as he walked into the barn. His appearance caused some of the archers to leap from their pallets, hurriedly saluting their commander. Others, those without even the discipline of town militiamen in their background, simply nodded their heads, if they bothered to acknowledge the officer at all. Hock gave no notice to either discipline or disorder, but continued on his way, deeper into the makeshift barracks. Soldiers hurried to hide the evidence of a small campfire, a half-cooked chicken disappearing even more rapidly. Even quicker to vanish were several jars of cheap wine and tepid beer that the Sollanders had broken out as soon as they were certain there were no officers around. Hock paid even these sights little mind; many Koeblitz farmers would be missing chickens before the army moved on, and the bottled spirits were a problem that could wait until later. Right now, the general had bigger fish to fry.

He found his man in the loft, rubbing a pungent-smelling polish into a long yew pole. General Hock climbed the short ladder leading up into the loft, feeling it sigh beneath his weight. He felt comfortable only when the solid planking of the loft was under his feet. That comfort faded when his eyes chanced to fall upon the coarse leather quiver resting beside the bowman. It was scarred with a riotous array of hash marks, too many to be easily counted. Hock knew that each mark represented a life that had ended with an arrow. Three of the hash marks stood bright and livid, freshly scarred into the leather.

'General,' the bowman sitting in the loft said, though his eyes never left the yew bow he was polishing. 'If I had known you were going to pay a visit, I would have kept the men in some semblance of order.'

'Not at all, Ekdahl,' Hock replied. 'I keep your mob around to fight, not to look pretty. The count has the Sablebacks for that sort of thing.' The general snickered at his own joke, but the levity brought no response from Ekdahl. Feeling awkward, Hock glanced around the loft, moving to a bale of hay situated across from the bowman. With a grunt, the heavy-set officer lowered himself onto the improvised chair. His eyes again turned to the quiver and its freshly cut notches.

'You're short some men, I hear,' the general said.

'Expired from injuries sustained in battle,' Ekdahl explained. He dipped the rag he was holding into a small clay pot and began rubbing a fresh layer of polish into his bow.

'I understood they were caught deserting and killed.'

'You understood wrong,' Ekdahl rejoined. 'It is all in my report. Their families can use the restitution. It is still three crowns for any man killed while serving in the count's army?'

General Hock stroked his long moustache. He didn't feel like challenging Ekdahl over the matter. The bowman kept a strange sort of order among his Solland ruffians, but there was no denying that he did keep order. Besides, he had more important matters to discuss with him.

'Ekdahl, I have a job for you,' General Hock told the archer. He wasn't a man to mince words or waste time over pleasantries, much less in a setting as pungent as the old barn. 'Baron von Rabwald is leading a small force into the Solland.'

'Mustering more troops is what the men think,' Ekdahl said, continuing the maintenance of his bow.

General Hock's voice fell to a hush. 'The men have it wrong.' The statement caused Ekdahl to lift his eyes from his weapon for the first time since Hock had entered the loft. 'The count has consulted the Crone of Morr and her ghosts,' Hock said. 'They've told him that our enemy is a good deal worse than some vengeful necromancer. It's one of the Dark Lords of Nagash.' That brought a touch of fear into even Ekdahl's steely eyes. 'They've also told the count how to destroy the enemy. Baron von Rabwald isn't leaving to gather more troops. He's going to look for the lost Runefang of Solland.'

Ekdahl set down his bow, leaning forwards, studying the general's face, searching for any sign of jest. 'I thought the baron a better man than to be squandered on a fool's errand!' he scoffed. 'Find Grudge Settler? Are they mad? It's a little late to try to pick up the Ironclaw's trail!' Ekdahl shook his head in disbelief as he saw General Hock's expression remain grave. 'They really think they can find it?' he asked.

Hock shrugged his shoulders. 'The witch thinks she can, and they're taking a dwarf along who claims it might be locked away in some old crypt in the Black Mountains. The whole thing stinks of sorcery, but the count is convinced. He feels we have nothing to lose trying to find Grudge Settler, and everything to gain.'

'Grudge Settler,' Ekdahl muttered. Like any Sollander, he had been reared on tales of the lost realm of Solland, and the vanished glories and honours that had been theirs until the Ironclaw's horde had despoiled the land. The runefang that had been stolen from Count Eldred's butchered corpse was a thing of legend to the people of the Solland, a link between their miserable present and their glorious past.

'I don't need to impress on you what the sword means,' General Hock continued. 'The count is considering it as only a weapon, a tool to use against his enemy, but it is more than that, much more. It's a symbol, a symbol of power, and symbol of rule.' Hock's voice dropped into a low hiss. 'If the sword is found, the count isn't the only one who will want it.'

Ekdahl's face tightened into a stony mask. 'What are you saying?'

'You were a road warden, Ekdahl, back when the count could still afford to have them in Solland. If there are six men alive who know that area better than you, I'm a goblin with the gout. Von Rabwald's little gang has a dwarf to guide them in the mountains and a witch to guide them to the sword. I want you to go along to make sure they get to the mountains.'

'And to make sure the right people get the sword, if they find the sword?'

General Hock smiled, his eyes dropping again to the scarred quiver. 'I am quite confident that you are perfectly suited to addressing that contingency as well.'

THE HALFLING LET his head linger over the pot, drinking in the aromatic smell trapped within the steam. He patted the bulge of his belly as it grumbled in response to the teasing of his senses. Soon enough now, soon enough. It wouldn't be seemly not to let the stew simmer fully. The hardest thing for any halfling devoted to the culinary arts was allowing his endeavours to cook for long enough. The rich, savoury smells were torture to a halfling's delicate senses and rapacious appetite.

Most cooks would alleviate the problem by snacking while they worked, but Theodo found that led to distraction and, worse, a befouling of the taste buds. What was the sense in slaving to create some fantastic delicacy if an aftertaste of raw turnip was lingering in your mouth? No, far better to firm the old resolve and tighten the belt. The tall folk had some proverb about the artist suffering for his art, and Theodo could think of nothing more artistic than a lavish meal and its satellite soups, sauces and entrées.

It was not, however, as if the current expression of his talents was particularly extravagant. There weren't enough raw materials to be had in Koeblitz to make that happen, even for somebody with a purse full of army silver. Radishes were about the most exotic thing to be had in this little Wissenland backwater. One had to be closer to the river to get anything really fantastic. Perhaps he'd see about a furlough to Nuln in the near future, to see if that little shop in the Tilean quarter was still selling basil and making those stringy little egg noodles he was so fond of.

Theodo's ruminations over his future meal faded away when a shadow fell over him. He turned to scold Ghrum for what felt like the hundredth time. If a halfling had little patience waiting for food to cook, an ogre had absolutely none. He'd had to give Ghrum the better part of the beef he was cooking just to placate him. Theodo had no delusions that the concession would satisfy Ghrum's prodigious appetite, but he had hoped it would keep him busy until the rest of the meat had finished cooking.

When he turned around, however, it wasn't Ghrum looming over him, but a slim-faced man with greying hair and a steel breastplate. Theodo's first impulse was to reach for one of his cooking knives, but he quickly recognised that his visitor wasn't Brueller or one of his friends. Officers didn't mix with the common soldiery, at least not officers from General Hock's staff.

The officer leaned over Theodo's pot, letting the savoury smell wash over his face. The man's lean face pulled into a smile and he closed his eyes, losing himself in the moment. Theodo took the opportunity to ransack his memory. There were so many officers, barons, margraves and knights running around the camp that it was hard to keep them all straight. Most of these blasted Wissenlanders looked alike to him anyway. Finally a name suggested itself from the depths of Theodo's mind, and a swift glance reassured him that there was a silver eagle on the officer's scabbard.

'Captain Markus,' Theodo beamed with a fellowship he didn't feel. 'What a pleasant surprise. If I'd known you were coming I would have prepared better and arranged some schnapps or something.' The halfling bit down on his thumb, considering how stupid it was to mention the schnapps and wondering if he'd remembered to hide what was left or if he'd left it sitting out in the open next to the salt.

'No schnapps,' Markus said, turning to face Theodo. 'Wine and beer only, general's orders.' He swung his head back around to the pot, indulging in the smell of the simmering meat. 'Shallya's mercy, but I'm going to miss that smell.'

Theodo licked his lips, a thrill of suspicion racing through him. 'Why… Why captain, you are welcome at my table any time.' He hurried to fetch an extra plate and knife from a wooden box lashed against the side of the oversized cart that acted as his kitchen.

'I'm afraid I don't have the time,' Markus said regretfully. 'I have to get the men ready. The count wants us to deploy to Bergdorf.'

Theodo set the wooden plate back in its box. 'Well, perhaps when we get to Bergdorf then. If you can arrange a bit of beef or mutton, I'll get something special whipped up for you.'

Captain Markus smiled sadly. 'You're not going to Bergdorf.'

Theodo's eyes narrowed, a lump growing in his throat. 'What?'

'New orders,' Markus answered. It seemed to Theodo that the smile wasn't quite so sad now. 'You're leaving with Baron von Rabwald. He's leading a small detachment into Solland to muster more troops or something.'

The halfling felt his gorge rise. Solland was nothing but a diseased expanse of mangy villages, goblin-ridden woods and stinking marshes. The roads were nothing but dirt paths littered with sharp rocks, the streams toad-infested sludge. There wasn't a decent eatery or tavern within a thousand miles of the Solland, much less anything resembling proper food. Crows and rabbits were the best he could expect, and maybe the odd potato, if some bandit didn't brain him first.

'The general wants me to leave with von Rabwald?' Theodo asked.

'Certainly,' Markus said, and there was no mistaking the grin on his face for anything resembling sympathy. 'Can't have a baron living off hard tack and salted pork after all. You'll go along to ensure his lordship is accommodated in the manner he is accustomed to.'

'This is some kind of sick jest, isn't it?'

'No,' Markus said, his face pulling up into a sneer. 'This comes straight from the general. Of course, I have to admit, I might have given him the idea. I don't like my men being cheated by some fat little camp follower. I don't like them being smashed up by that animal of yours.' The captain stabbed his finger at Theodo's chest. 'I don't like you. So here's what you're going to do. You're going to pack up all of your crap, you're going to hitch that brute up to your cart and you're going to follow Baron von Rabwald out of Koeblitz. If you get any silly ideas about, I don't know, maybe heading north instead of south, it will be my very unpleasant duty to have the boys from Kreutzhofen practise their marksmanship.'

Captain Markus turned around, pausing to take one last whiff of the steam rising from the pot. Theodo watched the officer march off, all the colour slowly draining from his face. He was still standing there, frozen in shock and horror when Ghrum lumbered back from whatever dark corner he'd been gorging himself in. Theodo spun around, balling his fists in impotent fury. He kicked a hairy foot against the side of the pot, singeing his toes and splashing the stew.

'Come on!' he snapped at the gawking ogre. 'We're leaving with Baron von Rabwald! Help me get the cart loaded up!'

Ghrum watched the small cook as he scurried around the cart, tossing pots and pans into the back, heedless in his anger of the disordered clatter. The ogre scratched his head, and then turned his eyes to the spilled stew.

'You gonna eat any of that?' Ghrum's voice boomed. He decided his friend wasn't interested, when a copper bowl came sailing from behind the cart and glanced off his leg. Taking no further notice of the halfling's distemper, the ogre leaned over and retrieved the muddy meat from the ground. In quick order, it vanished down his gaping maw. Ghrum smacked his lips noisily and dug a finger into his teeth to free trapped bits of gristle.

'Too much sand,' he muttered as he considered the taste.

Another bowl came flying at him from the other side of the cart.

CHAPTER FIVE

BARON VON RABWALD'S small expedition headed east from Koeblitz before turning, seeking to avoid a chance encounter with Zahaak's legion. Only when they were a day's ride past the town of Rötenbach did they feel safe enough to turn south. If Zahaak had reached this far, then the town could not have failed to know about it.

Ernst considered them a curious assemblage, and he wondered if the hinterlands of Wissenland had ever seen their like. Marshal Eugen, honouring his oaths and his order's obsession with the lost runefang, had mustered his remaining knights and insisted on accompanying what he considered a great and noble quest. He rode at the head of the column, the sun gleaming from the reddened steel of their armour. Ernst was pleased to have them. He had seen them fight in the battle against Zahaak and knew that he could ask for no more fearless warriors. That the once mighty

Order of the Southern Sword had faded to a mere handful of knights still seemed unreal to him. He could see
that forlorn, bitter knowledge stamped in the faces of
the knights, from old Eugen to Gustav, the youngest of
them to escape the swords of Zahaak's monsters. Ernst
thought of all the faded glories of Solland and wondered if this last remembrance of those glories was
destined to fade away too.

The soldiers drawn from the army by General Hock
were a disparate group. While many were from
Kreutzhofen, there was a smattering of troops from
Grunwald and Beroun as well. It was not difficult to
pick out the men from the infantry regiments from
those that had been drawn from the Kreutzhofen
Spears. They sat ill upon their horses, uneasy as they
urged them into a canter, horrified by the prospect of a
fast trot. Still, these were men who had done their part
in the battle. Ernst was certain they would acquit themselves well if there was more fighting to be done. Their
commander was one Sergeant Ottmar Geyer, one of the
few under-officers who had been left among the
Kreutzhofen Spears. Ernst found him to be a firm and
capable leader, keeping his ad hoc regiment in line and
ensuring that discipline did not suffer in the unusual
conditions.

Skanir the dwarf was more uncomfortable than any of
the infantrymen, perched in the saddle of a dappled
mule that had an unsavoury penchant for biting anyone
who got too close to it. Dwarfs were notorious for their
surly, gruff manners, and days in the saddle did nothing
to improve Skanir's disposition. He kept to himself,
smoking his pipe and carefully nursing the keg of thick
dwarf beer he had brought with him. After breaking the
nose of a soldier who had tried to steal a drink from the

iron-banded barrel, Skanir had earned the cautious respect of Ottmar's men, especially after Skanir promised to brain the next would-be beer runner with his hammer. According to Skanir, the keg represented the only decent drink until they reached the Black Mountains. If it was unwise to come between a dwarf and his gold, it was doubly mad to come between a dwarf and his beer.

Bringing up the rear of the column were the supply wagon and the bulky wooden cart employed by Theodo Hobshollow as a sort of mobile kitchen. While a pair of doughty oxen pulled the wagon, Theodo's cart was drawn by the huge ogre who accompanied him. Ghrum's enormous strides and monstrous endurance allowed him to keep easy pace with the horses. It was the nervous agitation the ogre evoked in the animals that had compelled Ernst to position the cook and his cart at the rear of the column, a position Theodo loudly protested. The halfling was worried that being at the back of the column would invite the ambitions of every brigand in the province. The baron hardly agreed with Theodo's assessment. It was his experience that very few bandits had the nerve to tackle an ogre, much less one with two dozen mounted soldiers and knights within shouting distance.

Perhaps it was the company he would be keeping at the back that was really the source of Theodo's agitation. If the horses were uneasy around the ogre, they positively hated the Crone of Morr and her companion, a Black Guardsman named Kant. Ernst could sympathise with the animals; there was a sinister, morbid atmosphere about the pair. Even he could feel it, like the echo of childhood fears, a clamminess that made the skin crawl. It was drastically more pronounced around the crone than it was her protector, so much so that Ernst wondered how the temple had ever managed to train a horse to carry her. Witchcraft and sorcery were things no man liked to think upon, but the aura of wrongness about the crone was something older, more primal. It was the unsettling feeling of an open grave, a foreboding of death and mortality. Ernst understood the reasons for the augur's inclusion in his expedition, but it took every bit of restraint not to order her back to Koeblitz just the same.

At the head of the column, well ahead in fact, rode Ekdahl, a bowman from the depths of Solland, hand-picked by General Hock to accompany them. According to Hock, there was no better scout or archer to be had in Count Eberfeld's army. So far, the man had displayed a cool professionalism that impressed Ernst, but there hadn't been any real cause to test his talents. That would come later, when they crossed the Sol and were in the backlands of the province, places where even a good goat path would seem like a gift from the gods.

Ernst hoped that they were paying attention, Taal and Rhya and even grim old Morr. It was a long way to the Black Mountains, and a long way back. He prayed that the gods would speed their way. He prayed that they would give the count the time he needed, but, most of all, he prayed that all of this wasn't some mad fool's venture.

A WEEK OUT from Koeblitz, the expedition made camp in the rocky hill country overlooking the forgotten remnant of the ancient road that had once connected Bergdorf to the dwarf stronghold of Karag Dar. The stronghold was gone now, its caravans of copper and iron barely a memory. Bergdorf's fortunes had faded with those of the dwarfs and the road that had brought prosperity to the town became nothing more than a scar on the landscape. A useful scar, however, according to Ekdahl. The going would be easier along the old road and eventually it would emerge from the hill country and connect with byways of a more recent vintage, which they could use to get to the river and its many settlements.

Baron von Rabwald dismounted from his saddle with a grunt and a sigh. Kessler hastened to assist the nobleman, but the baron waved him away with a curt gesture.

'I've covered more ground in the last week than I have in the last year,' Ernst commented, 'but I don't care how raw my backside is, I can still climb off my own damn horse.'

The effect was somewhat spoiled when his boot stubbornly refused to come free of the stirrup. Kessler kept his face rigid, but Ernst could see the amused light in his eyes.

'Not a word,' he scowled, finally freeing his foot. Standing on solid ground again, the baron stretched his body, trying to work the kinks out. Around them, the rest of the men were busy setting up camp. Three of the knights were rubbing down their horses, tending to their animals and those of their comrades before helping to construct their pavilion. The genuine cavalry among Ottmar's men did the same, knowing that the care of their mounts was more important than their own comfort. The infantry, however, had no such discipline. Several were already pitching tents and digging fire pits, a few others were leading their horses out to pasture, saddles still on their backs. They did not get far before Ottmar's curses had them quickly removing the saddles and fetching water for their steeds.

Ottmar turned away from the scolded soldiers and strode towards the baron and his enforcer. He was a broad-shouldered man, his face leathery from years of marching under the sun. A battered suit of chain peered from the rents in his tabard and there was a long scratch along the side of his kettlehelm where the blade of a skeleton had nearly ended his career. He snapped a quick salute before addressing the nobleman. 'Your lordship, I'll have some of the men prepare your quarters.' It was an elaborate way to describe a long canvas tent, but the sergeant was careful about maintaining every courtesy in his dealings with the baron. 'If your lordship has a preference as to situation, I shall have the men start on it right away.'

Ernst nodded in appreciation. 'Anywhere that's not too close to the latrine and well away from the ogre. I'm afraid he snores.' The remark managed to bring a grin to the sergeant's face. The baron only half noticed, however. He was looking past Ottmar, to where the crone and her guardian were standing. The templar had already started assembling the wooden framework of the augur's tent. 'Well away from them, too,' he added.

Ottmar followed the baron's gesture, grimacing as he saw the two figures cloaked in black. 'Aye, your lordship. They give me the shudders. I don't think simple decency keeps that templar sleeping outside on the ground. Even one of Morr's black knights isn't able to stand being close to that hag for too long.'

'Afraid of a woman, sergeant?' Kessler joked. There was no levity in Ottmar's face when he replied.

'You would be too. Carlinda ain't a normal kind of woman.'

'So she does have a name then?' Ernst mused.

'Keep calling her "crone", your lordship,' Ottmar advised. 'It suits her better.'

'You sound as though you know something about the witch,' Kessler observed.

Ottmar was slow to reply. When he did, it was in a hushed tone, as though he were afraid his words might carry across the camp to the crone's ears. 'She comes from a village not far from my own,' he confessed, 'though it was a black day when such as her was born. She were brought up natural enough, father a decent farmer from down near Litztbach. It was when she was married off that she took a turn.

Her husband was a farmer named Greber. Not long after they was married, she was with child, but in the winter when the time came for the babe to be born it came out of her stone dead, cord wrapped about its head like a noose. That was the start of it. Greber's farm had been one of the best in Litzbach, but his fields began to struggle, always giving him a late harvest. His wife became withdrawn, which was just as well since folks didn't care to be around her either.

'Greber didn't see any of it though. He just thought he'd had a turn of bad luck that would soon enough burn itself out. When his wife was with child again, well, he thought things had turned around, but they hadn't. They were getting worse. Second child came out like the first, cord strangling it while it was still inside her. Things really got bad for Greber then. His crops were failing and what little lived was too sickly looking to feed a hog. His livestock started dying off too.

'Pig-headed man, Greber. Everybody told him that his troubles had started with his wife giving birth to a corpse, so he figured the only way to break that hex was for her to have a live one. By this time folks could hardly stand to be in the same room as his wife. Just the thought of touching her was enough to sober the worst tosspot in the village. Looking at her was like looking at a vulture. There wasn't a man in Litzbach still thought of her as a woman. Even so, stubborn Greber bought the strongest ale that Anton the tavern keeper had to sell and went home to try again.

'Third time was just like the first two. Dead, with a noose around its neck. All the animals on Greber's farm died that night and the fields turned so desolate they weren't fit to grow rocks. Greber took one look at that little dead thing and just up and left. They found him the next morning swinging from the tree he hung himself from.

'By this time the midwife wouldn't have anything to do with Carlinda, so Greber had to have a priest from the temple of Morr attend her. That's the only thing that kept folks from burning her as a witch, there and then. The priest told them she'd been marked as the bride of Morr and that all the tragedy Greber had suffered was Morr's way of telling him his wife belonged to the temple, not to him. Good people of Litzbach weren't about to argue with a priest, and when he said he was going to take her away the attitude of most folks was that Morr was welcome to her.'

Ernst was silent. He wasn't sure what he had expected to hear, but it certainly hadn't been the ugly account Ottmar had related. So that was how Morr went about choosing his augurs. If he'd been uneasy about having the witch in his camp, her history certainly hadn't reassured him.

'Max,' the baron said, turning back to his horse and unstrapping the saddle. 'See if Theodo has anything edible prepared. If he doesn't, ask him to whip something up.' Ernst paused as a thought came to him. 'Speed over taste this time. I'd rather not be eating supper for breakfast.'

KESSLER PROWLED THROUGH the camp, making his way towards Theodo's cart. He could see the hulking ogre helping the halfling pull a motley array of pots and pans down, arranging them in some semblance of order on the grass. Theodo already had a small fire smouldering under a big iron cauldron. The faint smell of mutton suggested itself to the swordsman as he approached.

Across from the cook, the templar was fitting the heavy black cloth of the crone's tent to its wooden supports. Kessler glanced across at the activity. The crone was still seated on her horse, her face hidden beneath her hood. She looked like a patch of night that the sun had neglected to clear away, a sombre intrusion into the wholesome light of day. Kessler wondered if she truly possessed the awful powers attributed to her. It wouldn't be the first time priests had used mummery to make a prophetess out of some old half-witted hag.

Kessler was so intent on his study of the crone that he barely noted Skanir's arrival in the camp. The dwarf was growling oaths into his beard, glaring murder at the animal he dragged after him. The ill-tempered mule had thrown him about an hour before they had reached the campsite and stubbornly refused to allow him to remount. There was a malicious humour in the mule's eyes as Skanir forced it into the camp.

The animal's wicked temper crumbled into fright when Ghrum suddenly stood upright as he finished arranging Theodo's pots. Perhaps the brute had failed to smell the ogre, or perhaps it was simply too stupid to connect the smell to the creature until Ghrum rose up. Whatever the case, it set up a braying protest, jerking hard on the reins clenched in Skanir's hand. Now it was the dwarf's turn to be dragged, as the mule retreated from Ghrum, its hooves flailing in crazed kicks.

The mule's panic brought it closer to the black tent. The templar turned to arrest the animal's approach, but a kick from its back legs sprawled him in the dust. Another kick cracked into the flank of the crone's horse. The mount reared in alarm, neighing in fright. The horse galloped away from the mule, some of the brute's panic transferring to it. The crone gave voice to a surprisingly animated shriek and locked her arms around her mount's neck, holding on with all her strength as the wild horse ran through the camp.

Kessler reacted automatically to the charging mare, throwing himself at the horse. One hand caught at the animal's mane, another wrapped itself in the drooping reins. Kessler felt a surge of pain as the horse's momentum dragged him across the ground, burning the muscles in his powerful arms. He strained to turn the animal's head, exerting his immense strength to halt its reckless charge. The horse fought him for a moment, still blinded by the mule's panic, and then slowly allowed its pace to slacken. When it had come to a halt, Kessler reached up and grabbed the frightened rider, intending to lower her to the ground.

He froze in mid-motion. The body beneath his hands wasn't that of some withered old hag. It was firm and supple, strong and young. The hood had been thrown back somewhat by the violence of the wild ride. He could see smooth, pale skin, like polished alabaster, devoid of either blemish or wrinkle. The face hidden beneath the hood was young, not some gargoyle countenance ravaged by age. Kessler stared in disbelief at that face, at the soft delicate features, the bright green eyes. In that instant, he wondered if he had ever seen a more beautiful face.

That realisation made him hurriedly set her down. He knew what he looked like, his face with its ghastly scars and broken bones. He'd been captured by goblins, and when they'd tired of using clubs on him they'd started with their knives. It wasn't until he stopped screaming that they had lost interest, by then what was left wasn't really much of a face.

Kessler waited for the familiar look of revulsion and loathing. He waited for the woman to turn her head in disgust. Instead she kept looking at him, a strange, sorrowful light in her eyes. It wasn't pity, but something more despondent. It was Kessler who finally looked away.

'She isn't one of your tavern whores,' a chill voice snarled at him. The Black Guardsman must have run after them once he had picked himself off the ground. The templar stood before him, one hand on his sword, the other clenched in a fist. 'Keep your grubby paws off her, sell-sword.'

Crimson began to fill Kessler's vision. His hand started to reach for the greatsword slung across his back. He glared back at the templar. Then he glanced away, staring back at Carlinda. The woman was still looking at him, that strange sadness in her eyes. The anger that had flared up inside him withered. Kessler backed away, watching in silence as the templar recovered the woman's horse and led both animal and brute back towards the black tent. Once, only once, she turned, and he could feel her eyes staring at him from beneath the hood that once more covered her face.

'Crone,' Kessler muttered, spitting into the dirt. 'Somebody wasn't paying much attention when they handed that title out.'

KESSLER WALKED AWAY from the camp. It was a rare thing for him, backing down before anyone, for whatever reason. He didn't like the way Carlinda had looked at him. Loathing, disgust, horror: these were reactions he expected to find in a woman's eyes when she looked at him. It was something different with her, something that made him uneasy. It was a look of understanding.

The swordsman kicked at a bluish shard of flint lying in his path. Maybe she did understand, he reflected. The others in the camp regarded her scarcely better than they would a leper. He thought about what Ottmar had told him, about the way death followed her wherever she went. He stopped walking towards the trees, glancing back at the camp, at the black tent with the templar standing outside it. Death held no fear for him. It was life that plagued him, filling his dreams with phantoms of what might have been. The laughter, the joy of others was like salt in an open wound to him. To see children, to see lovers walking hand in hand, these were tortures worse to him than even the knives of the goblins.

She'd looked at him, looked at his ruin of a face, not with revulsion and not with pity. She was so young, so beautiful to be hidden away behind the foul title of 'crone'. Kessler's ugliness was on display for all to see, it was something he could not deny. That was how he could endure, because he knew it was there. Carlinda's ugliness was something that people imagined they saw, a spectral taint that had grown around her, fed by the superstitious gossip of ignorant peasants until even she came to believe it. Kessler had not felt the icy breath of Morr when he had reached out to touch her. He had not seen his flesh wither as his hand grasped for her. Superstition and imagination, that was all. He smiled as emotion filled him. It was strange that he, of all people, could find pity for another. He'd never found any for his many victims. Perhaps he wasn't as dead as he sometimes felt, to be moved by the tragedy that had made Carlinda both pariah and witch.

Kessler turned back towards the trees, not liking the desperate, hopeless thoughts that came to him. He'd left that all behind him long ago. The goblins had cut it out of him. Now he was a killer, nothing more. Someday, he would meet someone better than him, stronger or quicker. Then it would end. There was nothing else. There could be nothing else.

The swordsman's boot kicked out at another shard of flint. This time, Kessler watched it fly away, clattering across the rocky ground. It landed near a strange jumble of stones. Curiosity took root and he walked over to the pile. Staring down at it, at first the pile didn't seem anything more than some freakish caprice of nature. Something nagged at him, however, and he began to circle the stones. Gradually, he became aware of a subtle arrangement of stones that were somewhat darker than the others. Once the observation was made, he fancied he could make out a jagged arrow-like shape formed by the darker stones within the pile. He tried to shake off the impression, but the more he looked at it, the more convinced he was that it was there. Kessler looked up from the stones, staring in the direction he thought the arrow pointed. He saw a scraggly little bush and a few pine with moss clinging to their sides, but nothing more.

He started to walk towards the bush when he heard a sound behind him. He saw Ekdahl emerge from the undergrowth, a brace of hares slung over one shoulder, his bow in his hands. The scout nodded as he matched Kessler's gaze, and then glanced aside at the stones. Ekdahl walked over to the pile, staring down at it for a moment.

'Looks like a hunter's sign,' Ekdahl said, scattering the stones with his boot.

'Seemed like it was pointing over here,' Kessler said. Almost unconsciously, his hand had closed around the hilt of the sword slung across his back. Ekdahl gave no reaction to the menacing gesture, keeping his eyes trained on the hard, rocky ground. He stepped away from the scattered pile, striding confidently towards the bush. Kessler followed him, keeping just enough distance between them so that he would have room to work his greatsword.

Ekdahl leaned down, studying the bush, resting the butt of his bow against the ground. He pawed at the dirt for a moment, his hand emerging with a piece of tanned goatskin. The scout stared at the skin briefly, and then reached up to offer it to Kessler. He accepted it with his left hand, keeping the right firmly closed around the sword hilt. There was writing of some kind on the back of the goatskin. Kessler had never learned to read, but he was familiar enough with the letters of Reikspiel to recognise them. What was written on the piece of hide was unlike any writing as he had ever seen.

'What does it say?'

Ekdahl shook his head. 'I don't know,' he admitted. 'Those symbols are the same as those used by woodsmen and rangers, but the way they are put together doesn't make any sense. It must be in some kind of code.'

Kessler digested that. He held the goatskin to his face, smelling the charcoal that had been used to make the signs. He pressed a finger against one of the symbols. When he pulled it away, most of the black dust clung to it. 'Seems recent.'

'It is,' Ekdahl said.

'As recent as our making camp?'

'Possibly.'

Kessler mulled that over as well, but didn't like where it led. Ekdahl nodded in agreement.

'Yes, it might mean somebody is tracking us,' the archer said. He turned and stared into the woods. 'He could be watching us right now.'

Kessler folded the goatskin and stuffed it under his tunic. 'Unless he's already inside the camp.'

Ekdahl's eyes narrowed as the swordsman spoke. He rose from where he squatted beside the bush, fingering his bow.

Kessler slowly let his hand drop away from the hilt of his greatsword. 'I'll take this to the baron,' he said. 'See what he makes of it. Maybe somebody down there can tell us what it says.' Without further comment, Kessler started back to the camp, carrying himself with unconcerned confidence.

Ekdahl watched the baron's champion leave, and then turned his eyes back to the trees.

CHAPTER SIX

THE FIRST THEY were aware of trouble was when Ekdahl drifted back to the column and conferred with the baron. They had been riding for two days through the rocky hill country that formed part of the border between Solland and Wissenland proper. In all that time, they had not seen a single soul, only the occasional hill goat and river wren. Ekdahl had explained that the hill country was very sparsely inhabited. The ground was too rocky to plant crops and the timber too difficult to harvest to support woodsmen. The only size-able settlement was a village called Murzklein, built right where the hill country ended and the compara-tively fertile river plain began.

Ekdahl, riding ahead of the column, was the first to see the village. Even from a distance, he could see that something was wrong. It was midday and there was no sign of life about the place, no farmers out in the fields, no cattle out in the pastures.

Baron von Rabwald pondered Ekdahl's report, deeply troubled by the sense of unease that tinged the bowman's words. Foremost in his mind was a hideous thought. Had Zahaak turned back south after all? Was this the work of his unholy legions?

'How much time will we lose going around?' Ernst asked the scout.

'This is the only path,' Ekdahl reported. 'I'm sure we could find another way down through the hills, but it'll be hard going with the horses. We'd have to abandon the wagons.'

The baron considered that. They could replace the wagons and provisions at one of the river settlements, assuming the undead had not already been there, but he wasn't sure if he could trust the amateur horsemanship of some of Ottmar's men over such unforgiving terrain. He thought about the old Reikland adage about the two daemons, the one that was known and the one that wasn't. He decided to risk the unknown.

'Sergeant!' Ernst called out. 'Have your men ready their weapons. It looks like trouble up ahead. Marshal Eugen, have your knights fan out. Give support to the sergeant's men.'

The old knight nodded in understanding and began to spread his riders out.

'Think somebody is waiting for us down there?' Kessler asked, nudging his horse closer to the baron's.

'Could be,' Ernst replied, thinking about the strange, indecipherable message the swordsman had found. 'Head to the rear. Make sure the witch and the dwarf stay safe.'

Kessler's eyes narrowed, his crooked face lifting into a scowl. 'My place is up here, making sure you stay safe,' he growled.

The baron planted a good-natured slap on Kessler's arm.

'If we lose the witch and the dwarf we'll never find what we're looking for,' he said. 'Make sure that doesn't happen.'

Kessler gave the nobleman a reluctant nod and pulled his horse around, moving through the column to the back of the line.

Ernst watched him go, and then turned back around. 'Warden Ekdahl, if you would lead the way.'

THE VILLAGE OF Murzklein was a shabby, run-down cluster of hovels, mud walls showing through cracked and pitted plaster, thatched roofs bowed and crushed by too many heavy snows. There was an atmosphere of decay and ruin about the place that impressed itself on the baron from the start. The fields surrounding the village were scraggly and yellowing, and the nobleman felt sorry for anyone trying to scratch a living from whatever bleak harvest such a crop would yield.

Ernst quickly noticed the eerie quiet that had set Ekdahl on guard. The village was as quiet as a tomb; not even a bird flew above the hovels. The scout was right. At such an hour there should be some sort of activity, even if it was nothing more than a few goats grazing in the pasture. The baron's hand dropped to his sword and he found himself glancing over his shoulder to make sure that the men following him were likewise on their guard. Ahead, Ekdahl dropped from his horse. The scout jogged back to the column, leading his steed. He quickly handed the reins to one of Ottmar's riders and turned towards Ernst.

'I'll check ahead and see if I can see anything,' Ekdahl said.

The baron waved his approval to the man. Ekdahl turned back towards the desolate village, unslinging his bow. Nocking an arrow to the string, he slowly advanced up the rocky path, sometimes lingering behind a post or a boulder, studying the dreary walls with his hawkish gaze. After what seemed like hours, the bowman reached the foremost of the buildings. His back pressed against the crumbling plaster, Ekdahl edged around the corner of the structure and disappeared into the lifeless street beyond.

A moment passed, and then Ekdahl reappeared, waving the column forward.

Ernst repeated the gesture, and with a clatter of hooves and the rattle of armour, the riders hastened to join the scout.

Ernst and the others headed into the village. The stink of death greeted them as they approached the buildings. The baron drew his sword, his eyes narrowing as he scrutinised the decaying buildings. Ekdahl leaned on his bow, watching the riders draw near, his face the expressionless mask of the true professional.

'I've found the villagers,' he said by way of greeting. He nodded his head down the dirt street that squirmed between the depressing hovels.

Ernst followed the scout down the little lane, Ottmar's men forming up behind him. The dark, vacant windows and doorways of the village buildings seemed to watch them as they rode past. The baron saw what looked like blood splashed across the plaster front of one building, manoeuvring his horse around the broken ruins of a door that lay strewn across the lane. Cautious murmurs rose behind him, the soldiers watching the empty houses with ever-increasing anxiety. The stench of death continued to rise the deeper into the village they drew. Ernst was just beginning to consider that perhaps they should head back into the hills when his horse emerged from the narrow street into the stone-lined plaza that formed Murzklein's miserable square. He gagged at the grisly sight.

A great mound filled the middle of the square, a heap of butchered heads and dismembered limbs. A quick glance told Ernst that the heads were both male and female, and had been taken without regard to age. A spear stood above the mound, the brawny body of a man impaled upon it. The crude approximation of a splintered skull had been daubed upon the body's chest in blood.

'Greenskins,' Eugen spat, glaring at the grisly massacre. 'I've seen that sign before. It's the totem of Uhrghul Skullcracker.'

'I thought he was slain at the Battle of Rötenbach,' Ottmar said.

'We broke his army, but we were never certain the warlord was among the dead,' Eugen explained. 'It appears he pulled through, and found some more followers.' The knight rode closer to the mound of decaying humanity, waving away the thick cloud of flies that buzzed around it. He closed a gauntlet around the tip of the spear, knocking it down with a savage tug.

'First skeletons and now orcs,' Ottmar grumbled.

Ekdahl rose from his examination of the bloody tracks scattered throughout the square.

'What do you expect?' the scout asked. 'Count Eberfeld has drawn every available man north to join his army: no more patrols along the roads, no more rangers watching the wild places. Lots of things that were keeping their heads down will be growing bolder: bandits, beastmen,' he looked back at the gruesome pile of heads, 'orcs.'

Baron von Rabwald held a hand to his nose to stifle the stench. 'Sergeant, have some of your men form up a burial detail. Ask the crone if she can give the rites of Morr to these people.'

Ottmar turned around in his saddle, barking out orders to his men. Several soldiers reluctantly dismounted and started to approach the mound, a few opportunistic rats retreating from their approach.

'I shouldn't do that.'

Ernst spun around, finding Skanir grinning at him from the back of his mule. The dwarf took the pipe from his mouth and pointed with it at the base of one of the mud-brick walls that enclosed the square. It took the baron a moment to realise that he was indicating a strange object jumbled against the crumbling plaster. It was a bizarre collection of rubbish: bits of iron and copper, scraps of cloth and wool, old bones and sticks. All of it was tied together with rags. Ernst was reminded of the bundles they had seen refugees from the towns threatened by Zahaak carrying as they fled their homes, but what sort of idiot would bother about such junk? Skanir stabbed his pipe at another wall, and Ernst saw two more bundles of garbage. Now that he knew what he was looking for, the baron could see several more clustered around the plaza. He directed his puzzled gaze back at the dwarf.

'Somebody's been doing a bit of looting,' Skanir commented, tucking his pipe back in his belt. 'Probably waiting for nightfall before making away with it.'

'Looting?' Ernst scoffed. 'Who would bother stealing that kind of junk?'

'Same ones that have been watching us since we rode in here,' Skanir answered. 'They're watching us right now.'

'I don't see anyone,' Ottmar said, not quite keeping a note of uncertainty from his voice.

Skanir smiled back at the sergeant. 'I don't either. I also don't see any crows. Ever know crows to keep away from a free meal without good reason?' He stared back at the shadowy windows and doorways. 'They're here all right. A dwarf knows when grobi are around.'

'Goblins,' Ottmar hissed. The soldier drew his sword, sweeping his eyes across the crumbling buildings.

'Keep calm,' Skanir growled. 'They haven't attacked us yet, which means there can't be a lot of them. If you don't provoke them, they'll probably let us go. Grobi are all cowards at heart and all the steel we're carrying isn't going to make them any heartier.' The dwarf stroked his beard and sighed. 'Much as it disgusts me, we can probably ride on out of here without a fight.'

Ernst thought about Skanir's words. Was it his imagination, or did he see beady little eyes watching him from the shadowy hovels? He glanced back at the pile of severed heads. It sickened him to think about leaving the villagers unavenged, to leave them to rot beneath the sun. He also knew, however, that if Skanir was right, then even now they were in danger, standing in the eye of the storm. The longer they tarried, the greater the chances that the storm would break around them. His mission was more important than avenging a few hundred peasant farmers on a mob of greenskins. The fate of Wissenland had been entrusted to him.

'All right,' he told Skanir. Ernst looked over at Ottmar. 'Sergeant, recall your men. We're getting out of here.'

'You there!' Skanir suddenly yelled. 'Get away from that!'

One of the soldiers who had dismounted had walked over to a wall, intent on examining one of the strange bundles of trash. Even as Skanir shouted to him, it was too late. The soldier reached down for the bundle. At that instant, a black-feathered arrow sprouted from his chest. Before he could fall to the ground, three more struck him.

'To arms!' the baron roared. 'We are under attack!'

Scrawny, snarling shapes exploded into the square from every building. The marauders were only a little taller than Theodo, but there was a wiry strength in their wizened arms and a savage malice stamped on their sharp, toothy faces. The leathery hide that covered their bodies was varying shades of sickly green, and the cruel little eyes staring from their howling faces were leprous and cat-like. They wore tattered strips of armour and leather, the skins of rats and dogs, and necklaces of bone and sinew. Some sported rusty metal bucklers, the small shields perfectly sized to protect their diminished bodies. Wooden bowls and iron pots served some as helmets. Clenched in the hands of each goblin was some manner of blade or bludgeon, the sharpened hip bone of a goat serving alongside the rusty residue of a gladius. A few of them lingered in the shadowy door-ways of the hovels, firing arrows from short bows strung with sinew.

Ernst spurred his horse into the shrieking horde of goblins, trampling the gruesome creatures under its hooves and slashing at them with his sword. A black arrow glanced from his breastplate, clattering across the stonework of the plaza. Others were not so lucky. The spotty goblin marksmanship had brought down two of Ottmar's men, and Ernst could see at least half a dozen horses peppered with arrows.

Skanir gave voice to a fierce dwarf war cry, freeing his hammer and swinging it above his head. The goblins glared back at him, ancient hate overcoming their instinctive cowardice. A dozen of the snarling monsters scrambled across the square to confront him. Skanir swung a leg from the saddle of his mule, trying to free his boot from the stirrup. The brute pulled back in protest to the shift in weight and the clamour of battle. Skanir cursed the animal, trying to bring it under control so that he could quit the saddle. As he persisted, the mule reared back, throwing Skanir from its back. The dwarf crashed against the ground, his hammer falling from his fingers.

The dwarf rolled onto his side, ignoring the pounding throb of pain coursing through him. He could see the goblins still rushing towards him, their voices raised in savage laughter. Skanir hurriedly looked for his hammer, cursing when he saw it a few feet away, a slavering goblin standing over it. The goblin grinned at him and fingered its notched iron sword. Skanir scowled back. He wasn't sure which was more humiliating: getting killed by a goblin or putting a mule in his book of grudges.

THE REARMOST PORTION of the column was still in the narrow dirt street when chaos engulfed the square. Taken by surprise, several men and horses were cut down when goblins suddenly erupted from the silent, brooding hovels. The frenzied monsters slashed at legs and punctured bellies, spilling mounts and riders into the narrow lane and springing on the fallen with abominable glee. The screams of man and animal mixed into a loathsome din with the merciless laughter of the goblins.

Kessler smashed the first goblin who sprang at him with his boot, mashing its face. The creature wilted into a little heap, choking on its own teeth. The swordsman tried to slash a second with his blade, but the greatsword was too big to wield effectively from the saddle. The goblin darted under the stamping hooves of his steed to open its belly with a bronze axe. The horse reared and screamed, trying to escape the slaughterhouse of the street. Kessler pulled one leg from the stirrup, and then freed the other. He had just dropped down from the saddle when his terrified steed stumbled on its own dangling entrails and crashed against one of the mud-brick walls, stoving it in. A thin shriek sounded as the animal fell, and Kessler only hoped it was the goblin who had killed his steed that had been crushed beneath it.

The swordsman felt a sharp bite of pain in his back, the warm trickle of blood running down his side. He spun around, splintering the short spear that had been stabbed into him with his sword. Before the goblin could retreat, Kessler reversed the stroke and brought the edge of his blade chopping through the creature's hip. Almost severed in half, the dying greenskin flopped and writhed in the dust.

There were few men still standing within Kessler's range of vision. He could see one of Eugen's knights still holding his own against the attackers, the thick armour he wore and the heavy steel barding on his horse thwarting the efforts of the goblins' ill-kept weapons. Carlinda and Kant were the centre of a strange island of calm amidst the carnage raging around them, the goblins apparently less than eager to close with the sinister servants of Morr, sensing the deathly aura they seemed to exude.

A bellowing roar caused Kessler to look away from the crone and her guard. The side of a building exploded in a cloud of dirt and plaster as something immense bulled its way through. As the dust settled, Kessler found himself looking at a mammoth bulk, twice as tall as a man, with long ape-like arms and thick, column-like legs. The entire shape was clothed in knobbly, scaly skin, slate-grey fading to leprous white on the stomach. The brute's head was wide and squashed in appearance, almost devoid of any forehead at all. Great, floppy ears drooped from the sides of the monster's skull, torn and tattered like a moth-eaten rug. Small, pitch-black eyes glowered from either side of a huge crooked nose. Beneath the nose, a fanged canyon of a mouth gaped wide.

Beside the horror, a hook-nosed goblin shrieked, gesturing madly with what looked like a cattle goad. Kessler felt his spine crawl when the goblin locked eyes with him. The greenskin's face spread in a maniacal grin, jabbing the immense brute beside it with the goad. Slowly the troll's head swung around, the idiot fury in the monster's eyes training on the swordsman.

The brute took one ponderous step that Kessler was certain shook the entire street. Goblins scattered before its advance, scarcely willing to trust their lives to the troll's capacity to distinguish friend from food. Another quaking step and Kessler could see the enormous claws that tipped each of the troll's boulder-like hands. He braced his feet, tightening his grip on his greatsword. The troll didn't react to his defiance, but kept lumbering forwards.

Suddenly, the troll stopped, turning its head to stare at the street behind it. Only a few goblins continued to harass the beleaguered knight, but the troll looked past them. Its interest appeared to focus on Carlinda and the Black Guardsman. The goblin with the goad didn't appreciate the troll's distraction, screaming at the brute and jabbing it savagely with the goad. The troll swung back around, its dull eyes staring at Kessler for a moment. Then it looked down at the goblin. With surprising speed, the troll's claw closed around the goad. The goblin squealed in horror as the troll lifted it into the air, never thinking to release the weapon in its hands. The troll stared at the shrieking goblin, and then stuffed both goad and greenskin into its craggy maw. The goblin's screams were silenced by a sickening crunch as the troll's jaws ground together in a sidewise, cud-chewing motion.

With the goblin herdsman gone, the troll turned its back on Kessler and began to lumber off. Whatever relief the swordsman felt vanished when he realised where the troll was going. The strange, deathly aura that surrounded Carlinda might have repulsed the goblins, but it was attracting the troll. Scavenging carrion-eater as much as it was predator, the troll was no stranger to the touch of death, but in its tiny brain death equated to food. The monster's mouth dropped open in a hungry groan, dislodging the half-chewed carcass of the goblin. The goblins around the mounted knight scrambled like rats as they saw their mangled comrade fall from the troll's jaws, darting through doors and leaping through windows.

Freed from the goblins, the knight turned to arrest the troll's advance. His horse whinnied in protest as he urged it to charge the monster. Finally, his persistence prevailed and the knight drove against the troll's side, slashing it ruthlessly with his sword. The troll took a few more steps before becoming aware of the deep, hideous wounds the knight's sword had gouged into its scaly flesh. With a deafening roar, the troll turned on the man, bringing a mallet-like fist smashing down. The force of the blow collapsed the man's neck, causing his head to sink sickeningly into his shoulders. The lifeless corpse flopped across the saddle as his horse bolted up the winding street. The troll's body shook as a satisfied belch rumbled up from its belly, and then it turned and started towards Carlinda and Kant once more.

As the knight's horse ran past him, Kessler lunged down the street, rushing the troll from behind. He used his momentum to help drive his greatsword into the monster's back, thrusting it through the troll's armoured hide like a harpoon. The blade transfixed the monster, the point erupting from its belly in a spray of acidic juices.

The troll took another ponderous step, dragging Kessler and his sword with it. The champion fought to free his blade, worrying it from side to side in the wound. The troll moved again, still taking no notice of the hideous injury Kessler had dealt it. Then, abruptly, it threw back its head, giving voice to an ear-splitting bellow of pain. Kessler's sword was torn from his grasp as the maddened brute turned on him. The monster slashed at him with its claw, hurling him from his feet. Kessler landed twenty feet up the road, the carcass of a goblin only partially cushioning his fall. The swordsman struggled to rid his vision of the flashing sparks that filled it. He willed his body up, but the shocked, bruised flesh refused to listen, stubbornly content to lie sprawled in the street.

The troll lurched back up the street after him, anger in its dull little eyes. Then it stopped, glancing down at the sword sticking out of its belly. The troll jabbed a taloned finger at the steel protruding from its stomach, a confused look replacing the rage that had contorted its face a moment before. With an almost human shrug, the monster dismissed both the weapon and the man who had put it there. A black, slug-like tongue slavered across its scaly lips and the creature plodded back towards the crone and the promise of food.

Kessler tried desperately to force his body to obey him, frantic to stop the troll. He could see the Black Guardsman move his horse forward, placing himself directly between the troll and its prey. Kant looked back at Carlinda. Kessler thought he heard the templar say 'Don't,' and then, '*He* might find you.'

Then the troll was upon him. The templar's horse was a finely trained destrier, but even the fine warhorse could not control its instinctive fear of an abomination like the troll. The horse struggled to back away from the monster, foiling Kant's efforts to close with it. The troll was not so timid. Snarling, the brute lunged at the templar, its gigantic claws slashing through his destrier's neck. The horse reared back, a liquid scream bubbling from its ruined frame. With only one hand on the reins, Kant was ill-prepared for his steed's violent agony. He was thrown into the street, landing in a clatter of armour and dust.

The troll stared down at the Black Guardsman, a cruel intelligence briefly asserting itself in the monster's dull, idiot gaze. As Kant struggled to lift himself from the ground, the troll brought its massive foot stomping down. The foot smashed into the templar with the force of an avalanche, smashing flat both the helm and the skull within. The troll watched Kant's body twitch as life drained out of it, and then turned its hungry eyes towards Carlinda. A rope of drool slithered down the brute's face as it started to move once more.

Kessler shouted for the woman to run, to flee. Her horse had already started to become agitated, mimicking the panic that had thrown Kant at the troll's feet. Carlinda heard him, but instead of trying to move, she closed her eyes and folded her hands across her chest. Kessler could see her lips moving, but whatever she was saying was too low for him to hear. The swordsman struggled again to rise, roaring at his own feebleness. He grabbed a rusty goblin helmet from the ground beside him and threw it at the troll, trying to distract the monster, yelling at it to get its attention, but the brute kept plodding on.

Just as Kessler abandoned hope, something nearly as enormous as the troll hurtled down the street, the hovels shaking as Ghrum charged past them. A gigantic sword was clenched in the ogre's fist, a blade so enormous that it made Kessler's greatsword look like a boning knife. The ogre rushed at the troll, lifting his huge sword and bringing it slashing down into the monster's shoulder. The keen edge cleaved through flesh and bone like a butcher's knife and the troll's arm plopped to the ground, scrabbling in the dirt with spastic motions.

The troll stared stupidly at its severed limb, and then shifted its gaze to the ogre. Ghrum sneered at the monster. 'Hey, ugly,' the ogre roared. 'You want fight, fight Ghrum!' He brought his sword slashing at the troll once more. Instead of backing away, the beast lunged forward, clawing at Ghrum with its remaining arm, snapping at him with its powerful jaws. Kessler watched

in horror as the troll's teeth dug into the ogre's neck,
dark blood gushing from the wound. More hideous
still, the wounds the knight had chopped into the troll's
side had closed, without even a scab to mark where they
had been. Kessler shifted his gaze to the stump of the
troll's shoulder, sickened to see that it was no longer
spurting gore but instead appeared to have a bulb of
new flesh growing from it.

Ghrum howled in pain as the troll's teeth bit into his
flesh. He dropped his sword, closing both hands
around the monster's head. Slowly, agonisingly, he
forced the head back. With a wet, meaty sound, the
troll's fangs tore free of Ghrum's neck. The ogre kept his
hands locked around the gruesome head, struggling to
ignore the blood gushing from his wound. The troll
glared at him, spitting corrosive bile at Ghrum's face.
The acidic filth sprayed the ground behind him, sizzling
as it dissolved the dirt. Ghrum clenched his jaw, straining his muscles against the troll's resistance. By degrees,
he forced the monster's head to turn, and then, with a
roar more primal than even the troll's bestial bellows,
he snapped its neck. The brute's body struggled against
the ogre for several more minutes before accepting that
it was indeed dead. The scaly body went limp and
crashed to the ground with all the grace of felled timber.

The ogre closed a hand on his wound, pressing it
tight. He staggered against the closest wall, collapsing it
as he put his weight against it. Several goblins scampered from the ruptured building, but whatever fight
had been in them was already gone and they retreated
down the road. A frantic cry brought Kessler's attention
away from the fallen ogre. Theodo came sprinting down
the street, displaying a surprising agility for someone of
his girth. A slender dagger was in his hand and the

halfling had thrown a coil of thin rope over his shoulder. He hastened to the collapsed building, picking his way to the ogre beneath.

Kessler forgot them as he watched Carlinda dismount. The woman started to walk up the street, pausing where the halfling tended to Ghrum until Theodo's furious shouts made her turn away. She looked up at Kessler, holding his gaze as she strode towards him.

'Looks like that monster finished me after all,' Kessler said as Carlinda knelt beside him. Her cold, smooth hands pulled at his armour, probing the flesh beneath. She shook her head.

'The Sisterhood of Shallya are not the only ones versed in the healing arts,' she said.

Whatever retort was on Kessler's lips vanished in a grunt of pain as her probing fingers found a tender spot. Kessler shut his eyes as sparks started to flash before them once more. 'Sounds like the fight's over,' he said through clenched teeth. The crash of arms and the screams of the injured had faded away from further up the street. 'I wonder which side won.' He winced as another spasm of pain seared through him.

Carlinda looked down at him, frowning. She laid a hand on the side of his face. 'If you wake up alive, you'll know it was our side.'

Kessler felt a slight pressure against his head, and then everything vanished into darkness.

THE MEN CAREFULLY made their way through the gore-splattered square. Goblin bodies were strewn alongside butchered horses and the decaying carcasses of the people that had once called the village home. Here and there, they found a fresher corpse, a victim of the blades and bows of the goblins. When these were discovered, a cry of excitement rose from the men. They fell upon the corpses like wolves, tearing off boots and clothes, and scavenging weapons and armour. Like wolves, they snarled and snapped at one another.

'Find your own!' a short, scruffy looter with scraggly hair and a mouth of brown teeth growled, trying to keep the other vultures at bay while he simultaneously discarded the threadbare brigandine he wore and doffed the studded hauberk he was stripping from a corpse. The other jackals jeered and snarled at him, one darting beneath his kicks in an effort to steal the body's boots.

'Belay that, you scum!' a gravelly voice called out. 'There'll be time enough for that later! Keep your minds on what you're being paid to do!' The human jackals scowled at the speaker, a slim grey-haired man with chiselled features and deep, brooding eyes. Like them, his armour was tattered and worn, his boots scuffed and scarred, but the sword at his belt was still sharp, as some within the motley band of killers and cut-throats had already learned.

'Yes sir,' called back the scraggly-headed scavenger. 'We'll find it straight away.' He slapped at one of the other looters, and then delivered a kick to the man still trying to pull the boots off the corpse. 'C'mon,' he snarled. 'Let's find the damn thing and get it over with.'

Their leader watched the ruffians slowly spread out, scouring the plaza for a different kind of treasure. He shook his head in disgust.

'I told you to get me men, Baldur, not this vermin.' Baldur turned as he heard his name. The man who had accosted him was taller than him, with broad shoulders and an arrogant, aristocratic cast about his features.

Unlike the rest of the men scouring the battlefield, the armour he wore was fine chainmail, the clothes he wore new and well-maintained. There was a sword hanging from his belt too, but he'd had no need to draw it. Why should he when he had Baldur to do all his killing for him.

'What did you expect, Rambrecht? The Averheim city guard?' Baldur pointed back at the scavengers picking around the plaza. 'It takes time to get good men, and it takes money to buy their loyalty. Good men are expensive.'

'You weren't,' observed Rambrecht. 'Though I have not been terribly impressed by your performance thus far. Perhaps I should reconsider our arrangement.'

Baldur clenched his fist in silent rage. 'The agreement stands,' he snapped. 'I help you, you reinstate my commission. That's the deal.'

'The deal also required you to provide me with soldiers, not this brigand trash,' Rambrecht growled. 'I wouldn't trust this vermin against a pack of street urchins, much less real fighters.'

'The goblins have made a dent in their strength,' Baldur pointed out. 'Let's hope your friend on the inside can skew the odds a bit more in our favour.'

Rambrecht nodded. 'We'll have to hit them before they reach anywhere they can take on new recruits.'

'It would help if we knew which way they were going,' Baldur said. A sudden shout from the plaza caused them both to turn around. A small cluster of bandits came running over, pushing and pawing at one another in their haste, fighting over the object they had found like dogs with a bone. Baldur glared at the men in disgust, snatching it away as soon as they were close enough. He handed the thin strip of goatskin to

Rambrecht. The aristocrat studied the piece of hide, his eyes devouring the strange symbols scrawled on it. Laughing, he tossed it aside, walking across the plaza towards where they had tethered their horses.

'Ask and you will receive, Baldur,' Rambrecht laughed. 'Ask and you will receive.'

CHAPTER SEVEN

COUNT EBERFELD STARED in consternation at the map spread across the dark polished wood of the table. No pavilion for him in Bergdorf; the banquet hall of Bergdorf's magistrate was spacious enough to plot a dozen campaigns within. The footfalls of the scouts echoed hollowly from the brooding stone walls as they came and went. With each report, Eberfeld's spirit darkened. Each mark General Hock made on the sprawled map to reflect those thoughts only added to the frustration and depression that threatened to overwhelm the count.

Heufurth was lost. After their defeat on the Dobrin road there had been nothing the count's army could do to protect the town. Hock had sent riders to sound the alarm. Some of the town's populace had evacuated. Many had stayed behind, placing their trust in the thick stone walls that surrounded the settlement. The undead legion had fallen upon the settlement in a great, silent host. For two days they had lingered outside the walls. Hock's scouts reported siege engines among Zahaak's horde, archaic scorpions and onagers. The antiquated weapons seemed unequal to the task of breaching the thick walls of Heufurth, yet on the second dawn that saw Zahaak laying siege to the town, the undead had quit the fields outside and were in possession of the town. In the course of a single night, somehow the deathless host had broken the defences. It did not make the count feel any easier that the scouts insisted the walls of Heufurth still stood largely intact, that there was no evidence of siege towers among the legion's arms. Yet still Heufurth had fallen with such rapidity that it chilled Eberfeld to the core.

The legion had turned northward upon leaving Heufurth, following the road that would eventually bring it to Bergdorf. General Hock found reassurance in the fact. Resting upon a great hill that commanded the land for leagues, he considered that Bergdorf offered a significantly superior location from which to mount a defence. To heighten their advantage, Hock had sent entire regiments out to clear the surrounding forest and increase the range of visibility from the town. The felled timber was then used by the populace of Bergdorf to construct an outer palisade surrounding the stone walls of their town. Behind this, peasants from a dozen villages, pressed into service by Hock's troops, were busy digging a series of trenches and pitfalls. Hock was determined that any siege engines Zahaak brought to Bergdorf would find getting within range of the walls a difficult, if not impossible, prospect.

Count Eberfeld felt a pang of conscience as he considered those indentured workers sweating to bolster the town's defences. They had been dragged away from their farms at a time when the harvest was far too near. If they did not return to their homes quickly, their crops might spoil, leaving them with nothing. Even if his army crushed Zahaak's horde, the centre of Wissenland might be trading invasion and massacre for famine.

Scouts and officers continued to report to him, announcing the arrival of fresh regiments drawn from all across his realm. From the bleak foothills of the Black Mountains to the tranquil banks of the River Aver, they had come, marching to answer the call of their liege: bowmen from the forests, peasant spearmen from the moors, knights resplendent in their armour of steel and chain. The sorry remnant that had left Koeblitz had swollen to three times its number and still they came. There was a bravado about these reinforcements, a sense of strength and purpose that bound them into something stronger than simple flesh and steel. These were men who had come to defend their count and their homeland; to what nobler purpose could they aspire? General Hock was careful to keep the veterans from Koeblitz well away from the newcomers. They would discover the horror of Zahaak's legions soon enough. There was no sense having their courage eroded by the repeated tales of those who had already confronted the undead.

Some had not come, however. The call for men from Neuwald had gone unanswered, and Count Eberfeld wondered if even now the greedy burghers of the town were fleeing across the border to the safety of Nuln. Baron Volstadt had refused to bring his soldiers to Bergdorf, arguing that his own lands were more imminently imperilled by the enemy. Eisendorf was a settlement fully as large as Bergdorf, situated some distance to the west.

Eberfeld had briefly considered mustering his forces there, but the greater defensibility of Bergdorf had finally decided him. If Bergdorf fell, then Eisendorf would soon follow. The argument had made little impact on Baron Volstadt, who maintained that he had to see to the safety of his own people and lands before he could meet his obligation to his count. Eberfeld realised that it would be useless to try and persuade him, and foolish squandering the troops necessary to impose his will on Volstadt. The Eisendorf militia were some of the best equipped in the district, sporting thick armour and heavy blades courtesy of the rich iron mines running beneath the town. They would be missed. Eberfeld knew that for all their quality, there was little the Eisendorfers could do by themselves against Zahaak, yet for all of that, he still wished Volstadt luck.

Count Eberfeld looked up as yet another scout appeared before the map table. The dust of the trail was still thick on the man, coating him from crown to heel in a dingy grey. The man's face was almost black with dirt, a young face that tried to contain its weariness with the composure due a sovereign. Somewhere beneath the dirt and dust, Eberfeld recognised the livery of a river guard branded into the leather of the soldier's hauberk. He'd drawn many troops from the border outposts, but they had arrived days ago. From the look of him, this man had ridden hard for at least that long. What had compelled him to set out so long after his comrades had already left to answer the count's call to arms? The sickening feeling that had started to rise in his throat intensified when Eberfeld noted General Hock standing beside the scout.

'A report from the river,' Hock told him, his voice troubled. Count Eberfeld nodded and motioned for the

scout to speak. The soldier dropped to one knee, genu-
flecting before his liege. Eberfeld waved aside the
formalities, impatient to hear whatever dire news the
man had to convey.

'I have ridden from the Upper Reik,' the soldier began,
his voice a breathless wheeze. 'Two days in the saddle,
excellency, stopping only to change horses whenever I
felt them expiring beneath me.'

Count Eberfeld handed the gilded goblet resting
beside his maps to the soldier. He quickly up-ended the
cup, all but draining it of wine in a single, ravenous
gulp. Some semblance of vigour began to reassert itself
in the man as he wiped a dirty sleeve across his mouth
and continued.

'My post is a fortalice two leagues from where the
Reik splits from the Sol. The fort sits on an outcropping,
offering a good view of the river, and what is on the
other side.'

Eberfeld glanced aside at Hock, catching the general's
grim expression. The far bank of the River Reik marked
the territory of Averland. The river guard was officially a
constabulary force, monitoring the river for smugglers
and pirates. Averland maintained its own series of forts
and towers on the other side of the river, expressly for
the same purpose. However, it was a thinly veiled secret
that the forts were too large and too well-manned to be
there simply to deter smugglers. For the past two hundred years, the river forts had grown in both size and
number, guarding not against pirates but against unwel-
come advances from the other province. Sometimes, as
in the recent past, the forts weren't enough to deter the
ambitions of the men they were built to keep away.

'What is happening in Averland?' Eberfeld asked, feeling his heart go cold. 'What did you see?'

Even beneath the crust of dust, Eberfeld could see the soldier's face go pale. 'Excellency, Count Achim is massing troops on the other side of the border!'

Eberfeld smashed his fist against the table. He had dreaded as much, for all that he had expected it. The withdrawal of troops from the river forts had been necessary. They represented the single greatest concentration of soldiers he could draw upon within a week's march. He had hoped, however, that it could be accomplished without their counterparts on the Averland shore becoming aware of what was going on. Strict orders had been issued that the men were only to leave at night and that the reduced garrisons left behind should take measures to deceive the Averlanders that the castles were still fully manned. Somewhere, however, the stratagem had failed.

'How many did you count?' The question came from General Hock. The soldier shrugged.

'More than I could number,' he answered. 'Certainly more than I have ever seen before. Maybe not as great as the army encamped here, but if more Averlanders continue to muster they will not be far behind.'

'They have seen our soldiers leaving the forts,' General Hock mused aloud.

'That much is obvious,' Eberfeld snapped. 'Otherwise, why would Achim move his army.' He turned his eyes back to the map, glaring at the river where even now the Averlanders might be ready to cross. Zahaak's legion was enough of a plague to tax Wissenland's resources. The last thing they needed was Achim deciding to seize the opportunity to redress old wrongs.

'Perhaps it is a defensive posture,' Hock suggested. 'Perhaps Count Achim has misinterpreted the withdrawal of our troops. He may think we are pulling them back for an offensive into Averland.' The general averted his gaze, embarrassed to speak his next words, but knowing that he must. 'That was what your father did before he mounted his invasion.'

Eberfeld shook his head. 'Too many are already fleeing before the advance of Zahaak's legion. Some of them will have scattered east, and even the border forts and the river won't have stopped them. Achim knows full well our situation.'

'But does he believe it?' The general's question lingered in the air, like a frosty wisp of doubt and confusion. Eberfeld leaned back in his chair, pondering the questions that Hock's observation raised. It was possible, then, that Achim's actions were not belligerent.

'The memory of your father casts a long shadow,' Hock said. 'The siege of Averheim was not so long ago that it is easily forgotten. Would Count Achim truly believe that the land of his old enemy was beset by a supernatural foe torn straight from the pages of legend? Or would he consider it a ruse, a deceit to allow the armies of Wissenland to march again into his lands?'

'I would not countenance such deception,' Eberfeld said. 'I have too much honour for that.'

General Hock smiled gravely. 'To Achim, you are your father's son.'

The count turned his eyes again to the map. This time he did not see the armies he had drawn from across his province, nor did he see the deathless legions of Zahaak. This time he looked at Averland, filling it with burning villages and slaughtered towns, mentally depopulating his neighbour the way his father had thirty years before. He rose from the table, a decision reached.

'General, gather the Sablebacks and whatever other cavalry we still have left from Koeblitz. Before we plan any action against Achim, and before we do anything that might force him to act, I think we had best send an emissary to the border and find out his intentions.'

Hock saluted, turning to leave, when a sudden thought occurred to him, a suspicion that quickly worked its way onto his face. 'Excellency, who are you going to send?'

Eberfeld smiled at the officer's suspicion. 'The only emissary I can trust, general.

'Me.'

CHAPTER EIGHT

ERNST DABBED THE ragged strip of linen against his face for the umpteenth time, blood still pooling in the gash running beneath his right eye. Only his quick action had prevented the goblin spear from blinding him. Typical of the malicious creatures, the idea of killing an enemy cleanly was absolutely foreign to the goblin brain. The nobleman knew he should just relent and allow the injury to scab over, but he knew goblins often coated their weapons in the most unspeakable filth and was horrified by the thought of blood poisoning.

He was careful to keep his fears off his face as he walked through the camp. Laying over for the night in Murzklein had been out of the question. Even beyond the repugnance of sleeping among the bodies of so many slaughtered men and horses, there had been the very real concern that their vanquished foes would return in the dead of night. Many of the goblins had escaped when they found the battle going against them, scattering back into the hills. Skanir warned that as soon as they stopped running, their spiteful hearts would turn to thoughts of revenge. If there were more goblins in the hills, no doubt they would accompany the survivors on their vengeful foray. More unsettling had been Ekdahl's concern. The evidence that orcs had taken no small part in the massacre of Murzklein's populace was undeniable: the warband of Uhrghul, a warlord who had once threatened all of Wissenland. There was no telling how far the orcs had strayed from the massacre. They might be days away or they might be much closer. When the goblins returned, it might not be with more of their own cringing kind, but with hulking orc warriors eager for the taste of blood and slaughter.

Walking past tents and cook fires, Ernst was struck by just how gravely the goblins had injured them. Scarcely a man among them did not have some cut or bruise to nurse, and three had such wounds that it was doubtful they would survive the night. More injurious to the expedition had been the loss of horses. Fully a dozen had been crippled by goblin arrows and blades, forcing them to be destroyed. Others had run off during the battle and there had been no time to round them up again. Aside from the massive destriers of the knights, there were only five other horses remaining among them. Now Ernst was confronted by the unpleasant decision of how they should proceed. Let those with mounts range ahead and leave the others to fare as they would, or slow their progress to allow the, again, dismounted infantry to keep up.

The thought sickened him, especially in light of Ekdahl's continued warnings about orcs. There was little enough chance for them if they were beset by orcs, and if the remaining cavalry and Eugen's knights were removed from the battle, the chances would drop to none at all. Count Eberfeld had impressed upon him, that time was of the essence, but Ernst could not bring himself to abandon men under his command.

The baron's eye caught a group of figures standing around a roaring fire at the perimeter of the camp. He set his face grimly and strode over to join them. Ottmar and Eugen hastily saluted him as he emerged from the gloom surrounding the fire. Ekdahl continued to stare out into the night, eyes locked on the vague outlines of boulders and brush. Ernst went cold as he saw the intense concentration that was coiled throughout Ekdahl's body. Did the scout think their enemies so near to warrant such vigilance? If the greenskins were to find them wounded and weary, they could overwhelm the camp almost without a fight.

'Another of my men expired, your lordship,' Ottmar reported. The sergeant's leg was stiff, wrapped tight in leather thongs to keep the bones straight. A goblin axe had worked terrible mischief on him, but somehow the old soldier had pulled through.

'That brings your command down to fourteen,' Ernst said. They'd left a lot of good soldiers behind in the village and still their strength was being leeched away.

'Thirteen,' Ottmar corrected him. 'I don't think Felix will last the night, not with a goblin arrow skewering his lung.'

Ernst nodded. It was a terrible thing, to linger on in such a condition, dying from your wounds, but still desperately, hopelessly clinging to life. 'Thirteen then, plus Marshal Eugen's three knights, the cook and his ogre, Skanir and ourselves.'

'My knights may not be of much use,' Eugen said. 'The other ox from the supply wagon died. Our destriers are the only animals in camp strong enough to pull it. Either we leave the wagon and most of the supplies behind, or we put two more of my men out of the saddle.'

The baron bit back a curse. He'd been counting on using the wagon to move the worst of the wounded. The thought made the decision for him. 'Then we'll have to use the destriers. It is still a long way to the river and we can't leave the wagon behind. Your men will have to take some of the coursers.'

'What about your champion, that man Kessler?' Ekdahl did not turn as he asked the question, keeping his face turned towards the darkness.

'The templar was killed in the battle,' Ernst answered. 'Kessler is taking his place as bodyguard to the crone.'

Ottmar grunted, spitting into the blazing fire. 'I don't envy him the job,' the sergeant said. 'I'd rather be back with the goblins than shadowing that witch.'

Ernst laughed. 'Actually, he suggested it.'

KESSLER STEPPED AWAY from the black shroud of the tent as he finished assembling it, grunting as he inspected his handiwork. He reached out his hand and pulled back a fold of the heavy cloth, holding it wide to allow entry to the enclosure within.

A faint, appreciative smile briefly suggested itself on Carlinda's pale face, and then the augur carefully removed the blankets from the back of her horse. Kessler could see the animal shudder at her touch. Even her horse was instinctively repulsed by her presence, the priests of Morr having only taught it to repress its instincts, not deny them. He wondered at that, and questioned again why he had felt compelled to linger around that same presence. He was not a deep man, given to profound thoughts and imaginative insights, yet he felt he knew why just the same. It chilled him, chilled him in a way that Carlinda's eerie presence failed to.

The woman paused before entering the tent, bowing before Kessler. 'Thank you,' she said, her voice as soft as a winter whisper.

'It is only right that I show you courtesy,' Kessler replied, feeling colour pulsing into his scarred features, 'after all you have done for me.' He nodded his head towards the centre of the camp where the moans of the wounded rose into the darkening night. 'I should be over there with them after tangling with that troll,' he said. 'Instead, here I stand, fit and firm as the day I first took up the sword.'

Carlinda's sombre gaze looked into his, catching his eyes and holding them with their compelling intensity. 'The priests of Morr have taught me many of their secrets. There are rites, powers that can be invoked to ease the suffering of those soon to pass through the Gates of Morr. Some of those powers are of benefit to the living as well as the dying.'

The swordsman sighed and looked away. He didn't like her talk of spells and magic, calling upon the powers of the gods. It was too much like witchcraft for him. Perhaps a more cultured mind, a more learned mind, could understand the difference, but to him all the supernatural arts were nothing more than sorcery, the stuff of warlocks and wizards. For all that he had benefited from it, it still made him uneasy, evoking a superstitious dread almost as primitive as the horse's instincts. He did not like to think of the magic that had allowed him to recover from his wounds. Even more, he did not like to think of Carlinda as a witch.

'You had best retire,' Kessler said, hastily turning away from the talk of magic and gods. 'The baron will want to make an early start tomorrow, put some distance between us and the goblins.'

Carlinda continued to linger. 'What about you?' she asked. 'You'll have even more need of rest than I. It takes more strength to march than it does to ride.'

Kessler's hand closed around her arm, gently guiding her into the tent. Even through the heavy, coarse cloth of her vestment, he could feel the coolness of her skin. 'I'm taking the templar's place,' he told here. 'I'll stay out here and make sure you are not disturbed.'

'No one in this camp would speak to me, much less disturb me,' Carlinda said, her voice coming to him from inside the tent. He could hear her rummaging about in the darkness, making her bed. There was no scorn or self-pity in her voice, simply a statement of fact. She had lived too long as an exile to be hurt by the ostracism of her fellow man. 'Except for you,' she added.

Kessler stiffened, shifting uncomfortably from one leg to the other. 'Someone has to look after you with the templar gone,' he said, 'and I feel I owe it to you.'

'There's something more than that,' Carlinda persisted. 'You don't look at me the way the others do. You look at me almost… almost as if…' She broke off, catching the tremble in her words. 'Do you find me repulsive, Max Kessler?'

'You are a handsome woman,' Kessler replied awkwardly.

'Something need not be ugly to be repulsive,' she said.

The words cut into Kessler like a knife. He held a hand up to his mangled face, the face no woman could look at without horror. Maybe you didn't need to be ugly, but it certainly helped.

'They say you are touched by Morr,' Kessler said, his pain feeding cruelty into his words, 'that you are a thing of Death, that no living creature could bear to touch you or even look at you. Maybe they're right. Maybe that's why I don't look away. I've faced death so many times in the arena that I no longer recognise its horrors. I've killed ten men for every year I've drawn breath into this twisted carcass of mine. I guess me and Death are old friends by now.'

Silence stretched across the minutes and Kessler began to repent the callousness of his words. He was unused to speaking to a woman, any woman. He didn't have the tongue for subtle words and flattering praise, for empty reassurance and impossible hope. It had been a long time since he'd had any hope to call his own. That had been cut away along with his face.

'I'm sorry,' he said at last, trying to make the apology less gruff than it sounded. 'Forget the bitterness of an old bastard who's seen too many winters and not enough springs.'

Carlinda's face appeared as she pulled back the tent flap, a white moon against the darkness of the cloth. Her features were drawn, haunted, her eyes pained. She stared into Kessler's face and he could see the hurt in her eyes deepen. 'You wish they had killed you?' The question struck him like a physical blow, so abrupt did it come, so keenly did it cut.

When he answered, it was with a slow, measured pace. 'They did,' Kessler said. 'I was only seventeen. My father was a militiaman in Rabwald, and wanted me to follow in his step, but I wanted better, needed better. So I took up with a merchant caravan as a guard. The pay for that one trip was more than my father would see in a year. Of course I never saw any of it. Halfway to Nuln we were attacked by goblins. The lucky ones were killed. The rest of us they captured and dragged back to their caves. There's only one thing in the world a goblin enjoys and that's causing pain to something else. They enjoyed me for a long time.' He felt his ruined face again, imagining the hot knives grating against the bones of his skull and jaw. 'Somehow, I survived and crawled back to civilisation. The chirurgeons did what they could, but some things just can't be fixed.'

'But you were alive,' Carlinda pointed out.

'What came after wasn't living,' Kessler scoffed. 'I couldn't show this,' he shook his hand before his mangled face, 'without children running away screaming. Men shunned my company and women sickened at the sight of me. The only one who would have anything to do with me was the baron. Maybe it was pity, but just the same the baron gave me something to latch onto, something to fill that big empty hole the goblins left inside me when they cut away my face.'

'By killing.' There was no recrimination in her voice as she said it.

Kessler laughed, but the sound was hollow even to him. 'A lot of men would still be alive if the gods had let the goblins finish the job.' He shook his head, playing absently with the black tassels dangling from his sword. 'It's not a substitute for living, for having a real life, but it's something to find pride in: Max Kessler, the Baron's Champion.'

Carlinda reached a hand through the black mouth of the tent, touching Kessler's shoulder. There was no mistaking the unearthly cold behind her touch, but he did not pull away. 'So much hurt, so much loneliness,' she said. Kessler felt her fingers kneading his flesh, sending little icy tingles flashing through his body. 'We could almost be the same.'

His first instinct was to laugh at the idea that the powerful, deadly swordsman was the same as the small, hermit witch, but as he saw the earnestness in her face, Kessler found it impossible to find any amusement in her words. He closed his hand around hers, feeling the warmth drain from his fingers as they clasped.

'You don't have to stay outside,' Carlinda told him. He started to pull his hand away. Her grip tightened, became desperate. 'Please,' and Kessler felt himself shudder at the wretched, grovelling that was woven into the plea. It had been a long time since he'd felt pity for anything, man or beast.

He allowed himself to be drawn into the darkness of the tent. What came was too desperate, too needy to be called love. They were two lost, forsaken creatures trying to forget their aloneness in each other's arms; two broken, ruined souls trying to make themselves whole. Instead of filling the emptiness, their pathetic embrace only reminded them of what they had lost, what they could never have again. Yet even that miserable echo of life was more than they had before.

It was long into the night before silence returned to the Crone of Morr's black tent.

'GRIMNIR'S BEARD! THAT smells good!' Skanir said, extricating himself from the nest of blankets that covered him. As soon as he did, dull pain throbbed in his head. He raised a calloused hand to gingerly examine the huge knot he felt rising from his scalp. A goblin had cracked his skull with its sword, nearly penetrating the steel helmet the dwarf had been wearing. Even so, the blow had darkened his vision, making his head swim with a befuddled confusion. In such a state, he couldn't have warded off a determined cave rat much less a pack of howling goblins. Before they could overwhelm him, however, Eugen and his knights had come to his rescue, driving the determined greenskins from their crippled enemy. Eventually the remorseless steel and thick armour of the knights overcame the ancient hate of the goblins and they had broken before the assault. Skanir had tried to recover his hammer and pursue the cowardly grobi, but the effort was beyond even his dwarfish constitution and he had succumbed, wilting to the bloodied floor of the plaza like a weary flower.

The next thing that had intruded upon his senses was the thick, meaty smell that wafted across him. At first he was not sure if it was a real odour or simply a phantasm of his imagination, some echo of a dream that lingered in his waking mind. But, no. As Skanir drew in a deep breath of air, the aroma was still there. Cursing the aches and pains that still beset him, the dwarf resolutely pulled himself from his coverings. He found that he was in a small wagon, the walls lined with shelves, the roof studded with hooks from which dripped a riotous array of pots and pans. It did not take any great exertion of his intellect to realise that he had been billeted with Theodo Hobshollow, in the halfling cook's cart.

Skanir crawled to the mouth of the cart, peering from the opening. He could see a great cauldron set over a roaring fire, boiling water bubbling over the lip and sizzling as it struck the flames below. Theodo was standing on a big wooden stool, a stained apron covering his foppish vest and vividly stripped breeches. The halfling was stirring the contents of the pot with a great bronze fork, sometimes pausing in his labour to fish a hand into one of the pockets on his apron and add a dash of herbs or a pinch of spice to the stew.

The ogre was sitting near the halfling, the better part of an ox lying beside the hulking monster. The ogre noisily chomped on the leg he had torn free from the carcass, his massive jaws crunching against the bone with every powerful bite. An unsightly patch of leather was stitched against Ghrum's neck, bandaging the terrible injury he had suffered in his battle with the troll. Skanir nodded his head in grim appreciation. Few creatures could expect to recover from such a wound, but ogres were notoriously robust and difficult to kill. Certainly, the experience had done nothing to stem his prodigious appetite.

Again the heady aroma drifted to the dwarf. Biting down on the pain and dizziness that swirled through his head, Skanir lowered himself from the cart and staggered towards the cauldron. There could be no question, his nose hadn't betrayed him. He looked up at Theodo on his stool, Skanir's face a mixture of respect and shock.

'Surely that isn't kulgrik I smell?' he finally asked.

The halfling diverted his attention away from the boiling cauldron, smiling down at the dwarf.

'I am pleased to have my talents appreciated,' Theodo beamed, 'especially by one of the mountain folk. After all, your people invented the art of kulgur, though there are terribly few who appreciate the culinary discipline outside the mountain halls.' Theodo gestured towards the tents around them. 'I fear that troll meat will never catch on with the Empire.'

Skanir grinned beneath his beard. 'Just as well,' he said. 'It's a hard enough delicacy to come by as it is, and not to be squandered on those who don't appreciate it.'

Theodo hopped down from his stool, wringing his hands in the folds of his apron. 'You'll join me then? Good, I was despairing of eating it all by myself and... well, troll doesn't agree with ogres. Gives them gas, you know.'

The dwarf glanced aside to where Ghrum sat. The ogre had removed the head from the carcass and was staring contemplatively into the glassy eyes of the ox while gnawing at a rib bone. 'More for us, then,' Skanir said. Theodo hurried back to the cart, pulling a pair of plates from a small box fixed to the side.

'Quite so, quite so,' the halfling agreed. His eyes lit up as he saw Skanir produce a small silver knife and fork from a pouch on his belt, fixating for a moment on the elaborate workmanship of the cutlery, his mind turning over a mental list of silversmiths and money lenders who might be interested in such bric-a-brac. Theodo shook himself from his avaricious stupor. 'It would seem such a shame to waste any more of it. I had to leave most of the troll behind in the village, but I made sure to carve off the flanks and thighs. Even the best cuts, however, would be a bit much to manage on my own, and, of course, one can't let troll meat sit uncooked for too long.'

Skanir nodded, appreciating the slight shudder that went through Theodo. The regenerative properties of troll flesh were legendary and never to be underestimated. There were many stories of dwarf chefs who returned to their larders to fetch a chunk of troll meat only to be confronted by a furious, fully regenerated troll.

Theodo led his guest to a large box lying on its side. The halfling threw a chequered cloth across it and began setting down the dishes. Skanir only half-watched him, his eyes lingering instead on the animal tethered to a post behind the cart. The mule matched his baleful glare.

'Won't be done for some little time yet,' Theodo was saying. The halfling removed his apron, tossing it into the back of his cart. His fat little hands darted into the pocket of his vest, removing a set of heavily-used cards. 'I thought we might do with a bit of diversion while the troll finishes cooking.'

Skanir didn't attend the halfling's words, instead concentrating upon his stare-off with the mule. The animal pulled its lips back, displaying its blunt teeth in what seemed to him like a mocking sneer.

'Your ogre doesn't like troll,' Skanir observed, facing Theodo once more.

'How does he feel about mule?'

THE RUINS OF Murzklein were three days behind them when Ekdahl abruptly called a halt. Ranging ahead of the column on one of the few remaining horses, the scout came galloping back in haste, eyes scanning the trees and underbrush with obvious alarm. Savagely, he reined his horse in before Baron von Rabwald's, dismissing courtesy and decorum as he quickly snapped his report.

'Orcs!' Ekdahl gasped, stabbing a hand over his shoulder to indicate the trail down which he had charged. 'A camp of them laid out along the path!'

'Waiting for us?' inquired the baron.

Eugen shook his head, even as his hand fell to the sword sheathed beside him. 'Orcs don't wait,' the knight said. 'They are many things, but patient isn't one of them. If they knew we were here, they'd be on us already.'

'Then we might surprise them.' Ottmar and the other foot soldiers had clustered around the baron and Ekdahl, nervously listening to the exchange. 'Not much of an advantage, not against orcs, but we can use everything we can get.'

Ernst shook his head. 'We can't risk a fight,' he decided. 'We'll have to go around. Our duty is more important than killing a few greenskins.'

'Begging your pardon, baron,' Ekdahl said, 'but going around might not be terribly wise. If even one of those orcs catches our scent they'll be on our tail until they overtake us or we drive them off. Either way it will still come to a fight. If it were my choice, I'd prefer to have it here, when they aren't expecting it.'

'Hold on a moment,' Eugen protested, raising his mailed hand. 'We don't even know how many there are. You propose we blindly charge in? I've fought orcs before and believe me when I say that such an attack won't scatter them. They'll recover from their confusion almost instantly and then make for the closest thing they can find to kill, laughing while they do so.'

With one fluid motion, the scout slid down from his saddle. Landing on his feet, the black-garbed road warden began to unsling his bow. 'Of course not,' he answered the knight's challenge. 'I'll range ahead and find their numbers.' He turned, once more studying the treeline. Finally he pointed his hand into the brush. 'You can take shelter among those rocks until I return,' he said. Ernst could dimly perceive a jumble of bluish grey stone behind the trees. He glanced back at the scout.

'Whichever way we decide, it would be useful to know just how many of those monsters there are,' the baron said. Ernst stared hard at Ekdahl's face, watching for any betrayal of hidden emotion. The strange message was still fresh in the baron's mind, a message the scout had found only after Kessler had nearly tripped over it.

Ottmar seemed to share the baron's suspicions. 'If it pleases your lordship, I should like to go with him,' he said. 'If the orcs get one of us the other might still be able to get back to warn the rest.' Ekdahl gave the sergeant a curious look, but slowly nodded his head in acceptance.

During the exchange, Kessler had advanced upon the scene, leading Carlinda's horse by its reins. He glanced back at the woman. Her pale face was edged with concern, her dark eyes staring at him intently. He closed his hand around the augur's, giving it a reassuring squeeze. Carlinda's flesh was as cold as marble beneath his touch. Then he turned back to face Ernst.

'I'll go too,' Kessler told the baron. He didn't even try to hide the heat in his gaze as he looked at Ekdahl. The scout favoured him with what might have been a mocking bow. Kessler grinned back, adjusting the enormous sword lashed across his back. 'With three of us, there's a better chance of everyone making it back.'

'All right, Max,' Ernst agreed. 'We'll lay up in those rocks and wait for you to come back. Don't worry about the crone, I'll look after her while you're gone.' The baron hoped he was able to suppress the shudder that shot up his spine as he considered the prospect. He knew how intimate Kessler had become with the witch, for all that he could not understand it. Grace to the gods that he should ever become desperate enough to take such an abomination into his bed.

'It's not far,' Kessler said. 'Shouldn't take too long to determine what's what.' The swordsman sneered at Ekdahl, fingering the tassels dripping from the pommel of his weapon. The scout's eyes narrowed, but his mouth stayed close. He turned and started into the underbrush beside the trail, leaving his horse behind. Ottmar and Kessler were soon following him, vanishing into the scraggly growth of bushes and saplings.

Ernst waited until they were completely lost to sight, and then raised his fist, motioning for the column to withdraw towards the rocks. Foremost in his thoughts were his suspicions. He was sure Kessler could take care of himself; however great the odds, somehow the swordsman always managed to come out on top. He only hoped that whatever untoward thing was going on, they'd uncover it before it was too late.

SLIDING THROUGH THE undergrowth, the three men sketched a path parallel with the trail. Ottmar acquitted himself well, making scarcely more noise than Ekdahl, but the subtlety and caution of the woodsmen was beyond Kessler. Several times, as a stick broke beneath his boot or a branch snapped beneath his hand, Ekdahl motioned for a quick halt. Sometimes the scout would give Kessler a venomous glance before turning his attention fully upon the wilderness around them. Like some granite effigy, Ekdahl would freeze, his every nerve trained upon his surroundings, listening for even the slightest sound. After what seemed an eternity, he would allow them to proceed.

They advanced in such fashion for at least half a mile before they drew near their objective. Through the bushes, Kessler could see the encampment that had alarmed Ekdahl: a cluster of crude huts of straw and river mud, the shoddy things already sagging inward as they collapsed beneath their own weight. A jumble of rusty weapons was piled pell-mell all around the camp and in the centre a great pit had been dug. The stones that lined the pit were blackened with soot and the thing that was impaled upon the spit that hung above it was loathsomely human. Kessler felt his gorge rise at the thought of the hideous scene that must have unfolded here only hours before. He drew his sword, almost unconsciously drifting forward, eager to remind these beasts why it was unwise to feed upon man. Ottmar also produced a weapon and started to follow him.

'Hold,' Ekdahl hissed and there was such command in his voice that both of the men froze. The scout had not moved from his position facing the camp, but his gloved hands had nocked an arrow to his longbow. His eyes were like chips of steel as he looked at the other men. 'Get back here and keep quiet,' he said. Ottmar fingered his blade while Kessler's scarred face twisted into a scowl. There was no choice, both men had seen the deadly precision of Ekdahl's marksmanship.

'Where are they?' Kessler wondered. He had braced himself to be confronted by a mob of murderous monsters. Prepared for such a sight, finding the camp empty was unsettling. Where were the orcs?

'They're asleep,' Ottmar snapped when he had fallen back. 'We'll never have a better chance at them!'

Ekdahl just shook his head.

'Something's wrong,' he said. 'Too clean and orderly for an orc camp.' He tapped the side of his nose. 'Doesn't smell right. You never forget the dung heap stink of an orc pack.'

'Who else would cook a man's body?' Kessler growled. 'Or are you going to tell me that's not what they have spitted over their fire?'

'Oh, it's a man all right,' Ekdahl conceded. He glanced aside at Ottmar. 'You should recognise him, he's one of yours. They must have brought him all the way from

Murzklein. Same place they got those goblin weapons from.'

Kessler felt the hairs rise at the back of his neck. Was Ekdahl admitting there was a spy? Admitting that someone was following them and that they had set this whole phoney camp up? The swordsman began calculating the distance between him and the scout, how many steps it would take him to bury his blade in the Sollander's gut.

'Just who is "they"?' Ottmar asked, giving voice to the question foremost on Kessler's mind as well. Ekdahl stared at the two men for a long moment. Suddenly he spun, and before either man could react, he let loose the arrow from his bow. There was a sharp shriek, and a scruffy-looking man wearing a poorly mended hauberk toppled from the branches of a big oak tree, his bow falling from his hands as he hurtled to the earth.

The scream acted as a signal. Soon the trees seemed alive with bowmen, their arrows slashing down through the brush. Kessler saw more men come rushing out of the 'orc' huts, their hands full of brutal looking bludgeons and axes. Ekdahl had already loosed a second arrow, sending the shaft slamming into the chest of one of the attackers.

'Ambush!' Kessler snarled, an arrow zipping past his ear.

'Get back and warn Baron von Rabwald and the others!' Ottmar roared, keeping low and scrambling to join Ekdahl behind the cover of a tangled mass of briar. The shouts and war cries of the attackers intensified as arrows slammed all around their position. 'We'll keep them off!' the sergeant promised as Kessler lingered.

The swordsman nodded, watching as Ekdahl sprang from cover to send an arrow shooting into the charging foe. Another man crumpled to the ground, his throat transfixed. Even with the scout's keen aim, Kessler knew they would be overwhelmed. Ottmar was right, all they could do now was get word back to Ernst and warn him about the danger.

With a last look back at the trapped men, Kessler sprinted away. Without the need for caution, he crashed through the undergrowth with all the grace of a mad bull, arms pumping as he urged his powerful frame on to greater effort. For a time, arrows continued to whistle around him, but soon he had drawn past the range of the unseen archers, losing them in the maze of trees. Behind him, the sounds of combat died away and he wondered if perhaps Ekdahl and Ottmar had already been overcome. Wondering if their killers were already redoubling their efforts to catch the man who had sprung free from their trap.

Kessler expected to feel the sharp stab of an arrow in his back as he bulled his way through the forest. Every tree, every shrub was a potential hiding place for some lurking assassin, every shadow a refuge for some slinking killer. He was not afraid of death, the hardships of his life having inoculated him against that particular brand of terror. Even the pain of dying did not trouble him, and he almost welcomed the cruel bite of steel against his flesh. Ernst had often commented upon his capacity for pain, remarking that he seemed to enjoy it the way a dog enjoyed a bone or a drunkard his ale.

No, the fear that drove Kessler, that spurred him on even as the air became thin and hot in his lungs, was the fear that he should fail, that he should let down Ernst and Carlinda. They had to be warned, had to know about the men who had set up the ambush. Somehow, Kessler felt there was more than simple banditry behind the attack.

Screams and the clash of steel made Kessler pause in his race through the trees. The sounds came from ahead of him. For a moment, he wondered if he had somehow doubled back, if he had circled around to where Ekdahl and Ottmar continued to fight for their lives. He quickly disabused himself of the idea. Whatever fray was unfolding, it was greater than even two determined men could occasion. A horrible suspicion came over him and he ran forwards, a new determination firing him.

It wasn't the men he'd left behind he was hearing, it was Ernst and the column! The attackers hadn't pursued Kessler; they'd made straight for the very people he intended to warn!

Kessler bit back a curse. He was already too late to warn them. He might also be too late to save them, but as long as there was still a pulse in his body, he could still make their killers pay.

ERNST VON RABWALD thrust his sword into his attacker's chest, watching dispassionately as a gout of blood erupted from the ruffian's bearded face. The thug sagged weakly on his blade, threatening to tear the weapon from Ernst's fingers. He tried desperately to pull his sword free, crying out in pain as he reflexively tried to lend his left arm to the effort. It wouldn't move, pinned to his side by the arrow that had pierced it. Cursing, Ernst watched as the sword was torn from his grasp by the dying man. The baron quickly drew his dagger from his belt and limped away from his writhing victim. There were far too many of the man's comrades to linger and finish him off.

Their attackers had broken all around them with the fury of a tempest, smashing against them from all sides. They had taken refuge among the rocks that Ekdahl had directed them towards, there to await the return of the scout and his companions. The sounds of combat had drifted faintly back to them and he knew that the scouts were in trouble. Whether the orcs had discovered them or

the Sollander had sprung whatever subterfuge was behind
the strange message, Ernst knew that they needed his help.
He had already unhitched the destriers from the wagon,
anticipating that they would be needed in their former
capacity. Eugen's knights had strapped barding onto their
reclaimed warhorses with a practiced speed that impressed
even their marshal.

Just as the baron and the mounted element of his force
were emerging from the rocks, they had been met with a
withering hail of arrows. At least a dozen archers had set
upon them, their slipshod aim still sufficient to sink
arrows into the horses. Ernst and his men were thrown
from their stricken steeds, several of the men still struggling to recover from the fall when the second assault
started. What seemed a score or more of men, all wearing
shabby, piece-meal armour, had come rushing from the
trees. They offered no quarter, falling upon the wounded
with hideous glee. Ernst saw one of the knights stabbed
through the visor of his helm with a skinning knife, and a
soldier pinned to the ground by a brigand spear.

His injuries were serious. He'd suffered the wound to his
arm in the initial burst of bowfire, and his leg had snapped
like a twig when his stricken horse had thrown him. Ernst
fought to remain clear-headed, to keep command of the
situation. He quickly looked across the battlefield. At least
five of his men were down, two of them Eugen's knights.
Only a handful of brigands were on the ground, and it
looked like they were losses the scum could easily afford.
Eugen, his last knight, and a pair of soldiers were sorely
beset by the bandits. Ignoring the melee, other bandits
scrambled towards the rocks. The foremost fell back, his
chest collapsed by Skanir's hammer. The dwarf glowered at
his attackers, spitting at their cowardice and taunting them
to try again and share their friend's fate. Some of the

bandits tried to skirt around Skanir, but as they scrambled
into the rocks they found something more terrible than
the dwarf's hammer waiting for them. They retreated,
howling in fear, the slowest of them cut in half by a
gigantic sword as Ghrum loped after them.

Ernst spotted the ogre and saw more bandits rushing
towards the rocks. Instantly he thought of the wounded
men lying in the wagon and the sort of mercy they could
expect from such brigand vermin. 'Ghrum!' he shouted.
The ogre skipped a step, turning his huge face in the
baron's direction. 'The wagon! Get the wagon out of here!'
The ogre nodded in understanding and turned to rush
back to the rocks. Bandits scattered before him, their panic
increased rather than lessened by the frantic bowfire that
pursued the ogre back into his refuge.

Sharp flaring pain in his back told Ernst that he had
been stabbed. He started to turn to face his attacker, but
was slashed again, this time from the side. He fell, blood
gushing from his body in a torrent. Above him, he could
hear his killers arguing.

'Leave off! This one's mine!' roared a short, scraggly ruffian with a thin, reedy voice.

'You leave off Kopff! I'm the one that killed him!'
shouted a taller scallywag with a grimy, weasel-like countenance.

Kopff had already dropped to his knees beside Ernst,
struggling to rip the medallion from the baron's neck. 'I
stabbed him first Schmitt, that means he's mine! Go and
kill your own!'

Schmitt brandished his sword at the smaller looter, displaying his brown teeth in a savage snarl. 'He was still
twitching when I slashed him. Makes him fair game.'

The other bandit shook his head fiercely, stuffing the
purloined medallion down his breeches as he glared back

at Schmitt. 'I'd like to see you take that up before a magistrate!' he sneered.

Ernst bit down on his tongue, urging what little strength he had left into his right arm. He tightened his grip on the dagger, and started to raise his arm to lash out at the jackal perched on his chest.

'Look out, Kopff! He's still trying to stick you!' Kopff reacted swiftly, diving on Ernst's rising arm and crushing it to the ground.

'Oh, that's a beauty!' Kopff chortled, straining to pry Ernst's fingers apart. 'Just look at that knife, Schmitt!'

'It's not decent Kopff, you taking all the choice gewgaws,' protested Schmitt.

Kopff looked up, favouring the other bandit with an exasperated look. 'Are you going to stand there gawking or are you going to help me get his hand open? He's a strong bastard!'

Schmitt started to help Kopff when an enraged roar brought both men scrambling to their feet. They turned to see a huge shape emerge from the forest, a massive sword clenched in his hands, his face a mass of scars and fury. The killers scattered before him, in their panic imagining that somehow the ogre had circled around from the rocks to come at them from behind.

Kopff slashed ineffectually at the swordsman, only to have his blade batted aside by a brutal counterstroke. The bandit leapt back before the greatsword could cleave him from breastbone to hip. 'He did it! He killed him!' he whined, stabbing a finger at Schmitt even as he retreated before the attacker.

The look Kessler directed at the other bandit had the brigand cringing back like a whipped cur. He started after the retreating men, intent on cutting them to ribbons. Only the pained groan that came from the broken, bleeding thing at his feet brought him up short. The two bandits seized the opportunity, taking to their heels and plunging into the trees.

Ernst uttered a pained laugh as he saw Kessler leaning over him.

'Max,' he coughed. 'I think… we walked… into… a trap.'

RAMBRECHT WATCHED FROM the trees as the brigands fell upon the Wissenlanders. With real soldiers, the ambush would have gone smoothly, especially with the intelligence they had been given. As it stood, they'd been forced to make a fight of things. Baldur knew the scum he had gathered well enough to direct them to fire at the horses rather than the riders, and even so the vermin had barely managed to hit their marks. Now they were in there among the survivors, trying to finish them off. It wasn't going well, but well enough to satisfy him. It didn't matter to Rambrecht how many men they lost, just so long as they got the job done.

The knights that hadn't been immediately killed after falling from their horses were putting up a hellish defence, as was the hammer-wielding dwarf who was holding his ground among the rocks. Rambrecht hoped the bandits remembered Baldur's injunction that he wanted the dwarf alive. He didn't care how many of them the dwarf killed, he wanted him taken alive.

The ogre had been an unexpected surprise. The message left behind in Murzklein said that the beast had been injured, but he was still hale enough to toss Baldur's dogs around like ninepins. It was fortunate that the big brute had retreated back into the rocks, re-emerging lugging a large wagon behind him. Those brigands who thought to capitalise on the ogre's preoccupation were soon driven off by the distinctly accurate bowmanship of the halfling perched atop the wagon. The escape of the wagon did not overly trouble Rambrecht, since there was nothing there that he needed.

Despite the wretched discipline of Baldur's men, enough of them had remembered their orders to strike out after the objectives they had been given. Rambrecht felt a deep satisfaction as he saw a pair of them make it into the rocks and set upon the mounted witch. They pulled her down from her horse, and then dragged her back across the battlefield, to where Rambrecht eagerly awaited his prize. With the witch safely in tow, there might not even be any need to take the troublesome dwarf alive.

'They're butchering my men,' Baldur complained. Rambrecht laughed incredulously at him.

'What do you care?' Rambrecht scoffed. 'Soon you'll be commanding Averland guards, not this trash!' He dismissed Baldur's complaints and concerns, watching avidly as the battle continued to unfold. The knights were alone, fighting back to back with nearly a dozen brigands surrounding them. Several more were converging on a hulking swordsman who was trying to carry a wounded man back into the rocks. The aristocrat laughed again. The fool should have let his friend lie; now they were both doomed. There was no way he could wield his greatsword with one arm supporting his friend.

Rambrecht was not the only one who noted Kessler's situation. As she was dragged through the carnage, Carlinda saw the swordsman's travail. Despair surged up within her and she redoubled her struggle to pull away from her captors. The bandits growled at her, striking her and urging her forwards, but Carlinda barely attended their violence, her entire attention riveted on the killers closing upon Kessler and the baron. She knew he would never leave the baron, and she knew that he would die if he didn't.

Carlinda closed her eyes, a quiet litany rasping past her lips. She opened herself to the waves of power she had tried to block for so long, trying to focus it in her mind, trying to use it to help Kessler. The bandits holding her pulled away, releasing her as they recoiled in fright. Her skin grew icy, and her breath turned to mist as all the warmth drained away around her. She could feel the breath of Morr blowing all around her, coursing through her. She started to bind it to her will, to force the power to her purpose.

The augur's eyes snapped open in horror, horror that was echoed all around her. Bandits, knights and soldiers, all set up cries of alarm and terror. A great cloud of darkness was gathering, swirling in the empty air above the fray. Carlinda felt her soul shrivel as she beheld it, felt ancient fears rekindle inside her. In her desperation to help Kessler, she had gambled and tried to harness the breath of Morr for the first time since the ritual had been profaned by Zahaak's sending. Now she knew that she had lost that gamble.

The black cloud slowly began to resolve into a shape, the outline of a hooded skull. Eyes of fire gleamed in the sockets of the skull, glaring hungrily at Carlinda. Dimly, she heard the brigands' fragile courage shatter, heard them scurrying like rats back into the depths of the forest. Dimly, she heard Kessler shouting her name. She dared to look away, dared to watch as he took a trembling step towards her, torn between his concern for her and his loyalty to the injured man he carried.

She only managed to look at him for an instant, and then her eyes were drawn back to the sending. She could feel the infernal will of the monster that had sent it stabbing into her, fiery worms that seared into her brain and lashed her soul. She could feel the thing pawing at her mind, clawing away at her memories. She knew she could not let it find what it was looking for. She had to stop it, if it was not already too late.

Carlinda struggled to look once again at Kessler. Briefly, so briefly, he had made her whole again, made her almost a woman once more. She hoped she had helped him, in her way. Now that was all over. There was only one more thing she could do to help Kessler, to help them all.

She closed her eyes, willing the dreadful energies she had called upon, the energies Zahaak had used to find her and connect with her mind, to converge upon her own flickering life force. She felt her limbs grow leaden, and the icy numbness of the grave flowed through her. The heart in her breast faltered and grew still. The last thing she heard was Kessler shouting her name.

CARLINDA'S BODY CRUMPLED to the ground like a broken marionette, her limbs already rigid, her flesh already grey and cold. The wispy skull hovering above her snarled as she died, seething with wrath. Then the sending reared back, seeming almost to laugh as some new thought came. The image of Zahaak was still exuding pitiless malevolence as it faded back into the nothingness from which it had come, only the cold, still body of the augur testifying that it had ever been there.

Kessler stared at her, overcome with horror. He did not begin to understand what had happened, and knew that he didn't want to. Carlinda was dead, and her death was a thing of blackest sorcery. He wanted to go to her, but fear held him back, terror of that ghastly shape that had formed above her and had laughed at her passing. He felt shame and guilt and all the other self-despising emotions a man can know, but none was strong enough to draw him closer to that bewitched corpse.

Shuddering, Kessler turned his mind to helping the baron. Eugen and his surviving knight, a youth named Gerhard, came to help him build a litter for the stricken nobleman, while Skanir and a pair of surviving soldiers kept a watch on the trees against the return of the bandits.

When the litter was built, the men hurried to pursue Ghrum and the wagon. Kessler could not deny that he shared in their eagerness to put the battlefield and Carlinda's eerie death far behind them.

As much as he hated himself for it, even he didn't look back.

CHAPTER NINE

THEY DIDN'T STOP running until the gloom of night forced them to stop. Some ran to outdistance any pursuit from the men who had ambushed them. A few, those who had seen the crone's ghastly dissolution, were spurred on by something deeper, more primal.

It was with no small measure of reluctance that Marshal Eugen called a stop to their retreat, lest their already reduced numbers be further savaged by blind wandering through the benighted forest. What strength they still had lay in their numbers, and they could ill-afford to have that strength scattered and lost in the wilds.

Kessler was thankful for the pause. As soon as Eugen allowed them to stop, he was scrambling to the supply wagon. Ghrum had pulled the heavy wagon for hours, even the prodigious endurance of the ogre tested by such a feat. To lighten his burden, almost everything had been stripped from the wagon. All the remaining supplies had been abandoned save for a cask of water and a side of salted beef. The sides of the vehicle had been broken off, leaving only the flat bed behind. The wounded languished upon it, the ogre's loping gait across the hard broken ground threatening to spill them from their tenuous refuge at every turn. When the constant bump and bounce of their passage opened their wounds afresh, Theodo did his best to minister to them. Often it was not enough, and the grim-faced halfling would motion to the soldiers marching stoically beside the wagon. These men would sombrely close upon the wagon, grabbing whatever poor soul Theodo indicated. The dead man would be deposited in the brush and the ogre's burden would lighten just a little more.

Throughout the long march, Kessler had watched the morbid spectacle with dread, waiting to see the broken body of his master dumped unceremoniously in the forest. Somehow, Baron Ernst von Rabwald managed to cling to life until the time when Eugen finally allowed them to rest. Kessler tried to force cheer and hope onto his gruesome face, but even without the horror of Carlinda's death clouding his mind, he was a stranger to such moods and ill-fitted to suggest them to another. Ernst accepted his hand, holding it with a pathetic grip that spoke even more of the baron's flagging vitality than did the pallor of his face.

'I've done all I can,' Theodo apologised, climbing between the wounded to stand over the baron. 'He needs a real healer, not a camp cook playing at surgeon.'

Ernst tried to tighten his grip on Kessler's arm, as though to refute Theodo's words. He saw the way Kessler's expression sagged at the feeble exertion. The baron leaned back, his breathing becoming shallow. 'Who's left?' he asked. The question troubled Kessler, for it was one he had asked every time the swordsman had approached near enough to the wagon to catch his eye.

'Skanir, Eugen, one of his knights and three soldiers still fit enough to be called such.'

The baron closed his eyes, nodding as he considered the grim report. After a time, he gave a weak, dismissive wave of his hand. 'It doesn't matter,' he said, his voice struggling to rise above a croaking whisper. 'All Wissenland depends upon us. We must endure. We must prevail!'

Kessler looked around, almost embarrassed by Ernst's desperate outburst. Every man was watching the wagon, their faces a mixture of defeat, guilt and pity. They did not need to be reminded how much had depended upon them. It was Eugen who emerged from their ranks to quietly reprove the baron's feverish cries.

'My lord, we are too few,' the knight said. 'We must turn back, and let some other take up the task and succeed where we have failed.'

Ernst turned eyes desperate with denial towards the knight. 'We have to do it,' he insisted. 'Us, no one else. There isn't time for anyone else. Every day, every hour we tarry, that much longer does the enemy ravage our land! We must do it!'

The knight sighed, his voice becoming soft, patronising, like that of a patient father trying to dissuade a child of some fantastical delusion. 'My lord, we can't. We have no horses, no supplies–'

'Get them,' Ernst whispered. 'Requisition whatever you need wherever it is found.' His bloodied fingers fumbled at the torn ruin of his once elegant tunic. A folded length of stained oilskin dropped away from his hand as it emerged. Theodo bent and recovered the parchment from the bed of the wagon. The halfling whistled appreciatively as he read the elaborate calligraphy on the page.

'A letter of marque,' Theodo rasped, 'bearing the count's seal!' Almost reluctantly, he handed the parchment to Eugen. 'He's right. Carrying that, you can commandeer anything that isn't nailed down, anywhere in Wissenland.'

Eugen read the letter and then shook his head again. 'Even with this, we are still lost,' he explained. 'The witch is dead and without her we can't find the crypt.'

'Hrmph!' grunted Skanir. The dwarf was leaning on his hammer, trying to stuff the bowl of his pipe with a particularly pungent selection of crushed leaves. 'I don't need some manling sorceress to tell me how to find a dwarfish war-tomb!' He removed a small firebox from his belt and began to work the grinding mechanism to create an ember to light his pipe. 'Or maybe you've forgotten why exactly your count wanted me to come along? If it was just to nursemaid you lot, I'd have stayed put with my cannons!'

The dwarf's surly remarks were seized by Ernst, a feverish light creeping into his eyes. 'You'll carry on?' he asked. 'You'll find the crypt and bring back the runefang?'

Skanir drew a deep breath, expelling a plume of grey smoke from his nostrils. 'I gave my word, and Skanir Durgrund is no umbaraki. Let faithless mongrels like Uthor Algrimson shave their beards and break their oaths.' The dwarf paused, inhaling another lungful of thick smoke. His beard and eyes glowing in the smouldering light of his pipe, Skanir turned his head and looked at each of the men surrounding the wagon. 'I gave my word to your count, but I haven't made any oaths at the Shrine of Grimnir. I won't go rushing off to some lonely doom, my bones lost and forgotten. If the rest of you turn back, then I reckon my word has taken me as far as honour demands.'

Ernst focused his attention back on Eugen. 'You have to do it!' he pleaded. 'Otherwise all is lost!'

'No, your lordship,' Eugen replied, his voice heavy. 'If we try, weakened and ill-equipped, with no chance of success, if we try and fail, then all is lost. Our own glory means nothing, the recovery of the runefang and Solland's honour is what matters. If the gods have decreed that others should accomplish this, then who are we to question their will?'

A spasm of pain contorted Ernst's face and the wounded man sagged back against the hard planks of the wagon. 'We can't... You can't go back. It has to be now! It has to be us! Zahaak will kill everything his legion touches!'

'Then let it die,' Eugen said gravely, 'if that is the will of the gods. We can't selfishly cling to this chance to recover the Southern Sword. It is too important that the sword be found!'

Ernst favoured the knight with a disgusted wave of his hand, dismissing Eugen from his presence. The baron turned his desperate, pleading eyes on Kessler, fixing the swordsman with his imploring gaze. 'You must lead them Max,' he said. 'Take them to the gates of hell if you have to, but don't give up! Don't abandon the people. Don't prostitute hope to ambition! Take command, Max, and do a better job of things than I did!'

It took some time for the baron's words to eat away at Kessler's sense of defeat, and longer still for him to convince the bloody-handed swordsman that he should take command of the ragged remains of their company. It was the last thing Ernst had the strength to attain, and once he had impressed his last, wretched hope upon Kessler, he settled back and lay still. Kessler stood by his side, waiting through the long hours of the night as the baron's life slowly drained away.

Sometime after midnight, he joined Eugen and the others around the tiny fire they had made.

'He's gone then?' Eugen asked as Kessler lowered himself to the ground. The swordsman replied with a sombre nod, and then focused a haunted gaze on the crackling flames.

'A good man,' one of the soldiers said. 'He should have had a noble death, something more heroic.'

'Death is death,' Kessler said. 'There's nothing heroic about it. However it comes to you, you're still just as dead.'

'Cling to life with both hands to the last, eh?' Theodo laughed. The halfling was more than a bit deep in his cups and the others around the fire had long ago given up the fruitless effort of getting him to share whatever potent spirit was lurking within his hipflask. 'Only way I'd prefer to cross the gate is grey-headed in a bed big enough to smother a dragon and with a brace of saucy…' The cook's inebriated jocularity grated on Kessler's already worn nerves. He rose and turned on Theodo. The halfling remained oblivious to the threat, but Ghrum was a good deal more aware. The ogre lurched up onto his feet, looming in the darkness like a small hillock. The men around the fire shuffled uneasily, almost unconsciously drawing away from Kessler.

Kessler met the ogre's menace with a stare of smouldering fury. Ghrum's eyes retained an almost brutish

level of tolerance as he met that stare. Beside him,
Theodo continued to concoct increasingly unlikely and
amoral qualifiers to what he would consider an agree-
able demise. The ogre cracked one of his knuckles, the
sound booming like the crash of a hammer against an
anvil. Kessler took a step towards the looming monster.
Ghrum's face twitched with what might have been
amused respect.

There was no question which way the uneven contest
would resolve itself. Even a big man like Max Kessler
was hardly a challenge for an ogre. Before the mauling
could begin, however, furtive, rustling sounds from
beyond the camp arrested everyone's attention. Even
Theodo's drunken posturing drifted into silence as the
sense of menace impacted even his befuddled senses.
Weapons emerged from scabbards as eyes strove to penetrate the dark. Eugen's whispered orders passed
around the fire and men began to separate, to assume a
rough approximation of a skirmish line.

The tension continued to mount as the sounds drew
nearer. Theodo was fumbling with his bow, trying to
remember how to nock an arrow to the string. Ghrum
stood beside him, the ogre's gigantic sword clenched in
his boulder-sized fists. Eugen and Gerhard, the last of
the Knights of the Southern Sword, fixed the centre of
the line, imposing despite the absence of their heavy
steel armour. The surviving soldiers held the ground to
either side of the knights, nervous sweat dripping down
their faces. Kessler unlimbered his zweihander and
secured the left flank, placing himself close to the
wagon and his dead master's body.

It was Skanir's cry that broke the tension. His vision
sharper than that of man or ogre, his eyes more accustomed to the dark of tunnel and cavern than the light of

day, he was the first to recognise something familiar in the figure stealing towards them in the night. Even so, it was not until the man emerged into the dim circle of light provided by the fire and all could see for themselves the veracity of the dwarf's claims that any within the camp felt obliged to lower their weapons.

Bloodied, bedraggled, his armour torn, his clothes soiled by mud and briar, Sergeant Ottmar all but collapsed as he gained the camp. He seized the first waterskin he saw, draining its contents with ferocious greed. Then he sank gratefully beside the fire, trying to warm limbs numbed by the chill of the forest. Only when he had partially succeeded in this effort did he acknowledge the questions that bombarded him from every quarter.

THE WOUND OTTMAR had received was ugly, but neither crippling nor life-threatening: a deep gash in his upper arm, delivered by a sword stroke that had been more zealous than accurate. Theodo was too out of sorts to tend the injury, so Ottmar was forced to endure a tightly bound compress until such time as the flesh could be properly stitched together.

After they had sent Kessler back to warn the others, Ottmar and Ekdahl had tried to hold off the brigands. In this, their ambitions had exceeded their abilities and in short time they were nearly overrun. Both men had tried to lead the bandits off through the forest, thinking to mislead them from the real location of the column. However, when they heard the sounds of a terrible fight unfolding behind them, they knew they had failed in this purpose. They turned at that point, thinking to retrace their path and lend what support they could to Baron von Rabwald's men, but they had been followed by a handful of bandits. These came upon them suddenly and without warning. Ottmar was brought down by a sword stroke, left for dead by his attackers. When he recovered from his injury, he was alone with no sign of either Ekdahl or the bandits.

Ottmar had made his way back to the rocks, discovering the carnage left behind by the battle that had raged there. He saw the path the survivors had taken, Ghrum's enormous prints convincing him it was his comrades and not the brigands who had departed that way. The rest of the day, he had struggled to follow after them, but his wound vexed him terribly and he had never quite been able to catch up. Indeed, he had almost despaired of ever achieving his objective until he saw the light of their fire beckoning to him in the night.

'No, I saw no sign that anyone but me followed you,' Ottmar replied to Eugen's question. The knight breathed a sigh of relief.

'That is something, at least,' he decided. 'We can strike out for the river, recover at the first village we come across and send word back to Count Eberfeld regarding our losses.'

'We won't be staying that long,' Kessler told him. Eugen's eyes narrowed at the swordsman's reproach. 'We'll be here for just long enough to take what we need before we press on.' The statement brought incredulous curses from the soldiers and an impious oath from Gerhard.

'What we need is more men,' Eugen pointed out. 'We're not even strong enough to fight off a pack of bandits, much less go gallivanting through the Black Mountains. There's still a fair number of orcs prowling the mountains and more goblins living beneath them than a weirdroot fiend's worst nightmare could conjure!'

'Then we'll get more men,' Kessler countered.

'Where?' Eugen objected. 'Count Eberfeld has picked the region clean of militia and guardsmen to fight Zahaak.'

Kessler shook his head, glancing back at the wagon. 'I don't know, but we'll find a way. The baron would want me to try.'

'You?' protested Gerhard. 'Surely you don't think we're going to take that seriously? You're a baron's champion, an arena fighter, a trained killer. What do you know about command? Marshal Eugen is the natural choice to carry on as leader.'

Kessler glared back at the outraged young knight. 'Everything you say is true, but the baron trusted me more than the marshal to see this thing through. I intend to follow his final order.'

'We should put it to a vote,' suggested one of the soldiers. 'I say we follow Marshal Eugen. He has the right of it. We've done everything we could do. There's no shame in turning back.' The sentiment was echoed by the man's comrades, and brought a satisfied grin to Gerhard's face.

'There will be no voting,' Eugen said, silencing the dissent. 'Kessler is right, the baron made his choice and we are bound to that decision.'

'But the runefang!' Gerhard exclaimed. 'You said yourself it is more important that the Southern Sword is recovered, regardless of who gets the glory of doing so.'

'Yes, I did,' Eugen conceded, 'but maybe I was wrong. Maybe the baron was right. There are lives in the balance, lives that are not rightly ours to spend.'

The argument might have continued, but for Ottmar's decisive interruption. With a loud, piercing whistle, he silenced the conversation. All eyes turned upon the wounded sergeant. 'This bickering gets no one anywhere,' he said. 'Why not wait until you reach civilisation again. See what Kessler can do before you go making any rash decisions.'

'Besides,' Ottmar added, pleased with the effect his words had had, 'wouldn't it be better to wait until you are certain there are no enemies on your tail before falling out?'

That seemed to settle the matter and the conference broke apart as each man found his bedroll and tried to capture such sleep as the night might yet allow him.

Kessler found Ottmar before the sergeant could fall asleep. 'I want to thank you,' he told the soldier. Ottmar waved aside his gratitude.

'There's nothing to thank,' he said. 'I've been leading soldiers around by the nose for longer than I care to remember. The trick is to cloak your coercion in a bit of common sense. It gives them the illusion that they're making their own decisions.'

'I'll bear that in mind,' Kessler said.

Ottmar shifted deeper into the heavy blankets he had been given. 'You've got better things to think about,' he told Kessler, closing his eyes, 'like what you're going to do when you reach the river. It'll have to be pretty good to keep this lot together after what they've been through.'

Kessler turned away, stalking back towards the wagon. The sergeant was right, he would need to do something to prevent the entire expedition from disintegrating. He stared down into Ernst von Rabwald's cold, pained face. That was a question that would wait. Now he had a friend to bury.

* * *

THEODO SMACKED HIS head against the side of the oak as he tried to dredge up whatever was left in his capricious stomach. Nothing came up, so he decided that the worst was over, although his body didn't seem to agree, reflexively convulsing and heaving to purge itself of the fermented poisons the halfling had tortured it with the night before. He squinted at the faint glow on the horizon. Dawn was such an unholy hour, something to be shunned every bit as much a physical labour. It always reminded him of such thankless drudgery, the long years on his father's farm. There were much better ways to make a living.

Tending wounded tall folk wasn't one of them. Theodo shuddered again as he considered all that cut and torn humanity he had struggled so mightily to attend. He tried to prevent himself from empathising with others, it was a quality no serious-minded gambler could afford, but it was very hard not to absorb some of that suffering when you were so close to it. That was why he had let himself go so badly, guzzling down the last of his extremely private, extremely secret and extremely final supply of schnapps. At the time it had seemed like a good idea, and improved with every snort he drew from the flask. The spirits had helped so marvellously to blur all those ugly images swirling around in his head, all those ugly memories of screaming, dying men he simply couldn't help.

Now, all Theodo could think about was what a waste it all was. Drinking for enjoyment, he could understand and approve of. Drinking to forget, guzzling down expensive, quality stock until its very taste became an abstraction, that he could never condone. He didn't care for drunkards, they were weak, miserable, foolish things, even when their name was Theodo Hobshollow.

The halfling pulled away from the tree and his self-recriminations. He shook his head, trying to clear the butterflies from his skull. The creeping rays of the sun weren't helping matters, not in the slightest. Reflexively, he turned his back to the fiery despot, wondering if he could somehow convince Kessler to delay the march until noon.

Suddenly the halfling pulled back, blinking his eyes in alarm. He'd heard snippets, snatches of hushed conversation between Kessler and the baron before they had reached Murzklein, suspicious whispers about ranger signs and strange messages left by someone in the camp. Theodo turned around, looking over his shoulder at the men busily packing what meagre gear they had left. Were any of them looking his way? Was anybody watching him?

Theodo dismissed the paranoia. Tall folk never paid much attention to the doings of halflings. They might as well be invisible for all that men cared most of the time. It was a frustrating, insulting tendency, he admitted, but an enterprising fellow never lacked opportunity to put it to good use. He decided to put it to good use now.

The halfling crept forward, timidly approaching the crude stone arrow that his sharp eyes had discerned. Silently, he followed in the direction it indicated, discovering a big old oak with a knobby, nose-like knot in the trunk. Above the knot was a narrow hollow and in the hollow…

Theodo stared at the little scrap of goatskin for sometime before deciding that whatever was written on it was beyond his capacity to understand. He glanced back at the camp and a cold smile wormed its way onto his face. Somebody back there understood what it said.

The gibberish written on the hide would be valuable to them.

With an avaricious twinkle in his eye, Theodo secreted the goatskin securely in the vest pocket that had formerly held his flask of schnapps. His step was a good deal more confident when he returned to the camp. The butterflies were all gone. Like scruples, they simply had no place when a fellow's mind turned towards business.

CHAPTER TEN

COUNT EBERFELD KEPT his face set, his expression firm and confident. The effect was somewhat spoiled by Captain Markus standing beside him. The officer was the embodiment of anxiety, shifting nervously from one foot to the other, head constantly turning as he struggled to watch every corner of the tent simultaneously. His fingers tapped against the hilt of his sword, as though he was frightened to have the weapon away from his touch. That was something, at least, the count considered. The Averlanders hadn't requested their weapons.

Of course that fact didn't really comfort Markus. Armed or unarmed, there was little mischief the captain and the twenty knights who had accompanied Count Eberfeld across the border could work against the considerable host Count Achim had assembled. They'd be like mites nibbling at a dragon's scaly hide, and could be crushed just as easily.

Eberfeld thought about that vast encampment, the immense field of tents and pavilions, the timber corrals filled with warhorses and the wooden racks filled with spears and lances. From even a casual glance, he could see that Averland had worked hard to recover her strength after the last war. He knew that every man in the encampment was a tried and tested fighter, rotated from across the province to guard the notorious Black Fire Pass against greenskin marauders from the mountains and ruthless raiders from the lawless realms of the Border Princes. He could see the echoes of battle in the eyes of the soldiers, who turned their smouldering, hateful gaze on him as he was led through the camp to meet with their leader.

These men knew the ways of sword and spear, and had practised the art of war in pitched battle time and again. In the heart of each burned the sting of defeat, the slight against their national pride visited upon their people in the aftermath of invasion. Eberfeld knew well how far a man could drive himself out of love and loyalty and devotion. He also knew that hate could carry a man further. Beside the soldiers dressed in the black and yellow of Averland, Eberfeld's troops were little more than a motley collection of peasant militia.

The colours of Averland were not the only ones in evidence among the banners of Achim's army. Eberfeld noted the standards of several mercenary companies, their tents pitched well away from the regular soldiery. A loud and raucous band of horsemen, practising their reckless brand of mounted acrobatics, galloped around the edge of the camp, their shaved heads and long top-knots marking them as Ungols from the lands of the Tzar. More disturbing still was the bright blue banner with the green griffon splayed across it. Eberfeld knew the heraldry well, and knew what manner of soldiers rode beneath it. The Order of the Griffon, one of the knightly orders devoted to the protection of Altdorf and the Great Cathedral of Sigmar, served the Prince of Reikland and for them to be present in Count Achim's camp meant that the pretender to the crown of the Empire had sent them. Averland would be a staunch ally for the prince, helping him against the other claimants to the crown, the Count of Middenheim and Lady Magritta of Marienburg. Eberfeld frowned as he considered how much deeper Reikland's commitment to Achim might run and how substantial their support would be if Averland moved against him.

The tent they had been led into was clearly that of some knight or officer rather than Count Achim's own pavilion. Their escort had conducted Eberfeld and Markus into the canvas-walled room, and left promising to bring news of his presence to Count Achim. There was no hiding the hostility in the voices of the Averlanders, but as Eberfeld had hoped, the sheer audacity of his visit in person to their camp had confounded them. If that confusion rose as far as Achim, he might get his audience, might be allowed his desperate gamble to convince his neighbour that he was not his father and that Wissenland's troubles were genuine, her plight authentic. He had to trust that Achim would take his presence in the Averland camp as an act of faith, a testament to the truth of his words.

Of course, even if Achim believed him, there was the possibility that Averland would move across the border anyway. It depended how deeply ambition and hate ran in the old count, and how strongly the virtues of honour and humanity held his heart. If Eberfeld had overplayed his hand, rather than driving the wolf from his door he might be inviting it in.

The tent flap was suddenly pulled back, snapping Eberfeld from his troubled thoughts. Two men entered, stalking into the room with a wary, cautious quality. The foremost was a thin, middle-aged man with sharp patrician features and finely cut clothes trimmed in ermine. Behind him came a taller more powerfully built specimen, his imposing frame encased in an elaborately engraved suit of plates, the armour shining a steely blue as the flickering light of the tent's lamp glistened off it. The older man glared at Eberfeld with the same smouldering hostility the soldiers had regarded him with, but the knight's expression was more subdued, an unimpassioned watchfulness, the calculating regard of a predator sizing up its prey.

The thin Averlander studied Eberfeld, his sullen eyes scrutinising every inch of the nobleman. The man's gaze lingered on the jewelled cavalry sabre hanging from the count's belt, and his lean face pulled up into a sneer. Eberfeld clenched his jaw. At General Hock's insistence, he'd left the runefang of Wissenland behind. It was bad enough to risk the ruler of the province in such a dangerous and reckless endeavour, but to risk the symbol of the legitimacy of that rule was something Eberfeld was unwilling to do. The ruin of Solland was an imposing example of what happened to a land that lost its power to rule.

The Averlander's impertinent air of superiority grew as he reached beneath the heavy fur-trimmed cloak he wore, eyes still fixed on the mundane blade in Eberfeld's scabbard. The count could almost read the thoughts in the Averlander's mind, the understanding that the bold Wissenlander was not as confident as he pretended to be. The old man drew a sword from beneath his cloak, the blade almost seeming to glow in the gloom of the tent. Captain Markus muttered an oath and started to draw his own steel, but all Eberfeld could do was gasp and stare.

Before Markus could react to what he imagined was an attack against his lord, the thin Averlander plunged the blade he had drawn into the ground between him and Eberfeld, stabbing the sword deep into the living earth. Eberfeld only dimly heard the sigh of relief from his officer, his attention fully riveted upon the sword. There were slight differences in ornamentation, in the scroll work upon the jewelled hilt and the engraving upon the guard, the stylised flames that writhed along the dark metal of the blade, but there was no doubting its kinship with the blade Eberfeld had left behind with General Hock. There were only twelve such swords in all the world, and Eberfeld knew that he gazed upon the runefang of Averland, the legendary sword sometimes known as Mother's Ruin.

The thin Averlander gloated in Eberfeld's shock, folding his arms before him and waiting for the nobleman to regain his composure. When he was satisfied that Eberfeld would attend, the man spoke, his words at once snide and imperious. 'I am Graf Dietrich Kuhlmann,' the Averlander introduced himself, feigning only the rudest approximation of a courtly bow, 'seneschal to His Imperial Excellency Count Ludo Exeter Johannes Achim von Leitdorf, Warden of the River Aver, Guardian of the Grey Forest and Protector of the Black Fire.' Kuhlmann bowed again as he recited the titles of his lord and master. 'Count Achim extends the courtesy of his camp to the delegation from our neighbour. Courtesy, and nothing more.' The old man's hand extended in a casual gesture, pointing at the runefang thrust into the ground. 'I was told to bring this talisman to display the sincerity of my master's promise of safety. If any sword in this camp were to be raised against Eberfeld of Wissenberg, it would be this one. Count Achim would never endure any hand but his own to strike down an Eberfeld.'

Eberfeld looked from the sword into Kuhlmann's leering face. 'Am I to take it then that Count Achim will not allow me a personal audience and that I must make do with one of his... functionaries?'

'Count Achim fears that if he were to be in the same room as you, the compulsion to avenge himself would be too great to deny,' Kuhlmann replied coldly. There was such intensity in the seneschal's words that Eberfeld almost forgot the ridiculousness of the scene they evoked. Achim was an old man, more than half again as old as himself. Eberfeld's agents in Averland had repeatedly described the eccentricities of Achim, but never had they reported anything that suggested delusions or madness. 'His sons were murdered in the Rape of Averheim,' Kuhlmann continued. 'The impulse to kill the son of the man who killed his sons is one that has haunted his excellency ever since you succeeded your infamous predecessor.'

'Why then has your lord not acted before now?' Eberfeld growled. 'Why does he wait to pounce upon my lands when they are already besieged? I know there can never be friendship between Wissenberg and Averheim, but I had thought Achim a man of honour, the noble eagle who would swoop down from the open sky to strike his enemy. Instead I find him playing the part of a lurking vulture, waiting to pick clean the carcass of a land already struggling to survive!'

For the first time, Kuhlmann's smile was genuine and almost warm. 'Count Achim's dispute is with the House of Eberfeld, not with our brothers in Wissenland. We have no ambitions to seize territory or plunder the countryside. We are content to leave such tactics to Eberfelds and orcs. This army, this great host drawn from every corner of the province is not here to invade Wissenland, it is here to aid our neighbour in her time of need. We have ten thousand infantry, two thousand cavalry and a dozen ogres from the hills of Ostland, all ready to march to the aid of Wissenland's people. There are stores of grain and bread, which Count Achim, in his benevolence, intends to bestow upon the people displaced by the conflict being waged within Wissenland. As a people who have suffered the ravages of war, we Averlanders understand what it is to spend winter with an empty belly.'

Eberfeld's mind turned over the claims Kuhlmann was making, wondering how good the Averlanders' spies in his realm were. If they had reported the true extent of the fight against Zahaak's legion, they would understand that there was no need for subterfuge. Eberfeld had nothing to spare to stop them should they move across the river, certainly nothing that could delay an army the size of the one Kuhlmann boasted. No, Achim had to be playing a more subtle game. Eberfeld was quiet as he pondered what it might be. Something stood out in the seneschal's speech, something that he had perhaps let slip without fully understanding its import. Achim's feud was not with Wissenland, but with the family that ruled her.

Again Eberfeld's mind fled back through the years, to his earliest youth, when his father had still been alive. Walther Eberfeld had been a ruthless, ambitious man and hadn't allowed his tenuous claim to the crown of Wissenland to prevent him from seizing the title from the weak, corrupt von Stirlitz family. Averland had tried to support the von Stirlitzs against what they considered a usurper. Despite the aid of Averland and assistance from their masters in Nuln, Walther had deposed Hermann von Stirlitz and pronounced himself Count of Wissenland. Perhaps at first Walther had been moved by something loftier than his own pursuit of power. Certainly, he had used breaking the corruption of the von Stirltitzs as the rallying cry to draw support for his cause, to end the exploitation of Wissenland by the city-state of Nuln through their puppets in the court of Wissenberg.

Walther revelled too much in his new position as count to forget or forgive those who had opposed him. Across Wissenland, nobles who had stood against him were stripped of their lands and titles, and very often their lives. Assassins were dispatched across the Empire to exterminate the von Stirlitz family, root and branch. The states that had stood against him and supported his enemy soon found themselves at war. The resources and thick walls of Nuln had thwarted Walther's attempt at retribution, but Averland was not so fortunate. Much of its western counties were plundered and put to the torch, and the capital of Averheim besieged for months before threats from Reikland and Stirland forced Walther to relent and retreat back within his own borders.

Eberfeld hadn't even been born when his father had laid siege to Averheim, yet that event cast a long shadow over his rule. Count Achim's sons had been killed defending the capital and their deaths prevented any hope of reconciliation between the two rulers. Indeed, Achim had taken to wearing the names of his sons, Ludo and Exeter, a morbid affectation to posthumously allow his heirs rule over the province. Some wounds were too deep to heal. With Nuln, reparations had normalised relations between the city-state and Wissenland, but Eberfeld had learned after many fruitless efforts that Achim would never accept the hand of an Eberfeld.

Still, did Achim truly dare to move so boldly against Wissenland? To do so would possibly set a very complicated nest of alliances and treaties into action. Any move to invade Wissenland might see Averland invaded in turn. There was no love lost between Averland and her northern neighbours Stirland and Sylvania. Indeed, action against Averland was probably the only cause that could bring the two querulous backwaters together. Achim was too old a politician not to appreciate the dilemma.

However, perhaps he had a different strategy. The claims of offering aid to the people of Wissenland while spurning the legitimacy of its ruler would be a clarion call to every dissident in Wissenland. Far from an invader, Achim might be cast as some sort of liberator. Eberfeld's father had left many enemies when he died, and many barons might welcome the coming of a more pliant, less resolute count than Eberfeld. With Achim's army they'd have the strength to make it happen.

'I regret that I cannot accept Count Achim's generous offer,' Eberfeld said.

The knight who had accompanied Kuhlmann into the tent spoke for the first time. His accent was deep and guttural, thick with the tones of the Reik valley. Instantly, Eberfeld recalled the Reikland banner he had seen flying in the camp. 'I understand your hesitancy, Herr Count,' the knight said. 'There is much bad blood between your lands, and it is not easily forgotten or set aside, but at times like this, men must put aside their differences to muster together and fight the common foe.'

'Lord Hugo von Rhineholt,' Kuhlmann said, introducing the knight, 'captain of the Knights of the Griffon.'

'I have been sent here by Grand Theogonist Gottolf to mediate the dispute between your provinces,' Lord Hugo stated. Unlike Kuhlmann, there was no hostility in the knight's voice, only a suggestion of frustration and weariness.

'With due respect, you do not look like a warlock, Lord Hugo,' Eberfeld replied, 'and it would tax even a warlock's infernal tricks to blot out the history between Achim and my family.'

'Your lands are beset by inhuman abominations, despoiled by horrors from the grave,' Lord Hugo persisted. 'If Wissenland is to survive, then you must rise above your personal feelings. You must remember the example of Lord Sigmar, who showed us that the common blood of men is more important than the petty ambitions of tribes and chieftains. Men must stand together against the powers of Old Night.'

'Perhaps the Prince of Reikland will renounce his claim as Emperor then?' Eberfeld countered. He could see the knight's expression darken. 'No, Lord Hugo, I cannot afford to accept Averland's offer of aid, even if I trusted it. Perhaps Count Achim truly means to help my province, but there are those who would see it as weakness on my part to allow him to do so. Ambitious men would use this tragedy for their own purposes and the presence of so many foreign troops on Wissenland soil might embolden them. Perhaps, too, there are men in Averland who might rethink the purpose of their mission once their soldiers are across the river.'

Eberfeld looked from Lord Hugo to Kuhlmann, and then at the runefang standing between them. 'I cannot afford to accept the potentialities of Count Achim's assistance, nor the favours that might be expected of me from Reikland in facilitating such aid. Send the food if you will, I can't refuse my people such succour no matter the consequences, but keep your soldiers on this side of the river. I came here not to ask for help, but to assure Count Achim that the distress besetting Wissenland is real, that any fears he has that I am preparing to move against Averland are unfounded. If he is not convinced by his own spies, I invite him to come and see for himself the deathless legion that is laying waste to my land. If he comes, however, his delegation must be small. I will construe any move by this army to cross the river as an act of war.'

Eberfeld nodded to the two men, and then looked one last time at the Runefang of Averland. 'I promise you, any victory Achim draws from such a war will be a hollow one.' Without waiting for either knight or seneschal to speak, Eberfeld stalked from the tent, Captain Markus close behind him.

What could be done, had been done. The Averlanders would march or they would stay. Eberfeld could not spare the worry for them. The relentless march of Zahaak's legion was enough trouble for his mind. He wondered how far Baron von Rabwald's expedition had travelled and whether they had reached the Black Mountains yet. He wondered whether they had found the dwarf war-crypt, and whether they had found the runefang of Solland.

Was Wissenland's nightmare almost over, or had it only begun?

CHAPTER ELEVEN

FRITZSTADT WAS A miserable, timber-walled settlement on the banks of the River Sol, plaster facades covering walls of mud brick and raw stone. It was large enough to call itself a town and important enough to local tradesman to maintain a small dock, but it was still a far cry from the immense battlement-enclosed cities further north along the river. Yet to the tired, battle-weary men who emerged from the wilderness, it looked as safe and sturdy as the towers of Altdorf.

Kessler led the sorry remains of his company through the log gates of Fritzstadt, noting the thickness of the walls with some relief. Goblin or brigand, a foe would find getting past such a barrier a difficult prospect. He was less comfortable with the sullen, hostile regard of the two men positioned in the tower above the gate. There was something naggingly familiar about them, something Kessler could not quite place. He did not waste undue time pondering the problem, however. He'd lost count of how many times a face in the crowd had reminded him of some foe he'd faced in personal combat. Still, there was no denying that the two militiamen had seemed to recognise him.

The swordsman shook his head. He had more pressing concerns right now. There were wounded to be tended, stores to be requisitioned, horses to be commandeered. He patted the pocket that held the letter of marque from the count. The little slip of parchment gave him the authority to take whatever he needed from Fritzstadt. He just hoped that the place had what he needed.

Eugen appeared at his shoulder, almost as though the knight had read Kessler's thoughts. He directed Kessler's gaze to the cheap plaster walls, the dirt streets and thatch roofs. Whatever else Fritzstadt might be, prosperous was not among its claims. 'I don't think these people will be able to help us much,' the knight told him.

Kessler watched some of the coarsely dressed, dishevelled inhabitants of the town hurry along the street. Their eyes narrowed with suspicion as they passed, the faintest snatches of subdued whispers reaching Kessler's ears. Some went so far as to make the sign of Taal as they scurried past the group of strangers, before vanishing behind locked doors.

'It's certainly not Nuln,' Kessler agreed, 'but we'll manage. We have to.'

Eugen caught at his arm, arresting Kessler in his steps. 'Look at this place,' he said. 'You think there's more than two or three capable swordsmen in the entire town? We need fighters, not fishermen playing part-time soldier.'

Kessler pried the knight's hand from his arm. He matched Eugen's demanding stare. 'You want to turn back?'

'We could,' Eugen stated, 'just take a boat back up river, tell Count Eberfeld what happened, and get him to give us more men.' He saw the way Kessler's face darkened at the suggestion. 'It's more important that the runefang is recovered. Dying in the attempt won't do anyone any good.'

It was the umpteenth time Kessler had heard the knight make the statement. Each time he hated to hear it. The words made too much sense, but at the same time evoked a terrible guilt within him. To turn back was to admit failure, and that felt too much like betrayal for Kessler to accept. He had never failed Baron von Rabwald in life, and he would not fail him now.

'Every hour we delay, those ghouls slaughter a little bit more of Wissenland.' Ottmar edged his way between the knight and Kessler. The sergeant glared at Eugen as though looking at a leprous pig. 'Maybe you might think about that before you start imagining new glories for yourself.'

The accusation had Eugen's hand around the hilt of his sword. Ottmar took a step back, and then smiled, almost daring the knight to draw steel. Slowly, Eugen composed himself. 'The baron left you in command, Kessler,' he said. 'The decision is yours to make.'

Kessler sighed. He wasn't sure if the knight was aware of how uneasily the weight of command rested on his shoulders, but he had an ugly habit of reminding him of the fact. The swordsman turned away, looking down the street, towards the town square. The faint aroma of cooking fish drifted back to him.

'Then, as leader, I say we see about getting something to eat before we continue this talk.' At that moment, Kessler could have said nothing better as far as his soldiers were concerned. Theodo's eyes lit up at the mention of food, the halfling darting ahead to 'scout the way'.

The men followed after the halfling, emerging into the open plaza that formed the centre of Fritzstadt. A granite statue of some whiskered general stood large at the centre of the plaza, a representation of the founder of the settlement. For an instant, Kessler could not help but be reminded of the grisly totem they had discovered in Murzklein. Glancing around the square, he almost expected to see the vicious faces of goblins snickering at him from shadowy doorways. Instead, he saw a few street vendors and grubby fisherwomen hurriedly gathering their wares. Some scrambled for the massive doors of the town hall, a huge structure built of thick stone blocks and sporting the only iron fixtures Kessler had yet seen in the settlement. Others sought refuge in the plaster-walled temple of Taal that stood opposite the hall. A few, perhaps bolder than the rest, squirmed their way between the strangers, and then hastened down the street.

'Aren't we the popular ones?' Skanir scowled, lighting his pipe while keeping an arm crooked around the heft of his hammer.

'They certainly seem afraid of something,' Kessler agreed. They were the only living souls still in the square.

'They're afraid of your ogre.'

Kessler spun at the sound of the voice, his hand flying to the sword lashed across his back. The men with him were no less startled, some even drawing their weapons.

Kessler had reason to be thankful that the strange attitude of the townsfolk had made them more alert. As he looked at the man who had spoken, he had every reason to consider Fritzstadt no less hostile to them than goblin-infested Murzklein.

The speaker was descending a wooden staircase, which led into a large, rambling inn that fronted the square. Three men were with him, among them one of the familiar guards from the gate. Kessler knew why the man was familiar now, and where he had seen him before. He had last seen him in Koeblitz, along with the bearded Nordlander who had called out.

Kessler dragged his zweihander from its sheath, staring hard into the belligerent faces of the mercenaries. Some of the sell-swords responded in kind, but the Nordlander simply smiled.

'The baron's lapdog,' he laughed. 'I told you we'd meet again, only this time I'm on top.' The mercenary nodded his head towards either corner of the square. Kessler kept his eyes fixed on the menacing axeman, not daring to look away. Ottmar's whispered curse told him what the Nordlander wanted him to see.

'More of them!' Ottmar spat. 'All around us! At least twenty!'

The mercenary paced across the square, flanked by his comrades. He fingered the edge of his axe meaningfully. 'You put quite a scare into the good folks of Fritzstadt bringing that beast in here,' he said, pointing a finger at Ghrum, some of the bravado flickering off his face as the ogre growled back at him. 'They figure he's going to eat their daughters and molest their swine. As the duly appointed, and paid, protectors of this community, it would be remiss of us to neglect our duty.'

The smile broadened on the Nordlander's face as he tugged the axe free from his belt. He started towards Kessler with hate in his eyes. 'Who says you can't mix business and pleasure?'

'Raban!' The barked command brought the Nordlander up short as he started to close with Kessler. The other mercenaries took faltering steps away from the soldiers. Ghrum's huge frame sagged as he sighed with disappointment.

Kessler saw someone emerging from the town hall, recognising him at once as Valdner, captain of the Schwerstetten Brotherhood. The officer paced warily around the Wissenlanders, moving to join the axeman Raban. The Nordlander found it difficult to meet the reproach in his eyes.

'What's going on here? Explain yourself!'

Challenged, Raban remembered the emotion that had gripped him only moments before. He pointed his axe at Kessler, scowling at the swordsman. 'It's that scum from Koeblitz, the one that helped Baron von Rabwald cheat us of our pay!'

'And you thought to collect it from his hide?' Valdner asked. He shook his head in disgust as Raban's grin reasserted itself. 'Did you stop to wonder why this man is here? Did you stop to think that Count Eberfeld's entire army might be right outside the gates?' The huge Nordlander seemed to shrink into himself as his lack of thinking was illuminated. Valdner left Raban to nurse his burst ego and turned to Kessler.

'What are you doing here?' he demanded. 'Where is your master, the baron?'

Kessler met Valdner's stern look. He was silent for a moment, and then, deciding there was nothing to be gained holding back the truth, he told Valdner what he wanted to hear. 'We've come here to resupply. As for Baron von Rabwald,' Kessler paused, trying to force the words onto his tongue, finding them as bitter as the memory behind them, 'he's dead.'

The words provoked a strange reaction in the mercenary captain. His face became drawn, losing much of its colour. He staggered on his feet a moment, as though losing strength in his legs. With haste, Valdner gestured to his men. 'Go back to your posts,' he called out. The command brought groans and sullen stares, but the mercenaries did not hesitate to obey. Even Raban, his head held lower than that of a whipped cur, did not challenge his captain. With a last, malevolent look at Kessler, the huge axeman withdrew back inside the inn.

'So long as your men do not abuse the hospitality of this settlement, you are free to do as you will,' Valdner said, turning his attention back to Kessler. 'I advise the ogre to stay here in the plaza. It will rest easier with the town if they know where he is and where he isn't.'

'Thank you, captain,' Kessler said. He stared hard at Valdner, trying to read the thoughts running through his mind. The man had the same reason to hate him that Raban did, the same grievance against Count Eberfeld that his men shared. So, why the pretence? What game was he playing? Did he intend to let them get comfortable, to let their guard down and then unleash his sell-swords? That made sense to Kessler. Valdner was an old warrior, and he knew that he would lose men in a fair fight, even more so with Ghrum involved.

Valdner's next words made less sense to him.

'You are called Max Kessler?' When he received a nebulous nod of agreement, Valdner continued. 'You were there when your master died?' The question seemed an ill fit for Valdner's precise, clipped tones. 'I would like to hear how he died.'

'We were ambushed by bandits on the road from a place called Murzklein,' Ottmar said.

Valdner seemed to digest the question for a time. There was a suspicious shine to his eye as he questioned the men again. 'When we left the count's service,' he began, doing an admirable job of keeping resentment from his voice, 'the baron was attached to the count's army. Why should he be wandering the wilds far from where the war is being fought?'

'That, I fear, is our business,' Kessler said. Valdner nodded grimly, favouring the swordsman with the sort of look a serpent might give a sparrow.

'Perhaps you should tell him,' interjected Ottmar. The sergeant hurried to explain before Kessler could object. 'If we are to press on, we need more men. Captain Valdner's soldiers might be willing to set aside their grievances if they understood what was at stake.'

'They're mercenaries,' protested Eugen, 'sell-sword scum! The only thing they understand is their filthy blood money.'

Kessler motioned for the knight to hold his peace. Valdner seemed to take the outburst in his stride, more interested than insulted by the exchange between the three men.

'Are your services for hire, captain?' Kessler asked. He still did not trust the mercenary, but what Ottmar said was true, they needed more men if they were going to make it to the Black Mountains. Valdner's mercenaries were literally the only game in town.

'They may be,' Valdner answered. 'It depends on the price, and on a full explanation of what it is you expect of my men.' His voice dropped to a dangerous hiss. 'And a full accounting of how Baron von Rabwald died.'

'Agreed,' Kessler decided, ignoring the warning look that Eugen directed at him.

Valdner turned, extending his hand to indicate the town hall. 'I am on rather excellent terms with the burgomeister. I am sure he will lend us his council chambers to discuss the matter at length.' He smiled as the three Wissenlanders followed him to the stone-walled building. 'After all, devils always lurk in the details.'

THEODO HOBSHOLLOW WAITED outside the town hall of Fritzstadt, for the negotiations with the mercenary captain to conclude. From his perch outside the window of the council chamber, he had been able to hear much of what had transpired. He'd heard much that was of interest, and one or two things that were of extreme interest. As the meeting broke up, he stamped his foot down on the massive palm supporting him. Ghrum quickly lowered his arm, forcing Theodo to clutch the ogre's thumb to keep from falling.

The halfling glared up at Ghrum once he was safely on the ground again. 'Don't take up pottery,' he said, adjusting his dishevelled vest. Noting the dull look his friend gave him, Theodo rolled his eyes. 'You'd smash all the pots with those clumsy meat hooks of yours!' he explained irritably.

'Rather be hunting,' Ghrum decided after a moment of thought. 'Tastes better than pots.'

Theodo shook his head. It wasn't that ogres were stupid, though it took their minds a long time to mull over anything too complex, it was the fact that everything with them boiled down to 'can I eat it?'. The halfling smiled and patted his own prodigious gut. That was probably the reason they got on so well.

Theodo left Ghrum to puzzle over some of his other careers of choice and squirmed around the side of the building to watch as the men left the town hall. Valdner's expression was hard to read, but at least there was no outward show of hostility. Kessler's step was less heavy than it had been, so something must have turned around for him. Ottmar looked more at ease too. It was Eugen who was the black spot, the fly in the ointment. The scowl the knight wore looked like it had been borrowed from a witch. While the other men walked towards the inn, Eugen took his leave of them, stalking off towards the streets of Fritzstadt. The halfling nodded his head knowingly. He waited for a few seconds, and then scurried after the knight.

Eugen wasn't quite as dull-eared as most men, and he caught the halfling following him after turning only a few corners. Of course, Theodo wasn't putting any special care into being quiet. He made a broad gesture of showing his hands to the knight as Eugen rounded on him, favouring him with his most ingratiating smile. The tension drained from the knight's body as he found that his pursuer was nothing more menacing than a halfling cook.

'Going for a walk?' Theodo asked.

'Yes,' Eugen replied, turning away.

'Mind if I come along?'

Eugen turned back. After the meeting with Valdner, after failing to convince Kessler to turn back, he was in no mood for the halfling's company. 'Yes,' he said.

'Oh, that's too bad,' Theodo said, shaking his head sadly. 'I thought you might need some help.' Eugen's eyes narrowed as he stared at the halfling. 'I'm quite good at hiding things,' he explained cheerfully. He reached into the pocket of his vest, displaying the strange message he'd found. He chuckled as the knight backed away. 'Of course my services aren't cheap. Costs a lot to feed an ogre.'

The scowl on Eugen's face became almost murderous. 'I've never seen that before,' he growled. He had seen the strange message Ekdahl and Kessler had discovered and brought to the attention of Baron von Rabwald. He knew that it was evidence of a spy in their midst. He knew that Theodo was aware of the fact too.

'You've seen it now though,' Theodo continued. 'Other people might see it too, if I let them.'

The knight lunged at the smirking halfling, closing a fist around his throat. 'You scheming toad!' he snarled. 'You dare accuse me, a knight, of being a spy!'

Before Eugen's grip could tighten, the knight was hurled back. He smashed into a mud brick wall with enough force to drive the air from his lungs. By the time the black spots stopped dancing in his eyes, Theodo was adjusting his rumpled clothes. Ghrum was towering over the halfling, violence smouldering in the ogre's monstrous face. The halfling laid a restraining hand on the ogre's gigantic boot. So incensed had he been by the halfling's insinuations, he'd failed to hear the ogre lumbering up the street.

'Now, now,' Theodo scolded. 'If you kill him, how do I make him pay?' It was more the tone than the words that appeared to make Ghrum subside. Theodo focused his attention back on Eugen. He tapped the strip of goatskin he'd shown the man, and then carefully replaced it inside his vest.

'Think things over, marshal,' Theodo told him. 'Nothing good comes of being too hasty, after all. Once

you've reached a decision, you know where to find us.
I'm sure you'll make the right choice when the time
comes.' He raised his eyes meaningfully to the hulk
looming above him.

'You know what will happen if you don't.'

CHAPTER TWELVE

JANOS GRUBNER WATCHED the motley, mismatched group of men ride out into the breaking dawn. The innkeeper looked across the dirt expanse of Fritzstadt's tiny town square. Every doorway and window was filled with drawn, haggard faces, eyes blazing with resentment. The burghers had paid Valdner and his men good money to protect the town, and now they were gone, riding off with this man who bore the count's letter of marque. It had taken most of the horseflesh in town to outfit the gang, and Valdner's mercenaries had availed themselves of the opportunity to ransack the Fritzstadt armoury, blatant looting made legal and just by the letter from the count. Even if half the able men in town hadn't marched north to answer the muster, there was nothing now to arm them with.

Janos could see the fear and spite in the eyes of his neighbours, the sense of betrayal and violation their town had suffered. Burgomeister Paulus had hidden in his manor, refusing to answer the outrage of his citizens. The innkeeper couldn't blame him, between the count's letter and the brutish swagger of the thug who carried it, there had been nothing Paulus could do to recover the situation. Now all he had left was to bury his head in the sand and trust that everything would blow over soon. The situation up north would stabilise and he'd be able to send his complaint to Wissenberg and receive compensation for what had been commandeered. The town guard and militia would return, preferably before any goblins became aware of what ripe pickings and low risk Fritzstadt offered in its current circumstances. Paulus had to have faith in his optimism that things would get back to normal, and he had to try to impart that faith to the good people of his town.

The innkeeper knew he was affected as much as anyone else by the departure of Valdner's men, that he shared the same dangers as the rest of the undefended town. Somehow, he couldn't help but smile as he watched the last of the sell-swords trot out through the gate. He touched the breast of his tunic, feeling again the heavy leather bag hidden there, the bag he'd been given in the dead of night by one of the ragged warriors who had marched into town the day before. There was a wonderfully calming quality about gold, especially in the right amount. The warrior didn't even want Janos to do very much to earn it, just give a letter to a man who would be calling at the inn within a day or so, nothing more. Then Janos would be free to close up his inn and relocate to Pfeildorf or maybe Nuln until things quietened down. With his late night windfall, he'd be able to do so in style for quite some time.

Only one thing troubled Janos. He wasn't a man who enjoyed riddles, and the puzzle left behind by his furtive guest had been gnawing at his mind. He'd opened the letter to discover what sort of message he'd been entrusted with. There were no seals upon it, so there was no risk in having a peak. The problem was that what was written on the parchment wasn't anything he was familiar with. The characters were just a meaningless jumble of signs and marks, certainly not the letters of Reikspiel or the sharp runes of the dwarfs.

Janos shrugged. It was a mystery, and doomed to remain so. Once he was in Nuln, he'd have plenty of distractions to take his mind off the enigma.

'GET THAT FOUR-LEGGED cripple out of my way, baron-boy!' The roar came from the bearded mercenary Raban. There was a gloating, self-assured mix to the anger darkening the sell-sword's face, the tell-tale taint of a brute spoiling for a fight. Kessler kept his expression cold as he turned in the saddle. He let his eyes shift across Raban's hairy face, and then swept his vision to the jumbled piles of slate that lined the path.

'Yes, I mean you!' Raban snarled, genuine irritation in his voice. Kessler stopped looking for the imaginary target of Raban's baiting. He could feel the eyes of everyone in the column fixed on him. The mercenaries would, of course, be watching his every move, ready to leap to the aid of their belligerent comrade. Kessler wondered how many of his own men were silently rooting against him. Without him, Eugen would have little problem turning their rag-tag command around and heading back to Count Eberfeld. Some of the soldiers were solidly with the knight, Skanir's attitude was ambivalent, and he wouldn't expect Theodo to put his neck out for anyone. Indeed, the only source of support he could firmly count upon was Ottmar, who shared his sense of urgency. Kessler didn't think that would be enough.

Kessler bit his tongue and started to nudge his horse towards the side of the path, grinding his teeth as he saw the triumphant smirk beneath Raban's beard. The mercenary didn't wait, plunging his steed forward and pushing Kessler to the edge of the dirt path.

'Something to say, baron-boy?' Raban growled as he passed, a feral, lupine quality to his eyes. Kessler glared, matching the challenge he saw reflected back at him in Raban's savage gaze. The smirk hardened into something dangerous. Kessler started to reach up for the sword lashed across his shoulder even as Raban's hairy hand dropped for the axe swinging from his belt.

Before the tense atmosphere could explode into violence, Raban's horse reared back, nearly throwing the fighter from the saddle. His fingers just grazing the grip of his zweihander, Kessler risked a look back to see what had startled the horse. Captain Valdner was close behind Raban's steed, a riding crop clenched in his gloved fist. The captain's face was stern, reproving, a mixture of disappointment and anger that comes easily to the best officers and fathers.

'I have something to say,' Valdner said, his voice cutting at Raban like a lash, striking him as sharply as the riding crop had the flank of his steed, 'something perhaps the rest of your comrades in arms might find useful to hear before you get cut down by Herr Kessler here.'

'Your faith in me leaves me speechless, Bruno,' Raban scowled, recovering his balance if not his dignity. Valdner pounced on the remark.

'Yes, let us suppose you can do what a hundred other men have failed to do,' Valdner said, thrusting his finger at Raban like a spear. 'Let us suppose you get that big axe of yours buried in Herr Kessler's head before he can split that thick skull with his sword. What then?' Valdner stretched his arms beside him in a helpless, frustrated expression. 'We lose our patron, we lose our contract.' He raised his finger as he came to the most important point, the one that would reach down to the very core of his men, 'And we lose our pay.'

'If these heathen Wissenlanders will pay,' sneered Anselm. The Sigmarite had dismounted and approached them on foot, one hand clenched around the hammer icon he carried. 'There is no honour among such swine!'

Valdner turned on Anselm, like a bear rounding on a hound. 'Would I be included in that statement?' he demanded. The bravado wilted in Anselm's pasty features and the Reiklander seemed to cower in the shadow cast by his hat. 'Have I given you, any of you, cause to doubt my word and the compact shared by our Brotherhood?'

'No, captain,' came the response from a scar-faced Sylvanian maceman. 'You've dealt square with us ever since Schwerstetten.' He reached to his belt, pulling free the ugly, black-iron weapon he carried. 'You even stole our weapons back from that fat pig Hock!'

A knowing smile replaced the last traces of anger in Valdner's expression. He nodded sadly to the Sylvanian, and then levelled his gaze on the rest of his men. 'I apologise, Minhea, but in that matter I must confess to deceiving you, deceiving all of you. I let you think that I made some fantastic foray into Count Eberfeld's camp to steal back our arms. The truth of the matter is that they had already been stolen away from Hock, and all I did was go out and collect them.' Valdner gestured at Kessler. 'This man's master stole them back for us: Baron von Rabwald, whose sense of honour, whose devotion to his own word made him turn against his sovereign to redress a wrong that had been worked against us. That is the kind of honour a Wissenlander knows!'

The short speech had its desired effect, all the agitation and hostility in the mercenaries smothered by a mixture of shock and guilt. Even Raban looked sheepish as he walked his horse down the path, directing not even a single glance in Kessler's direction. The Wissenland soldiers breathed easier as they saw the tension drain out of their mercenary companions. Valdner edged his horse beside Kessler's and together the two men watched their ragged company march past.

'Thank you, captain,' Kessler said in a subdued voice. 'I am afraid I have little aptitude for command. I'm more comfortable using steel than psychology to settle my arguments.'

'Then you have something in common with Raban,' Valdner said. He looked at the grotesque swordsman, studying the brutish stamp in what remained of his features. 'I must confess I was quite dubious when you told me that the baron had passed command of this vital expedition over to you.'

Kessler bristled at the statement. 'I doubt either of us is fit to judge the decision of a man like the baron.'

'Not so,' Valdner corrected him. 'There was a time when I was the baron's closest confidant.' He chose to ignore the incredulous expression Kessler directed at him. 'This was well before he was *Baron* von Rabwald, of course. Back when he was just Ernst.' He nodded as he stared again at Kessler's twisted face. 'As I said, I was quite dubious that he should give such an important duty to a man so clearly unfit to lead. I see it now, however. I see what Ernst saw, what made him trust you with so grave a task.'

'And what would that be?'

'You're too stubborn to let anything go,' Valdner laughed. 'You're like one of those fighting dogs that locks its jaws around its enemy so tightly that it won't let go even when it's dead. The baron knew what he was doing when he put you in command of this fiasco. He knew he could trust you to drive these men as long and as far as you have to, no matter the cost. You won't admit failure, won't even accept it as a possibility. That sets you apart from, say Marshal Eugen or Sergeant Ottmar.'

Kessler thought about Valdner's assessment of his tenacity, and had to agree that it was precise and accurate. It reminded him in many ways of the snap judgements Baron von Rabwald would make when meeting a person. He'd been uncannily accurate in such initial impressions. Maybe Valdner was right, maybe his determination to see a thing through was what had made Ernst place such trust in him.

'Will it be enough?' Kessler asked, only realising he had spoken when Valdner answered him.

'In a day, perhaps two, we shall be in the Black Mountains,' Valdner told him. 'So far we have had easy riding, good weather and pleasant countryside. All of that changes when we reach the mountains.' The mercenary shook his head. 'It is a ridiculous thing to consider, but the closer we get to where we are going, the harder the journey becomes.

'Save your questions until then,' Valdner concluded. 'When we are in the Black Mountains there will be doubt and fear enough to go around.'

IT WAS DIFFICULT not to allow doubt and fear to overwhelm him as Kessler stared at the monolithic expanse of the Black Mountains. Like a great wall, the imposing spires of dark grey rock clawed up at the sky, struggling to cut their way through the misty grey clouds that gathered around their spire-like peaks. Sometimes the sun reflected in dazzling brilliance from the surface of some glacier trapped within the high mountain valleys, sometimes it would struggle feebly to penetrate the shadowy stands of pine that dotted the slopes, but always the deep grey walls of the mountains dominated the scene. Even the foothills that crouched in the shadow of the mountains were merely dim echoes of their gigantic kin, jagged stumps of craggy grey rock stabbing up from the earth like the shards of a titan's blade.

Looking at the mountains, Kessler could understand how they had come to consume the dwarfs, devouring their culture and society until it became impossible to separate the two. He could appreciate the formidable barrier, the great fence that protected the Empire from the howling hosts of greenskins that infested the lands beyond the mountains. If any man doubted the might of the gods he had but to see what Kessler saw, a vision of such awesome magnificence that even a hardened, brutish killer could not help but feel its power.

Kessler could tell that his companions felt the same power pressing down upon them, the cold, passionless might that demanded respect from all it touched. The faces on the Wissenland soldiers grew drawn, their expressions stiff. Even those among Valdner's crew who had served in Averland at the infamous Black Fire Pass and had seen the mountains before were subdued, perhaps because better than any of them, these veterans knew the capricious spirit of the mountains and the dangers of trying to cross through them.

Skanir dismounted from the pony he had been given in Fritzstadt, a creature a good deal more pleasant than his missing mule, though the dwarf bristled at the indignity of riding an animal the men in the company regarded as fit only for children and friars. Still, there was no malice in him as he walked away from the pony, holding his head high and shielding one hand across his brow as he studied the jagged slopes of the mountains.

'There,' he said at last in a voice made small by the weight of ages. The dwarf's stumpy finger pointed to a great gash in the face of one of the mountains, as though a god had cleft the stone with his axe. 'That is it, the place where Zahaak was destroyed once before: Drung-a-Uzkul. There is a great war-crypt of my people dug into the mountain not far from the battlefield. It will give us a place to start looking for the Sun-Fang.'

Kessler nodded as he listened to Skanir speak, his eyes fixing on the valley where Zahaak had been defeated so long ago. Carlinda had been leading them to this place; somehow he knew this as surely as if the augur were standing beside him, whispering it into his ear. Could the war-crypt Skanir spoke of, the tomb that held the dwarfish dead from that ancient battle, be the one they were looking for? Skanir claimed that the Black Mountains were littered with such tombs, making their task still more immense. Somehow, though, Kessler could not shake the conviction that they were close, that the gods or perhaps the wraith of a dead witch had brought them here. Drung-a-Uzkul, where it had all started ages ago. It would suit the caprices of fate if this place would also play its part in ending the nightmare.

The swordsman lowered himself from the saddle to speak with Skanir when a sharp cry from his left brought his sword leaping into his hands. One of Valdner's men fell from his horse, an arrow lodged in his face. Shouts of alarm and panic echoed from every quarter and men scrambled to find cover.

An ending indeed, Kessler thought, but perhaps for them not Zahaak!

'Oooh, lookit that one Kopff!'

The short, toad-faced brigand followed the direction of his weasel-like comrade's pointing finger. A greedy grin crawled onto Kopff's face. He glanced quickly up the hillside. Nearly fifty bandits were scattered up the slope, hidden behind clumps of scrub and jagged outcroppings of dark rock. A quick inspection assured him that none were looking in his direction. He let his eyes linger longer on the pile of stone behind which he knew Baldur and Rambrecht were sheltering.

'That trim on his helmet is gold, sure as Sigmar,' Kopff hissed, turning his attention back to Schmitt. Schmitt licked his lips hungrily. Kopff nocked an arrow to the string of his bow and started to rise from behind their cover. Schmitt's hand closed around his arm, pulling him back down.

'Baldur said to wait for his signal!' Schmitt warned. Kopff rolled his eyes.

'And let some opportunistic thief nab that helmet?' the bandit asked, sounding almost wounded by the suggestion. The observation rattled Schmitt and he released his hold. Kopff started to rise again.

Schmitt pulled him back down. 'I saw it first,' he said, fitting an arrow to his own bow. 'I should be the one to knock him down.'

'You couldn't hit the backside of a castle at twenty paces,' said Kopff, shaking free of the other man's grip.

'The helmet's still mine,' Schmitt persisted. 'I saw it first. Fair's fair! The helmet's mine!'

Kopff sighted down the length of his arrow, watching as his target slowly rode nearer. 'I'm surprised at you, Schmitt! Trying to profit from another man's hard work!' He released the string and the arrow flew down the slope, slamming into the warrior he had marked for death. The mercenary cried out, dropping from the saddle. Instantly, the hill was alive with shouts and curses, hastily launched arrows shooting down at the riders in a lethal shower of iron-tipped mayhem.

ALL AROUND KESSLER was shock and confusion, men and beasts running and roaring as arrows fell all around them. Several found marks in the sides and flanks of the horses, sending the animals mad with pain and fear. Kessler clung tight to the reins of his own animal as the panic of the injured animals threatened to overcome it. He saw thrown riders scrambling across the rocky ground, trying to dodge the stamping hooves of the enraged beasts.

Theodo's sharp squeal of terror rose even above the screams of the horses. Tossed into the dirt by his burro, the halfling was beset by Eugen's raging horse. The knight fought hard to regain control of his animal, but the flailing hooves pounded the ground all around the tiny cook, threatening to grind him into the dirt. Every effort Theodo made to scurry to safety seemed to drive Eugen's horse wilder, its frantic efforts to crush the halfling becoming more intense. Finally, Ghrum's enormous bulk rose beside the maddened steed. With a display of monstrous strength, the ogre seized the horse by the neck and forcibly jerked steed and knight to the ground. Theodo did not spare a glance for the stunned animal or its equally overwhelmed rider, but darted for the closest bunch of scrub, vanishing into the foliage as completely as a frightened rabbit.

Most of the Wissenlanders and all of Valdner's men had already quit their saddles, taking shelter in a dry stream-bed that offered at least some cover from the ragged fire driving down on them from the slopes. Kessler saw a few of Valdner's men trying to reply in kind, but there were few bows among the mercenaries and none among the Wissenlanders. A loud boom thundered from nearby and acrid grey smoke blew across Kessler's face. The swordsman glanced aside at Skanir, finding the dwarf cursing lividly at the pistol clutched in his hand.

'Give me a solid cannon any day over one of these mouse-croakers!' he snarled, his face almost completely veiled by the smoke rising from the barrel of his weapon. Several arrows slammed into the ground nearby. Whatever the effect his shot had failed to have, it certainly drawn the attention of their attackers.

'Get back with the others!' Kessler yelled, and then decided that he should take his own advice as an arrow glanced from his hauberk. Sickened, he pulled his horse around, using the beast for cover as he sprinted towards the stream bed. When he was close enough, he broke away, diving into the depression. Slime and mud splashed across his face as he landed in the dregs of the stream. He quickly glanced down the length of the stream, observing that most of the men seemed to have reached it without serious injury. Keeping on his belly, he crawled along the trench to where he saw Valdner, Ottmar and Anselm. Before he could reach the mercenary captain, a dazed Eugen dropped into the trench, his tabard quickly soaking up the slime of the stream. The knight paused to wipe the filth from his chest, and then laboriously followed after Kessler.

Valdner was barking orders to his men, trying to coerce those close enough to make a break for the stream, urging others to keep low and use whatever shelter they had found. Two of his men were beyond listening to his commands, their bodies pierced by arrows, one of Ottmar's soldiers keeping them company. The captain snarled at the two archers in the gulley, trying to provide covering fire for the men still trapped in the open. The demand was more than their ability to meet and one of the mercenaries was struck down as he rose from behind a dead horse and made a rush for the stream.

'Any idea who's up there shooting at us?' Valdner growled as he saw Kessler and Eugen crawling towards him. Kessler nodded, fury gleaming in his eyes.

'Same ones who set that ambush before,' he said. 'I recognised the men who killed the baron. They must have followed our trail all the way from Fritzstadt.' Valdner clenched his jaw tight and glared back up the slope.

'Not much we can do until it gets dark,' the captain swore. 'They have the high ground and a damn sight more bowmen than we do. If they'd waited for us to get a little closer...' Valdner shook his head. 'Let's just hope they give us the chance to make them regret that mistake.'

* * *

BALDUR SWORE, POUNDING his fist against his leg. He rounded on Rambrecht. 'Brigand trash, just like I told you!'

The ambush should have worked perfectly, cutting down all of the Wissenlanders in one swift, certain stroke. The plan was to draw them close, up on the slopes and then fire into them from such range that even the slovenly marksmanship of bandits and outlaws couldn't fail to find their marks. Again, events had impressed upon Baldur the quality of the men he now led. What he wouldn't give for a score of Averheim guards!

'The tactics were sound,' Rambrecht snapped. 'It is your leadership that I find lacking.' The aristocrat's tone dropped, becoming dangerous. 'Recover the situation, Baldur. Do what you're being paid to do.'

The bandit chief glared at his arrogant patron. It never ceased to amaze him how the nobility always expected something from nothing. Quickly his mind turned over the possibilities. 'I have an idea, but it'll cost you.' Baldur felt a slight sense of satisfaction as he saw Rambrecht's expression sour. 'Your man down there tells us that the reinforcements they took on are mercenaries.'

'Meaning?'

'Meaning we offer them a better deal,' Baldur said. He didn't wait for his patron's approval. Cupping a hand to his face, he leaned out from behind the boulder and shouted down to the men sheltering in the stream bed.

'We only want the dwarf!' Baldur shouted. 'Give him up and we'll spare your lives. Whatever Wissenland is paying you, I can guarantee you more! Give up the dwarf and nobody else has to die!'

His piece said, Baldur darted back into cover. There had been little evidence of archery on the part of the men below, but he knew that there had been a few casualties among his brigands. He was firmly determined not to join them.

'Now what?' Rambrecht demanded.

'Now we let them think it over,' Baldur said. 'I'm sure–'

But the rest of his thought went unspoken. A terrible scream tore apart the tense silence that had followed Baldur's ultimatum. The bandit chief spun around, horror flashing through him. How had the Wissenlanders managed to get men behind them on the slope? All of them should have been accounted for if Rambrecht's spy had dealt true with them.

The full horror of the situation was impressed upon him when Baldur saw one of his bandits rolling down the side of the hill, a black-feathered arrow lodged in his back. Even as the echoes of that first scream started to fade, the air was split by a horrendous din of shrieks and war cries. More arrows clattered against the rocks as the upper slopes exploded with violence. Small, scrawny figures were charging from every crag and cranny, yellow teeth glistening from their green, leathery faces. Beyond them, large, brutish shapes bellowed and roared, crashing savage axes and immense cleavers against their shields of steel-banded lumber. The taste of acidic sickness was in Baldur's mouth as he saw the huge monsters lunge down the hill, smashing the smaller goblins aside in their ferocious charge.

Baldur had little enough faith in the ability of his men to fight human soldiers. Against the savagery of orc warriors, he had none at all. He had laid his trap too well, only the Wissenlanders weren't the only ones who had been caught by it.

CHAPTER THIRTEEN

FROM THE NATURAL trench of the stream bed, Kessler
watched in amazement as roaring, howling orcs lunged
down the hillside, eager to cleave bandit flesh with rusty
orcish steel. The small weedy shapes of goblins cringed
and crawled around the hulking monsters, loosing arrows
at every opportunity, caring little if their missiles struck
man or greenskin. In short, brutal order the ambushers
had become the ambushed, their cries of surprise and fear
ringing out even above the bellows of the orcs.

Eugen pointed a mailed fist at the hillside, indicating
a scrawny, mail-clad orc standing apart from the rush of
its fellows. The monster wielded a great rod of twisted
iron in its leathery paw, a collection of shattered skulls
dangling from the rusty cross-beam lashed across its
mid-length. A scrap of flayed skin flapped above the
broken skulls, its decaying surface branded with the
crude, jagged glyph that Kessler had seen in Murzklein.
'Uhrghul Skullcracker,' Eugen hissed, his voice filled

with a mixture of fear and loathing. Kessler looked away from the grisly standard and the crippled orc that held it, turning his attention to the knight. Eugen's sword was in his fist, his body rising from the stream bed, his face a mask of grim determination.

The knight was not looking at the infamous warlord's standard, rather, he was fixated upon a great ghastly figure that lumbered down the rocky slope with all the malevolence of an avalanche. Kessler had heard stories that orcs never grew old, they simply kept getting bigger and bigger until someone or something finally cut them down. The orc he was looking at was immense, easily eight feet in height even with its slumped, apish shape. The muscles that bulged beneath its ragged tunic of piecemeal armour looked capable of crushing a man's chest like a walnut.

The orc carried an huge length of cruelly sharpened steel that seemed halfway between halberd and butcher's knife. Kessler doubted if even he could lift such a weapon, much less carry it with the practiced ease the orc displayed. A great horned helmet covered the small, brutish head, bronze spikes jutting from the crown. The front of the helm was open, displaying a grotesque face that was terrible and murderous even among the savage orcs. The heavy, lantern jaw seemed to sag beneath the weight of the steel-capped tusks that curled beneath the monster's face.

The forehead was thick and low, scarred with the marks of claw and blade. Small crimson eyes glimmered from the depths of the face, twinkling with a malign, inhuman cunning. The dry, leathery hide of the hulking orc was darker than that of its comrades, more black than green to Kessler's eyes.

'Uhrghul Skullcracker,' Eugen growled again, still staring at the immense orc warlord. The orc had reached the foremost of the bandits, men who struggled futilely

they savaged. Even the notoriously tough feet of a halfling were unequal to the trail, Theodo preferring the indignity of being carried by Ghrum than suffering the cuts and bruises that afflicted the others. The cook resembled nothing so much as a smug house-cat, perched on the ogre's mammoth shoulder.

For the rest of them, there was no relief from the inhospitable terrain. The horses they had managed to hold onto during the ambush would never have made such a steep and arduous assent. Reluctantly, Kessler had agreed to leave the animals hobbled in a clearing at the base of the mountains, hoping that the surrounding hills would shelter them from enemy eyes. Two days had passed since the ambush and they had seen no sign of either brigand or greenskin, but Kessler did not think such luck would hold forever. That the bandits were the same killers that had attacked them before was undeniable, and that the arrival of Uhrghul and his orcs was in retaliation for the battle in Murzklein was almost beyond doubt. Valdner suggested that the vengeful goblins had been tracking Kessler for quite some time, but at some key juncture they had mistaken the trail of the bandits who were also shadowing the Wissenlanders for that of their intended prey. Hence, when the orcs and goblins struck, the brigands had been the target of their assault.

Skanir was taking no chances that whichever foe had emerged victorious would find picking up the hunt an easy matter, and so he took them on a circuitous, winding route through the hills. It almost seemed that the dwarf had some sixth sense that allowed him to find the ugliest, hardest patches of earth the slopes had to offer. There was a cold logic behind Skanir's insistence that they take the most arduous track. Any pursuer tracking them would be less than keen to follow in their footsteps.

At times, the rocky slopes of the mountains would sport stands of stunted, twisted trees somehow eking a precarious existence from the sheer, cliff-faces of the towering giants. These discoveries would greatly excite Kessler's men. Early in their assent, Skanir had shown them that wherever they saw a tree on the slope they would find refuge from the biting attentions of the howling mountain wind, a place where the capricious formations of rock and earth had conspired to create a bastion against the fury of the elements. Such brief respites from the cold winds almost seemed like gifts from Skanir's grim dwarf gods.

At other times, they would stumble upon evidence of those same gods, or at least the diminished culture that had worshipped them: patches of mountainside that were too smooth to be the work of wind and rain, stretches of slope too regular to be some freak of nature. Shards of broken stone sometimes suggested the mark of hammer and pick, and fragments of crumbling rock occasionally resembled ancient brickwork.

Finally, Skanir allowed them to abandon their circuitous route through the mountains, leading them along a path that was too easy to be any natural formation. It was the ruin of some ancient road, winding its way among the black rocks and jagged peaks. Rock slides and windstorms had worn it down, grinding away at it through the long centuries, but the dwarfs had built against the ages and still their ancient work managed to serve its original purpose. The elements had rendered the old roadway all but invisible to the eye, but there was no deceiving the feet that followed the path. Sometimes a jumble of stone would rise beside the road, and beneath the moss and rubble the vague suggestion of carving could be discerned. By degrees, Kessler recognised a kinship among the broken shapes. They might once have been life-sized representations of dwarfs, hands closed around large tablets or plaques, which they held against their stony breasts.

'Mile-rocks,' Skanir explained when he saw the swordsman examining one of the broken statues. 'Markers to let those travelling the mountain paths know how far they had come and how far they still had to go.'

The dwarf nodded his head sadly as he bent to brush pebbles from the disembodied face of the worn statue. 'The mountains were once full of them, watching over the travellers who traversed their roads. That was before the greenskins came, before my people abandoned the roads above for the security of the Underway beneath them.'

He straightened, gesturing with his hammer at the sweep of the mountains around them. 'Once the strongholds of my people stretched across the spine of the world, from the steaming mire of the south to the icy shadow of the northern wastes. Then came the Time of Woes, when the mountains shook and the earth spewed its fires into our cities. Much was lost to earthquake and volcano. Those who were left no longer had the strength to cull the greenskins and had to retreat behind walls of stone and gates of iron.'

Skanir's mouth twisted with bitterness and he nodded grimly as he turned away from the toppled mile-rock. 'The days of glory are done, they will not come again.'

The dwarf marched down the roadway, slinging his great hammer over his shoulder. 'This way, manlings,' he called. 'The runes on the mile-rock say that we are not so very far from Drung-a-Uzkul. If you keep to a decent pace, we should be there in a few days.'

* * *

THEY DID NOT leave the ancient dwarf trail to make camp. A sheer drop into the canyons marked one side of the path, the craggy slopes of the mountain the other. Instead, they settled themselves in the trail itself, finding what comfort they could in the few blankets and cloaks they had left. Teeth chattered in the bitter chill of the night, and men huddled together for warmth as the cold gnawed at their bones. No fire had been built, Valdner warning that at such height, a light could be seen for leagues. If Uhrghul or the bandits were still hunting for them, the smallest fire would be as good as a beacon to them. So, they were left to the dark and the cold.

Guards were posted at either end of the trail, the only approaches any enemy could use to sneak up on them. It was a lonely watch, long hours stretching into a small eternity as the numbing night crept beneath the watchers' skins. The soothing blackness teased the eyes, tempting the mind behind them with the promise of succour and slumber.

It took a disciplined mind to stave off the lulling lure of the clammy caress of the night, to keep vigilant even as the tedium of the vigil dragged on. Raban the Nordlander was an uncultured, rough fighter, a man who lacked the spit and polish of many regular soldiers, but he knew his duty and he knew what was expected of him. When he heard rocks shift behind him, his axe was raised in an instant, his powerful frame spinning around. Raban's eyes glared into the darkness, his face twisted in violent challenge. Even when he discerned the visage of the figure that approached him, the challenge did not leave his face.

'You!' Raban accused, tightening his hold on his battle axe. 'I thought you were standing guard opposite me!'

'Have no fear,' the voice in the shadows assured him. 'Nothing is going to overrun my post.'

The mercenary sneered. 'You abandoned your position. I thought you were some kind of old hand at soldiering, not some young-blood to wander away from his duty as soon as he gets bored.'

'Don't be stupid,' the man in the darkness retorted. 'I wanted to speak to you. That is why I left my post.'

'You could have spoken to me any time today,' Raban said suspiciously.

'Not without someone else listening in. Listen, Raban, I think you are the sort of man I can confide in, someone I can trust.'

Raban laughed. 'Save the flattery, Wissen-worm. If you've got something to say, spill it.'

'Very well. You heard the offer those bandits made just before the orcs attacked?' Raban shrugged his shoulders in response. 'I happen to know that their offer was quite genuine and quite sincere. Furthermore, I am in a position to guarantee that the offer still stands.'

A grin crossed Raban's brutal features. 'You must have been watching a different fight than I was. I don't think they'll be paying anybody from the belly of an orc.'

'Then the men they were working for will,' the voice snapped. 'There are persons in Averland who would pay well to keep the runefang away from Count Eberfeld.'

'So that's the deal, is it?' Raban asked.

'The Wissenlanders have betrayed you once, do you really think this thug Kessler will treat you fairly? Help me recover the runefang and I promise you more wealth than you can imagine.'

Raban considered that, resting his axe on the ground as he thought about what his visitor had said. 'Is this offer just for me, or for all the Brethren?'

'All of you. We may need their help. I trust to your candour in broaching the subject with your fellows.'

Raban's smile widened as his last concern was dispelled by the man's words. Putting a knife in Kessler's back would be easy, betraying the Schwerstetten Brotherhood was something else. There was only one other thing that nagged at Raban's mind. He shook his head. 'All right, I'll be discreet mentioning this deal to the men, but there's one thing bothering me. What's your angle? I mean why should I trust a man who is betraying his own province, leaving Wissenland to her enemies?'

'Because Wissenland isn't my home! I am a Sollander, one who has grown weary watching Wissenland pick clean the carcass of my home, stripping away our legacy until there is nothing left!'

'You think Averland will treat you better?'

'They already have,' came the response as Raban's visitor drifted back into the night. Raban watched as the man's shadow vanished in the darkness, his ears picking out the sound of his boots as they carefully moved back through the camp. He tried to follow their progress, but soon his attention was drawn to a faint light burning just beyond the camp, in the direction where his visitor should have been keeping watch.

The light burned for several minutes, and then was quickly snuffed out. Just the time, Raban judged, it would have taken his visitor to retrace his steps. The mercenary nodded his head grimly. It seemed that his visitor was hedging his bets: beacon to bring any surviving brigands, a bribe to woo the loyalties of the Schwerstetten Brotherhood.

CHAPTER FOURTEEN

BERGDORF'S DEFENCES WERE more monumental than
when Count Eberfeld had last seen them. In his leader's
absence, General Hock's army had been quite busy. A
stone restraining wall had been constructed beyond the
inner line of ditches. A long trench surrounded the
crude wall, a zigzag ditch designed to disrupt the formations of the enemy and channel them into specific
areas, areas where they would be easy prey for the
army's bowmen. As he looked upon the elaborate
preparations his generals had made, the count felt reassured. Man, daemon or undead liche, Zahaak would
not easily breach such defences. The slaughter of the
wight's legion was almost assured.

The count felt a chill run up his spine. What good did
it do to kill a thousand, to kill ten thousand of the
fiend's host if they would not stay dead? Few bodies
had been left behind by the legion on the Dobrin road.

Both their own dead and those lost by the Wissenland army had vanished with the marching legion. He had a loathsome idea where they had gone.

A knot of horsemen rode out from Bergdorf to meet the returning count. He was surprised to find Baron von Weidinger leading the cavalry, a small retinue bearing the livery of Bergdorf. The riders' faces were pale, their expressions grave. Count Eberfeld raised his eyes, noting for the first time the scarcity of defenders visible on the walls. Something terrible had happened, Hock's fortifications had been completed, but there were no soldiers manning them. The count did not try to guess what had happened, training his intense gaze upon von Weidinger, waiting for the baron to give him an explanation.

'Your excellency!' the baron cried. 'Praise all the gods that you are back!' The intensity of von Weidinger's relief brought dampness to his eyes and a ragged choke to his voice.

'What has happened, baron? Where is Hock? Where is the army?' The questions came in rapid succession, the count keeping any trace of panic from his words and all hint of emotion from his face.

'Gone, excellency,' von Weidinger said. 'General Hock has led the army to Neuwald!'

Count Eberfeld blinked in disbelief, unable to credit what his ears had heard. After all the careful preparations, all the cautious plotting of strategy, what had possessed General Hock to cast it all aside and march the army to Neuwald?

Von Weidinger answered the question before it could be asked. 'General Hock ordered the army to Neuwald three days ago,' the baron said, regaining some control of his voice as he related events rather than emotion.

'Two days before that, from these very walls, we watched the enemy march past us. Through the fog that surrounded them, we could see their ghastly shadows, tramping in eerie unison. Not once did they turn to face us, not once did their march falter. Arrows sent into the fog went unanswered, challenges shouted into the mist went unmet. It was as though, for the shapes within the fog, Bergdorf and all within the city didn't exist.

'General Hock was sorely vexed by the puzzle, terrified that the enemy was following some stratagem he could not fathom, poring over his plans trying to spot any weakness in the defences that he had failed to see. He was convinced the legion would be back, that their silent march past the walls was simply a ploy to entice the army to sally out from behind the walls. He still expected the battle to be fought before Bergdorf's walls when the first scouts arrived informing him that the legion was laying siege to Neuwald. It was then that Hock realised he had been tricked, that the legion had bypassed Bergdorf not to draw out the army but to attack a weaker target.'

'Hock rode out to lift the siege?' Count Eberfeld was unsuccessful in keeping the dread from his voice. He could imagine the general's agonised deliberation before making such a pivotal decision. Staying safe behind the walls of Bergdorf while Neuwald was butchered was a decision that would have haunted him to the grave. The uncertainty of a quick, improvised attack was one that would have held little appeal for him, but at least he would know he had tried to do something.

Baron von Weidinger nodded slowly. 'The general took all the cavalry and light infantry with him, anything he felt could move fast enough to do Neuwald some good. In all, he should have nearly three thousand fighting men.' The baron's face grew pale again, his hand pulling close the neck of his sable cloak. 'But what man can say how many the legion numbers, or how many of the living it takes to destroy the dead?'

'Compose yourself,' the count warned. He saw the way the baron's display of fear was infecting the horsemen around him. Von Weidinger licked his lips, trying to keep the tremble from his face.

'Stay here,' Count Eberfeld told the baron. 'Keep your men alert and see that the walls stay manned. I will ride on to Neuwald and assess the situation for myself. I'll send word back to you about what I find.'

Von Weidinger saluted his count, worried that his leader was riding into such danger, but deeply relieved that he had not been asked to ride with him. Count Eberfeld turned away from the nobleman, regarding Captain Markus and the other members of his small entourage. Their expressions were no less grave than that of the riders from Bergdorf, a resigned sort of fear that the men were not ashamed to show. The count knew these men were not cowards. They had gone with him unquestioningly into the camp of Count Achim, Wissenland's most determined foe before Zahaak had emerged from his lost tomb. Loyalty to their land and their sovereign had made them follow him, and he knew that they would not desert their honour now.

Count Eberfeld looked past his small bodyguard, eyes alerted to a cloud of dust that rose from the road beyond them. Their hands fell to the hilts of their swords as a company of horsemen appeared galloping towards Bergdorf. The count knew they could not be refugees from Hock's army; Neufeld lay in the other direction. For a moment, he considered that they might be late answers to the general muster that he had proclaimed, perhaps knights who had gathered from the wilds of the Grey Mountains or the hinterlands of Solland.

Tensions, just beginning to ease, swelled back into full hostility as the identity of the riders became obvious. They were knights, but not knights of Wissenland. The shining steel armour and vivid crimson surcoats of the riders proclaimed them as Reiklanders, the warrior-monks of the Order of the Griffon. The massive figure of Lord Hugo von Rhineholt rode at their head. He raised his gauntlet as his company drew close to Count Eberfeld, bringing the riders to a swift and sudden halt. Lord Hugo lifted the visor of his helm and bowed his head to the count.

'I see Count Achim reconsidered allowing me to escape his hospitality,' Count Eberfeld remarked. The comment brought swords rasping from sheaths as the Wissenlanders bared their steel. Upon the walls of Bergdorf, arrows were nocked to bows.

The Sigmarite knights did not move, letting their blades rest within their scabbards. There was almost pain in Lord Hugo's face as he gazed at the weapons bared before him.

'Count Achim is not my master,' Lord Hugo stated. 'I answer to Lord Sigmar and Grand Theogonist Gottolf.'

'And they tell you to violate my borders, invade my land and ride against my people?' Count Eberfeld snarled.

'They tell me to ride against the enemies of mankind,' the knight snapped back, 'to rise above the petty squabbles of counts and barons and strike against real threats to the empire that Sigmar forged.' The knight pointed a steel finger at Count Eberfeld. 'Are you willing to do the same?'

Count Eberfeld was silent, feeling the weight of Lord Hugo's words, feeling the accusation in them like a knife twisting in his gut. Doubt gnawed at his resolve. Was it the welfare of his land or the welfare of his pride that made him spurn Count Achim's offer? Was it the survival of Wissenland or the survival of Count Eberfeld that was the object of his war?

'I make no promises of treaty or favour to Gottolf or the Prince of Altdorf,' the count said.

'I ask for none,' Lord Hugo responded. He gestured a steel-clad arm at the ranks of armoured knights behind him. 'If you are truly beset by the black curse of Nagash, I have three-score and six seasoned warriors who would ride with you. All they demand is the opportunity to bring Sigmar's holy wrath down upon the skulls of these abominations!'

The count's sword hissed back into its sheath and he extended his hand to Lord Hugo, welcoming the strong grasp of his stern grip. 'If that is all your men ask, they shall find more than enough where we are going.'

THE KNIGHTS OF the Griffon stood their horses upon the small rise, staring down at the grey fog that had settled around the town of Neuwald, the towers of the settlement rising above the murk like the masts of a sunken ship reaching up from the black clutch of the sea. Screams and shouts rose intermittently from the unseen walls of the city, but within the fog, almost perfect silence held dominion, broken only by the snap-crack of catapults hurling missiles into Neuwald.

Lord Hugo had ridden to the battlefield with Count Eberfeld. They encountered General Hock's army in a shambles, a desolate, dejected body of men held together only by their common fear. Twice they had marched into the fog, and twice they had been repulsed by the rotting warriors of the legion. It was a testament to their discipline that they had not routed long before Count Eberfeld's arrival. That the count, with a few words and a display of his determination, was able to rally his men towards a third effort spoke of how well he was loved by his people.

The weakness in General Hock's desperate but ill-advised effort against the legion lay, Lord Hugo was convinced, in his attempt to engage the enemy across too broad a front. This was no living foe, to be broken by force of arms. They had to be destroyed, destroyed to the last warrior. Hock, in his despair, had gambled that a half-effort would be enough.

Count Eberfeld was yet unwilling to abandon the town, however, and so conferred with his officers to decide on a plausible course of action. While they had no immediate means to break the siege, it was decided that a concentrated attack might be able to punch through the lines of the legion. Their object would be to destroy the legion's onagers and spare Neuwald from at least the attentions of the siege engines. Lord Hugo had insisted his knights spearhead the charge. Supported by the Sablebacks and a regiment of irregular cavalry from Bergdorf, it was believed that they would be able to drive straight to the catapults. The legion was an infantry force, and though its ranks were deep and its mindless warriors devoid of fear or doubt, the onagers needed room to operate, and the ranks could not be thick around them.

Lord Hugo stared into the fog, watching the still, fence-like line of shadows standing just within the veil. The sound of the catapults told him that here was a good place to strike, since the onagers could not be more than a few hundred yards behind that fence of living corpses. He raised his sword high, shouting a prayer to Sigmar. The oath was echoed by the knights behind him, even a few of the Sablebacks and cavalrymen on his flanks picking up the cry. Then Lord Hugo lowered his sword. Hundreds of horsemen galloped forward as one, roaring their war cries at the silent enemy.

There was movement within the fog as the knights barrelled down the rise. A ragged, stumbling mass emerged from the mist. Shouts of horror rose from the charging cavalry as their eyes closed upon the grisly things. Torn flesh clung to broken bones, strips of bloodied cloth dripping around mangled frames. The things moved in stiff, awkward stumbles, sightless eyes staring emptily at the oncoming chargers. The Wissenlanders were struck dumb with revulsion as they saw the things, as they recognised the liveries of Heufurth and Kreutzhofen among the rags the things wore, as they found a ghastly familiarity in some of the decaying faces that gawped at them from the fog. From some of the zombies, those in which a faint echo of life stubbornly clung, there issued low, anguished moans, the sound both piteous and terrible.

Horses shied and panicked as the stench of unburied carrion struck their senses, as the unholy taint of the zombies reached them. The animals jerked against the men who tried to command them, spilling riders into the dust. The charge degenerated into a confused mess of desperate men and terrified beasts. Lord Hugo tried to maintain some cohesion among his knights, tried to pursue the attack despite their animals' fear. Scarcely a third of the men who had followed him down the slope were still in control of their animals and still able to lend themselves to the charge.

The empty, rotting visages of the zombies watched the men thunder towards them, oblivious to the pounding hooves, the lowered lances and the bared swords. Slowly, the things raised their own swords and spears, holding them with ungainly hands and vacant stares. They seemed almost to welcome the destruction descending upon them.

As Lord Hugo's charge neared the waiting line of zombies, more shadows emerged from the fog. These moved not with the uncertain, stiff motions of the zombies, but with a horrible grace and speed, an abominable parody of the galloping horses of the Sigmarites. When the Wissenlanders had fought the legion on the Dobrin road, there had been no cavalry among the lifeless horde. Horsemen had not been a fixture of warfare when Zahaak had walked the land as a mortal king, nor had they been part of the legion it had led into the Black Mountains to support its infernal master. Zahaak, however, was not like the mindless things it controlled, it still had intelligence. It could adapt to the tactics of an enemy, and even use them.

In life, they had been the Knights of the Southern Sword, these horrors that galloped from the fog. Now they were knights of Nagash, loathsome shadows of the warriors they had once been. Their flesh was withered against their bones, shrivelled by the fell sorcery of Zahaak, their faces were empty skulls picked clean by the beaks of carrion crows. Their armour was tarnished with decay and the filth of battle, the steeds beneath them were the skeletal husks of their stalwart destriers. Hooded cloaks of flayed skin covered their wasted frames while shroud-like tabards billowed about their mounts. Upon the breast of each cloak, instead of the Southern Sword, they bore the cruel whorl of the Ghoul

Star, that ancient symbol of horror and madness passed down from the hoary lore of Nehekhara.

The undead knights did not hesitate in their charge to meet Lord Hugo's men. Zombies were crushed beneath dead hooves as the lifeless riders spurred towards the battle, the rotting things remaining eerily silent even as their bones snapped beneath the galloping knights. Again coils of unnatural terror closed around the charging riders, this time striking man and beast alike. Men wrenched desperately at the reins of their steeds, trying frantically to turn their animals about. Horses pitched screaming to the ground as their terrified riders struggled too recklessly to turn them, and men hurtled screaming from saddles as their animals refused their efforts to control them.

Into this rout came the legion's riders, charging into the confused ranks with cold, passionless havoc. Blades black with crusted blood slashed down into the bodies of floundering men, hacking at them like cordwood. Neither scream nor curse caused the swords of the undead to hesitate. Horses pitched to the earth, their necks cut open by the blades of the dead, men falling in butchered heaps to breath their last in the blood-drenched dust.

Lord Hugo and a handful of his knights tried to fight back, to blunt the awful counter-attack of the undead riders. He slammed his sword into the collar of one wight, nearly severing the faceless head from its unclean body. The hooded skull flopped obscenely against its shoulder, grinning malevolently at Lord Hugo as it continued to slash at him with its sword. The knight tried to finish the job with another strike at its neck, but even as he did so, his horse screamed beneath him. The animal pitched to the ground, its lung punctured by the thrust of another wight's sword. Lord Hugo was thrown by the dying beast, tossed through the air like a child's doll. He landed in a blinding burst of agony, feeling his leg snap like a twig beneath him.

The knight groped for his sword, horrified by its loss in his fall. Lord Hugo looked frantically for his men, but the only ones close were the mangled, dying bodies strewn across the ground. He could see the undead riders pursuing the rest, driving them from the field. The sight had broken the faltering spirit of Wissenland's army, and they were retreating from the battleground in a disordered mob, defying the best efforts of Count Eberfeld to rally them. If the count was lucky, they'd stop running once they reached Bergdorf.

The sound of movement close by brought Lord Hugo's attention back to his immediate distress. The black knights had pressed their attack across the field, chasing after the fleeing horsemen, but they were not the only elements of the legion stalking out of the fog. Lord Hugo gasped in horror as he saw the festering zombies shambling forwards, limping and crawling on their snapped and broken limbs. He tried to lift his body from the ground, but fell flat as his leg buckled under him.

Driven by despair and fear, Lord Hugo began to crawl. A prayer to Sigmar whispered across his lips as he tried to scramble away. Behind him, the zombies loped onwards, slowly gaining on the wounded man. The knight redoubled his efforts, frantic energy crackling through his nerves. He cried out as the bones in his leg scraped against each other, and then bit down on his tongue, horrified that the cry might spur his pursuers to greater efforts. The zombies displayed no eagerness, however, pursuing him with the same mindless persistence.

Lord Hugo's desperate fight for escape ended as he felt again the icy, unnatural terror close over him. He saw armoured boots lined across the ground before him. Lifting his eyes, he found himself staring into the empty skulls of the undead knights. The creatures, dismounted from their ghastly steeds, stared back at him with the pitiless regard of the dead. Lord Hugo screamed, covering his head with his arms as the wights lifted their swords. The blades chopped down into his body, slicing through flesh and bone. Again and again, the swords of the undead rose and fell, rose and fell, never pausing, never relenting, attacking until the last drop of life had been driven from the knight's veins.

It was a long time before the knights of Nagash sheathed their swords. When they did, what they left behind them could scarcely still be called a man.

CHAPTER FIFTEEN

THE GLOOM OF night cast its ebony shroud across the slopes of the Black Mountains, smothering the twisted trees and misshapen bushes in a lightless murk of shadow. The hard stones and piled rocks cast down from the mountains took on weird, lurking shapes in the darkness, like a legion of hungry monsters waiting to pounce upon their unsuspecting prey.

Schmitt was not much given to imagination or deep thought, yet even the rat-faced outlaw could not fail to be impressed by the almost tangible menace of his surroundings. He was a hard man who had led a hard life, with only a knot of greed where most men had a conscience. Yet even he couldn't quite suppress a shudder as he watched the upper slopes of the mountains, wondering what else might be up there staring back at him. The cries coming from the camp behind him did little to ease his nerves.

Before the orcs attacked, there had been over forty men in Baldur's band of brigands, poachers and outlaws. Now they numbered seven, clustered around a tiny fire that was shielded by a motley array of cloaks and coats, lest some flicker of light betray their presence to some prowler of the night. The survivors were clustered around the fire, nursing their wounds with fistfuls of damp leaves and bandages torn from blankets. Baldur was no stranger to such sorry spectacles, indeed, the aftermath of the border skirmish that had seen him exiled from Averland had been still more miserable in its scope and enormity. For all that the men he looked upon were criminal vermin, Baldur could not set aside his sense of responsibility for them. As their leader, he still felt some obligation towards them.

Baldur clenched his fist and turned on his patron. Rambrecht sat in a canvas camp chair, honing the edge of his blade with a stone, eyes intent upon the sparks that slid from the steel. He was less concerned with the pitiful moaning that rose from the worst of the wounded. It was Rambrecht's ruthless leadership that had allowed them to escape the orc ambush, at the expense of their comrades. Gathering what men were close to hand, Rambrecht had given the order to withdraw while the orcs were still engaged with the bandits further up the slope. It was a decision that sat ill with Baldur. He still considered himself an officer, a captain, and no captain liked to abandon his men in the middle of a fight.

'Something you want?' Rambrecht asked, looking up to find Baldur standing before him. The aristocrat set his sword across his lap, tossing the sharpening stone into the brush. He gave the disgraced officer a superior, challenging glower that dug at what remained of Baldur's pride.

'I want to know when we turn back,' Baldur said. 'We've lost too many men, and those that are left haven't the strength to go on.'

Rambrecht laughed. 'Those dogs? Wave enough gold under their noses and watch them pick themselves back up. They'll go to the walls of Khemri for us if we promise them enough gold!'

'And what will they be when they get there?' Baldur snarled back. 'Tired, broken men facing trained soldiers and mercenaries. Don't forget, the Wissenlanders outnumber us, and we've certainly lost the element of surprise.' As if to punctuate Baldur's words, a sharp moan rose from the camp.

A sinister gleam came to Rambrecht's eyes. 'Don't forget that we still have a man on the inside,' the aristocrat said. 'That counts for a lot. When the time comes, we'll surprise them.'

Baldur shook his head, biting back a curse. 'We're too weak to go wandering around the mountains!' He stabbed a hand in the direction of the brooding black peaks. 'We don't know what we'll find up there!'

'On the contrary,' Rambrecht corrected him, 'we know exactly what we'll find: a ragtag mob of Wissenlanders and a relic that means power and wealth for both of us!' The aristocrat's lips were moist as he imagined the bounty he would claim when he presented the lost runefang of Solland to the royal court in Averheim. A barony would be the least he might expect. Count Achim had a granddaughter as yet unwed, and it was not impossible to dream of gaining entrance into the royal family if he brought his bold scheme to fruition.

Baldur could see in Rambrecht's face that he had lost his argument, but with the tenacity of an old soldier, he tried again to make the aristocrat see reason. 'What

about what else we might find up there? What about
the orcs? What if they pick up our trail again? What if
they are out there even now looking for us? Do you
think they'd have a hard time finding us if they wanted
to?' Again, a piteous moan of pain rose from the camp.
Rambrecht looked past Baldur at the bandits gathered
around the fire. He singled one of them out.

'You! Kopff, isn't it?' the aristocrat snapped. The squat
brigand nodded sheepishly and took a step forwards,
his hands folded across his chest. 'Who's making all
that racket?'

'It's Stampf, Herr Rambrecht, your lordship, sir,' Kopff
replied, keeping his voice at what he hoped was a
servile tone. 'Half his arm was chopped off by an orc–'

'Shut him up,' Rambrecht growled, 'unless you want
his whining to lead every greenskin in the Black Mountains to us!'

Kopff licked his lips and bobbed his head in agreement as he backed away, almost stumbling over his own
feet. Rambrecht dismissed the bandit from his
thoughts, turning again to glower at Baldur.

'Maybe you've lost sight of what you have at stake,
captain,' Rambrecht hissed. 'Maybe I was wrong seeking
you out. What's wrong, *captain*? Now that what you
have dreamed of for so many years is nearly within your
grasp you find it frightening? Don't you want your commission restored? Don't you want to return to your
family and see your home again? To stop living like an
animal out here among this scum?'

The anguished moan started to rise again, and then was
cut off, replaced by a ghastly gurgle. Baldur felt his stomach lurch as he heard the sound, and saw the triumphant
superiority written across Rambrecht's face. Kopff emerged
from the darkness, wiping a bloody knife on his leggings.

'Herr Rambrecht, sir, your lordship,' the toad-faced bandit whined, 'Stampf's going to be quiet now.' Kopff blinked and drew away when he saw the enraged look that Baldur directed at him. Quickly, the bandit leader turned on Rambrecht. Before the aristocrat could react, the ex-soldier's hands had closed around his collar, pulling him from his seat.

'Damn you!' Baldur raged. 'It was bad enough leaving men behind to be butchered by orcs, but now we're murdering our wounded! I'm still an officer, Rambrecht, whatever they say in Averheim. I still have honour. I still have a sense of duty and obligation.' He glared into Rambrecht's eyes, pleased to find, for the first time, a tinge of fear in them. 'These are my men! *Mine*! I won't let you slaughter them for your own mad ambition.'

The other bandits from the camp had drawn close during the exchange, watching as their leader argued with his patron, nervously gazing from one to the other. Rambrecht saw the uncertainty on their crude faces, the blind stupidity of a mob just rousing to action. The aristocrat's breath was laboured, his pulse quickening as he realised which way they would turn when that action came. They had all heard Baldur's arguments, and had time to digest his words in their villainous minds.

Then, suddenly, the situation changed, in a way that Rambrecht was quick to turn to his advantage.

Schmitt came scrambling into the camp. Words were tumbling from his mouth even before he was aware of the tense stand-off he had intruded upon. 'Lights!' he cried. 'Lights on the mountain, just like you said to look for!'

The smile was back on Rambrecht's face and he pulled himself free of Baldur's suddenly slackened grip. 'Lights on the mountain,' he repeated for Baldur's benefit. He looked at Schmitt, and they stared at the other bandits. 'Tell them what kind of lights you saw.'

Schmitt nodded and hurried to obey. 'Just like the nob said to look for,' he stammered. 'A light that burned long, then short, then long, like a pattern.'

'The signal fire proves that my spy is still active,' Rambrecht declared, 'still with the Wissenlanders and still marking their trail for us. All we have to do is follow them and they will lead us to the treasure.' He glanced aside at Baldur and sneered. 'Or we can do as your chief here suggests: turn tail and leave the treasure to Count Eberfeld. Which will it be?'

Rambrecht already knew which way the brigands would vote; he could see it in the avarice shining in their eyes. A babble of excited voices rose in a confused chorus as the bandits stumbled over each other to agree with the aristocrat. Rambrecht pounced on their excitement. 'I'll pay any man who stays with me three hundred gold crowns against an equal share of the treasure,' he bellowed, struggling to make his voice rise above the din.

'Thank you, Rambrecht.' The aristocrat swung around, confused to find Baldur smiling at him. 'You've allowed me to wash my hands of these men with a clear conscience.'

'I didn't think you were a coward,' Rambrecht said. 'Stick with me and you'll still get your commission.'

'You and these fools can commit suicide,' Baldur snapped. 'I'll pass, if it's all the same to you.' The ex-captain turned and stalked away, his hand resting against the hilt of his sword.

'Don't send anybody after me, Rambrecht,' he warned as he vanished into the night. 'You've already lost enough men.'

* * *

THE SHEER SIDES of the canyon loomed above Kessler like the walls of a tomb, pressing in upon him with their enormity. Only a thin sliver of sky snaked its way overhead, reminding the swordsman that he still walked the earth, that he was not entombed deep within it. This, so Skanir told them, was Drung-a-Uzkul, the site of the ancient conflict that had seen the ruin of Zahaak the Usurper. Of that long ago battle there was little sign, patches of corrosion lying forgotten among the rocks and dust of the canyon, the sorry echoes of iron weapons and bronze armour.

Of more recent violence, there was ample evidence. The sheer walls of the canyon had been lovingly adorned with runes and carvings, by the dwarfs, to commemorate their dead, lost in the battle with Zahaak. Most of them were defiled, defaced and disfigured. Crude goblin glyphs were scratched over the dwarf runes, the bearded faces of bas-reliefs smashed into oblivion. Skanir's mood became still darker as he studied the havoc that centuries of goblin vandals had worked upon the monuments, his eyes burning as they glared across the canyon. Dwarfs held their ancestors and their history in the deepest reverence, and this was more than destruction to Skanir, it was desecration. Kessler could well imagine the vengeful thoughts stirring in the dwarf's heart. The way his eyes glowered at the landscape, it seemed as if Skanir was begging the mountain to produce a horde of greenskins for him to smash into pulp with his hammer.

A light tug on his sleeve pulled Kessler from his contemplation of Skanir. The swordsman glanced in the direction of the summons. He found himself staring into Ghrum's enormous gut. The tugging continued and he lowered his gaze to find Theodo's nimble fingers coiled around his arm. The halfling was a miserable sight, one side of his face swollen and discoloured where he had been struck by a horse's hoof, his once resplendent clothes frayed and tattered, his curly hair tangled and matted. Seeing that he had Kessler's attention, the halfling quickly glanced around, a furtive quality in the motion. When his turn brought him around to where his vision was filled with the ogre's leg, Theodo shrugged. There was little chance of being inconspicuous when his bodyguard was the biggest thing within a league, excepting perhaps the mountains.

'I need to have words with you, Herr Kessler,' Theodo said. 'We have a spy in our midst.'

Kessler copied the halfling's quick glance around the canyon, trying to note if anyone was paying attention to their discussion. Ottmar and the surviving soldiers were up near Skanir, and Valdner and his troop were somewhat behind Kessler's current position. Eugen and Gerhard were across from Kessler, inspecting some carving on the far wall. The swordsman looked back at Theodo and nodded for him to continue. The halfling reached into the breast pocket of his vest, producing a folded square of tanned hide. Kessler didn't need to look at it for long to recognise it as another of the cryptic notes.

'Where did you get this?' Kessler demanded, his voice a low growl.

'I found it in the woods, the morning after we buried your boss,' Theodo answered. He saw the anger flare in Kessler's eyes. 'I didn't tell you sooner because, well, I wasn't about to stick my neck out without knowing who would be looking to cut it.' He felt there was no need to inform Kessler about his ambitions to make some easy gold by blackmailing the spy.

'And have you figured out who the spy is?'

Theodo's smile became hard, his eyes narrowing with spite. 'Your friend over there,' the halfling said, thrusting a thumb over his shoulder, 'the old knight, Eugen. I've been suspicious of him for a while now. In Fritzstadt, I decided to confront him about my suspicions.' Theodo put a hand to his swollen face. 'Curious that a knight, a cavalryman, should completely lose control of his horse like that. You'd almost think he was intentionally trying to stamp me out.'

Kessler shook his head. It was too outrageous to consider. He knew knights, knew the rigid codes of honour and conduct they lived by, which were more important to them than their lives. To believe a knight guilty of such subterfuge and treachery... No, Kessler couldn't accept it. Yet there was no denying that Eugen's horse had attacked the halfling. Theodo wore the evidence across his face. Still, Kessler resisted the implication. He stared hard at the halfling. He'd heard about the cook's crooked ways and his reputation as a card sharp and scoundrel. It was easier to believe that Theodo was the spy than Eugen.

'If you believe what you're telling me, why haven't you taken action?' Kessler pointed at Ghrum's colossal figure. 'It would have been easy enough to have your ogre toss him off the mountain when we were climbing up here.'

'I'm sure that would have gone over quite well with the rest of you,' Theodo said. 'Ghrum isn't exactly subtle, certainly less so than the knight. Why, you might even get the idea that I'm the spy.' Theodo's face twisted into a scowl when he saw the expression Kessler wore as he spoke. 'So that's how it stands, is it? You don't believe it's the knight? Just like the tall folk, pin the blame on the halfling! You think I imagined his horse trying to pound me into the dirt!'

Before Kessler could answer, a sharp cry caused him to turn away from Theodo. Ottmar and the soldiers had strayed ahead down the canyon, taking the front position. The men were clustered in the centre of the passage, their faces flush as they laughed nervously among themselves. The source of their anxiety was readily apparent, a curved loop of iron having erupted from the earth, its convex surface riddled with ugly spikes. In their advance, the men had sprung the trap. Only the decay of its mechanism had spared them as it had frozen in mid-strike. The soldiers pointed at the trap, chattering about their near escape. Then one of them stepped forward for a closer look. Every eye in the canyon had been drawn to the clamour, but it was Skanir's hardened gaze that saw a situation still rife with danger.

'Stay away from there!' the dwarf bellowed, rushing forward. It was too late. The soldier had nearly reached the faulty trap when the ground beneath him fell away. The man's howl of terror exploded into an agonised wail. Skanir roared at the men who ran forwards to discover the fate of their comrade, snarling at them to keep back. The violence in the dwarf's voice and the horror of the burbling moans that rose from the exposed pit caused emotion to retreat before caution.

Skanir carefully made his way towards the pit, probing the ground with the butt of his hammer. Once, the ground he tested collapsed, uncovering a second pit. Kessler understood the diabolical ingenuity of the diseased minds that had constructed the traps. The iron loop had been a blind, never intended to inflict harm. It was bait, bait to draw the curious into the real trap, the pits that pock-marked the canyon floor.

At length, the dwarf reached the edge of the hole that had claimed the soldier. In his approach, Skanir had revealed half a dozen other pits, each wide enough to swallow a man. He scowled as he stared down at the hole, muttering into his beard as painful moans continued to rise. He looked back at the men watching him.

'Come up if you like,' the dwarf called, 'but it ain't pretty. Follow my footprints in the dust. Don't stray from the path.'

After several tense minutes, a small crowd had joined Skanir at the pit. Below, they saw the moaning soldier, his body pierced in a dozen places by the spikes that lined the floor of the hole. It was a sight that sickened even a veteran killer like Max Kessler.

'See that yellow crust on the spears?' Skanir asked, pointing to the few spikes the soldier's body had failed to hit in his fall. 'Grobi poison. They boil it down into a resin so it sticks better and lasts longer.'

'Then this is a goblin trap?' Ottmar asked, resolutely keeping his face turned from the hideous sight in the pit.

'If there's one thing grobi find more amusing than graffiti, it's setting traps,' Skanir said. 'The more fiendish the better. They make them good, too,' the dwarf reluctantly conceded. 'This arrangement might have been sitting here for a hundred years waiting for somebody to stumble into it.'

Kessler barely heard Skanir's words as he studied the walls of the pit, looking for hand holds, anything that would carry him down to the trap's victim. The dwarf noted the swordsman's efforts. He closed his thick arm around Kessler's shoulder, pulling him back.

'Better to forget it,' the dwarf said sombrely.

'We have to do something for him,' Kessler snapped. The sentiment was echoed by the other men standing around the pit. Skanir shook his head.

'You can't help your friend,' he said. 'The grobi poison is already running through him. They make some nasty poisons, things that make you die by inches rather than all at once. Goblins think suffering is funny, and they like to watch things take a long time to die.' Skanir set down his hammer, drawing the pistol from his belt. He aimed the firearm down into the pit. 'The only thing you can do for him is make the end quick.' Skanir hesitated for a moment as he made the pronouncement, waiting for any protest to find voice. None came and the agony from the pit was silenced by the boom of the dwarf's weapon.

Skanir turned away from the hole, shoving his pistol back into its holster. 'From here on, everyone follows my lead. You can bet the grobi have left plenty more surprises around. Anybody stumbles into one,' he paused and stared hard at the men around him, 'just hope it finishes you quick.'

THE STENCH OF roasting flesh seared its way into Baldur's pain-wracked senses, oozing past the red wall of agony that filled his vision. The man's eyes flickered open, fighting to focus through a film of tears. A leering, toothy-green face slavered over him, its inhuman visage made all the more monstrous by its evil mirth. The creature leaned over him, its long pointy nose hovering above his, its rodent-like eyes staring into his own. A thin, knobby fist cracked against Baldur's face, splitting his lip. The bandit scarcely felt the blow through the pulsating agony that already filled him, but his body reacted reflexively to the hit. Wicked, wispy laughter tittered from the goblin and the creature spun around.

'Hey, boss! The humie's wakin' up!' the goblin hissed, sadistic anticipation in the monster's voice.

Hulking shapes loomed from the darkness, their massive bodies swollen with muscle, and their leathery hides pitted with scars. Scraps of armour hung from their massive frames, huge blades tied to their broad belts by strips of sinew and chain. Their faces were brutish and thick, huge lantern jaws drooping beneath their heads, weighed down by the yellowing tusks that protruded over their lips. Tiny, piggish eyes shone from the deep recesses of their skulls, glaring at the world around them with scarcely restrained malevolence. Clawed fists clenched in savage anticipation, eager to feel flesh tear beneath naked fingers. They stomped forward at the goblin's goading cries, only too ready to glut their primitive need for violence.

A still larger figure emerged from among the mob of orcs, pushing his way through the inhuman warriors, smashing the heads of those too slow to clear a path for him, crushing ears beneath a fist that struck like a steel bludgeon. Those stricken cringed away, glaring hatred at the brutal master who had maimed them. The warlord paid no heed to the loathing of his minions. An orc ruled its fellows through fear and cruelty, the simple concept of loyalty alien to their savage brains. So long as he remained stronger and more vicious than those who followed him, he would remain warboss. The moment he showed the first sign of weakness, they would fall on him like a pack of wolves and sate the malice they nursed against their warlord. Until that time, they would obey their master. At least, they would if they knew what was good for them. There was not a knight in all the Empire who had killed more orcs than Uhrghul Skullcracker had.

The huge warlord marched from the ranks of his warband, his dark hide black in the shadowy night. The orc held a hunk of charred meat in one giant fist, gnawing at it as he approached the goblin and the prisoner whose body the malicious greenskin straddled. At Uhrghul's approach, the goblin sprang away, bowing and grovelling in deference to the warlord.

'He say anything?' Uhrghul demanded, his teeth ripping a ribbon of flesh from the meat clenched in his hand.

'No, boss,' the goblin fawned. 'He just woke up.'

Uhrghul's eyes blazed with annoyance, his mouth freezing in mid-chew. He glowered at the goblin, shreds of unchewed meat falling from his face as he snarled at the smaller greenskin. 'Start making the words then!' the orc snapped. 'I want to know where the humie's friends got to! The boys'll want something to kill soon.'

The goblin decided it didn't like the subtle threat behind those words. Barely a dozen of its kin were still following Uhrghul's warband, far too few to do anything should the orcs decide to slake their boredom on the goblins who followed them.

The goblin slapped Baldur's face again, its clawed fingers ripping open his cheek. The bandit groaned into full awareness, eyes widening with horror. The man's fright brought another laugh from the goblin, but a sharp bark from Uhrghul cut the creature's humour short. Quickly, the goblin forced its scratchy voice into the complexities of Reikspiel, putting questions to the prisoner in his own tongue.

Uhrghul watched the exchange carefully. Unable to follow much of what the goblin was saying, the orc struggled to read the creature's face for any sign of craft or deception. They had their uses, goblins, but it was a stupid orc indeed who trusted one. That was an easy way to wake up with a slit throat or a bellyful of poison. Still, there were times when the cowardly sneaks were handy. It had been goblins who had captured the bandit, falling upon him while they had been away from camp hunting. Uhrghul was pleased enough by the capture that he had ignored the more probable reason for the goblins being abroad: that the craven creatures were deserting and slinking back to their caves. It was probably time to kill a few of them and remind the others why he was boss.

The orc warlord snapped back from his murderous thoughts, focusing his attention back on the goblin interrogator. He saw the goblin's leathery face pull back into a grin as the captive told it something. Instantly, Uhrghul lurched forward, grabbing the goblin by the scruff of its fur tunic. The creature flailed wildly as the orc lifted it off the ground. Uhrghul held the goblin inches from his face, glaring into its sneaky little eyes.

'Well, what the humie say?' Uhrghul growled.

'He says his pals are headin' into the mountains, boss,' the goblin hissed in its most servile tone. Uhrghul mulled that over for a time, and then shook both his head and the goblin he held.

'No, don't sound right,' Uhrghul said. 'Ain't no humies dumb enough for doing that. They'd be scurrying back to one of their towns, not headin' where they'll find more orcs!' Uhrghul's heavy brow bunched forward as the orc strained to make sense of the problem. He saw the flicker of a grin play on the goblin's sharp face. The orc shook the little greenskin viciously, rattling its small body like a rag doll.

'What else the humie say?' he demanded. A few moments passed before he realised he would need to stop shaking the goblin if he expected an answer.

'He... he say his... his pals're lookin' for somethin',' the goblin stammered, trying to recollect its rattled wits. Uhrghul's face stretched into a menacing scowl.

'What're they lookin' for?' the orc snapped.

'He ain't telled me yet,' the goblin whined, throwing up its hands in appeal to the huge brute who held it. 'Honest, boss, he ain't said a word about it!' A cunning quality slipped past the fear in the goblin's eyes. 'You figure it's treasure, boss? Gold, rubies maybe?'

Uhrghul unceremoniously dropped the goblin, ignoring the squeal of pain that accompanied the creature's fall. Instead, he lumbered over to Baldur, sneering down at the captive. The man's arms were lashed to pegs by strips of dried sinew, his torso similarly bound. Only the man's head was free to move. He struggled to lift himself, spitting at his tormentor. Uhrghul dismissed the man's defiance, taking another bite of meat.

'Ask the humie again,' Uhrghul commanded the goblin interrogator. The smaller greenskin scrambled forwards, clutching an arm that had been bruised in its fall. 'Ask the humie how his legs feel,' the orc added, pulling another bite of flesh from the bone in his hand.

Baldur groaned in agony as the goblin pressed him once more with questions. Under the greenskin's goading, he lifted his head, staring not at his captors but at his own body tied to the ground. A piercing, tortured scream slashed through the night as his eyes saw the horror that had been visited on his flesh. His screams intensified as he noted the charred toes that protruded from Uhrghul's meal.

The orc warlord nodded, pleased by the prisoner's terror. 'Tell the humie he can die fast or slow,' Uhrghul said. 'That always scares the soft-skins. Tell him if he talks, you'll make sure he's dead before the lads start cooking their supper.'

CHAPTER SIXTEEN

PASSAGE THROUGH THE canyon had been slow and perilous. Kessler doubted they would have survived more than a mile without Skanir's sharp eyes. Not a single foot of wall, it seemed, had been spared the vandalising attention of the goblins. The filthy monsters had been no less industrious, leaving more lethal evidence of their intrusion behind. Covered pits, wolf-traps, rock-falls, even several devices of such complexity that Kessler found it hard to believe goblins could have conceived them, such were the relics the spiteful greenskins had added to the haunted atmosphere of Drung-a-Uzkhul. Skanir had spotted them all, warning his companions of their danger. After the hideous fate of the first casualty, none of them needed much reminder to watch their step.

Gradually, the canyon began to widen. The men found themselves standing in a large valley, the broken remains of a pair of dwarf statues lying sprawled across much of the ground. The spot had an air of desolation that was positively overwhelming, a clammy clutch that oozed into Kessler's pores. A huge section of one canyon wall had broken away, collapsing into rubble, exposing a yawning cave that stretched into the darkness. He didn't need Skanir to tell him that the dwarfs had entombed the carcasses of Zahaak and his legion here, long ago. Now, the secret tomb was open and its unholy occupants once again stalked the land.

'Grobi work,' Skanir decided, examining the heaped pile of stones. 'It would have been concealed to look like part of the mountain, but somehow they must have stumbled onto it recently.' The dwarf reached down and lifted the severed arm of a goblin, the flesh shrivelled against the bone. 'Probably thought they'd find some treasure to loot. I don't have to tell you what kind of surprise they found instead.' The dwarf let the sinister statement linger, and then turned around, scanning the heights that loomed over the canyon. 'The war-crypts will be up high, above the stink of the battlefield,' he said, almost to himself. Skanir studied the walls intently. With a sharp gasp, he pointed. The dwarf architects had blended the narrow twisting trail up the sheer face of the cliff so well into its natural setting, that Kessler had difficulty picking it out, even with Skanir's help.

Kessler started towards the base of the cliff, carefully picking his way through the rubble of broken statuary. Suddenly, he felt a tremendous force slam into him, bowling him to the ground. Kessler struggled beneath a powerful grip, trying to pull free. From the corner of his eye, he could see Raban's bearded face pressed close to him, the Nordlander's arms pinning him to the earth.

The mercenary cursed venomously as Kessler strove to push the man off him, only faintly hearing the cries and shouts from the rest of his small company. Finally, Kessler managed to drive an elbow into the axeman's gut, momentarily stunning Raban. He pulled free of the mercenary's slackened grip. Before he could pick himself back up, however, Raban's hand closed around his ankle, spilling him back onto the ground with a savage tug. This time he landed on his back. As he started to kick at the man who had felled him, Kessler saw a flash of steel cut through the air above him. A moment later, the scything blade flashed again, its lethal edge only a few feet above his face.

Kessler carefully began to crawl back the way he had come. Raban spat blood from a lip bruised by Kessler's boot and followed after the man, writhing along on his belly like some hairy lizard. When he was clear of the scythe, Kessler was able to see more clearly what had happened. A moon-shaped edge of rusty metal had exploded from the side of one of the statues, its tremendous momentum causing it to swing back and forth like some butchering pendulum. The blade was poised at a height designed to behead a dwarf, but would have worked nearly as much havoc slicing through a man's chest. While Kessler watched, Ghrum lumbered over behind the trap, the ogre's immense hand closing around the iron stalk that supported the blade. With a brutal tug, Ghrum snapped the corroded metal, ending forever the whirring threat of the pendulum. His dull eyes considered the lethal implement for an instant, and then, with a dismissive shrug, he tossed it aside.

Kessler quickly took stock of the situation. If Raban hadn't struck him, he would have fallen prey to the goblin device, that much was immediately clear. The swordsman stepped forward and helped the battered mercenary to his feet. Raban sullenly shook aside the assistance.

'You have my thanks,' Kessler said, trying to apologise for the way he had struggled against his benefactor. Raban leered at him resentfully.

'Keep it,' the Nordlander spat. 'Just be thankful you're the one footing the bill, otherwise I'd have let that thing skewer you.'

The way he said it, Kessler knew that Raban would probably have preferred that result. The sharp glance he directed at Valdner left no doubt as to why he had acted otherwise. Brushing the dust from his leggings, Raban marched over to the advancing officer.

'You should be more careful, Herr Kessler,' Valdner reproved him. 'So very much counts upon your remaining with us.'

'Don't blame him,' Theodo cried out, sharply. The halfling was pushing his way through the mass of gawking soldiers and sell-swords. There was a malicious quality to the cook's bruised face. 'There's the one that triggered it!' He thrust an accusing finger at Eugen. The knight was crouching beside the statue, beneath the murderous sweep of the pendulum. At the halfling's accusation, he straightened, glaring at Theodo.

'It was an accident,' the knight returned.

'Strange how many convenient accidents seem to surround you,' Theodo spat, touching his swollen cheek. The statement caused Eugen to see red, his hand dropping to the hilt of his sword. Before he could advance on the halfling, Eugen heard the rasp of steel sliding free from leather. He turned his head and found Kessler facing him, the immense greatsword held at the ready.

'You'd take the word of this… this burrow rat over mine?' Eugen scoffed, shock in his tones. Kessler did not reply, simply keeping his sword at the ready. Other weapons were now being pulled clear of their scabbards. Ottmar and Valdner both approached the knight, backing Kessler's move.

'I don't know what to think,' Kessler said, his voice a low growl. 'I'm not very good at it. I do know that there have been too many coincidences in this camp to suit me. I also know I'll feel better if you lowered your sword.'

The knight stared into the faces of Kessler, Valdner and Ottmar. He looked past them and saw the hardened countenances of the other mercenaries and Wissenlanders. Only the young Sollander, Gerhard, looked sympathetic. Eugen saw him start to reach for his own weapon. The move decided the veteran's actions. Nodding his head weakly, he let his sword drop into the dirt, holding his hands to his side in an expression of defeat. Valdner came forward and retrieved the fallen weapon.

'Minhea!' the captain called. The wiry Sylvanian emerged from the ranked warriors. 'Take charge of the prisoner. Don't let him out of your sight.'

Eugen barely heard the words, his attention fixed on Gerhard, silently urging the younger knight to make no move. When the Sylvanian came to lead him away, Eugen offered no resistance. There would be a time for that, but the time was not now.

Kessler watched him go, part of him relieved that the knight had been exposed, part of him sickened that a warrior of such honour could have fallen so low as to become a traitor and spy.

THE CROOKED PATH up the side of the canyon emptied onto a shallow plateau. Kessler wondered whether the space was natural or another example of the dwarfs' amazing engineering skills. He rather suspected that it had been constructed, carved from the side of the canyon. Perhaps a hundred yards wide, nearly half as deep, the table of rock jutted out from the craggy cliff, looking out over the canyon floor hundreds of feet below. Here, as in the canyon, every inch of the wall was carved, sporting the sharp runes and elaborate bas-reliefs of ancient artisans. Here, as below, the craftsmanship had been defaced by the clubs and axes of goblins, rude pictures and rough glyphs painted over anything too hard to be completely destroyed.

Kessler's attention lingered on the walls only briefly, his eyes soon drawn to the great portal set into the face of the cliff. Massive columns of marble flanked the doorway, even the attentions of the goblins doing little to deface their elegance. The doors were immense panels of bronze and steel. Two bas-relief warriors stared out from the panels, their armour scratched and chipped by vandals, their faces obliterated, replaced by crude goblin paintings that leered obscenely. A huge crater defaced the join of the doors, the dented ruin left behind by a battering ram.

'Looks like we're not the first ones to visit,' Valdner observed.

Skanir walked towards the doorway, shaking his head sadly. He placed a hand against one of the maimed relief figures, almost reverently. The dwarf's fingers pressed against the door, finding it solidly in place. His eyes turned away from the abused dwarf craftsmanship to the rough iron plates that had been pounded into the panels, reattaching them to the stone of the doorway.

'Orcs,' Skanir spat, 'broke their way inside looking for plunder.'

'But they sealed it up again when they left,' observed Ottmar, pointing at one of the iron plates. 'Seems an odd thing for an orc to do.'

'Not if you understand greenskins,' Skanir said. 'They never build anything that they can't steal from somebody else. They broke in here to steal the treasure and armour that was buried with the dead, but they came back later to do even worse.' He lowered his head, glaring at the grainy white sand that littered the plateau. Skanir turned over what looked like a bit of rock, with his foot. Slowly it dawned on the men watching him that the rock was a tiny fragment of bone. The white sand was actually pulverised bone, the crushed remains of ancient skeletons. 'The orcs dragged our dead from the crypt, smashing them to powder. Then they planted their own dead inside.'

Kessler nodded his head, appreciating the outrage Skanir was feeling, but unable to contain the excitement the dwarf's words provoked. 'You said the runefang would be in such a place, a dwarf crypt that had been violated by orcs, used to bury one of their own.'

Skanir looked dubious. 'These mountains are full of war-crypts that the greenskin vermin have defiled. It's asking too much of the gods that this is the one they planted old Gordreg in.'

The swordsman stepped closer to the doorway. A sense of belonging and purpose filled him. He could not shake the impression, the feeling that this was where he needed to be. A thrill swept through his body, a cold sensation that raced along his spine. For an instant, he imagined the smell of Carlinda's cool, pale body. The instant passed, and Kessler reached forward to touch the bronze doors.

'Who did your people bury here?' Kessler asked. His eyes were riveted to a parade of small bas-reliefs that ran along the arch above the door. Somehow they had escaped the vandalism of the goblins, standing as stark and clear as the day they had been carved. The armoured figures of dwarfs, the horns of their helmets reaching out from the arch, clashed with a horde of thin, spectral shapes. At the fore of the ghostly legion was a figure that caused Kessler to shudder. Tall and skeletal, cloaked and hooded, Kessler could not help but be reminded of the wraith that had manifested during the battle with the bandits, the awful sending that had devoured Carlinda with the terrible hunger of an icy flame. Opposing the figure was a dwarf, his armour more elaborate and clearly defined than those of his army, his horned helm sporting a tiered crown around its rim. The dwarf held a massive axe in his hands, brandishing it against the undead monstrosity.

Skanir ran his fingers along the door, trying to discern by touch the runes that the goblin graffiti had made indistinguishable to the eye. The dwarf almost seemed pale as he turned away from the door and looked up at Kessler. Skanir chewed his beard for a moment as he tried to convince himself that what he had read was true. He looked up at the carvings Kessler had been inspecting, shaking his head in disbelief.

'It's his tomb,' Skanir said, 'the crypt of Isen Fallowbeard, the King of Karag Dar, who used Zonbinzahn to defeat Zahaak!'

The exclamation brought the others forwards, all except Minhea and his charge. After travelling so far and enduring so much, all wanted to see what had been found, the proof that might mean an end to their journey. As they clustered around the doorway, a dozen voices raised in excited confusion, Theodo found something to dampen the spirits of his comrades.

'Excuse me,' the halfling shouted over the murmur of the men above him. He had to repeat himself several times before he caught anyone's attention. When he saw Kessler look his way, Theodo pointed up at the bas-relief. 'Aren't we looking for the Runefang of Solland, the "Sun-Tooth" this dwarf is supposed to have used to kill Zahaak?' Kessler felt a numb horror grip him as he looked back at the carving. He didn't need Theodo to point out what was wrong, but the halfling did so anyway.

'If we're hunting for a sword, why is he using an axe?'

THE JUBILATION OF a moment before sickened into a black despair, one that even Kessler's stubborn spirit could not escape. Every eye seemed to glare at the carving, as though it had betrayed them. The bolstered hopes of an instant crashed into pits of dejection. They had risked much and come far, with nothing but a legend and a prophecy to guide them. Now the prophetess was dead and the legend had been proved wrong.

The men did not have long to contemplate the horrible twist fate had thrown their way. Standing away from the gang gathered around the doorway, Eugen and Minhea were the only ones placed far enough away from the cliff wall to see danger rear its head. Or rather, heads, since a dozen or more sharp-beaked, serpent-like faces protruded from the rock. At first, the men thought the faces were simply more carvings, strange gargoyles placed by the dwarfs to watch over the tomb. They dismissed the imagined motion that had drawn their eyes upwards. Then the motion repeated, and they gasped as terror gripped their hearts. The serpentine faces had

moved, shifting in loathsome unison to stare down at
the men below. Two immense legs appeared beneath
the heads, great leonine limbs covered in plates of black
scale and tipped with axe-like claws.

Eugen found voice before the mercenary, screaming a
warning to the men at the doorway, his lungs burning
with the fury of his exertions. It was a single word, that
warning, the name of a thing so fabulous and rare that
only one in a hundred scholars would call it more than
myth, yet of such dreadful reputation that even as a
myth its image had been burned into the minds of
men.

'Hydra!'

The strange cry caused those at the doorway to spin
around, staring at the men they had left behind. Some
wondered if this were some trick on the part of the traitor.
Others, noting the pallor that had overwhelmed Minhea's
dark Sylvanian complexion, wondered if both men had
gone mad. Then a trickle of pebbles and dust fell about
them. Eyes turned upwards, and voices rose in screams of
horror and shouts of disbelief. Men scattered in every
direction, dragging weapons from scabbards.

Pale tongues flickering from fifteen beaks, the monster watched the men flee below it. The reptile lurched
forwards again, exposing its huge scaly body. Bigger
than a pair of oxen, its slinky body tapered into a long
barbed tail. Yellow stripes interrupted the pattern of
scaly black plates that encased it. Its heads were supported by a nest of writhing, snake-like necks, each as
thick as a man's arm and ten feet in length. The hydra's
four powerful legs stabbed into the face of the cliff,
pounding their talons deeper than a mountaineer's
piton. Heads facing down, the hydra scrambled lizard-
like down the face of the cliff, abandoning the fissure in

which it had lurked. The beast nearly reached the level of the bronze door before it coiled its body close to the rock. With a great lunge, the hydra launched off the rock, landing with a shuddering impact on the surface of the plateau. The incredible speed of the reptile caught Kessler's men by complete surprise. Several were still gaping in awe as the hydra landed among them, its heads snapping among them in a blur of violence and savagery.

One soldier fell, an arm sliced off at the shoulder by the monster's blade-like beak. A mercenary's shriek terminated in an obscene gurgle as his head was plucked from his shoulders. Another's screams of torment rose shrill and loud as three of the hydra's heads lifted him into the air, struggling to tear him apart.

Those not slaughtered or mutilated by the monster's attack broke, scurrying for cover. In his terror, one of Valdner's men pitched over the edge of the plateau, his scream rising up from the canyon as he plummeted to his death. One of the Wissenlanders sprang at the far wall of the cliff, trying to climb the defaced dwarf carvings. His groping fingers found a cunningly concealed tripwire. An instant later, the man was crushed beneath tons of stone as the goblin trap performed its murderous purpose.

Valdner struggled to rally the rest of his men, hoping to muster some manner of united defence against the rampaging beast. Kessler, separated from the others by the monster's bulk, tightened his grip on his zweihander, and prepared to sell his life dearly should the hydra turn his way. The few archers among the mercenaries peppered the beast with arrows, but the missiles merely glanced off the reptile's scaly hide. A crack and boom signalled that Skanir had fired his pistol into the brute.

Fire flashed from the hydra's side, reptilian treacle spurting from the injury. The hydra's primitive nervous system did not seem to register the wound, not even a single of its writhing heads turning from its gory feast of dead and dismembered men. Skanir threw the weapon down in frustration, roaring about the uselessness of the 'mouse-croaker'.

Eugen was more determined. The disgraced knight had broken free from the distracted Minhea, and Kessler could see the Sylvanian lying sprawled on the ground. The traitor brandished the mercenary's mace, swinging the spiked implement full into one of the hydra's feasting heads. The blow struck something more keenly sensitive than the spot Skanir had shot, for the entire creature lurched backwards, a scalding hiss rasping in ghastly chorus from its heads. Even the veteran knight froze in fear as he felt the malignity of the hydra's evil eyes focus on him. Like a coiling serpent, the hydra's necks retreated into themselves.

Before the monster could spring, Kessler flung himself at it, his greatsword flashing against the tip of its lashing tail. The scaly flesh parted beneath the force of his stroke, reeking filth slopping from the reptilian meat as a foot of tail was severed from the hydra's body. The bleeding was quickly staunched as slashed arteries collapsed and sealed, but the hydra's primordial fury was not so easily abated. With another sizzling hiss, the beast spun around, all of its heads glaring at the lone swordsman who had maimed it. Kessler struck at the monster as it turned on him, the serpent-like neck slithering from the path of his blade.

Then the beast was beset from the rear once more. Eugen had been joined by Gerhard, the two knights savaging the hydra's armoured flanks with mace and sword. Others were rushing forwards, emboldened by the example set by Kessler and the knights. Ghrum's enormous bulk loomed above them all, his gigantic blade chopping down into the hydra's leg like a butcher's cleaver.

The reptile shrank from the attacks, its heads writhing and lashing in chaotic disharmony. It crawled away from the axes and swords that stabbed at its armoured hide, dragging its crippled leg after it. Kessler was beginning to dare to hope that they would kill it without suffering further loss when he saw a flash of light shine from one of the writhing heads. Again, he saw a head spurt fire from its mouth. An instant later, the hydra regained enough of its primitive mentality to force its writhing heads to the purpose. Three of the heads dipped in unison, facing the reptile's abusers. As one, the beaked maws snapped open, searing flame exploding from their jaws.

The screams of dead and dying men echoed across the plateau. Gerhard fell away from the hydra, the young knight's flesh cooking within the charred ruin of his armour. Mercenaries tore at burning clothes, rolling across the ground in agony. Kessler saw a soldier, his tunic blazing like a torch, race across the plateau and throw himself into the canyon below, dropping away like some fading candle.

The screaming seemed to excite the hydra, its frenzied motions becoming still more crazed and erratic. Heads flailed, spewing fire at nothing, and claws lashed, raking the walls of the cliff. Men used the monster's delirium to slink away, none eager to join his incinerated comrades.

Skanir shouted at the retreating men, urging them to attack before the hydra recovered its senses. 'Over here!'

he called, standing on top of the wall the goblin trap had partially collapsed. 'Lure it over here!'

If no one seemed eager to follow the dwarf's suggestion, Kessler could hardly fault them. No man could struggle against that writhing fire spewer and come out alive, but if no man was up to the challenge, there was another to take up the dwarf's call. Still slapping at the smoke rising from his clothes, Ghrum returned to the attack, driving his sword into the hydra's side with the force of a siege ballista. The reptile shuddered beneath the attack, its talons slashing at Ghrum's body. The ogre ignored the hideous wound, wrapping his powerful arms around the nest of writhing necks. Crushing them together in a strangler's embrace, Ghrum kept the snapping heads and their deadly fire from reaching him. The ogre looked back at Skanir, again hearing the dwarf's frantic cry.

Like a Tilean athlete hurling an iron discus, Ghrum planted his feet firmly in the rocky ground and shifted his body. With a mighty effort that seemed beyond even an ogre's monstrous strength, Ghrum spun around, whipping the hydra's flailing mass with him. At the height of his turn, Ghrum released the reptile, allowing its momentum to carry it forwards. It crashed into the side of the plateau, just beneath where Skanir was perched on the wall. The dwarf uttered a sharp curse and jumped down, scrambling away on hands and knees in his desperate haste.

The hydra uncoiled its body from the bruised heap it had landed in. Heads writhed, hissing angrily and spitting fire in every direction. Flames flashed into the sky, licked at the ground and seared against the wall. A portion of the wall suddenly began to sizzle on its own, and then a tremendous explosion rocked the entire mountain. The cliff seemed to rear up on invisible legs, and then came crashing down in a sea of dust and rubble. The hydra vanished within the holocaust that its own flames had precipitated.

When the dust and smoke began to clear, stunned men slowly lifted themselves back to their feet, shaking their heads in an effort to clear the ringing that filled their ears. An avalanche of rock and rubble had crashed down upon the hydra, yards of cliff face sliding down upon it.

Skanir smiled proudly at what his quick thinking had brought about. Unable to harm the beast with his pistol, he had put the rest of his blackpowder to more practical effect, using it to blast apart the wall and bring it down onto the monster. Already weakened by the goblin trap, it had only needed the touch of the hydra's fire to set it off.

He was less pleased by what else his plan had caused. The dwarf cursed again as he saw an unplanned side-effect; the violent explosion had also brought some of the opposing cliff crashing down. A pile of jagged rock stood between the Wissenlanders and the door to the war-crypt. He walked over to Kessler, finding the swordsman likewise contemplating the second avalanche.

'Well, you're in charge,' Skanir said. 'We start looking elsewhere, or do we dig?'

Kessler stared at the pile of rock. Despite the incongruity of the carvings, he still could not shake the sense that this was where he needed to be. They had come too far to turn back now. Even if the dwarf legends were wrong, he could not doubt Carlinda's visions.

'We dig,' Kessler answered.

* * *

HOSTILE EYES WATCHED from the heights above as the Wissenlanders battled the hydra. The explosive conclusion of the combat had men diving for cover, shielding their heads against the shower of rock and debris that billowed up from the avalanche. A few began whispering prayers to Ranald and Khaine as they cowered from the blast.

Only one man remained standing. Rambrecht sneered as he saw the carnage the explosion had wrought. The mouth of the crypt was choked with rubble, and it would take the Wissenlanders hours to clear the opening. It was not quite as satisfying as seeing them all devoured by the hydra, but Rambrecht was content merely to have them delayed. If fortune continued to favour him, he would have the runefang long before the Wissenlanders finished digging.

The aristocrat turned, smiling as he saw the solid stone cairn that stood nearby. Fortune had smiled upon his decision to take the high ground. With his small crew of brigands and thugs, he hadn't been eager to risk a confrontation with the Wissenlanders in the canyon below. Instead they had opted to follow the progress of their enemies from the cliffs above. When Skanir began to lead the expedition up onto the cliffs, Rambrecht had a good view of the dwarf's destination long before any in the Wissenland company did. It would have taken a long climb to get down to the carved doorway in the mountainside, too long a climb to gain on the Wissenlanders.

Knowing this, and knowing a little about dwarf architecture, Rambrecht had set his scum looking for something like the cairn. Whatever their other faults, some of the bandits were quite accomplished woodsmen, and they had discovered the cairn in short order.

Removing a few of the massive stones revealed what Rambrecht hoped he would find, a narrow passage sloping down into the dark of the mountain. It was a ventilation shaft, constructed by the dwarfs to circulate air down to the workers constructing the tomb below. The same shafts would be used to extract the workers when they finished their labours, sealing the doors from the inside to better protect them from thieves. One of those exits would serve Rambrecht and his crew as an entrance.

The Averlander looked back down the cliff, laughing as he watched Kessler's men attack the blocking pile of rocks with a frenzied effort. Rambrecht laughed. Let them break their backs. By the time they forced their way inside, the runefang would already be on its way to Averheim, and he would be on the road to absolute power.

CHAPTER SEVENTEEN

THE FINEST WINE from the royal cellars tasted bitter to Count Eberfeld as he sat in the war room of his palace. All the comforts of Wissenberg were hollow to him now, less real than the horrors he had seen, the ghastly threat that continued to wreak havoc upon his land.

The sputtering torches cast weird shadows along the thick stone walls of the war room. Forgotten generals and long-dead knights seemed to stare accusingly at him from old tapestries and antique paintings. These were their people too, the descendants of his ancestors. It was a terrible weight, to be the one responsible for saving them, to preserve the legacy of the Merogens, to keep the realm of Wissenland from fading into the pages of history as had the realm of Solland before it.

Generals and captains gathered around the huge oak war table jumped as the count's fist slammed against the oak. The nobleman's fingers closed around one of the many maps littered on the table, holding it before his officers as though displaying something profane.

'Look at it, gentlemen!' the count demanded. 'If any man here can make sense of it, I'll give him his weight in gold!'

The men gathered around the table did not need to have the problem explained to them. They had been studying similar maps for days. Great black splotches marked those communities that Zahaak's legion had razed to the ground. There seemed no pattern or reason behind them. The wight had brought the full force of his legion against hamlets and villages that weren't even in the path of its march while ignoring entire cities that had watched the undead horde pass within sight of their walls. It was obvious that Zahaak was making some use of the roads and trails that dotted Wissenland, but it was strange the way the legion would sometimes follow a road for days, only to veer off and push through solid wilderness for weeks.

If there was a pattern to the legion's movements, no one had been able to fathom it. Indeed, many suspected that, as well as being undead, the general of the spectral army was also insane.

The turning point, for Count Eberfeld, had been Bergdorf. With all the careful preparations and defences, the city had been ignored by Zahaak, his legion converging on Neuwald instead. The attempt to break the legion's siege of Neuwald had proven disastrous, worse than disastrous, for now they knew the fate of those who fell to Zahaak's horde. The once proud Knights of the Southern Sword had been brought into abominable service as knights of Nagash, their corpses infused with the unholy semblance of life. How many others had been slaughtered only to swell the ranks of

Zahaak's army? It was a question that chilled the noble-man's very soul.

'We cannot afford any more half measures,' the count said, impelled to speak by the dark thoughts swirling in his head. 'Unless there is a reasonable chance of victory, no more lives are to be thrown away attacking the legion. Any town in its path is to be evacuated, at the point of a sword if need be.'

'How can we know if a town is in its path or not?' protested one of the generals. 'These fiends strike with-out pattern or reason! We can't just abandon half of Wissenland because they might show up!' The count raised an eyebrow at the emotional response, but let the outburst stand. They were all suffering from the strain, and courtly manners were the last thing that would bring a solution to the crisis.

Heads turned as the iron-bound door to the war room creaked open. The robed figure of Vadian, high priest of Morr, slowly crept into the room, his aged form casting an almost skeletal shadow against the brooding walls. A young disciple walked beside the old priest, his head trimmed into a tonsure above his white-trimmed robes. The acolyte's arms were filled with a collection of mouldering scrolls and wrinkled parch-ment. Vadian bowed before the seated officers and nobles, and then approached the far end of the table, where Count Eberfeld held court.

'Your excellency,' Vadian said, 'I think I have discov-ered something that may reveal the reason behind the enemy's campaign.'

The statement brought chuckles from the soldiers and barons seated around the table. Old hands at the art of war, these men had wracked their brains for any strat-egy that would make sense of the legion's advance through Wissenland. They had found none, not even the wanton bloodlust of an orc warlord or the feral hate of beastmen. Nothing militarily made any sense of Zahaak's movements.

'What have you found, father?' the count asked, directing a scowl at the chuckling officers to stifle their mirth.

Vadian nodded to his acolyte. The young priest set his burden of scrolls down on the table. Vadian leafed through them for a moment, and then unrolled one for the count to inspect. It was a map, a very old map, its edges frayed and tattered, much of it worm-eaten and crumbling into powder. Yet still it was unmistakably a map of Wissenland, the rivers standing stark against the frame of the Black and Grey Mountains. The count studied it for a long time, and then shook his head, not understanding what he should see.

'Notice the settlements, excellency,' Vadian prompted.

Count Eberfeld looked at the map again, the parchment crumbling under his fingers as realisation flashed through him. He looked at the more recent map, the one he had used to admonish his officers with. Again and again, he checked and compared the two, trying to make certain there was no mistake.

The settlements on Vadian's old map were the same as those that had been attacked by the legion. The ones that were absent were those Zahaak had ignored! Somehow the priest had discovered the answer. Count Eberfeld squinted harder at the old map, finding Neuwald, but seeing only an empty place where Bergdorf should be. Roads existed in places where not even a goat path now pierced the wilds. Where roads should be were only forest and glen.

'What does it mean?' Count Eberfeld asked. The room was silent, the earlier humour forgotten in the intensity of the count's question.

'This map dates from one hundred years after the reign of our Lord Sigmar,' Vadian stated, pressing a finger against the faded legend at the bottom of the scroll. 'Your excellency, this creature, this abomination, thinks it is still fighting against the Merogens, still helping its unspeakable master make war against Sigmar! The cities it has bypassed, the roads it ignores, it does so because in its mind they do not even exist! For Zahaak, all the centuries that have unfolded since it was destroyed by the dwarfs have never been. For Zahaak it is still the year 15, and he makes his war against the world of that time!'

Officers and noblemen rushed forward to inspect the now all-important map, looking anxiously to see if their own homes would be found, if their own cities had been marked for doom by a fiend fighting battles from millennia past. General Hock raised a grim face to his sovereign.

'Wissenberg,' Hock gasped. 'He'll follow the river straight to Wissenberg.'

Count Eberfeld nodded, feeling the horror of the revelation sink in. He rose from his chair, eyes watching the anxious faces staring back at him.

'We must evacuate the city!' Baron von Schwalb declared, his heavy features growing as pallid as the ermine trim of his cloak. 'We must petition Nuln and Altdorf for aid. Every vessel on the river, to the last scow, must be pressed into service to remove Wissenberg's wealth to safety.'

A wave of fear spread through the room, dozens of voices rising in panic. Few of the nobles assembled did not have property in the provincial capital, fewer still did not have family or friends among the city's inhabitants. For the others, the symbol of Wissenberg as the enduring strength of the realm was enough to unman them, the thought that the ancient stronghold would suffer the same fate as Neuwald and so many others.

'I won't run,' Count Eberfeld said. Though spoken in a soft, almost weary tone, his words brought silence to the room. Noblemen and officers looked at their sovereign, disbelief and horror on their faces. 'If we flee now, if we throw ourselves upon the charity of our neighbours, if we abandon our homes and our land to this evil, it will be the end of us. We may have our lives, but whatever heritage and dignity we can claim will be gone. We will have betrayed the blood in our veins, the line of our ancestors back to the first Merogen warriors. We will be a vagabond people, wretched and abhorred, no better than wandering Strigany thieves. Even if we come back, even if this shadow passes from Wissenland, there will be nothing for us here. Towns and villages can be rebuilt, but how can you rebuild the pride of a vanquished people? Would you have us become like Solland, a bitter tear and a lingering sorrow?'

'But Zahaak cannot be destroyed!' protested Petr Grebel. The priest of Myrmidia made the sign of his goddess as he spoke. 'One of my order was the only man to escape from Neuwald. He was there when the gates fell. He saw Baron Volstadt and his bodyguard cut their way through the legion's skeleton warriors, unto the armoured mass of its elite. He saw Zahaak enter the city, saw him defy the baron's men. The wight slaughtered many, but Baron Volstadt's guards would not break. At last they struck the wight down, hewing him with their swords, scattering his bones before the feet of their slain baron. Then he saw Zahaak rise again, rise from his own ruin, as terrible and monstrous as before. The horrified guards did not raise a hand against the resurrected wight, but stood gaping in terror even as he cut them down.'

'It is true, excellency,' one of the assembled captains shouted. 'I have heard that an assassin bearing a dagger blessed by the Sisters of Sigmar crept into the undead encampment and hacked the skull from Zahaak's body. Yet the next day the legion marched on, with the wight still at its head.'

'Some dark power protects this monster,' Baron von Schwald swore. 'The black power of Nagash!' he added, making the sign of the hammer as he spoke the profane name.

Count Eberfeld glowered at the frightened men. He had heard the rumours and tales before, the claims that Zahaak could not be killed. He had tried to fire his men with courage and determination, but hope was the only salve for the fear that ruled them.

'Zahaak was destroyed once before,' Vadian reminded the noblemen, 'put back into the grave for almost two millennia by the dwarfs. The runefang of Solland put him there. Grudge Settler brought the wight to ruin once. When Baron von Rabwald returns with it, the runefang will do so once again.'

Count Eberfeld could see the men around him trying to take encouragement from Vadian's words, but there was too much doubt and despair to overcome. Two centuries had passed since Grudge Settler was stolen by Gorbad Ironclaw. Men had searched in vain for the sword, lost their lives looking for it. Many believed it would never be seen by the eyes of men again. No, the promise of bringing Zahaak to destruction with the fabulous lost sword was too remote, too fantastic to bolster their courage. They needed something substantial, something certain, if they were to overcome their fear and stand with him against the wight lord. And stand they must, for if Wissenberg fell, Count Eberfeld knew that Wissenland would never rise again. It would be carved up between the feuding provinces, absorbed into the realms of other counts and princes. Like Solland and Drakwald before it, Wissenland would be nothing more than a memory.

The count let his hand fall to the jewelled scabbard that held the runefang of Wissenland. 'There's nothing the Grudge Settler can do that Blood Bringer can't do better,' Count Eberfeld swore, patting the hilt of his sword, steel in his voice as he stared into the eyes of each of the men gathered around him. 'We'll make this grave-cheating ghoul sorry it ever crawled out of its tomb.'

CHAPTER EIGHTEEN

'STOP FOOLING WITH the damn ogre and help us!' Raban's furious voice rose above the grunts and curses of the men labouring at the rock pile. They'd been working at the mound of rubble for hours, tempers falling ever fouler the longer the labour progressed. Kessler clung to the belief that this, indeed, was the right tomb. Right tomb or not, the promise of treasure had quelled complaints from other quarters. Only Eugen hadn't been fired by the promise of looting whatever riches the orcs had buried with their warlord. Already branded a traitor, the knight couldn't realistically expect any share of the plunder, or any part in the glory should they find the runefang. Kessler had been perplexed by the knight's bravado during the fight against the hydra, but Valdner soon set him right. Even a traitor was threatened by the mindless beast, and Eugen had acted to protect his own hide, not save the expedition. The mercenary captain set Anselm to watch over him, trusting that the Sigmarite would make a more attentive custodian than Minhea had been.

Theodo looked up as Raban challenged him. Following the fight with the hydra, the cook had raced to his wounded friend, tending Ghrum's leg as best he could. Though the ogre was covered in scratches and burns, it was the deep injury he'd sustained to his leg that troubled Theodo. He'd seen Ghrum take a lot of punishment over their years together, but never had he seen so noxious a wound. The hydra's claw had stabbed clear through the meat, scraping against the bone. It bled profusely, forcing the halfling to make a tourniquet for the mangled limb while he tried to stitch it back together. Valdner considered the halfling's ministrations to be a lost cause, a sentiment that most in the camp shared. Ghrum was beyond an opinion either way, fading in and out of consciousness.

'Let him bleed out already and get over here and help us,' Raban snapped when he saw that he had Theodo's attention. Theodo scowled back at the mercenary.

'If he dies, you're next,' the halfling promised, darkly. The threat brought a laugh from Raban. The axeman threw the stone he was hefting in Theodo's general direction.

'Any time burrow-rat,' Raban grinned, turning back to his work. He laughed again when the rock he moved exposed a strip of bronze. He tugged it away, causing a small slide that brought curses from the workers lower down the pile.

'Captain!' he called, pointing triumphantly at the exposed section. Valdner and Kessler approached the axeman. They could see that the bronze panel was badly dented and warped by the avalanche. Raban drew their attention to the cold, clammy draft.

'The rocks broke down the doors,' Skanir agreed, climbing stones to join them. He studied the twisted bronze, and then forced another rock from the pile. Instead of revealing more of the door, he exposed a vacancy, a section of blackness that betokened the crypt beyond.

'Another hour of this and we should be through,' the dwarf promised. As he made the declaration a black-fletched arrow glanced from the rocks beside his head. The attack had barely registered among the men before savage war cries were roaring in their ears.

A pack of hulking orcs was charging up the narrow path to the canyon, blades and clubs waving above their heads. Kessler saw the gruesome standard of Uhrghul Skullcracker rising above the throng, the ghastly trophy rack that marked the presence of the infamous warlord. A handful of wiry goblins was already on the plateau, ahead of the rushing orcs, crude bows of bone and gut clasped in their hands. The goblins laughed cruelly as they saw the fear in their enemies' eyes, and let fly another salvo at the men. One mercenary fell victim to the slovenly bow fire, his belly punctured by an arrow. The man dropped in a screaming heap.

Valdner barked commands. Men leapt from the rock pile, scrambling to reclaim the weapons they had set aside when they started their work. Seeing their foes armed, the goblins abandoned their archery, scurrying behind fallen rocks, content to wait for the orcs to confront the men.

The orcs were not long in coming. Valdner had time to arrange the men in a ragged skirmish line before the brutes reached the plateau. The mercenary captain did not seem to have any great illusions about their chances. Blade for blade, they were no match for the ferocious greenskin warriors. In desperation, Valdner snapped a command to Anselm and Eugen, ordering the prisoner and his guard to continue clearing the doorway. Within the confines of the crypt, they might at least prevent the orcs from completely overwhelming them.

Kessler did not give the mercenary's hope undue attention. If the plan was to hold off the orcs until the door was clear, then he didn't think their efforts would buy them enough time. It would be all they could do just to keep the orcs from crashing through them like a stampede. The swordsman shook his head. He'd always known his doom would be to die with a sword in his hand. There was a rough justice that he would meet his end fighting against the kind of creatures that had destroyed his face.

Howling like blood-mad wolves, the orcs surged onto the plateau, their rusty axes gleaming crimson in the dying sunlight. Iron-shod boots ripped at the earth as the immense greenskins rushed towards their prey. As Kessler watched them come, something in his mind snapped, rebelling against the fatalism that had claimed him. With his own war cry screaming from his chest, Kessler ran to meet the hulking brutes. His heavy greatsword, its black tassels dancing around his wrists, described a great arc as he swung it at the foremost orc, tearing the brute's belly open clean to the spine. The roaring monster crumpled, folding in half as his body collapsed around the hideous wound. Kessler's boot cracked into its skull, smashing its jaw and knocking the mangled orc prone. The dying brute was trampled beneath the iron heels of its charging comrades.

Kessler turned to face a horn-helmed warrior that lurched at him from the ruin of its fallen fellow. Before he could meet the monster's axe, a heavy warhammer cracked into the orc's ribs, bits of scavenged plate and looted chainmail flying from the impact. Bloody froth exploded from the orc's fanged mouth and it stumbled back. Kessler saw Skanir follow it, raising his weapon to finish the job he had started. The orc lashed out at the dwarf with a sloppy sweep of its axe. Skanir skirted from the path of the murderous stroke, leaving the orc extended and unbalanced. Before the monster could recover, Skanir brought his hammer plummeting down in an overhead blow, bursting the orc's helm and smashing its head into pulp.

All around him, Kessler found others meeting the charge of the orcs. Emboldened by his example, perhaps gripped by the same impulse of defiance in the face of certain doom, soldiers and mercenaries were grappling with the powerful greenskins. The sudden counterattack caught the orcs by surprise. Creatures ruled more by instinct than strategy, they were slow to react to change. In those first few moments, the skill and training of the men prevailed against the raw, brute power of the orcs. Five of the monsters were brought down, slashed by halberd, smashed by hammer and stabbed by sword. The first few seconds of battle belonged to the men.

It was not enough.

The smell of blood, the crash of battle, the feel of steel cracking against steel broke any confusion that had entered the dull minds of the orcs. Raw, brute power asserted itself in gory magnificence. One soldier was cut in half by the sweep of an orc cleaver, the hulking mass of sharpened steel carving through him as if he was a butchered steer. A mercenary found his arm snapped like a twig beneath the impact of an orcish bludgeon, bones bursting through the links of his mail under the power of the blow. Another mercenary had both hands chopped from his body by the slashing edge of an orc sword as he slashed at its owner with a halberd. Before the man could begin to scream, his attacker lunged forwards, closing its fanged jaws around its victim's throat.

Foot by foot, the orcs pushed their foes back, the sheer mass of their huge bodies allowing them to bully their human adversaries across the plateau. The dark-skinned bulk of Uhrghul rose up behind the press of battle, goading his warriors on. The warlord barked a command to his warriors and the thick, violent laughter of the orcs rose above the screams of dying men.

The ferocity of the orcs seemed to abate. Their attacks were pulled short, jabbing at men to keep them moving, but without the intention of cleaving flesh and smashing bone. Those with shields used them to batter their enemies, pushing them back, turning them aside. Kessler could almost believe that the monsters were fighting defensively, trying to conserve their strength, but it was virtually unheard of for orcs to hold back in battle. Then the first wailing shriek sounded from the edge of the plateau. A mercenary had been pushed back too far, his feet finding nothing beneath them but empty air. The coarse laughter of the orcs rumbled again as the man's scream faded with his fall. With sadistic cunning, the orcs had turned the men, moving them so that their backs would no longer be to the doors of the crypt but to the edge of the plateau. Certain of victory over their outnumbered foes, the orcs had decided to make sport with them, to give them the choice of dying upon steel or plummeting to the canyon far below.

Valdner made the same realisation, shouting orders to his men, trying to reverse the terrible path the orcs were trying to herd them down. Men redoubled their efforts to break through the line of green monsters that pressed upon them, but neither training nor discipline could offset the strength and mass of the orcs. Foot by hideous foot, they were forced back, pushed closer and closer to the precipice.

EUGEN AND ANSELM watched in horror from the rock pile as their comrades were forced towards the edge of the plateau by the orcs. The Sigmarite made the sign of the hammer, praying to his god for deliverance, for triumph over the ancient foes of humanity. Eugen paid the mercenary's prayers little notice. Seizing a rock, he brought it cracking against the man's leather hat, dropping him senseless to the ground. The knight quickly removed Anselm's sword from its sheath. For an instant, he looked at the doorway behind him. A black vacancy now gaped near the top, a space just big enough for a man to squirm through. He immediately dismissed the thought.

Already branded a traitor and a murderer, Eugen would not earn the epithet of coward. The Knights of the Southern Sword had been scoured from the land, driven into the dust that had claimed Solland. He was the last. The order would fade with him, and in time even its memory would vanish. He was bitter that everything would end with him. He had hoped he might see the legendary Sun-Blade, the Runefang of Solland, set eyes on the sacred talisman he had served for most of his life. That hope was gone, however, and all that remained was to acquit himself well in his final moments, and perhaps to buy some hope for his comrades. He had not betrayed them before, and he would not do so now.

Eugen saw the iron-fanged hulk of Uhrghul Skull-cracker towering behind his warriors, urging the monsters to brutal effect with his deep bellows and roaring curses. The knight's fist clenched tighter around the hilt of Anselm's sword. Killing the warlord was the one thing that might throw the orcs into disorder and allow his friends to escape the deadly trap. The orcs were wholly fixated upon pushing their enemies over the precipice, and had totally ignored the two men. No greenskins stood between him and the warlord, and a quick sprint would bring him face to face with the malevolent Uhrghul. Eugen grimaced at the thought. His entire order had failed to destroy the monster, and now he would have to do it on his own. The longsword in his hand looked as threatening as a paring knife beside the enormous armoured monster. Still, no other plan of action suggested itself to him.

Just as he started his run, motion beyond the warlord drew Eugen's attention. At first, he thought he had seen a goblin scrambling among the rocks, but when the movement was repeated, he saw that it was something very different. The heap of boulders and rubble that had buried the hydra was shifting. While he watched, he saw a serpentine neck clear the rubble, waving dizzily in the air. Another soon followed it, and then a clawed paw was pulled free. Eugen felt a chill of horror as he realised that the hydra yet lived. Then a thrill of hope surged through him as a new, mad plan occurred to him.

The knight bolted from the doorway, racing past the battleline. Several orcs turned away from the foes before them to howl at him as he ran past, yet none were quick enough to block his path. Uhrghul was turning towards him, glowering at the armoured man who charged at him. The warlord lifted his brutal weapon, ready to dash the life from the knight. Eugen ducked beneath the murderous blow, slashing at the orc with the slender sword he held. The tip scraped across Uhrghul's face, dark blood beading behind the blade's sweep. The warlord roared in rage, driving his weapon again at the knight. Eugen ducked away from the attack, jeering at the gruesome beast.

Uhrghul snarled, drool dripping from his tusked jaws. The orc smashed his weapon against his chest in a savage display of fury, and then lunged forward, pursuing the knight who dared to mock him. Other orcs broke away from the fight to assist the warlord, lessening the pressure against the men still struggling on the battleline. Taxing his every muscle, Eugen continued to avoid the warlord's powerful blows, striking back at the brute when the opportunity presented itself. The cuts were not enough to cripple the warlord, just enough to keep his rage and attention focused upon Eugen.

Eugen led the orc across the plateau, risking a look over his shoulder whenever he could. The knight smiled. In a way, the plan was a grim parody of the sport the orcs had been making with their enemies, except that the monsters didn't know it yet.

The hydra was free from the pile of rubble, its reptilian heads waving around in confusion, still stunned by the violence that had crashed down upon it. Eugen jabbed one last slash at Uhrghul, opening a wound in the orc's thigh. Uhrghul was so intent upon the knight and so consumed by anger that he failed to notice the hydra until he had been lured to the base of the rockslide that had buried the beast. As Eugen danced away

from him for the last time, the orc's crimson eyes
strayed from the retreating knight, widening in alarm as
the writhing nest of the hydra's heads filled his vision.

Eugen turned his back to the shocked orc. He shifted
his hold on his sword, gripping it by the blade just
before the guard. With all the strength still in his body,
he hurled the improvised javelin at the disoriented
hydra. The steel stabbed into one of the necks, sinking
deep into the scaly flesh. The writhing nest of the reptile's heads snapped around, the fresh pain from this
new injury cutting through the confusion that gripped
it. The hydra's snake-like eyes narrowed with malice, as
one of its beaked mouths snapped open. Eugen opened
his arms wide and laughed as the concentrated flame of
the hydra engulfed him.

Let Uhrghul Skullcracker try to add these skulls to his
totem, was the thought that filled the knight's mind as
death's fiery breath swept over him.

THEODO DROVE HIS dagger into the goblin's sharp face,
piercing its eye. The greenskin flopped away from him,
rolling on the ground in agony. Some of its fellows
actually paused to point and laugh at their maimed
comrade before turning their attention back on the
halfling. While the orcs had charged into battle with the
men, their goblin allies had looked for softer prey, prey
less likely to present them with a fight. The small
halfling and the insensible Ghrum looked to them like
a gift from Mork, the sneaky greenskin god of cunning
and trickery.

He could have run, and tried to find cover, but
Theodo was not about to abandon his stricken friend.
For a time, he had been able to keep the goblins at bay
with his keen archery, but while he had been sticking

arrows in the goblins to the fore, others had crept upon him from the flank. Now they were all over him, crawling across Ghrum's body like lice in their effort to settle their score with the halfling. Two of the goblins had discovered that Theodo knew how to use a blade as well as a bow. Unfortunately, the others didn't seem terribly impressed.

A goblin with a crooked sword and a chewed nose circled Theodo, chopping at the halfling's feet with its blade, laughing at the way he hopped to avoid the biting edge. Another, wearing a cowl of animal skin and a shirt of finger bones jabbed at him with a spear, trying to push him into the flint axe of a third goblin. Blind in one eye, the axe goblin made wildly inaccurate strikes at the halfling's head, almost overbalancing with each attack.

Theodo felt his blood boil at the mocking, degrading laughter of the goblins. He was sure it was quite a novelty to the spiteful beasts to find an enemy smaller than them. Used to the humiliating disdain of humans, the snickering contempt of the goblins was more than he could endure. He struggled to keep his wits about him, to prevent himself from throwing his life away in some reckless assault. That would only play right into the goblins' hands.

When he looked up at Ghrum, however, all restraint left the halfling. More goblins were swarming over the ogre, stabbing at him with cruel knives and cutting him with barbed hooks, giggling like fiends all the while. Snarling like a cornered beast, Theodo flung himself at the spear-wielding goblin. The monster's weapon stabbed into his side, but Theodo had the satisfaction of splitting its face with his dagger. Then he was crushed to the ground as a pair of wiry arms wrapped around his middle, squeezing the air from him. A fist cracked against his skull and red spots danced before his eyes. More hands closed around him, hoisting him upwards. The whispery, cackling voices of the goblins filled his ears, their laughter scraping against his nerves. Suddenly, they dumped him on the ground and pinned him in place.

The one-eyed goblin with the stone axe shuffled into view, grinning down at Theodo. He screamed as the goblin raised its axe over its head, and then brought the weapon smashing down. Instead of crushing his skull, it smashed against the ground inches away. The goblins laughed again and the axe was raised once more.

A great growl drowned out the cackles and titters of the goblins like a peal of thunder. The ground trembled as a huge shape rose, spilling goblins to the earth. Others clung to charred garments as the figure picked itself from the ground. Ghrum's massive hands pulled the clinging goblins free, crushing the squealing horrors into a paste in his massive fists.

The amusement the goblins had found in tormenting a lone halfling and a comatose ogre vanished with that first bellowing roar. Goblins scattered like rats fleeing a sinking ship, disappearing with a speed that seemed almost sorcerous. The goblins holding Theodo hesitated for a moment, but one look at the grisly residue that Ghrum wiped from his hands was enough to hasten their flight. The one-eyed greenskin was last to turn and run, crashing into a boulder in its hurry. Ghrum brought his foot stomping down on the fallen goblin, grinding it into the earth.

Theodo clutched at the dripping wound in his side, trying to ignore the pain. He looked up at Ghrum and smiled. 'Feeling better?' he quipped. Ghrum seemed to consider the question a long time, but at last he gave his friend a nebulous nod.

Theodo turned his attention to the battle with the orcs. He was surprised to find most of them at the far end of the plateau, at least until he saw the flickers of flame shooting through their ranks. The hydra hadn't been killed by Skanir's trap after all. He hoped it wasn't treacherous of him to wish it well against the greenskins.

Kessler and a handful of survivors were trying to fight their way clear of a few orcs that stubbornly insisted on pursuing the battle. Now the men outnumbered the orcs, but the contest still looked very much in doubt. Theodo looked up at Ghrum, and then pointed at the orcs menacing the men. Ghrum gave him another nod. With only a few steps, the ogre was upon the orcs, his enormous hands closing around the necks of two greenskins. Before the monsters could begin to struggle, Ghrum smashed their skulls together and threw the bodies over the edge of the plateau.

The ogre's timely intervention was just what the men need to tip the balance. The handful of orcs still fighting against them were not enough to combat both groups of adversaries. They were quickly overwhelmed, dying gamely beneath the men's steel and Ghrum's crushing fists.

Even so, the cost of battle had been hideous. Of the expedition, only Kessler, Ottmar and Skanir remained. Valdner still had Raban and Anselm, already starting to recover from the blow that Eugen had inflicted upon him. Each of the men looked across the plateau to where the orcs swarmed around the fire-spewing hydra.

'Whoever wins that fight,' Valdner said, 'we're in no shape to oppose them.'

Kessler looked at the doorway and the rubble still blocking it. 'We'll head down there,' he decided.

'Do you still think we can get the runefang for Count Eberfeld?' asked Ottmar. Kessler shook his head and smiled.

'No, but at least if we get to the tomb we can die rich.'

CHAPTER NINETEEN

WITH GHRUM'S POWERFUL assistance, the entrance to the war-crypt was cleared. The battered survivors gave one last look at the fight still raging across the plateau. The charred carcasses of orcs were littered everywhere, yet still the greenskins stubbornly attacked the hissing, shrieking hydra. As Valdner said, it was a contest none of them should stick around to see the finish of. Torches were hastily crafted from garments and weapons stripped from the dead. Skanir's tinder box soon provided them with flame.

Holding their torches before them like talismans to ward away the sinister, cloying darkness of the crypt, the men descended into the ancient tunnel that stabbed into the depths of the mountain.

The tunnel had been hewn from the living stone of the mountain, vaulted in the ponderous, heavy manner of dwarf construction. The large scale of the hallway allowed the men to easily navigate the wide, arched passage, but the ceiling was too low for Ghrum, forcing the ogre into an awkward, uncomfortable crouch. His great bulk almost completely filled the corridor, forcing the others to range ahead of him.

'At least we can close the door behind us,' observed Valdner. It was true, whether orc or hydra, any foe descending into the tomb would have to get past the living barrier of Ghrum's body to reach the rest.

'Keep your eyes open,' snapped Skanir, directing an intense gaze at each of the others. 'The goblins will have saved the deadliest traps for the crypt. The stuff down in the canyon and on the plateau will look like child's toys compared to what we're apt to find down here. Look at everything, and then look at it again. Ask me before you even take a breath and we might, *might* live to reach the tomb.' Skanir pointed at Theodo with the peen of his warhammer. 'Stay with the ogre. Keep him back a good twenty yards from the rest of us. I'll mark any triggers we find. Do your best to get him around them. Warn us if you can't.' Theodo nodded weakly, still clutching at his injured side. The halfling hobbled back to join Ghrum while the rest of the company followed Skanir's lead.

The clammy darkness of the tunnel oozed around them like a living thing, tendrils of shadow reaching out to smother their torches. The walls, like those of the canyon, had been richly engraved, bas-relief figures standing guard every few feet. These, too, had suffered the malicious amusement of the goblins, defaced by knife and cudgel, filth scrawled across them in chalk, blood and even fouler pigments. To the sinister aura of death and the hoary weight of time was added the poignant melancholy of things lost and defiled.

It did not take long for Skanir to order the little column to a halt. The dwarf dropped on hands and knees, inspecting something that was all but invisible in the gloom. He followed his line of inquiry to the wall, peering intently at the defaced lines of runes. A smile twitched at the dwarf's stern visage. He lowered his torch, allowing the light to play off the object that his sharp gaze had picked out in the dark. It was a line, a stretch of wire pulled tight across the corridor.

Skanir held up his hand, motioning for the others to keep back. He set his hammer down on the floor beside him. Removing his pipe and a lace from his boot, the dwarf hurriedly made a crude grapple. Leaning back, he tossed the pipe at the tripwire. The momentum of the tethered missile caused it to wrap the lace around the stretched wire. Skanir gritted his teeth and pulled back on the lace. The pressure tugged the wire out of line. Instantly, a bright flash of metal flickered in the darkness. With a howl, Skanir leapt forwards, smashing his foot down on something that started to rise from the floor.

Kessler came forwards. As he advanced, Skanir motioned for him to bring the warhammer he'd left behind. Returning the weapon to the dwarf, Kessler saw what Skanir had captured. It was a cruel, axe-like blade, ground down to an incredible thinness. It was fitted to an iron shaft, which drooped from a small crevice in the wall. It was in this hidden, finger-thin fissure that the deadly blade had been waiting, ready to spring when the tripwire was disturbed. Only the pressure of Skanir's foot prevented the blade from snapping back into its hiding place. Skanir accepted the warhammer with a grunt. Taking it in both hands, he brought the weapon smashing down into the axe head. The thin, ancient metal broke with a dull snap. Satisfied, Skanir removed his foot, allowing the iron shaft to whip back into the wall.

'Look at everything twice,' Skanir growled, glancing across the anxious faces of the men. A smile spread beneath his beard and he swung his warhammer up onto his shoulder. 'Then get my opinion before you decide it's safe.'

KESSLER HAD LOST track of how many times Skanir had called them to a halt. Each stop was an eternity of tension and horror, never knowing what new, ghastly trick the goblins had left behind to guard their warlord's bones. Spears that shot out from floor and ceiling, poisonous darts fitted into the walls, sections of floor that collapsed into the sort of hideous pits they'd seen in the canyon, all paled beside some of the more inventive measures the fiends had taken. The corridor had blazed into diabolical life for several minutes, the result of an incendiary fungus that the goblins had cultivated along one stretch of the tunnel, a trick that had nearly claimed even the sharp-eyed Skanir. The dwarf had explained the workings of another, even more violent trap. He'd found a grotesque, charred thing splattered against one of the walls. It had taken some time to determine that it was something like the hydra they had fought, perhaps some youngling of the monstrous tribe. It had fallen prey to the goblin trap long ago, its flesh dried almost into leather against its crumbling bones.

The trap that had claimed it was hideous in its cunning. Skanir indicated a small hole in the wall, and then pointed out little pieces of stone littering the floor. The goblins would make a hole in the wall, a little niche where they would then burn certain dried fungi and moulds. While these noxious weeds were still smouldering, they would seal the niche with plaster and rock. The smoke from the fungi would be trapped within the niche, making the air tighter and closer with every instant. A tripwire would be fitted to the cap sealing the niche. When some unfortunate stumbled across it, the cap would be pulled loose and the trapped smoke would escape from its prison with thunderous, explosive force.

The explanation was more than simple instruction, it was to impress on the men the importance of avoiding such a trap. One misstep could kill them all. Kessler felt a chill when Skanir pointed down the tunnel with his torch. He could see two more of the capstones in the small section of the hall illuminated by the reach of the light. Gesturing for the men to wait, Skanir headed forward to mark the danger areas.

'Wishing you were back fighting the crow feeders?' Kessler turned at the question. Valdner stood beside him, a set expression on the mercenary's face. The swordsman tried to look past that expression to see the thoughts brewing behind Valdner's eyes.

'I am where I need to be,' Kessler said, putting as much firmness as he could muster into his voice.

Valdner shook his head and smiled. 'If it's the right crypt,' he objected. He looked aside at the mummified reptile. 'It would be a shame to wind up like that for nothing.'

Kessler felt the hairs bristle on his neck. His doubt was crushed beneath the sudden irritation he felt. 'This is the right tomb,' he said with greater conviction.

Valdner looked away, watching Skanir picking his way through the tunnel ahead. 'There isn't any gold, is there?'

The question took Kessler by storm. He'd expected it for sometime after leaving Fritzstadt, had lain awake at night dreading it. To hear it now, to hear it in the heart of the Black Mountains, swallowed within the murk of an ancient tomb, stunned him. He'd tried to prepare something, some lie that he could tell the mercenaries, some appeal to their humanity. Whatever he'd thought he would say was lost to him now, silenced by the unreality of hearing the question. They had all risked so much and travelled so far. They had all lost so much.

Valdner nodded in response to Kessler's silence, sadness pulling at his face. 'I suspected as much in Fritzstadt,' he said. 'I'll have to talk to my men about this, what's left of them.'

Kessler caught at the mercenary's arm. 'There is still the treasure in the crypt,' he hissed. There were few enough of them already; he couldn't lose Valdner and his men.

'I don't think so,' Valdner said. 'Think about all the traps we've seen: all small, all easy to avoid if you know what you're looking for. There were no rockfalls, and nothing to block the passage or prevent a careful person from getting past, even if the traps were triggered. Whatever treasure was down here, I'd bet my bottom groat the goblins who put it there came back and stole it as soon as there weren't any orcs watching them.' He nodded at the hydra splattered against the wall. 'That thing got in here somehow, probably the same way the goblins got back out. Dwarfs build to last, but goblins are fair diggers too.'

The observation was like a stab in the chest to Kessler. The fleeting hope he'd nursed, the desperate need to believe this was the right place, the reckless conviction that somehow Carlinda had guided him here, all of it drained out of him. Even if everything he believed was right, there was still no hope. If the runefang had ever been here, if this was indeed the tomb of Gordreg Throatripper, then it had been stolen already, carried off by goblin looters, gods alone knew how long ago.

'It's hopeless then,' Kessler groaned. 'Even if it was ever here, it's not here now.' He looked up and stared hard into Valdner's eyes. 'If you knew there was nothing down here, why did you follow us into the crypt?'

Valdner smiled and laughed. 'You might have forgotten our playmates on the plateau, but I haven't. Whoever wins that fracas is going to be looking for blood. Down here, with solid stone to watch the flanks, I think we have a good chance to take more than we give. Besides, using a tomb to make a last stand appeals to the poetry in my soul.'

The remark brought a chuckle from Kessler. He shook his head again. He found it hard to read Valdner, the man was as much a mystery to him now as when he had encountered him in Fritzstadt. He didn't like mysteries. As Baron von Rabwald's champion, he'd never had much reason to puzzle over a man's motivations. Who he had to kill and why were always clearly defined for him before he unsheathed his sword. The mercenary captain, however, refused to fit neatly into any category that Kessler tried to class him in.

'I'll go talk with my men,' Valdner repeated, jabbing a thumb over his shoulder to where Anselm and Raban were holding a conversation with Ottmar. 'Don't worry, we'll stick with you. It's not like we're going to get a better offer.' The statement started as a joke, but before he finished speaking, a hardness came into his eyes. He lowered his voice. 'Keep your eyes open. You might have tapped the wrong man with Eugen.'

Kessler was still contemplating the warning as Valdner stalked back to speak with his men.

UHRGHUL HOWLED HIS fury to the stars, hurling the heavy orc cleaver at the retreating monster. The huge mass of butchering steel struck the hydra's flank, sinking into its armoured flesh. The creature's heads, those still imbued with some semblance of life, reared back in a wail of pain. Uhrghul took no satisfaction from the reptile's injury. Of concern to him was the fact that the blow had failed to stop it. Snarling, he stooped to another of his dead warriors, ripping an axe free from a charred hand.

The hydra leapt at the wall of the cliff, sinking the claws of its three good legs into the stone. Bleeding from dozens of wounds, gore bubbling from the severed stumps of heads and tail, one leg dangling broken and mangled, the hydra had lost any taste for the fight. It scrambled across the rock, displaying the strength if not the speed and agility of its earlier descent. Its intent was the same crevice from which it had lurked above the doorway.

The orc warlord saw the black mouth of the cave. Roaring, he threw the big axe at the fleeing monster. The cumbersome missile glanced off the rocks. The hydra scrambled to the opening, twisting its mangled bulk into the cave. A last glimpse of its bleeding tail, and then it was gone. A halberd crashed against the stones an instant later, bouncing away and clattering to the floor of the plateau.

Uhrghul spun around, frustration and bloodlust burning in his narrowed eyes. The warlord's armour was dented and battered from the fight, the flesh of his right side burned a still darker hue by the hydra's fiery breath.

Blood dripped from his left hand, where one of the hydra's beaks had shorn away a pair of fingers. One tusk, chipped by the hydra's flailing necks, hung broken from the corner of his mouth. Already a gruesome sight to his warriors, Uhrghul's hideous wounds only increased their fearful respect. They backed away as he prowled towards them. Uhrghul ignored them all, except for the fur-hatted orc who had thrown the halberd.

'What you do?' Uhrghul demanded of the warrior. He waved his hand at the cave above the crypt. 'The lizard gone.'

The harsh tones had only just rumbled free from Uhrghul's massive chest when the warlord's massive hands were closed around the nervous warrior's head. The orc beat savagely at Uhrghul with its fists, but the warlord maintained the murderous pressure on the warrior's skull. There was a sickening pop and the fists flailing at him fell limp. Uhrghul ran his tongue across the blood that splashed into his face, increasing the pressure, not stopping until his palms clapped together in the gory mush.

The warlord turned away from the flopping body of his dead minion. The rest of his mob, what remained of them, watched him with cringing, fearful eyes. Uhrghul snorted derisively. Fear didn't matter to him, so long as they respected him. A warlord without respect wasn't a warlord for long. The casual slaughter of their fellow would remind the other orcs that he was in charge, and why.

Uhrghul took stock of the situation. He'd lost a lot of good warriors fighting against the fire-spitting lizard. That didn't bother him; a good scrap was worth losing some lives. What angered him was that the lizard had escaped. There was no trophy to add to his totem, no hide to tan into armour and shield, no meat to add to the pot.

The orc grimaced, spitting at the cave the hydra had fled into. He still had a dozen warriors, more than enough to fish the creature from its hole. Maybe they could round up a few of the goblins and get them to rig up some sort of ladder to reach the hole. The weedy wretches had scampered off at the first sign of a real fight, but they'd be back soon enough to claim a pick of the plunder.

The thought of plunder brought Uhrghul's gaze lower. The orc grunted angrily as he saw the gaping entrance to the crypt. None of his orcs had opened the tomb, and the hydra had fled into the cave. That meant some of the humans had escaped, creeping down into the crypt to steal the treasure.

Uhrghul snarled, wincing at the pain from his shattered tusk. Stabbing a hand into his mouth, he ripped the offending tooth from its socket. He pressed his tongue against his gum to stifle the flow of blood. The humans were down there, trying to rob him of his treasure. Well, he'd have something to say about that!

'You lot!' Uhrghul bellowed at his surviving warriors, a bubble of blood trickling from his face as he spoke. 'Down the dwarf-hole! There's humies need killin'!'

CHAPTER TWENTY

NOT FAR BEYOND the deadly gas traps left behind by the goblins, Skanir again called a halt. This time, however, the dwarf stopped them not to warn of another trap, but to announce the end of the road. The tunnel widened before them, expanding to nearly twice its previous size, its vaulted ceiling stretching into the murk high overhead. A pair of immense iron doors loomed in the far wall, richly engraved with runes and sculptures. Despite the best efforts of the greenskins, the image of the long-dead king of Karag Dar was clearly visible. Again, Kessler noted the massive axe the dwarf held, rather than the sword he had expected to find. Bigger than life and cast in iron, Isen Fallowbeard stared forbiddingly from the door of his tomb.

Skanir stepped forward, running a reverent hand across the figure of the ancient king. The others were not so restrained. At the threshold of the tomb, with the dim hope of treasure still refusing to die from their hearts, the men rushed at the door, caution overwhelmed by greed. The thought of goblin traps paled beneath the lustre of imagined gold. Kessler joined in the rush, determined to discover for himself whether the runefang was there or not, to discover whether Ernst and Carlinda and all the others had died in vain.

The iron doors were much like those at the entrance of the war-crypt, bent and twisted by the orcs who had violated this place. They leaned against each other like weary children, their abused hinges slowly pulling away from their settings in the wall. Scraps of iron and bronze had been hammered into them to reseal the tomb after the orcs had dumped the body of their warlord inside. Kessler was not surprised to find that they had been pried away in the light of Valdner's suspicions that goblins had returned to loot their dead master's grave.

The men pushed open the abused doors, leaving Skanir in the antechamber to continue his study of the runes that covered them. The flickering light cast by the torches did not penetrate far into the chamber beyond, its high ceiling lost in the shadows, its far walls beyond the reach of the light. What they saw was enough to make them thankful for the darkness.

No gleaming piles of gold, no overflowing chests of silver, no heaps of rubies and diamonds greeted them. What they found was the musty stink of ancient death, the lingering odour of old bones and crumbling leather. The floor was littered with shards of bone, the empty sockets of smashed skulls staring at them wherever they turned. Shattered skeletons were everywhere, so thoroughly destroyed that it was only with some difficulty that Kessler decided they had belonged to dwarfs. Skanir had said that, as a king, Isen Fallowbeard would have been buried with his hammerers, those of the royal guard who had fallen with him in battle. When the orcs despoiled this place, they had not spared their fury on the bones of their enemies. He wondered which of the shattered skulls grinning at them had belonged to the king.

Shards of bone crunched beneath Kessler's boots as he moved into the tomb. Wherever he turned, it was the same, nothing but the wreckage left behind by the greenskins. Not a strip of mail, a scrap of steel or a piece of gold had escaped the looters. If the dwarfs of Isen Fallowbeard's time had developed the practice of filling their teeth with silver, then even these had been taken. Black despair crushed his last, desperate hope. If the runefang had ever been here, it was long gone.

Even as he turned away, the glitter of steel arrested Kessler's attention. He swung around, to be certain that his eyes had not imagined the gleam. No, he had not been deceived. It was there, gleaming from the shadows. More bone crunched under his feet as he ran towards it. The light from his torch gradually resolved shapes in the darkness, the smashed and broken debris of dwarf sepulchres. There were hundreds of them, all around the tomb, but it was the one at the centre that had drawn his attention. The king's casket must have stood here. The orcs had been especially violent destroying it, breaking the stone casket into great blocks, and fashioning a crude throne from them. The skeleton of a huge orc sat upon it, colossal even in such a desiccated state.

It was Gordreg Throatripper, ancient lieutenant of the Ironfang. The twinkle of steel caught by his torch had come from this decayed liche. The goblins might have looted everything else of worth in the tomb, but the craven creatures had not dared to despoil Gordreg, even in death. The warlord still wore his armour of steel scales and his helmet of bronze plates and iron horns. The enormous weapons he had carried in life rested against the sides of his throne: a mammoth axe with more steel in it than a suit of plate armour, a massive spiked club with a head bigger than that of an ox, and a ghastly looking flail that the ages had crumbled into an echo of its former terror.

Kessler looked at the weapons closely, circling around them, trying to find the one weapon that legend claimed Gordreg had inherited from his infamous master. He shifted the club, letting it crash to the floor with a dull echo. He kicked away the remains of the flail, scattering it along the side of the throne. He tried to move the axe, its weight defying even his efforts to move it. Gaining control of himself, he abandoned his futile efforts.

The runefang was not in the tomb.

Accepting that truth, Kessler looked again at the skeleton. This time he noted the peculiar positioning of its hands, as though Gordreg were holding something across his lap. In his mind's eye, he could almost see what it was, a slender length of dwarf-forged steel, almost too small for the huge fist of an orc. It had been here! This was the place!

Something else impressed itself on Kessler's mind in that moment. Dust hung heavily on the skeleton, tarnishing its armour and almost covering its weapons, but the warlord's lap was clean. The runefang hadn't been stolen by goblins long ago, it had been taken more recently.

How recently, was revealed to the swordsman when cold, sardonic laughter echoed from the darkness.

'LOOKING FOR SOMETHING?' a snide, gloating voice asked, rising from the shadows. Kessler saw a man, tall and straight, clothed in a suit of fine chain, with a sneer twisting his classical features. The swordsman let his gaze linger on the man for only an instant, and then his eyes were drawn to what he held in his hand. Despite the dirt that covered it, despite the nest of bones and other barbaric talismans that were tied around its hilt, Kessler could not mistake the weapon that the stranger carried. He had seen Count Eberfeld's blade too many times to fail to recognise its twin. The man who had challenged him from the shadows carried the missing runefang!

Other men were emerging from the darkness, producing torches of their own to fend off the gloom. Kessler recognised some of them, knowing them to be the same scum that had twice tried to ambush and murder him. He saw the brigands who had brought down Baron von Rabwald grinning at him with brown teeth. Somehow the vermin had found another way into the crypt and stolen the relic before Kessler could recover it. Then they had heard the Wissenlanders approaching, and had darted into the darkness to lurk in hiding.

'I must thank you for your perseverance, soldier,' Rambrecht told Kessler. 'Without your persistence we might never have found this place.' He raised the runefang before him in a mocking salute. 'Count Achim will appreciate your efforts, I assure you.'

Kessler reached a hand up for the sword lashed across his back. The motion brought a warning hiss from behind him. He felt the touch of steel against his neck. Shifting his eyes to follow the cold length of steel, he was soon staring into Ottmar's unforgiving gaze. There was no mercy or compassion in the sergeant's face, only the smirking triumph of a traitor revealed. Kessler let his arm drop back down, sighing with defeat.

'That's how you escaped and Ekdahl didn't,' he stated.

Ottmar smiled and nodded his head. 'He was suspicious at the end, which is how I was wounded. It made my story of a narrow escape more convincing though, didn't it?'

Kessler rolled his eyes, cursing himself for not questioning the soldier's good fortune. The brigands were chuckling, coming closer, and fingering their daggers and swords. Kessler turned his head, saw Valdner coming forwards, saw Raban holding his axe against Skanir's throat, and saw Anselm nonchalantly approaching the brigands.

Rambrecht reached into a pouch on his belt, producing a strip of tanned goatskin, strange marks stained into the hide. Kessler groaned, recognising it as a similar message to the one he had found before they had entered Murzklein. The Averlander tapped the document idly against his thigh.

'Aside from the dwarf and your men, did anyone else survive the hydra?' Rambrecht asked. Ottmar seemed surprised that the aristocrat knew about the fight with the monster, but quickly recovered.

'Only the halfling and his ogre,' he answered. 'They are back in the tunnels. Both of them are wounded. Even if they wanted to, they couldn't give us much trouble. We ran into some orcs before entering the crypt. The greenskins settled for the rest.'

Rambrecht's expression became smug, pleased by the spy's report. There'd been enough trouble already. It was about time things started running his way. 'We'll keep the dwarf, he might be able to find us a quicker way out of the mountains. I don't see why we need any of the others.' The comment brought a murderous gleam to the lurking bandits' eyes. Rambrecht snorted derisively as he noticed their eagerness. 'You can have your men deal with them,' he said, nodding at the mercenaries. He'd seen how competent Baldur's brigand trash were too many times in the past. Now that he had real fighters, he intended to use them.

Valdner walked towards the aristocrat, holding his sword by the blade, presenting the hilt to Rambrecht in the Estalian custom. 'Begging pardon, your lordship,' Valdner said, 'but I'm not taking orders from some traitor, deserter scum.' Ottmar glared at the sell-sword, colour rushing into the sergeant's face. 'I'll offer my sword to you, but not to this fork-tongued weasel.'

The Averlander laughed. 'I accept your offer of service, captain,' he replied. Rambrecht reached forward to touch the pommel of the offered sword, familiar with the Estalian tradition. He failed to notice the chill that came into Valdner's eyes as he stretched out his hand.

Suddenly, Valdner threw his body forward, smashing the hilt of his sword into Rambrecht's face. The stunned aristocrat staggered back, stumbling as he fought to recover. Valdner did not waste any further attention on the man. With what seemed like a single fluid motion, he flipped his sword into his other hand, catching it by the grip and spinning around. The mercenary's sword flashed out, raking across Ottmar's face. The sergeant screamed, his own sword falling from his hand as he clutched at his slashed eyes. Valdner left the spy to shriek on the floor, turning to face foes that were still in the fight.

At their captain's attack, Raban and Anselm sprang into action. Raban removed his axe from Skanir's throat, Nordlander and dwarf both shouting war cries as they rushed at the bandits. Anselm, already close to the enemy, darted forwards while they were still watching Ottmar bleed. The Reiklander's sword stabbed out, skewering a bandit just beneath the ribs. He ripped the blade free, leaving his foe to scream and bleed, turning to close with another.

As soon as Ottmar's blade was gone from his neck, Kessler's arm shot up and over his shoulder, his hand dragging his zweihander free of its scabbard. The swordsman glared at his foes with a hate stronger than anything he had ever felt in the arena. He did not have time to wonder why the mercenaries had turned against Ottmar and his patron; that was a question that could wait. There were men to kill and a sword to reclaim.

RAMBRECHT STAGGERED BACK, his nose split by the fury of the blow that Valdner had dealt him. More than the physical blow, the aristocrat was stunned by the sudden turnaround. Everything had been going his way. Every card had been clutched firmly in his hand. Now it had all degenerated into anarchy: a wild fray. They had outnumbered the Wissenlanders, could have picked them off from the shadows with arrows, or else simply sneaked away while they were still moaning over the loss of the runefang. Instead, thinking the three mercenaries safely in his pocket, he'd decided to gloat, to rub his triumph in the face of the vanquished. Rambrecht could not deny that he had caused the crisis, but he was too arrogant to accept the blame. He'd teach the sell-sword scum the folly of turning against him.

Even as the thought occurred to him, Rambrecht reconsidered the situation. His men outnumbered the Wissenlanders, but they were brigand trash against professional soldiers. At a glance, he saw that one of the bandits was already down and another hard-pressed by a mercenary swordsman. If they were going to recover the situation, they had to strike swiftly and overwhelm the Wissenlanders while they still had the numbers.

The Averlander looked over his shoulder at the two brigands behind him. Instead of finding the eager, feral killers of a few moments before, he saw nervous, frightened men, their blades hanging loose in their hands.

'Herr Rambrecht, your lordship, sir,' one of the bandits, the frog-eyed Kopff, stammered. 'We've reconsidered remaining in your employ.'

'We ain't dyin' for you, ya stuffed-up git,' elaborated his companion, Schmitt.

Rambrecht glared at the two craven curs, but before he could voice his rage, the men were already retreating into the recesses of the tomb, back into the rat-run of tunnels that led to the ventilation shaft. The Averlander started to pursue them, but something, some inner warning sense, made him turn back.

The full weight of Kessler's zweihander came crashing down at the aristocrat's body. More by instinct than thought, Rambrecht brought the runefang around, blocking the murderous blow with the ancient relic. Steel shrieked against steel, blue sparks flashing through the dark, the barbaric trophies lashed to the runefang's hilt jostling madly under the impact.

Repulsed, Kessler took a step back to recover and bring the enormous sword up once again. Rambrecht lunged at him with the runefang. This time, the Wissenlander was on the defensive. The zweihander froze in a blocking position, waiting to catch Rambrecht's blade. The runefang slammed into Kessler's steel with an impact that roared like the report of a cannon. A burst of sapphire light exploded around the point where the two weapons made contact. Kessler felt a surge of crackling energy pulse through his arms as he was hurled back, knocked through the air as though he'd been kicked by a troll.

The swordsman crashed down on his back, slamming hard against the stone. Air rushed out of him, black spots bouncing through his vision. The greatsword was knocked from stunned hands, clattering away in the gloom. Kessler rolled his head up in time to see Rambrecht rushing at him, slaughter in the Averlander's furious eyes. He kicked out his legs just as the aristocrat was swinging down at him.

Rambrecht howled as his knee buckled, and he was spilled across Kessler's body, the runefang pinned between them. Kessler could feel the weapon's preternaturally keen edge gnawing into his armour, could feel the little talismans of bone and rock clattering against his greaves. He struggled to pull the Averlander off him while at the same time keeping him pressed too close to use the runefang. Rambrecht's snarling face loomed above him, all the fury of Khaine's hells in his countenance. The aristocrat twisted and writhed, trying to wrench his sword free, trying to pull clean from Kessler's greater strength. He squirmed one hand free, using it to smash the swordsman's face. Kessler felt skin split beneath the vengeful blows and bones crack beneath the wrathful punches. The fractured pieces of his nose ground together, blood bursting across his face. Kessler simply grinned back at his enemy. Pain was too old a companion for him to pay it much attention. If the Averlander thought he was going to break free by hurting him, then he was going to be sorely disappointed.

It was not the blows to his face that made Kessler suddenly relent, but an icy, clammy numbness that swept through his body. In the struggle, as Rambrecht strove to free the sword, something hard and cold brushed against Kessler's bare arm. At first, he thought it was just one of the orcish talismans that dangled from the hilt of the sword, but the horrible sensation made him doubt. Strangely, it was not unlike Carlinda's chill, unearthly Carlinda, but magnified to a terrible, withering intensity.

Rambrecht pulled clear, darting back from the recoiling swordsman like a cat fleeing from a snake. The aristocrat stood panting, glaring at Kessler with more than hate in his eyes. There was a nameless terror there as well, a terror that made him hesitate, that made him cast a fearful gaze across the tomb.

Kessler could feel it too, as though the air were growing heavy, deadening all light and sound. The shadows seemed to twist and writhe in ways that he knew were dictated by something beyond the flicker of flame. The sounds of conflict faded as all within the tomb felt the creeping dread clutch at them. Breath turned to mist in the sudden chill, flesh pimpling with goosebumps.

A sense of impending doom gripped every man, causing the blood to curdle in his veins. Kessler felt his eyes drawn to Gordreg Throatripper's ramshackle throne, his gaze locked on the orc's mouldering bones.

Evil was coming.

CHAPTER TWENTY-ONE

OTTO KRAUS, LATE of the Dortrecht city watch, now a sergeant in the Fifth Dortrecht Militia, whispered a prayer to Taal and Manaan, the gods of forest and river. He hoped that the forbidding nature gods would deign to listen to the prayers of a mere man, one unversed in the holy sacraments and rites of priest and druid. He hoped that they might turn a sympathetic eye towards the men lined across the Westgate Bridge.

He prayed that they might prevail, that they could save the rest of the city from the ghastly power that beset it. More selfishly, he prayed for his own life, begging to be spared from the merciless swords of the enemy. He had rejected the blessings of the priests of Morr, who had stalked among the regiments earlier in the day, commending their souls to Morr's care so that they might fight without fear for their immortal beings. Kraus did not want to think about death, about the likelihood that he would not survive the day. He did not want to think of Morr, that sombre, cheerless lord of death and the grave. To him, Morr had more in common with the enemy than the frightened men who offered the god their prayers.

Kraus looked across the length of the bridge, to where the cobblestone span reached the shore that marked the market quarter of Dortrecht, sometimes called the 'new town'. Nothing lived in new town now. It had been evacuated on orders from General Hock, the officer who commanded everyone and everything in Dortrecht. Some had stubbornly stayed behind, avoiding the soldiers who had marched through the streets to enforce the general's orders. Sometimes a scream would rise from the haunted streets of new town, piercing the silence like a titan's spear. It had been many hours since the last scream. Nothing lived in new town now.

General Hock had arrived days ago, conferring with Baron von Schlaffen regarding the defence of the city. The baron had grown obstinate, refusing to sacrifice the market quarter and the docks as the general demanded, unwilling to give up even an inch of his city without a fight. The bold determination of their baron had been very popular with the people of Dortrecht, even as his soldiers made the rounds to recruit every able-bodied man in the city into a dozen fresh militia regiments.

Men possessed of moderate familiarity with arms found themselves appointed officers and sergeants, and men who had never before held anything more dangerous than a boat hook or meat cleaver found themselves being issued spears from the city armoury. The general sent by Count Eberfeld to lead the defence of the city was silent, while Baron von Schlaffen rallied his people, almost seeming to cede command to the baron. He allowed the men of Dortrecht to construct palisades and walls in the market district, to dig ditches and set up barricades around the docks. Meanwhile, the troops General Hock brought with him, soldiers from across the length and breadth of Wissenland, laboured upon an inner ring of defences, centred around Dortrecht's old wall and the small tributary of the river that lapped against its foundations. The high city, the old city, had been built upon a peninsula ages ago. Since that time, the peninsula had become an island, connected with the mainland only by a series of bridges. It was around these bridges that General Hock had based his strategy.

When the inner defences met General Hock's demands, he turned upon Baron von Schlaffen, ordering the stubborn nobleman's arrest. He immediately ordered all inhabitants of new town to be brought behind the thick walls of the old city, and all Dortrecht regiments to abandon the barricades they had built for their baron. Companies of soldiers were sent to clear all structures from the opposite shore of the river, demolishing them with sledgehammers and torches. A broad expanse of new town, several dozen yards in depth, was destroyed when the soldiers were through. Officers explained that the destruction had been necessary to create a killing field for the archers who would man the walls of the old city, but the explanation did not ease the hostile resentment of the Dortrechters.

This, too, the general had taken into account. From the moment he had set foot in Dortrecht he had been playing against time. He allowed the baron to implement his fruitless efforts to save the entire city in order to keep both him and his people occupied. He knew that when the time came, he would need to seize sole control of the city. The baron was too close to implement the full

ruthlessness that the position demanded. Hock would try
to save the city, at least as much of it as he felt could be
saved, but that was not his mission. He was trying to save
the whole of Wissenland. If he had to sacrifice Dortrecht
to do it, then he would do so.

Before the Dortrechters' hostility could foment into
rebellion, the enemy reached the outskirts of new town,
as General Hock had expected them to. The people of
Dortrecht had bigger problems to worry about beside
the arrest of their baron. Watching the hideous fog
sweep out across new town, seeing the shadowy shapes
marching silently within it, terror gripped the city. Hock
used that fear, exploited it the way a seductress exploits
love. The iron voice of command that led the people
was his and his alone, sending them running to the
walls to oppose the unholy force that intended to
slaughter them all.

Kraus wiped the perspiration from his face, trying to
keep a tight grip on his sword. Hock was a strong-
handed, uncompromising leader, but they had no
other. There was no time to question him, only to obey
and to pray that some of them would see the next dawn.

The militiaman looked at the pale, shivering men
around him. Stevedores and carpenters, chandlers and
wainwrights, street vendors and fishermen, all were
alike in the awkward, terrified way they gripped their
spears. Kraus felt his own pulse turn to ice. They were to
support a real regiment, a band of halberdiers from
Bergdorf who stood ahead of them on the bridge. He
didn't want to think about the chances of his militia
against anything strong enough to break through the
real soldiers.

Instead, he closed his eyes and prayed, trying desperately to banish from his mind the image of thin

shadows silently lurching their way through the fog, converging on the Westgate Bridge.

GENERAL HOCK STOOD upon the battlements atop the immense blocks that formed the wall of the high city. The thick stones had stood for millennia, watching over the river-front settlement as it grew from modest town to swarming city. Perhaps, in another hundred years, it might rival Wissenberg or Averheim, if it was in the cards that Dortrecht should see another hundred years.

Dortrecht was an old settlement. It was the city's ancient lineage that now imperilled it and all who lived there. Hock had memorised the crumbling, mouldy map that had been drawn from Wissenberg's musty archives. Every town, village and hamlet marked upon it had been razed by Zahaak's infernal legion. To the undead, it was as though all the centuries since Sigmar's battle with Nagash had never been. They followed the old roads, and made war upon the old places. Wissenberg would be one of those places, Dortrecht was another. There were still a few towns along the river that might draw Zahaak's legion before it reached the walls of the capital, but only at Dortrecht was there any real chance of stopping them, of holding them until Count Eberfeld was ready.

The general stared down from the height of the wall, watching the creeping mass of grey mist sweep through the deserted streets outside the wall. He felt a tinge of guilt with every scream that rose from that desolation, but he told himself that the wretches had brought their doom upon themselves by disobeying his orders and staying behind. He hoped there were not too many of them, not only to ease his guilt, but also because the enemy was numerous enough already. The legion did not need any more fresh corpses to swell its ranks.

Four bridges had originally connected the old city with the shore. Hock had ordered three of them to be readied for demolition. It had been the province of Thorir Hammerhand, an engineer from the Grey Mountains and a master of the strange fire-powder that the dwarfs used in their cannons. Thorir had rigged charges of the stuff to the bridges. If Hock squinted he could see the barrels lashed to the sides of the spans. The containers had been soaked in oil and pitch. They would take flame quickly when archers sent fire arrows slamming into them. The bridges, the dwarf assured him, would vanish as though they had never been there. Hock intended to wait before setting them off, until they were swarming with the lifeless legions of the enemy. Then would be the time to destroy the bridges, when they could blast hundreds of the foe into oblivion with them.

He had left the fourth bridge intact. It would act as a lure to Zahaak's troops once the others were gone. The entire legion would converge on the Westgate Bridge. To do so, they would need to cross the killing ground his men had cleared in new town, exposed to the hundreds of archers lining the walls of the old city every step of the way. The bridge was narrow, and easily held by a few score men. Hock had charged nearly two thousand men with holding it, reserve regiment upon reserve regiment ready to surge forward as soon as they were needed. He intended for the bridge to become a bottleneck, where the entire legion would be caught. The catapults in the old city's towers were already trained on the far end of the bridge. The havoc Hock intended them to visit upon the foe would be hideous.

If it was possible to prevail against this supernatural force, they would do so. If not, Hock intended to delay them for as long as possible. Every day, every hour, would bring more men to Wissenberg, and give Count Eberfeld more time to secure his defences. Zahaak would be stopped. Hock had to believe that was possible.

The sorcerous fog that travelled with Zahaak's legion, covering it like a shroud of grey shadow, was rolling through the market district, consuming street upon street, building after building. Hock could see the black shapes of the things that marched within the fog, dead things that had been called from their graves by a new and terrible master. Even from the wall, Hock could feel the unearthly chill of that fog pulling at his flesh with an oily caress of decay. He shuddered against the influence, putting a hand to his talisman of Myrmidia, goddess of strategy and war. The little bronze icon did little to soothe his unease.

Hock turned his head, staring at the man beside him. Unlike the others who stood upon the walls, he wore neither livery nor uniform, was neither soldier nor commander. The man was hairy and wild-looking, his unkempt beard seeming to cringe away from the filth-encrusted, brown, homespun robe that clung to his scrawny bones. His fierce, savage gaze studied the battlefield below with a fanatic intensity that even Hock could not match. Soft, whispered words tumbled from the wild man's grimy lips, forcing the general to strain to hear them. He shuddered at the snatches of nonsense he heard, like children's rhymes badly remembered. He had pinned much on the abilities of this madman. It was ghastly to think what would happen if he lost his feeble grip on reality.

'Magister,' Hock said, addressing the wild man. The lunatic's eyes rolled around in his head, trying to focus on the general without turning away from the scene beneath the walls.

'I am the saviour of the mud-fish,' the warlock said. 'The wind is my brother and it speeds them past the sound of the red, where all is peace and love and purple midnight.' A crazed grin crawled through the madman's beard. 'We must swim to the sun before the ice comes and drowns the mountains with smoke.'

Instinctively, Hock and his aides recoiled from the madman and his mutterings. The warlock had been practising his obscene craft for decades, using little spells to call the rain for farmers or ward away an early frost. Every year, his mind had degenerated, becoming more unhinged, and less capable of separating the world of reality from the insane visions of his wizard-sight. Finally, the farmers had decided he was more dangerous than useful and reported him to the authorities. Crimes of witchcraft and magic were punishable by death, but those charged with such villainy could only be executed on Hexenacht. Such was the law in Wissenland. Another two months and Albrecht the Doomsayer would have been lost to Hock. As the general stared into those blood-shot eyes, he wondered if that would have been a bad thing.

'Please, Albrecht,' begged the general, 'try to be sane!'

Hock's words seemed to reach through the madness. The wildly dilated eyes of the warlock focused cleanly upon him as Albrecht turned his head. An almost embarrassed look came across the shaggy face. He reached a hand to his temple, pressing against his head. 'I am sorry, general,' the warlock apologised. 'It is so difficult, like maggots burrowing through my skull. Can't you feel it? Can't you feel the evil? So much evil the very air is corrupt with it. So much my brother the wind cowers from it.'

Hock shuddered again, wondering if perhaps the warlock was speaking of the strange, oily feel in the air. How much worse must the sensation be to one attuned to such abominable forces? No wonder the man was mad.

'It is time, Albrecht,' Hock hastily said, trying to speak before the warlock could slip again into insanity. 'I need you to use your power to disperse the fog.'

The warlock nodded grimly. 'Such evil will not be burned away by the clean light of brother sun. It is too old and too strong. I shall call to brother wind, as you would have me, but the sun will not destroy the evil.'

'No,' agreed Hock, 'honest steel will do that. Now be about your sorcery, before the wind decides to disown his "brother".'

Half-said in jest, the threat seemed to galvanise Albrecht into action. The warlock pulled back the sleeves of his robe, exposing scrawny arms caked in dirt and rat bites. He waved his hands through the air, as though kneading clay. Hock could feel the atmosphere grow cold, his nose filling with the stink of ozone.

Throwing up his arms, the warlock began to screech and cry in tones that seemed to tear the sky. Albrecht's voice rose, higher and higher, until Hock thought the man's heart would burst from the effort of maintaining such volume and intensity. The coldness grew greater, sweat hardening into frost on the general's forehead. The wooden hoarding that cast its shadow across the battlements creaked and groaned as ice burrowed into the heavy timbers. A weird, supernatural glow gathered around the warlock. With a shudder, Hock realised that the strange illumination was not being drawn into Albrecht's body, but was somehow being exuded from it. The warlock was, in some strange way, the engine of the fell powers he commanded, at once both candle and flame.

Albrecht's voice rose higher and higher, and soldiers covered their ears. There were no words in the warlock's voice, at least none known to sane men, but those who heard the ghastly sounds knew terror just the same. General Hock looked across the pale faces of the men around him, feeling their fear infect him. He felt for the dagger on his belt, wondering what horrible mistake he had made trying to use the warlock, knowing the only sure way to stop him.

Before Hock could take more than a single, faltering step towards Albrecht, shouts of amazement echoed all along the walls. Men pointed excitedly at the desolate, fog-bound morass of the market district. Hock's hand lingered on the dagger as he looked down. A sharp gasp forced its way from his throat. He had asked Albrecht to perform a miracle, but now that he gazed upon it, he was dumbfounded by the sight.

All across the market district, the fog was in retreat, rolling back as though blown by a mighty gale. Hock strained his ears to catch the howl of such a mighty storm, but not even the faintest whisper of wind rewarded his efforts. Below, not even a dead leaf stirred in the ruined market district, the unnatural gale seeming to have power over the fog alone. Hock looked back at the warlock, finding the man's eyes glowing with sorcerous power, his face pinched in what was at once an expression of agony and ecstasy.

The general turned away as new shouts of alarm sounded from the walls. The retreating fog laid bare the shadowy shapes marching through the ruins, exposing them before the gaze of the men on the walls.

Hock felt his heart sink as he saw Zahaak's legion marching in deathless silence through the haunted husk of the market district. He saw skeletal things, the rusting tatters of ancient armour hanging from their bones, the corroded stumps of blades clenched in their talons, tramping through the streets with the unliving precision of a clockwork orchestra. He saw other things, things so freshly dead that hair dangled into their rotted faces, and flies buzzed about their gory wounds. With horror, he noted the grey and white liveries of Neuwald, Geschberg and Beroun, and with horror he recalled what his scouts had reported, that the legion left nothing dead behind as it marched.

The freshly dead did not display the precision of their predecessors, moving with awkward, stumbling movements that caused their ranks to be disordered and confused. Hock took small comfort from the fact that such mindless dead would not rout, however poorly they fought, and however many of them were put to the sword. Only by destroying them all, by slaughtering every abomination in Zahaak's unholy legion could they carry the day. Looking out upon the numberless host converging upon the bridges, Hock appreciated the enormity of such a task.

Hock shook his head, biting back his doubts. They had to try. There was no other way. If they failed, Wissenland was doomed. There would be no quarter from their undead foe, Zahaak would butcher them all and then infuse their corpses with an unholy simulacrum of life. They would rise to march with their killers, to march on Wissenberg and destroy everyone in the city. Count Eberfeld would be hard-pressed to survive against the legion at its present size, how much more impossible would be his defence against the legion as it would be if Dortrecht fell and all of its defenders were added to its nightmare ranks? General Hock's eyes blazed and he ground his teeth. No! He would not let that happen!

The general's body shivered, his iron resolve melting into watery slag. His eyes had found a black shadow moving among the lurching, shambling columns of the legion, gliding silently between the decayed ranks of the dead like some spectre of the netherworld. There was something obscene about the apparition, something foul beyond words or thought. The darkness about it was unreal, detached from the world around it, as though the sun refused to shine upon the ground the thing profaned with its touch. Hock had the impression of a tall, gaunt figure, a hood rising above its shoulders. Beneath that hood, Hock could feel eyes burning up at him, eyes that were colourless embers of hatred and malignancy. He could feel the weight of antiquity crushing down upon him, the hideous pressure of ages lost and despised. Who was he, a thing of blood and bone, with his two score and ten years, to stand before that which was ancient when the Merogens were still naked savages hunting reptiles in the primordial mire?

Hock was still gazing down at the black shape, feeling the enormity of his insignificance closing dead fingers around his pounding heart. His trembling hand began to rise from his belt, the cold length of his dagger pulling clear of its sheath. The general fought to drag air into his lungs, and tried to will the blood to speed through his veins as his heart grew ever more sluggish. He tried to close his eyes, tried to turn his face away from the thing that he knew to be Zahaak the Usurper: Zahaak, the Sword of Nagashizzar.

'Thorir!' the general shouted. 'The cannon! Fire the cannon!' Hock managed to stab his hand over the wall, pointing a quivering finger at the shadowy spectre.

There was little cause to impress upon the dwarf artillerist the target that the general desired. None upon the walls of Dortrecht failed to feel the ancient malignity exuding from its presence. They knew that here was a thing that had been drawn into the cursed ranks of the undead by Nagash's black touch. Its dark power was a thing that sickened the soul of those exposed to it, that sent frozen tendrils of terror writhing along the spine.

The dwarf roared at his veteran crew. The cannoneers pivoted their cumbersome weapon, training its wide-mouth upon the shadowy phantom. Thorir roared again, but the final notes of his command were obliterated in the louder roar of the weapon. Smoke and fire belched from the gilded mouth of the cannon, the pungent stink of blackpowder rolling across the walls.

The precision of the dwarf cannoneers was as exact as any piece of dwarf craftsmanship. The iron ball shot down from the walls, smashing straight through the ghastly shade that was Zahaak the Worm. Bone and armour, cloth and cloak, shattered beneath an impact that would have pulverised stone. The wight disintegrated, shards of its ruin spraying across the silent ranks of its army. A rousing cheer swept through the men on the walls, carrying down into the streets of Dortrecht and the soldiers standing guard on the one surviving bridge.

Hock dared to share the jubilation, smiling as he remembered the tales of horror and invulnerability that had surrounded the dread wight lord, but the smile died on his face, and the cheering faded into silence behind him. Upon the shore, where the cannon had struck Zahaak down, a billowing mass of shadow roiled and blazed. Hock's heart went cold as he saw the phantom essence of the wight lord form black, wormy fingers. It slithered across the ground, pulling itself from the crater left by the cannonball. The splotch of shadow coiled around one of the bronze-armoured skeletons of the legion, wrapping around it until the undead warrior was completely consumed.

The chill of the grave touched every man as the profane power of blackest necromancy drew all warmth from the sky. The skeleton entombed within the shadow began to move. With every step, the shadow seemed to withdraw into it, the darkness seeping into its ancient bones. By the time it had taken its seventh step, the skeleton was no longer covered by the inky blackness, but it was no longer what it had been. A shudder of despair and terror rumbled through the souls of Dortrecht as they looked upon the malignity they had thought slain. The cannon ball had destroyed only the husk, only the shell that had contained Zahaak. Now the Dark Lord walked again, only the smoking crater beside it providing evidence that it had ever been struck down.

The wight lord turned its hooded skull up to the walls of the city, its merciless eyes boring into the souls of those who had inflicted such indignity upon it.

Other shapes were moving through the columns of the legion, like patches of grey mist that had somehow resisted the retreat of the fog shroud. Hock dimly perceived that the shapes were not moving through the ranks of the legion, but instead were rising from it, ghostly shadows that oozed into the air like pillars of smoke, dancing to a wraith-wind unfelt by mortal flesh. There was the suggestion of a human form about them, lean bodies that might have been called supple when warm flesh yet clung to their bones. Grey tatters of grave shroud swirled around them, whipping in the spectral wind like shreds of mainsail from the mast of a ghost ship. Black tendrils of hair billowed around naked, gleaming skulls, waving with a horrible vitality at once beckoning and grotesque.

The apparitions hurtled through the air like meteors, racing upwards from the silent, plodding ranks of the legion. Cold, wicked blades were visible, clutched in their fleshless hands, the naked steel the only thing of substance about their incorporeal beings. Archers sent arrows whistling through the semi-transparent shades, the missiles passing harmlessly through the ghastly spirits. The things paid no notice to the fruitless attacks, converging instead upon the walls, flying towards the one man alone among the city's defenders who had drawn their attention.

Albrecht's spell faltered as he felt the empty eyes of the spirits focusing upon him. The warlock's arms fell to his sides, his voice dropping to a frightened croak. The spectral light bled away from him, leaving behind a pitiable, broken thing.

But the dead know not pity.

The fanged jaws of the banshees dropped open as they flew around the cowering warlock. From unseen realms of death and horror, the apparitions gave voice to a keening wail, a cry that none in the city could fail to hear. It reverberated through mind and soul, shattering men like a sledge against brick. In an instant, a hundred fell dead in their boots, a hundred more fleeing into shrieking madness to escape the shrieking torment of the banshees' wail. These were the chafe, the residue thrust from the dark by the searing scream of the ghosts. Against he who was the target of their malevolence, the ghastly chorus worked still greater havoc.

'They have come to kill the prophet!' Albrecht shrieked, and all the agonies of hell were in his tones. The warlock's hands tore at his raiment, and his teeth gnashed together, tearing his lip into a gnawed mass of pulp. 'They have come to kill the prophet!' he screamed again, his voice cracking with the effort to carry his tones above the wailing chorus of the banshee.

Blood bubbled from the warlock's ears, slopping down his neck and across his shoulders in a steady stream. 'They have come to kill the prophet!' he screamed, and the stream became a torrent. The warlock's shriek became a loathsome gurgle as his gnashing teeth sliced through his screaming tongue. The wail of the banshees howled around him unchallenged, rising to a crescendo. The blood running from Albrecht's skull became a thin mush and he pitched to the stones of the parapet, his face crashing into the porridge of his own brain.

The shriek of the banshees twisted into a terrible, malicious laughter. The ghosts swirled above the walls, cackling above the heads of the archers before streaking back down, hurtling back into the ranks of the undead legion. Soon they had vanished once more into the decaying host, only the echoes of their scream lingering behind to haunt the hearts of those who had seen them.

General Hock only vaguely appreciated the destruction of Albrecht the Doomsayer. Eyes locked on the black shape of Zahaak the Usurper, he could feel his life being leeched from him. Drop by drop, or perhaps hour by hour, his vitality was being bled away by a terrible, malevolent will. He could feel his arm lifting the dagger up, bringing the stabbing blade towards his throat. He could feel his arm moving, but he could do nothing to stop it. He knew that, even when he felt the sharp point of the blade against his trembling flesh, he would not be able to stop it.

Suddenly, fresh air seemed to come roaring back into his lungs, blood surging once more through his veins. With a grunt of horror and disgust, Hock flung the dagger from him, letting it fall to the river below. He sagged against the battlements, trying to recover his shattered thoughts, trying to control the terror that set his heart pounding like a hammer against his ribs. His body, his soul, were his once more. It was an effort, an effort such as he doubted himself capable of, but slowly Hock looked down at the ruins again. The black shadow was not looking at him but was racing through the ranks of its legion, retreating back through the market district, speeding to the earthen ramparts where the undead had pitched their silent camp in morbid mockery of a living army.

Hock could spare no more thought on what strange urgency had caused Zahaak to spare him. Though the wight lord was gone, its army remained. The legion was still on the move, marching silently, inexorably, across the bridges. On the Westgate Bridge, soldiers clashed with rotting horrors that had only weeks before been their countrymen, trying to kill with clean steel beings that were already dead and damned.

The men on the Westgate would need to fend for themselves. Hock watched the other spans, waiting tensely as the undead tromped across them. When the spans were all but lost beneath a press of bleached bone and mouldering skin, the general lifted his field baton, the gold-capped staff gleaming in the sunlight. He knew the gaudy talisman would be clearly seen by his officers along the walls, even if his voice did not carry to them.

One smooth motion brought the raised baton crashing down, as though smashing the skull of an invisible foe. Hock's deep voice boomed across the walls.

'Loose!'

Hundreds of bows released arrows on the general's command. Doused in pitch, the arrows were flaming brands as they hurtled at the bridges. Some fell short, some crashed into the massed ranks of the legion, but many more struck home, slamming into the charges prepared by the dwarfs. For long, tense seconds, the burning arrows continued to rain, their flames swiftly engulfing the oil-soaked barrels. Then the entire island was shaken as one after another, the charges exploded. Tons of stone were lifted into the air, crashing down into the market district, crushing dozens of skeletal warriors beneath them. Hundreds of skeletons and zombies were obliterated in the blasts, their shattered bits splashing along the river in a grisly rain.

A mighty cheer boomed across the walls as men watched the legion crumble. Archers began to fire into the ranks massed on the opposite shore, sending arrows stabbing into the dead husks of men. Hock had been careful to advise his marksmen to aim for the head of their foe, for only destruction of the skull seemed to disperse the hideous energies that gave these things their vitality. He was pleased to see that his order had been remembered as arrows shattered the heads of dozens of undead warriors.

Just as he was beginning to think there would be a chance, that perhaps they really could carry the day, the snap-crack of siege engines rose from the desolation of the market district. Hock saw large missiles come hurtling up at the old city, falling well past the walls. He was surprised by the comparative silence of their descent, the expected sound of collapsing brick and crumbling stone failing to reach him. A grim unease began to crawl along his spine as more and more of the quiet missiles were thrown at the city by the legion's catapults. There had been something obscene about the speed with which the legion had conquered Neuwald, the way Zahaak had so easily defeated the town's thick walls.

One of the strange missiles fell shorter than the others, landing just within the walls. Hock and his aides hurried along the battlements, intending to see what new horror the legion was inflicting upon Dortrecht. Soldiers gave way before them, nodding sketchy salutes to the general as he passed, all old resentments set aside for the time being. Soon, the buildings pressing upon the curtain wall gave way to a street, affording Hock a better look into the city beyond. He saw a knot of militiamen converging upon something in the distance. Closer, he could see the missile that had fallen short, dripping down from the iron cross-arm of a lamp-post like some gigantic bird's nest.

It was no stone or boulder that had fallen, but rather a grisly net crafted from strips of bloodied cloth and other unmentionable materials. Something moved within the net with a fitful energy, and while Hock watched, he saw a rusty blade emerge and begin to saw away at the confining 'ropes'. The net suddenly broke, spilling half a dozen bodies into the street. The things landed hard, but took little notice of their fall. Awkwardly, with jerky movements, the zombies lurched to their feet, fetching blades and cudgels from where they had been scattered by the fall. Lifeless eyes the colour of boiled eggs passed across General Hock and his gawping aides, and then focused on the angle of the wall beneath them. With the same slow, monotonous tread, the rotting zombies began to march down the length of the street, leaving behind those shattered by their violent descent.

'They're heading for the gate!' one of Hock's aides shouted. The adjutant raced along the battlements to warn the threatened portal. Hock spun around, feeling a sense of dread as he saw more of the missiles flying overhead. How many had landed? How many would they launch? If each missile carried half a dozen zombies, his soldiers would soon be scattered across the city mopping up small knots of the enemy. It was fortunate indeed that they had destroyed the other bridges and reduced the legion's means of a more meaningful ingress to one.

The thought brought Hock's eyes back to the opposite shore. Archers were still firing furiously at the legion, taking a slow but steady toll. However, the legion was no longer standing idly by while its ranks were whittled away. Column upon column of the skeletal warriors were marching into the river, not relenting even when the waters rose above their fleshless skulls and they vanished beneath the surface. Some of the river walkers were already emerging, climbing the foundations of the walls, lifting themselves onto the broken stumps of the bridges, pounding at the barred gates of the city.

There was no question of the undead forcing the gates. Their foothold upon the far shore was so tenuous that even the smallest battering ram could not be brought to bear. As Hock watched more of the ghastly nets go sailing over the walls, he knew that the undead outside had no intention of battering their way in. They were waiting, waiting to be let in by the steadily swelling ranks of zombies that each crack of the catapults sent flying past the city's defences. If even one gate fell, Dortrecht would be quickly smothered by the tide of lifeless warriors that would come streaming in.

The general snapped hasty orders, sending adjutants to pull men away from the Westgate Bridge, to reinforce the garrisons at the other gates. He only hoped the redeployment would be quick enough. He hoped they still had the strength to buy Count Eberfeld more time.

THE FIELD CAMP of the legion was silent, lifeless as the forgotten tomb that had been Zahaak's resting place for centuries. The wooden palisades and earthen ramparts were arrayed in precise, measured sections, relics of an age when war was a new art for man and approached as much as science as it was carnage.

At the centre of the camp, standing alone amid the cleared, barren ground, a great tent swayed slightly in the fitful breeze. It was of a style that had passed from the world when a deposed king had brought red vengeance upon his own people, when a broken man had accepted the unholy promise of a thing that had made itself a god.

The flayed skins of men stretched taut between poles of bone, held in place with ropes of sinew. The scalps of priests and virgins hung from the exposed tips of the poles, and the skulls of wizards grinned from the peaked crown of the tent. Ancient figures had been drawn in blood on the walls of tanned flesh, the primordial picture-scrawl of lost Khemri, cradle of sorcery and the black arts.

A shadow poured through the opening of the tent, seeping into the greater darkness beyond. Witchlights flared into putrescent life in obedience to an unspoken command, tiny wraiths swimming through the ether bound within the walls of skin. No furnishings stood exposed by the glowing spirits, only a short altar of black basalt and a statue of obsidian that stood behind it. A skeletal face leered or snarled from beneath the statue's crown, its iron hand stretched in silent demand.

Zahaak's ancient bones creaked into obeisance before the statue, the embers of the Usurper's eyes fading into a pallid light. The wight stood once more, pulling back the heavy hood that cloaked its skull. Time had hardened its bones into a stone-like consistency, yet even so, the hieroglyphs scratched into its forehead wept beads of crimson. Few mortal scholars would know the meaning of that script, fewer still would not be driven mad by such knowledge. It was the brand of obscenity, of the ultimate abomination. That which was the truth behind the great darkness that Zahaak had named master long ago.

The bleeding hieroglyphs continued to drip from its skull as the wight moved across the small confines of the tent. The armoured hand of Zahaak removed a sackcloth bag from a bone box. The fanged skull grinned down at the sack as something within it stirred into querulous, frightened life. For a moment, some little fragment, some echo of a man dead two thousand years, tried to make itself felt. The moment passed, more quickly than ever before. Each time, the echo grew less, consumed a little more by the great darkness waiting to devour it.

Let it end, the echo had whispered. But immortality had no end. Zahaak would see to that. The wight dragged the little pink, wailing thing from the bag. Pitiless fires stared down at it from the barren sockets of its skull. The wight could feel the creature's terrorised heart throbbing, pounding like a tiny drum.

There was danger. The wight had sensed it. The danger was somehow connected with the witch, the meddler it had destroyed and her paltry god. Now, somehow, someway, her essence had brushed against the weapon that had brought destruction to Zahaak long ago. The wight did not understand, nor did it question. If the weapon had been found, then it must be lost again.

Zahaak turned its skull away from the wailing, struggling thing it held. The Usurper looked again at the grasping, demanding claw of the statue. Again, the tiny pounding heart drew its attention back to the little life in its hands.

Slowly, Zahaak returned to the box of bone, removing a copper athame. The wight looked down at the crying pink thing, at the flutter of its racing heart.

The stretched claw of the statue reached out from the shadows, demanding payment for its power.

CHAPTER TWENTY-TWO

THE SKELETON UPON the throne grew dark, as though some great shadow had fallen upon it. By degrees, the blackness began to disperse, not by any influence of the light, but in some nebulous, unwholesome manner. To Kessler, it looked as though the darkness had seeped into the old bones of Gordreg Throatripper, absorbed into the skeleton like water soaking into a sponge.

The bony hand was the first thing to move, shifting from the skeleton's empty lap to slap listlessly against its armoured thigh. The second hand fell, brushing against the makeshift throne. The petty hates of men were forgotten as all within the tomb continued to back away. Mercenary, bandit or dwarf, none could deny the cold terror that crawled through their bodies.

With a slow, creaking motion, the fanged skull of the orc turned, staring at the men with its empty face. Talons closed about the grip of axe and club, legs fused to the throne by centuries of decay pulled free, armoured boots scraping against the bone-littered floor. The wight stood for a moment, tottering on its withered feet. It soon recalled its balance. Another turn of its fleshless face, and the orc warlord took a menacing step away from the throne. What colour remained in Rambrecht's face drained from it as the Averlander realised that the creature was moving towards him.

The stroke of the axe was slow, Rambrecht easily blocking it with the runefang. The sword briefly blazed with light, but whatever power it held failed to topple the wight. After centuries with the sword across its lap, perhaps Gordreg's old bones had become attuned to the runefang's power. Perhaps something still more powerful was working against it. Whatever the cause, the wight seemed to be emboldened by Rambrecht's attack. When it struck at him with its club, the blow was faster and less awkward than before. Again, the Averlander blocked the attack, the runefang exploding with magical energy as it connected with the pitted orcish iron.

Shouting a war cry, Kessler lunged at the reanimate. Watching the wight recover from the second attack, he could almost feel the thing's power swell. His greatsword crashed against the armoured side of the hulking skeleton, making it stagger.

'Stay away from it!' Kessler snarled at Rambrecht. The Averlander backed away, content to allow his enemies to fight among themselves. Already the wight was coming again, swinging the axe with a speed that at least resembled that of a living arm. Kessler felt his arms ring with the force of the stroke as he caught it upon his sword. He risked one look at Rambrecht to assure himself that the Averlander had obeyed his warning, and then the orc was upon him once again, bringing the club about in a murderous arc. Kessler dodged the effort, spinning his body around so that his zweihander smashed against the wight's ribs. Rusted links of armour splintered beneath the contact, ribs shattering under the force of the sword. Gordreg's bones didn't seem to mind, its arm already rising to hack at Kessler with its axe.

RAMBRECHT GAVE NO further attention to the uneven contest between mortal strength and deathless horror. If the fool wanted to play hero, Rambrecht was content to allow that. While the wight was finishing Kessler, he'd be getting clear of the tomb. Such were his thoughts, until he remembered the grim-faced men who had so soundly rejected his service. Valdner and his comrades were still there, including the dwarf Skanir with his formidable hammer. Of Rambrecht's rogues, those not lying upon the floor dead had fled back through the crypt.

Valdner glared at the Averlander, looking at the runefang, and then into the aristocrat's anxious face. 'Anselm, Skanir,' he called. 'Help Kessler. Raban, watch the door. If this scum gets past me, you get to kill him.'

The bitter hatred in the mercenary's voice chilled Rambrecht's blood nearly as much as the presence of the wight. The aristocrat stepped back, trying to move around the advancing Valdner while at the same time keeping his distance from the wight.

'Whatever that fool Ottmar promised you,' Rambrecht hissed as he retreated, 'I'll double it! I'll give you a captaincy in the Averheim Guard!' He had seen the blurring speed and terrible skill of this man. He was too accomplished a swordsman to think he had any edge over a seasoned soldier like Valdner. Against Kessler, Rambrecht had trusted the speed of the lighter runefang against the weight of the cumbersome zweihander. Here, he knew, the greater skill of the mercenary would be the deciding factor, magic sword or no.

'You are gracious, milord,' Valdner sneered, spitting at Rambrecht's retreating boots as he spoke. 'Tell me, does your offer also bring back all the men killed by your hired scum?' To punctuate his words, Valdner stabbed at Rambrecht with the point of his blade. The aristocrat retreated before the feint.

'I'll give you a real command!' Rambrecht swore. 'Real soldiers, not sell-sword vermin! The finest fighting men in Averland!' He danced away from another jab of Valdner's sword, nearly falling across one of the broken dwarf caskets. Valdner was on him in an instant, slashing at the aristocrat. Rambrecht only narrowly avoided disaster, rolling away from the edge as it licked across his body. Blood wept from the jagged slash across his chest.

Gore bubbled between the fingers that Rambrecht clutched to his chest. The aristocrat stared in horror at the determined, fanatical expression on his enemy's face. 'Black Gods damn you! What is your price? What do you want?'

Valdner's lip curled into a snarl. He paused, hateful eyes boring into those of the Averlander. 'I want my brother back, you bastard!'

As Valdner spoke, he thrust at the cowering aristocrat. Rambrecht started to retreat from the attack, but reversed the motion in a quick lunge when he saw Valdner crumple. The mercenary's foot had twisted beneath him, his boot slipping on the uncertain floor of splintered bones. Rambrecht drove down on him, intending to spit the avenger before he could recover.

The mercenary's sword crunched through Rambrecht's chest, burrowing through flesh and bone. A look of shock was the last expression to flow across the aristocrat's face, disbelief that the mercenary had recovered so quickly. He would hardly have credited that the fall had been deliberate, bait to lure him into recklessness.

Valdner rose, letting Rambrecht's weight pull the sword from his grasp. The Averlander flopped down into the carpet of bone, his body twitching as life fled from it. The mercenary reached down, ripping the runefang free from nerveless fingers.

'That's for Ernst,' Valdner snarled.

THE WIGHT'S AXE slashed down once more, coming so close that Kessler saw some of the tassels from his sword severed by the sweep of the blade. He braced himself for the brutal crash of the club. The wight was tireless and unstoppable, but also mindless, slave to its own routine. First would come the axe, and then the club, a pattern the horror was unable to break. It made it easy for Kessler to anticipate his enemy, to react to its attacks even before it made them. He knew, however, that anticipating the thing was not enough to bring it down. Unlike the wight, he was tiring, his muscles feeling like strips of raw fire burning beneath his skin. Every block, every strike was slower and weaker than the one before.

Relief came in the forms of Skanir and Anselm. They came at the wight from opposite sides, slashing at it with hammer and sword. The wight's leg buckled beneath the crack of Skanir's hammer, nearly pitching it to the floor. Anselm's sword scraped against the arm holding the axe, all but severing the limb from its lurching body. The wight fought back, bringing its axe around in a clumsy swipe at Anselm. It turned to face Skanir, some fragment of the ancient hate between orc and dwarf causing its fanged jaw to drop open in a silent roar. Skanir met the wight's hate, cracking its skull with his hammer as it loomed over him, all but ripping the jaw from its socket. The huge club came smashing down, narrowly missing the dwarf as he dove aside.

Before Kessler could warn him, Anselm was attacking again. Expecting the wight to maintain its attention on the dwarf, to continue trying to smash him with its club, the Reiklander rounded on the creature, delivering an almost blinding array of cuts to its body. Any one of the blows should have crippled a living thing. Against the wight, all they did was to shred its already rotting armour and chip away at its already fleshless bones. The axe came swinging around, catching Anselm before he could leap away. The man had no time to scream. Before he could understand what had happened, the Reiklander's head was torn from his shoulders, bouncing across the floor in a gruesome display.

Skanir rushed at the wight, expecting it to gloat after dealing death. A living orc might have, but Gordreg was far removed from the living. It lifted its club once more, repulsing the dwarf with a bone-jarring sweep of the weapon. There was blood in Skanir's beard as he picked himself up from the floor, more gushing from the gash in his forehead. The dwarf shook his head, bracing himself as the wight lumbered towards him, its axe at the ready once more.

Ignoring his protesting muscles, Kessler intercepted the orc skeleton, slashing at it with his zweihander, finishing the job that Anselm had started. The hand clutching the huge axe and most of the attached forearm crashed to the floor. The wight turned away from Skanir, and back towards Kessler. Without even looking at the arm lying beneath its lumbering feet, the bones of Gordreg stalked after Kessler.

Down came the club, crashing to powder fragments of bone. Kessler tried to strike the wight, but the effort was beyond his protesting muscles. Instead, he backed away, bracing himself for the sweep of the axe.

Then he remembered that the axe was lying on the floor. In its place came the club once more. Kessler's sword was torn from him as the murderous bludgeon caught him in the side. He slammed into the floor, his body lighting up with flickers of pain. The sensation urged him on, his fingers questing for the weapon that had been torn from his hands. Above him, the wight continued its deadly march.

Suddenly, a man was standing between him and the wight. Kessler shouted at the man to back away, but the warning came too late. Instincts honed on a hundred battlefields, reflexes fired in a dozen wars, it was almost without conscious thought that Valdner brought the runefang smashing into Gordreg's skull. Coming at the wight from its unprotected side, the mercenary found an almost contemptuous ease in planting the enchanted steel in the brutish head. Bone shattered beneath the blade, accompanied by an ear-shattering boom.

Even with its skull shattered, the wight of Gordreg Throatripper did not fall. Instead a black fog billowed around it, swirling and flickering with obscene energies. Valdner backed away from the fell power that exuded from the headless thing, almost letting the runefang slip from his stunned grip. Kessler scrambled for his sword, staring in mute horror as the bones of the orc warlord began to crumble. It was not the dissolution of the orc that struck him with horror, but the unleashing of that which had employed it as a vessel. Within the swirling black cloud, that darkness that was deeper than the natural gloom of the crypt, Kessler could see a shape, a shape that had haunted his dreams. It was the black outline of a hooded skull, the same hideous sending that had destroyed Carlinda.

The two men staggered back from the sending, their breath an icy mist that froze in their lungs. They could see tendrils of darkness, like a legion of shadowy worms, dripping from the thing. In the blink of an eye, an entire carpet of spectral maggots was writhing on the floor. The men watched in awed silence as the maggots began to spread, sinking into the numberless fragments of bone littering the floor.

As the bones absorbed the shadow-worms, they began to jump and shudder. Some began to lift into the air, forming into little whirlwinds of shattered bone. Faster and faster the whirlwinds grew, larger and larger as more of the litter was infected by the sending. Even the fragments beneath their feet began to move. Valdner gripped Kessler's shoulder.

'We need to get out of here,' the mercenary swore. The whirlwinds were joining into a cyclone, the shards of bone spinning ever faster in a tempest of darkness. Some fragments would rip free, streaking across the tomb at incredible velocity, gouging into the walls of the crypt. Valdner did not want to consider their terrible power against mortal flesh.

The men turned and ran. Skanir had already withdrawn to the doorway, his face a crimson mask from the cut in his forehead. Raban and Skanir shouted desperately to their friends, encouraging them to hurry. Neither man looked back to see the source of their fear, it was enough to see it in their faces. Once, Valdner staggered as a shard of bone punched through him, slicing through his armour as easily as a knife through cheese. Kessler caught him before he could fall, pulling the man along as the tomb behind them became a raging maelstrom.

It seemed they would never reach the beckoning figures at the doorway. More shards of bone struck them as they ran, opening Kessler's cheek and stabbing through the meat of his arm. Valdner's screams told how much greater was the toll on the mercenary. There was no chance to consider his suffering. It was all Kessler could do to keep moving. A flash of pain swept up his leg as a piece of bone punched through his thigh, another as his shoulder was shredded. Another man would have yielded to the pain, but Kessler charged on. As his master had told him so many times, he thrived on pain, and had never allowed it to overcome him.

Finally, hands were reaching out to Kessler, pulling Valdner from his shoulder and pushing both men through the door. Skanir and Raban hurriedly dragged the heavy metal doors closed. Shards of bone could be heard pattering against it, like rain against a windowpane.

The immediate danger over, Kessler sank to his knees, trying to rest his abused body. He began tearing strips from his shirt to bind his wounds, and then stopped as he saw Valdner lying against the wall. The mercenary was in poor shape, his body coated in blood. Kessler winced as he saw the enormity of his wounds, trying to determine where he could even start tending the man.

Valdner's eyes blinked open and he smiled at Kessler, trying to force a laugh from his tortured frame.

'Next time you go on a treasure hunt,' Valdner wheezed, 'don't invite me.' The mercenary brought his arm around. Despite the punishment he had endured, his hand still clutched the jewelled hilt of the runefang. 'This one was more than enough trouble.'

'So that's it,' someone said, with a sharp whistle. Kessler spun around, seeing the other occupants of the antechamber for the first time. Theodo came creeping forward, his steps awkward and pained, one hand still clutched to his side. Whatever weakness there was in his body, none of it showed in the halfling's eyes. Kessler could imagine him already trying to calculate the value of the relic. It was just as well the halfling hadn't been around to hear Rambrecht's offer.

'Grudge Settler,' Kessler agreed, 'the salvation of the realm: Zonbinzahn.'

Theodo nodded his head appreciatively, acknowledging the blade's value beyond monetary wealth. Behind him, crouched in a heap against the wall, Ghrum managed an impressed grunt.

'It's the runefang,' Skanir interrupted. He'd tied a bandage around his head, the blood-soaked cloth looking incongruous with his wild mane of beard. 'I'm not so certain it is Zonbinzahn, "Sun-Tooth".' The dwarf nodded grimly at the looks of horror his remark evoked. He stabbed a thumb at the doors behind him, at the image of King Fallowbeard. 'Remember, that's an axe he's holding. Now if I recall, some of the old runes–'

'Excuse me,' Theodo piped in. 'I do hope the lecture can wait. While Ghrum and I were catching our breath out here, some scruffy looking fellows ran past us.' He jabbed a thumb at the tunnel. 'Not too long after that, we heard them doing a fair bit of screaming.'

'The Averlander's scum,' Raban snorted. 'They must have run into some of the old traps.'

'Ever hear of a trap laughing at you while you died?' Theodo protested.

Valdner managed to rise from the ground, staring at the black mouth of the passage. 'That answers the question of who won the fight, the orcs or the hydra.'

'Maybe they're in as bad shape as we are,' Kessler said. The suggestion didn't seem to encourage anyone. Slowly, painfully, he picked up his sword from the floor, sending fresh flashes of protest from his muscles. 'I didn't think so either.'

THEY FORMED A ragged battleline at the mouth of the tunnel. Too injured to fight, Valdner was propped against the far wall, Theodo trying his best to stitch the worst of the man's wounds. Unable even to stand in the antechamber, Ghrum likewise crouched against one wall, a look of terrible frustration on the ogre's heavy features. To be left out of a good fight was about the worst thing that could happen to an ogre, beside the dreaded curse of 'half rations'. With few illusions as to their chances, Kessler, Raban and Skanir waited for the orcs.

A sharp bang punctuated by snorts of gruff laughter told them when the orcs had reached the goblin pressure traps. The tension in the antechamber grew as sharp as a knife, sweat dripping from the faces of the waiting men. A few moments later, the first of the orcs rounded the corner of the corridor. A huge bull with curling tusks and a breastplate of bronze, the brute came hurtling down the corridor. Raban met the monster's charge, chopping at it with his axe. The blade crunched into the orc's shoulder, the strength behind the blow forcing the monster to its knees. Skanir brought his hammer cracking around, smashing into the side of the brute's skull. Kessler slashed his greatsword into its arm, for good measure, nearly ripping it from the orc's shoulder. The mangled orc slumped to the ground, shuddering as its tiny brain came around to the reality that it was dead.

Snarls and bellows echoed from the tunnel, a series of savage grunts that were almost precise enough to be called speech. Skanir motioned for them to back away from the entrance to the passage. Clearly the first orc had been used by its fellows to clear any traps ahead. Finding enemies, the brute had been overcome by its natural viciousness and had attacked without waiting for the rest. Even so, its death had warned the others.

The men waited while hulking shapes stomped down the passage, their steps more cautious than the blind charge of their scout. Catching the scent of blood, the guttural snarls began again. A barking growl was followed by relative quiet.

'It's the warlord,' Skanir whispered, 'six or seven others with him.'

'You can tell what they're saying?' Kessler marvelled.

Skanir shrugged. 'Kill enough of them and you pick a few things up. This lot wants to rush in and kill us, but their boss isn't sure how many of us are left. It seems he's got bigger ideas than just stirring up a fight.'

A gruff voice snarled out from the depths of the tunnel, though Kessler would have sworn it was the bark of some beast rather than anything truly intelligible. Skanir's face grew drawn as the dwarf struggled to concentrate on the primitive speech, trying to work his mind around the unpleasant task of making sense from the violent growls of an orc. When he did, all the light went out of his eyes. Kessler had never seen a face so resigned to death as that which Skanir turned to him. More than death, it was the look of someone who knows he has brought doom to everything he believes in, everything he loves.

'It's Uhrghul Skullcracker,' Skanir snarled, all the ancient hate of his race in his voice. 'He wants the runefang.'

'Give it to him,' Raban growled back. 'If he agrees to let us go.'

'He's offering us a quick death,' Skanir shot back. 'Besides, we can't let him have the sword. To you, it's the runefang, but to his kind it's something else. It's the Blade of the Ironclaw, a warlord so terrible that even the lowest goblin still remembers his name. With a talisman like that to rally the greenskins, Uhrghul can put together a war host the likes of which hasn't been seen in lifetimes.' Skanir clenched his fists tight around the haft of his hammer. 'We can't let him have the sword.'

Kessler looked away from the tunnel, at the sorry remainder of their company. 'I'm afraid there's not much we can do to keep it from him.'

'Then we do like Raban says,' Valdner said from where he lay against the wall. There was a sardonic humour in his eye as he watched the shocked faces of his comrades. 'We can't keep it from him, so let's give it to him.'

CAUTIOUSLY, THE ORCS came marching from the tunnel. Hulking masses of swollen muscle and lurking violence, their beady eyes squinted at the flickering torchlight. Powerful hands held axes and cleavers at the ready, fingers twitching in eagerness to spill blood and butcher flesh. The greenskins gave voice to barking bursts of laughter when they saw the sorry condition of the men who had thought to oppose them. Only their leader, the dark-skinned beast that was Uhrghul remained on edge. The voice that had called back to him had been that of a dwarf. He had enough respect for the tough, foul-tasting stunties to know that they never gave up easily. They knew enough to understand that dying was better than giving up, it was the one reason he respected them. Still, they could be as tricky as an old goblin if pressed into a corner. This one had certainly been pressed into a corner with nothing but a few dying men and a wounded ogre to keep him company.

Uhrghul had given his warriors strict orders not to kill anything until he had the sword. After that they could start working off their frustration from traversing the trap-riddled length of the tunnel. Until then, the warlord wanted to puzzle over what kind of trick the dwarf had up his sleeve. Maybe he'd cut off an arm and have a look.

A sharp whistle drew Uhrghul's attention to a little figure standing beside a pair of massive iron doors. It looked like a young human, but Uhrghul gave that fact sparse attention, his eyes riveted to the heavy blade that the little thing was struggling to hold. The creature yapped at him in the snooty language of the humans. Uhrghul didn't understand the meaning of the words, he didn't know that they were 'If you want it, come and get it!' He only knew that the little creature tugged open one of the doors and dashed inside, taking the sword with him.

The warlord had enough sense to recognise a trap when he saw one, even if he didn't understand how it worked. His warriors, however, had displayed their inability to do the same quite eloquently in the tunnel, leaving half a dozen of their comrades scattered through the corridors. Unfortunately, they knew full well what Uhrghul was looking for and why. Each one harboured ambitions, each one imagined itself as war-lord of a mighty waaagh. As they saw the halfling dash through the door, carrying the runefang, every one of them gave voice to a savage cry. Thoughts of slaughter and ambition were forgotten as they charged the door, bursting through it and into the tomb beyond.

Cursing, Uhrghul rushed after his greedy warriors, his arrogance refusing to allow another orc to claim what he had already decided belonged to him. He under-stood there was some sort of trap at work, but he trusted that his faithless warriors would bear the brunt of it, leaving an open field for him to recover the sword.

As Uhrghul charged through the doors, they slammed closed behind him. Ghrum pressed his entire bulk against the panels, blocking them against retreat. The howls of the monsters as the tempest of swirling bone tore into them reached the ogre as a faint murmur.

'The runefang,' Kessler cursed. He took a step towards the door, but Skanir held him back.

'It was lost to us either way. Now, at least, the orcs won't have it.' Skanir stroked dried blood from his beard, staring again at the door. 'I didn't think the little fellow had it in him. He's bought us all our lives.'

Kessler turned reluctantly from the door. 'Maybe, but that won't help save Wissenland.'

'One battle at a time, Kessler,' Valdner said. Raban all but carried his captain as they started towards the tun-nel. 'For now, I'll be content with an open sky over my head. The ugly thing about tombs is that you never know how long you'll be staying in them.'

CHAPTER TWENTY-THREE

VULTURES SCATTERED INTO the air, croaking their displeasure at the men who emerged from the black opening of the war-crypt. The birds did not fly far, but found perches on the rocks. As Kessler hobbled out of the gloom of the crypt, he felt their hungry, expectant eyes on him. The swordsman staggered on, until his weary feet carried him to a large rock that had been torn loose from the cliff, one of the few spaces not littered with the bodies of men and orcs. Raban helped Valdner limp across the plateau to where Kessler was sitting. The injured mercenary grimaced as the Nordlander lowered him to the ground, cursing foully as a wound in his back began to bleed again. He waved away Raban's efforts to staunch the flow.

'Soon enough they'll have something else to pick clean,' Valdner commented. The boldest of the vultures had already descended back to the plateau, tearing at the mangled bodies that coated the ground. Raban threw a rock at the nearest bird. The vulture hopped away from the breast of a soldier, settling on an orc's back. It watched Raban with its glassy eyes, and then began to rip at the greenskin's bloodied flesh.

'Maybe you should have taken the Averlander's offer,' Kessler said. The swordsman nodded his head sadly. 'At least then the runefang might not have been lost.'

Valdner stared hard at Kessler. 'There are some things more important than gold, even to a mercenary. I lost men because of the Averlander's treachery, good men who had fought beside me for many years. There is a rough sort of honour that even sell-swords abide by. More than the bonds of loyalty and honour, however, there was the question of blood. Ever since Fritzstadt, I've been bound to your quest by ties older and stronger than your own. Ernst, the Baron von Rabwald, was my brother.

'Half-brother would be more precise,' Valdner continued before Kessler could react to the revelation. 'Ernst's mother, the baroness, was always a frigid, domineering woman. After producing an heir to the title, she considered her wifely duties at an end. Our father, the old baron, took a mistress to warm the bed his wife shunned. When she bore him a son, the baron raised the child with all the consideration and care with which he indulged his legitimate heir. I was raised very much as Ernst's equal in every matter and as we grew up, I became his closest friend and confidant. Of course, the baroness resented my presence, but she could never prevail upon my father to send me away.

'It was when the baron was killed hunting wolves during the winter of my twelfth year that my life came crashing down. The baron was scarcely in the ground before his wife sent my mother and me away. Over the years, Ernst would conspire to send money to us, allowing us to sustain ourselves. When my mother died some years later, Ernst invited me back to Rabwald, despite his mother's wishes. Ernst's intentions were good, but I knew there was nothing for me in Rabwald, so I enlisted with a mercenary company. The training and education I had received while my father was alive allowed me to prosper in the profession. Eventually, as you know, I became captain of my own command.'

As Valdner gave voice to his memories, a bitter melancholy grew within him, and a glaze came across his eyes. No longer did they stare at Kessler. What they focused upon were the phantoms of dead yesterdays and lost tomorrows. 'I wanted to reclaim the runefang more than you could understand,' he said at last. 'I wanted to bring it back to old gold-grubbing Count Eberfeld and say, "Here, here is the salvation of your land, bought with the blood of Baron von Rabwald. Baron von Rabwald, who was a better man than you." I would do that to honour my brother, to enshrine his name in the lore of our land. I would have made the people of Wissenland remember him into the days of their grandchildren!'

The emotion taxed Valdner, and he slumped back against the side of the rock, fingers closing a little tighter around the worst of his wounds. 'At least that is what I would have done had we captured the prize,' he sighed.

'No good to mourn the lost,' Raban commented. The hairy Nordlander paced among the dead, closing the dead eyes of men and kicking the stiffening bodies of orcs. 'The runefang is as gone as your brother. It is certain death to go back into that tomb. Only a mad man would dare to challenge whatever fell sorcery infests it.'

Kessler struck his knee in desolate frustration. 'Then there is no way to stop Zahaak,' he cursed. 'Wissenland will burn, its people put to the sword, because of my failure!'

'Unless you don't need the sword.'

Kessler spun around, staring in perplexity at Skanir. While the men had made haste to put as much distance between themselves and the forbidding crypt as possible, the dwarf had lingered behind. The swordsman had thought that perhaps he had been trying to reason with Ghrum, to convince the ogre to leave the antechamber. The ogre had resisted Kessler's efforts to make him see reason, stubbornly determined to hold the doors of the tomb closed against the orcs while at the same time insisting that he would wait for his friend Theodo. How the halfling would survive the maelstrom of black sorcery and flying bone, or how he would get through the doors that Ghrum was keeping closed, were questions that the ogre was unwilling to set his mind to considering.

Skanir, it seemed, had not stayed behind in the antechamber for long. Now, he was perched atop a pile of rubble, inspecting the runes carved into the archway above the war-crypt's entrance. His stumpy hands brushed against the stone in subdued reverence. He motioned for Kessler to come and see what he had discovered.

'It's been bothering me,' Skanir said, 'looking for a sword when King Isen Fallowbeard is clearly depicted wielding an axe against Zahaak. The dwarf wasn't born who would make that kind of mistake on the ornament of a king's tomb! So I decided to look closer. I couldn't make out enough on the doors in the antechamber, but I can read enough of the runes here to tell you that what we were looking for isn't the runefang. It never was.'

A strange mix of alarm and hope made Kessler sprint towards the dwarf. 'What are you talking about?' he demanded. Skanir didn't seem to hear him. A broad smile spread beneath his blood-stained beard. He jabbed a thumb at Kessler's chest.

'It looks like you picked up some souvenirs down in the tomb,' Skanir laughed. Puzzled, Kessler looked down at his body. Caught in the buckles of his armour were several strands of thin chain and crumbling leather. Tiny talismans, finger bones, old coins and bleached fangs, were attached to the strands. Kessler remembered the crude totems the orcs had fixed to the runefang's hilt. He remembered the struggle with Rambrecht, when the sword and its trophies had been pressing against his chest. The talismans must have torn off when Rambrecht wrested the runefang free.

Then Kessler's eyes were locked on one talisman in particular. It was a curved, crescent-shaped bit of stone, polished to impossible smoothness, deep grey in colour, but streaked with vivid veins of gold. Kessler did not even try to imagine the skill it had taken to carve the single rune the stone bore, to capture that radiant, sun-burst image so that its every curve was displayed in the vibrant gold, native to the stone. He was too busy staring at it, drawn into the masterless craftsmanship and the aura of power and antiquity that clung to it. As he touched the stone, he felt the faintest echo of the sensation he had experienced in the tomb, just before Gordreg Throatripper had risen from his throne. He sensed that some terrible force was connected to the stone, but that the force was spent, at least for the moment. Whatever menace was attached to the stone, for now, it lacked the power to strike.

It was an effort for Kessler to lift his eyes from the stone in his hand, to look again at Skanir's grinning face. The dwarf's thumb was pressed against the figures carved into the archway. Kessler saw again the sinister aspect of Zahaak, and the heroic Isen Fallowbeard opposing him. There was the great axe in the king's hand, and dangling from the haft of the axe a curved, fang-like object. Kessler's eyes were wide with wonder as he looked again at the stone in his hand.

'Zonbinzahn,' Skanir nodded, 'the Sun-Tooth. Alaric carved it, sure enough, but it wasn't one of your rune-fangs. It was a war-rune, a talisman to increase the power of an already mighty weapon. The art of crafting such powerful relics was all but lost even in Alaric's day. He must have used one of the elder runes to craft the Sun-Tooth, runes of such power that no runesmith dares carve them more than once in his life. That was the power he gave King Isen Fallowbeard to wield against Zahaak Kinslayer!'

After the misery of such defeat, Kessler could barely dare to hope that Skanir was right. The thing he held in his hand, the small smooth stone, could it really hold the power to destroy Zahaak? He thought again of the dread apparition that had appeared in the tomb. Zahaak's sending, a spectral vessel of the wight lord's wrath. Had it been to stop him from escaping with the runefang, or the little smooth stone that old Gordreg had fitted to its hilt?

Then it struck Kessler. The smooth, crescent-shaped stone, with its bright, sun-burst rune! The Sun-Tooth! A stone shaped like a fang, its surface pitted by a single rune! Their quest had indeed been to find a rune-fang, but not *the* runefang! What strange caprices of fate had caused both relics to become intertwined, so that hunting for one brought them to the other? What equally malicious twists of fortune had caused Grudge Settler to be lost again in the very moment of its finding?

Kessler might have laughed, but looking away from the Sun-Tooth, his eyes found something that killed his humour. A shadow, huge and bestial, loomed up from the steps of the war-crypt. It took a step into the light, blood dripping from dozens of gaping wounds, armour hanging in ragged strips from its tattered body. A single, beady eye glowered in hate and rage, while a torn jaw snapped open in a snarl of fury.

Before Kessler could shout a warning, the orc's axe was in motion, slashing out in a butchering arc. The blade caught Skanir just below the waist, hurling the dwarf from his perch on the rocks. Skanir crashed into a gory heap, one leg folding beneath him at an obscene angle. The orc barked a grisly laugh and stomped out of the shadow of the archway. Through the ragged, dripping wounds that peppered the monster's body, Kessler could see the gleam of bone, and the wet shine of pulsing organs. How the monster had escaped the sorcerous death trap that infested the tomb, Kessler could not guess, but only the savage, stubborn vitality of an orc kept it standing.

The swordsman quickly stuffed the Sun-Tooth down the breast of his tunic and pulled his greatsword from its sheath. Mangled as he was, Uhrghul Skullcracker managed to twist his face into a brutal sneer. The orc had not failed to hear the sigh of exhaustion, or see the look of strain as Kessler's weary muscles rebelled against him. He snickered again as he saw Valdner struggling to rise.

Raban's axe nearly chopped the sneer from the orc's face. At the last instant, the brute staggered back, catching with his shoulder a blow that was meant for his skull. The Nordlander's weapon bit deep into Uhrghul's flesh, crunching into the bone beneath. The orc howled in pain, closing a fist around the haft of the man's axe. Raban twisted his body, trying to free his weapon from the monster's inhuman strength. Uhrghul struggled in turn to swing his weapon around and bury it in his enemy's back. A deadly dance ensued, Raban striving to free his weapon while the orc tried vainly to turn him within reach of his own blade.

Summoning such strength as he had left, Kessler rushed to Raban's aid. Uhrghul caught the flicker of motion from the corner of his eye. Roaring like a trapped bear, the orc swung around to answer this new challenge. The violence of the motion caused Raban's axe to tear free, taking much of the orc's shoulder with it. The warlord bellowed again at the incredible pain. Halfway through his turn, Uhrghul spun back around on Raban. Unbalanced by the freeing of his axe, the mercenary was unprepared when the orc barrelled into him. Uhrghul's powerful jaw snapped shut around Raban's face, the knife-like tusks stabbing through his flesh. The mercenary's scream boomed across the canyon as Uhrghul wrenched his head back, ripping away most of the man's cheek and nose.

Kessler hacked at Uhrghul with his zweihander, severing the brute's already mangled arm. The orc, lost to his bloodlust, didn't pay the injury any notice. Towering above the screaming wreck of Raban, he brought his axe chopping down in a crimson arc, cleaving skull and breastbone, leaving the blade buried in the man's gut.

Kessler chopped at the monster again, scraping his sword across the orc's ribs. Dark blood spurted from the fresh wound. Uhrghul abandoned his axe, rounding on Kessler with a clenched fist. The mallet-like fist cracked against the man's chest, kicking him back. The zwei-hander clattered across the plateau as Kessler crashed to earth. The swordsman forced himself to his feet, taking a perverse strength from the flash of fresh agony that spoke of broken ribs.

Uhrghul dipped fingers into the fresh wound in his side, sniffing the dark blood that stained them. The orc knew he was dying, that fight as much as he would, there was noth-ing he could do to stave off the icy hand of death. The understanding simply made him more ferocious, more determined to glut the murderous malice that burned in his heart. Kessler tasted blood in his mouth, and felt the damaged ribs grinding together as he moved. He saw Vald-ner, unable to stand, and Skanir reduced to a twitching pile of debris. Even dying, the orc would outlast them all.

For the second time, a shadow loomed large at the mouth of the crypt. This time, the apparition held no terror for Kessler. It was his turn to sneer at the orc. Uhrghul's beady eye narrowed with suspicion as some of the warlord's old cunning fought through the red haze of slaughter. He turned in time to see Ghrum's immense arm come crashing down, slamming into the orc with the awesome power of a battering ram. If a sin-gle bone was left unbroken by that impact, Kessler would have been amazed. Uhrghul seemed to fold around the ogre's fist, collapsing like a punctured blad-der. The orc's body flew through the air as though shot from one of Skanir's cannons. It crashed among the dead, bounced high, and then plummeted off the edge of the plateau. Kessler could faintly hear the clatter of its descent to the canyon below.

Ghrum's face was contorted with pain and fatigue, yet there was a suggestion of guilt in the ogre's eyes as he looked at Kessler.

'Sorry,' Ghrum apologised in his slow, gruff tones. 'One got out.'

'You HAVE TO get the Sun-Tooth back to your people. We must finish the job we set out to do and send Zahaak back to his grave.' The words came in a frail whisper from Skanir's bloodied lips. The blow he had suffered from the orc had been worse than Kessler had dared imagine. One leg had been almost ripped clean from its socket. The blood bubbling up from the dwarf's mouth spoke of other, perhaps no less horrendous, internal injuries. He was dying, but like the orc, he was too stubborn to easily accept the fact. Kneeling beside him, Kessler could not fail to be impressed by the tragic dignity with which the dwarf struggled to keep his grip on life.

'Tell my people how I died,' Skanir persisted. 'Warn them where Ironclaw's sword was found. Let them put my name in the clan's book of grudges, that all the Durgrunds, all the generations that bear the name of Stonehammer, will know how Skanir Stonehammer found his doom.'

Kessler nodded solemnly to the dying dwarf. He felt the once-powerful grip around his fingers grow slack. When he looked again, the light had passed from Skanir's eyes.

'You're going to do what he told you.'

Kessler rose and faced Valdner. The mercenary was still leaning against the stone that Raban had set him against. The dark pool that surrounded him hadn't been there before they'd emerged from the crypt. Valdner didn't make a question of it, not even a statement. Despite the weakness in his voice, Kessler knew that it was a command.

The swordsman made no move, studying Valdner with an inscrutable gaze. Something inside him was repulsed by the suggestion. He'd killed many men, and seen many others die. He thought he was too old a comrade of death to ever rail against its approach. Now, however, the old acceptance felt hollow, indecent even.

'Ever think maybe we don't want you gawking at us while we're busy dying?' Kessler turned his head, looking down at Theodo's battered, bloodied body. When Ghrum had emerged from the war-crypt, it had taken Kessler several minutes to realise that the gore-soaked rag he was carrying was the halfling. That there was still any life in the rogue was even harder to believe.

Kessler stared, his face mask-like. There was something obscene about leaving the men here, abandoning them to the doubtful mercy of the mountain.

Valdner shifted uneasily, wincing with the effort. 'Staying here won't accomplish a thing, Max, but if you leave now, you might be able to get that dwarf gewgaw to Count Eberfeld while it can still do some good.' He smiled and closed his eyes. 'Get back to Wissenland while there's something to save.'

Kessler stood silent, hating the sense Valdner's words made. 'I'll come back,' he promised, loathing how empty the words sounded, even to him.

'Bring some decent brandy if you do,' quipped Theodo. Ghrum's belly growled in sympathy to what he thought was a request for food.

'A few courtesans with low standards and loose morals wouldn't be turned away either,' Valdner added. The effort of laughing caused the pool around him to widen.

Kessler nodded respectfully to the fading captain. Slinging his zweihander over his shoulder, the swordsman turned away, marching stoically down the twisting slope to the canyon below.

CHAPTER TWENTY-FOUR

FROM A HILLTOP overlooking Wissenberg, Count Eberfeld watched as his city was slowly surrounded. The unearthly shroud of fog that surrounded the legion gleamed weirdly in the moonlit night, like a great cloud crushed to the ground and bound to the earth. The fog bank was larger than the count remembered it from Neuwald. He did not like to think why it had to be so, did not like to ponder the hideous fact that it had to expand, because there was more for it to hide from the sun.

The sacrifice made by General Hock and the people of Dortrecht had given Count Eberfeld desperately needed time. Wissenberg was already a ghost town, its people evacuated to other settlements along the river, towns too recently built to figure in Zahaak's ancient battle plan. The only men still within the city were soldiers, fighting men drawn from the length and breadth of

Wissenland, tasked with holding the walls of the city at all cost. Count Eberfeld's strategy depended on those walls holding, and remaining in friendly hands.

Earlier battles against Zahaak had failed, because they had been fought against the skeletal horrors that made up his legion. Hard-earned experience had shown that such efforts were futile, like draining the sea with a thimble. Only the most grievously mutilated bodies were not raised again to unholy life by Zahaak's necromancy, and they were easily replaced by the mounds of Wissenlanders killed fighting against the wight lord.

Now Count Eberfeld intended to strike at the heart of the undead legion, the one element of that ghastly host that could not be resurrected by Zahaak's fell magic: the wight himself. The count let his hand fall to Blood Bringer, the sword that was the companion of the blade that prophecy said could kill Zahaak, and which Baron von Rabwald had left to recover so long ago. The council of his advisors and nobles had prevailed against him throughout the campaign not to risk him or his runefang in battle, warning of the dire ruin that could result from such a loss. So, Count Eberfeld had sat back, sat and planned, sat and let others fight his battles.

He had sat while his realm died around him.

Count Eberfeld glared at the glowing fog, at the shadowy wraiths that marched inexorably towards the walls of his city. No more. He had reached that decision when Dortrecht had fallen. He would not let his advisors hold him back any longer. If he did nothing, Wissenland was lost anyway. His ownership of Blood Bringer would mean nothing if the land it was sworn to protect became a graveyard. Wissenberg might be the last objective of Zahaak's old battle plan to destroy the Merogens, but who could say that the wight would not devise a new campaign once that task had been accomplished. The wight might just as easily turn his legion against all that had been built since the time of Sigmar as be content with the destruction he had already wrought.

A small cluster of officers stood with their count, beneath the shade of his pavilion, watching the play of emotion cross their sovereign's face. At length, through the morass of anger, guilt and shame emerged the emotion that the officers had waited for. An icy mask of grim determination overcame Count Eberfeld's face. He looked away from the walls of Wissenberg and the doom that marched steadily upon them. Zahaak would never breach those walls, instead the wight's legion would be broken upon them.

The count stood next to an oak table, its surface covered by a sprawling map of Wissenberg and its immediate environs. He could see every detail recorded in painstaking care; even the position of his encampment, his soldiers' tents, and his knights' stables had been marked. It had taken excruciating patience to watch and wait for the entire legion to close upon Wissenberg, for every last wisp of its spectral fog to fall within the landscape recorded on the map. Perhaps the hardest thing he had been forced to do in the course of the entire campaign was to let the spectre of destruction march right up to the walls of his city while he sat by and did nothing. This time, however, his restraint promised rewards.

Count Eberfeld nodded to the dark, soberly clad figure that stood beyond the table. Father Vadian of the Cult of Morr bowed in return. The old priest produced a strange silver pendant from within his robes. A small arrowhead was fitted to one end of the chain, the other end attached to a silver ring, which the priest slipped around his finger. He stretched his hand carefully over the map, so that the arrowhead swung idly above it. Closing his eyes, Father Vadian began to chant, the tones low and whisper-thin, like the rustle of leaves across a grave. Again, Count Eberfeld experienced the clammy, unearthly cold that heralded the power of Morr.

The pendulum hanging from Father Vadian's hand began to swing, slowly at first, and then with rapidly increasing revolutions. Wider and wider the circling arrowhead spun, dancing above the map with a frantic energy of its own. The priest's ritual increased in tempo and speed in time to the spinning pendulum. It moved faster and faster, becoming a silver blur to the men watching its revolutions with anxious eyes. Mouthing the words quicker and quicker, the priest's voice threatened to crack from the strain of forcing the prayers from his lips.

At last, the pendulum froze, the chain standing rigid above the map, thrust at a gravity defying angle as the arrowhead stabbed downward. Count Eberfeld and his officers rushed forward as Father Vadian's voice faded away. Their awed faces stared down at the spot the pendulum had chosen, almost unwilling to believe what they saw. Count Eberfeld decided them, tapping the spot with his finger.

'This is where he is,' the count stated. 'This is where we must strike. Mark the position well, men. We must throw everything we have into the effort. I don't care how many ranks of rotting nightmares that fiend puts against us, we must break through! If it costs every man in this camp, Zahaak must be destroyed!'

The count's words brooked no question, no challenge. His officers knew what was at stake. They knew that they would probably die in the attempt to save their land, but they also knew that their sovereign was not sparing himself from the same danger, not trying to escape from the same fate. That knowledge, more than anything else, steeled their hearts to the desperate gambit. If every man in their army had to die, their lives would be well spent wiping Zahaak's evil from the land.

The officers saluted and hurried to ready their regiments. Count Eberfeld stared hard at the map, imagining what carnage lay between him and the hideous wight lord. He wondered if this was how Count Eldred, last lord of Solland, had felt as he waited for the gates of Pfeildorf to break and for Gorbad Iron-claw to sweep his city into the dust. No, Eldred's stand had been one of defiance, a hopeless fight that was lost before it had begun. Here, at least, the illusion of victory, the ghost of a desperate hope, reached out to Eberfeld. Only if he dared to grab that intangible hand would he know if it was a thing of substance or simply a phantom of his own despair.

Count Eberfeld turned from the table. He would be leading the Sablebacks in the coming charge, and there was much to make ready before the attack could begin.

'Wait, your excellency,' Father Vadian said, his raspy voice arresting the count as he began to leave. Count Eberfeld gave the old priest a questioning, impatient stare. Vadian held up a pallid finger. 'You cannot ride yet against Zahaak the Worm,' Vadian warned. He saw the count direct a horrified look at the map stretched across the table. 'He is where the pendulum said he would be,' Vadian assured him, 'but you must wait. Ride against him now, and you throw away not only your own life, but those of all Wissenlanders.'

The count scowled at the priest's words. He had heard too many similar arguments in the past weeks. He had no mind to listen to another one. If Zahaak was not destroyed, there was no Wissenland to throw away. He turned to leave, not even deigning to argue with Vadian.

'No, your excellency!' Vadian shouted. 'You must wait!'

Eberfeld rounded on the pleading priest, his scowl turning into a snarl. 'Wait for what, bone-keeper?' he demanded.

Before Vadian could reply, a soldier in the livery of the count's household appeared at the door of the tent. Both men turned and faced the trooper. Long in the count's service, the man did not question the angry tone in his master's voice, nor the livid flush to his face. He merely bowed, doing his best to avert his eyes, fearing that some of the count's displeasure might be redirected towards him if he did not show proper deference.

'Excellency,' the soldier said, 'a messenger has ridden into camp, begging to speak to you. He says he is from Baron von Rabwald.'

The anger in Count Eberfeld's face was instantly replaced by shock. He turned to look at Father Vadian. The priest simply nodded his head.

'Speak with your guest,' Vadian told him. 'Then muster your courage. You will need it if you would send Zahaak's black spirit back to hell.'

By COLUMN AND rank, the grey and white uniforms of the Wissenland army surged from their encampment, closing upon the sinister mist billowing outside the walls of Wissenberg. Sergeants barked orders while priests raised their voices in prayers of protection, drawing upon the faith of the soldiers to steel their hearts against the supernatural horror that they were soon to confront. Halberds gleamed in the starlight, and spears rose above the massed ranks like a forest of steel. Swordsmen smacked the hilts of their blades against the bosses of their shields, producing a cadence of shuddering metal. Any mortal foe would find the sound terrifying. Against lifeless fiends it was made to reassure the soldiers and to fire them with the reminder of their numbers and strength.

The grim fog continued to drift towards Wissenberg, oblivious to the men marching towards it, like a raging lion ignoring the approach of an ant. Now the soldiers could see the shadowy figures beyond the veil, and could smell the corpse-reek of decaying flesh. Officers shouted commands, in their hundreds, calling upon discipline to keep their men going. The line faltered, and then surged forwards once more. Cries rang out from the foremost ranks as things emerged from the fog to confront them, festering husks of humanity with empty eyes and peeling faces. The crash of steel against bone echoed through the ranks. Battle had been joined.

Wissenland's captains shouted new orders, forcing their troops forward, driving them past the zombie scum and into the fog, into the lines of the legion proper. Flesh struggled against undead bone, and steel cracked against iron and bronze. Foot by bloody foot, the soldiers of Wissenland stabbed deeper and deeper into the fog, their thousands pitted against the legion's tens of thousands. The men fought with the ferocity of despair, cutting their way into the undead host.

Count Eberfeld watched from a hill as his infantry crashed into Zahaak's legion. The sounds and screams of battle drifted up to him, sending icy fingers of guilt burrowing through his heart. Every man who fell was a sacrifice, a sacrifice to buy him the chance that was their only hope. Killing a thousand, even ten thousand of the undead would not save Wissenberg. Force of arms could not win the day for them. Only the destruction of Zahaak would bring them victory.

The count tore his eyes away from the battle, watching instead the ghoulish mass of the fog. Slowly at first, and then with ever-increasing speed, it began to shift, sweeping outwards. Zahaak was addressing the attack on the legion's flank, moving to engulf the Wissenlanders. In doing so, the wight had thinned its lines, exposing the legion to an attack upon the opposite flank. Born in an age without cavalry, the wight consistently displayed an inability to appreciate the tactics of mounted warfare. Perhaps it could have reformed the ranks of its legion in time to thwart an infantry assault against the exposed flank, perhaps it had appreciated that the ground was too uneven for chariots. Whatever thoughts had whispered through its ghastly skull, Eberfeld was thankful that they had not moved Zahaak to defend against a cavalry charge.

Eberfeld looked at the riders gathered around him, almost a thousand strong: templars and knights, outriders and lancers, noblemen and warrior priests. Every man in the camp who had the skill and fire to fight from the back of a horse had been mustered into the count's command. The count prayed to any of the gods who cared to listen that he was not throwing away their lives. If they did not carry the day, if they did not strike Zahaak down, none of them would live to see another dawn.

The count looked again at the man who stood beside his horse. Father Vadian bowed his head in deference to Eberfeld's position and courage. The count paid the priest small notice, looking instead at the map he held and the silver pendulum poised above it. He fixed in his mind the spot that the pendulum had pointed to, the place where he would find Zahaak the Usurper. Then he turned in the saddle and faced his men. Blood Bringer rasped free from its scabbard and the count held it high above his head, letting all his fighting men see the rune-fang in his hand.

'For Wissenland!' the count roared, bringing his sword chopping down. Hooves thundered down the hillside as the riders charged towards the doom of their land.

BLOOD BRINGER CRASHED DOWN, smashing through the festering skull of something that might once have been a fisherman. Its broken husk crumpled, splintering beneath the flying hooves of Count Eberfeld's steed. Cries of rage and horror rose around him, ripping past the lips of his Sablebacks. The screams of horses tore at the night as the clutching claws and rusting spears of zombies dragged them down. The count could not say how many of his riders were still with him. He could not even tell if any of the other regiments were still keeping pace. All that mattered was the endless sea of rotting faces, the ghastly corpse legion with its empty eyes and decayed hands. There seemed to be no end to them, yet he knew there must be, there had to be. Somewhere beyond these horrors was the ultimate horror of Zahaak.

How many had already died? How many were even now dying to bring an end to that monster? Count Eberfeld thought of Baron von Rabwald and his men, lost and forgotten in the wilds where they had fallen. He thought of the man who had ridden so far to turn his phantom hope into a thing of substance. Max Kessler claimed to have killed five horses riding to reach Wissenberg, a journey that had brought him across the entire length of the province. The man had neglected his own hurts, ghastly wounds that would have crippled any lesser man. Kessler's determination exceeded even that of the count. Eberfeld was ready to die to try and save his land. Kessler had refused to die, forcing his body on when every fibre of his being must have called out to him to give in, to abandon the struggle and relent. Many of the wounds he had suffered were torn open by his fierce ride, others were alive with infection, oozing with pus and corruption. Even with such hurts, Kessler had violently warded away the attentions of surgeons and their leeches until after he had spoken with his sovereign, until he had given Count Eberfeld the key to destroying Zahaak.

It swung from the hilt of his runefang, the little crescent of rock with its spiral of gold. Count Eberfeld could feel its power, augmenting the ancient magics already bound within his blade. The undead hosts around him could feel it too, recoiling from him like slugs before a flame. He knew it was no effort of mortal valour that sped their passage through the lines of the legion, but the magical might of Blood Bringer and the talisman, the Sun-Tooth.

The Sablebacks plunged into a line of hoary skeleton warriors, their decayed husks encased in bronze scales, plumed helms rising from the grisly skulls. No mere zombies, no mindless skeletons, these things fought with a cruel semblance of life, a ghastly echo of mortal hatred. The blue blood of nobles gathered around the ancient warriors in puddles, as the fearless horrors hacked and stabbed at the charging horsemen. They did not quail before the power of the runefang as the lesser warriors of the legion had, but fought with a tenacity that Count Eberfeld would have called fanaticism in anything alive. His great courser was cut down beneath him, sinking to the earth with a bronze kopesh lodged in its belly. The count managed to free himself from the saddle as his horse dropped, slashing the skull from its killer before the fiend could recover its weapon.

Screams of horror sounded all around. Already tested to their utmost, the courage of his army began to crack. They had seen their champion, their leader, brought down, unaware that he had survived the slaughter of his steed. Count Eberfeld had been a living vessel of the hope of Wissenland, the only person in whom his people could place their trust and allegiance. With him gone, their discipline crumbled. Their ranks lost cohesion, and holes began to open in their lines. Fresh cries of terror sounded as the most ghastly of the legion's creatures galloped into those holes to butcher the enemies of their infernal master. The swirl of the melee did not close fast enough to spare Count Eberfeld the sight of his army being ridden down by the grisly knights of Nagash, the skeletal horrors that Zahaak had crafted from the once mighty Order of the Southern Sword.

The count's flesh turned to ice as the cold clutch of evil clawed at his heart. He turned away from the slaughter of his army to face the source of such pitiless malice. The bronze-armoured skeletons parted like wheat before a scythe. A tall spectre, girded in shadow and steel, strode between their silent, faceless ranks. A crimson cloak billowed around its shoulders, a hood drawn over its naked skull. Beneath the primordial evil that exuded from the being, Eberfeld could feel it gloating over him. This was the true enemy, the puppeteer behind the legion: Zahaak the Usurper, Zahaak the Worm.

Eberfeld tightened his grip on the hilt of Blood Bringer. He could sense Zahaak sneering at him. The wight stalked towards him, lifting its scythe-like staff. The man could feel the fell sorceries bound within the weapon grasping at him, stabbing at his soul with fingers of decay. He fought against the urge to throw himself down before the blade, to lift his neck and let the scythe take his head. It took all his strength to resist the suicidal compulsion, and the effort of his resistance pounded through his veins.

Such was the psychic duel that Eberfeld scarcely remembered the physical peril. While his spirit fought against the black sorcery, Zahaak stalked ever closer. The wight raised its staff. What would not be given could still be taken.

Less than a breath separated Count Eberfeld from death and damnation when, almost of its own accord, the runefang crashed against the descending staff. An electric pulse seared through Eberfeld's body, but he was rewarded to see the malevolent blade of the scythe shatter against Blood Bringer's burning edge. Zahaak staggered back under the violent exchange, its domineering self-assurance vanishing with its repulse. The sockets of the wight's skull smouldered with witchfire. At first, it stared at the count, and then its attention shifted to the blade he held.

Zahaak stepped away from the count, its unholy gaze locked not on the runefang but on the fang-like stone that swung from its hilt. The wight lord felt something it had thought never to know again, something that it had not felt since Black Nagash had taken from him that thing called ka, his very life essence.

It knew fear.

The wight had never expected to see the Sun-Tooth, the relic that had brought death to Zahaak, again. He had cast spells of terrible potency to ensure that it would not. However, Zahaak had not known how many centuries the Sun-Tooth had lain fixed to the hilt of Solland's stolen Grudge Settler. He had not understood the curious way its aura had mixed with that of the enchanted sword. Like the men who had hunted for it, Zahaak had confused Sun-Tooth and runefang, but where men had mistaken talisman for sword, Zahaak's sorcery had mistaken sword for talisman. The wight thought the Sun-Tooth was safely lost within Gordreg's tomb, yet here, impossibly, he faced it once more.

The wight continued to back away, exerting its will to motivate its numberless legion. The skeleton warriors did not move, frozen by the alien fear that tainted Zahaak's commands. Rage flared up within the monster, rage fuelled by royal pride. Claws splayed like knives, the wight flung itself at Eberfeld, determined to destroy the man who had forced it to know fear again.

Eberfeld swung the runefang at the lunging monster, the glowing blade smashing into the fiend's side. One steel talon slashed across Eberfeld's cheek, and then the ghastly wight lord was staggering, clutching at the wound in its side. Black serpents of midnight drooled from its ruptured side, striking the ground like oily worms, seeping into the earth. Zahaak struggled to rise again, but Eberfeld smashed the runefang down into the reeling monster. Through crimson hood and leprous skull, the magic steel cut its path, the stony crescent of the Sun-Tooth blazing with might. The sword cleaved through Zahaak's head, piercing socket and jaw. The witchfires withered and faded. A dry rattle hissed through the broken face. With a final shudder, the body collapsed to the ground, black scales crumbling into rust, the crimson cloak fraying into tatters, ancient bones turning to dust.

Count Eberfeld felt the monster's power vanish. All around him, the silent ranks of skeletons stood still, locked in the moment of their master's destruction. Then, like the body of Zahaak, they began to collapse, crumbling into a field of rust and bone. The eerie fog faded into nothingness, revealing the black tapestry of the starlit sky.

Where before only screams had risen, now cheers rose into the air, the joyous shouts of men redeemed from the brink of eternal horror. Eberfeld could see the survivors of his army picking their way among the dead, searching for their hero.

It would be some time yet before they found him. Count Eberfeld dropped to his knees, holding the runefang before him. Quietly, his voice solemn and subdued, he thanked the gods for his victory, and thanked the men who had given everything to save his land. They, not he, were the true heroes, the true saviours of Wissenland.

THROUGH THE LONG battle, Kessler fought to keep breath in his burning lungs. The efforts of the leeches and surgeons were useless. They could not even prolong his suffering, much less preserve his life. It did not bother him much. There was precious little to bind him to this world any longer. He was ready to die, but first he had to know. He had to know if it was victory or ruin.

Every second was agony, the poison of infection sizzling through his ravaged body, his failing strength draining from him with every drop of blood that oozed from his wounds. Kessler ground his teeth in a madman's grin, savouring the pain, letting it fill him. So long as there was pain, there was life. He would die, but not yet. Not yet. Not yet.

One of the surgeons, understanding the magnitude of Kessler's pain, raised a knife above the swordsman's head. Kessler saw the look in the surgeon's eye. Before the healer could strike, Kessler's hand was around his wrist, grinding the bones together. The healer cried out, the blade falling from nerveless fingers.

'Not yet,' Kessler growled, making certain that all around him knew his meaning. He almost smiled as he saw their awed fear, like an echo of the spectators who had watched him despatch the baron's enemies. They backed away, and Kessler knew that no other bold hand would rise against him.

A great cleansing wind rushed through the camp. The cloying reek of death was banished, and the nebulous clutch of ancient evil dissipated into the ether. Even the shadows of night seemed to become brighter, less filled with threat and malice. Kessler felt a surge of calm and peace wash over him, and he knew that the taint of Zahaak was being purged from the land. The Worm had been cast back into oblivion, and with him all the evil he had wrought. Only the scars would be left behind, the empty cities and the empty graves, and they would heal.

Kessler closed his eyes against the bright light that swelled within the hospital tent, but still the brilliance blinded him. For a moment, he struggled, and then, for the first time since goblins had cut his face from his body, Kessler no longer felt pain. He was dimly aware of something, something torn and mangled and putrid lying stretched below him. He could not remember what it was. As the light grew, he realised he didn't even care.

In the light, a smiling figure held her hands out to him, three tiny shapes clinging to her pale, slender legs.

He knew that he was gazing upon the Gates of Morr, where Carlinda had lingered to wait for him.

Her wait was over.

EPILOGUE

'I THINK I smell fresh air, Kopff!'

'You said that twenty smells ago, Schmitt,' growled the weasel-faced brigand's companion. Even in the pitch dark of the tunnels, Schmitt could see the disgusted sneer on Kopff's face.

'If we'd gone the way I said, we'd be out of here by now!' accused Schmitt. After deserting Rambrecht, the two men had tried to navigate their way back through the old goblin caves that they'd discovered in the rear of Gordreg's tomb. What they had hoped would be a quick, safe route to the surface had proven to be an apparently endless warren of twisting tunnels and blind corridors. The two bandits had been prowling the dark for weeks, living off cave-rats and other unmentionable squirming things, trying desperately to find some way back to sunlight.

'Stop your yapping!' Kopff ordered. 'If I hadn't led the way, we'd never have found our way back to the crypt and picked up this trinket.'

A greedy grin split the outlaw's face as he patted the jewelled sword thrust through the loop of his belt. In their blind rambling through the tunnels, the two bandits had rediscovered Godreg's tomb. The terrible necromancy that had raged through the chamber was spent by the time they came slinking back. Even thoughts of hunger had deserted the rogues as they pounced on the freshly slain dead littered around the crypt, looting the corpses of man and orc with equal abandon. It was during this frenzy of greed that Kopff had spotted the shine of the runefang's hilt, hidden behind a pile of rubble. The brigand lost no time in seizing the weapon and claiming it. He knew little enough about its pedigree, but he recognised that the richness of its decoration and manufacture would command a high price whatever market he found to dispose of it.

Kopff pulled himself from his avarice, eyes narrowing as they were drawn into the gloom of the tunnel. 'I think I see something!'

Kopff crept down the winding corridor, Schmitt close behind him. They'd seen no hint of goblins or orcs, but neither man wanted to press their luck too far. There was safety in numbers, or at least a chance that any monsters would strike after the other bandit.

Gradually, Kopff's claim of seeing light bore out, a faint glimmer shining from some crack in the mountain above the tunnel. The bandits grinned at the sight, rushing forward to wallow in the almost forgotten sunlight. In their haste, they paid little notice to the thick, cloying reptilian musk that washed over their other senses.

It was only the sound of something crunching beneath their boots that caused Kopff to pause. The bandit lifted his heels, trying to see what had broken beneath them. A sharp cry from Schmitt snapped him away from his inquiry.

Schmitt was scrambling away from something large and smelly lying in the centre of the corridor, right beneath the little ribbon of daylight shining down from the roof. Kopff thought his heart would stop as he recognised the scaly bulk of the hydra, as he discerned claws and heads among the sprawled mass. He drew the dusty steel of Grudge Settler from his belt, the runefang shivering in his trembling grip. He started to back away, thankful that Schmitt was between him and the beast.

'We've got to get out,' Schmitt gasped, trying to edge past Kopff, apparently having reached the same conclusion about keeping someone between him and the hydra. Kopff shoved him away, making a show of carefully studying the sprawled reptile.

'I think it's dead,' Kopff pronounced. Schmitt looked dubious.

'Maybe it's sleeping,' he objected.

'No, we'd hear it breathing,' Kopff decided. 'It's dead.' Schmitt's indecision began to show. Kopff gave him a shove towards the sprawling beast. Schmitt's boots crunched across the floor.

'Go make sure,' he told the weasel-faced brigand, bracing himself for a speedy retreat down the tunnel.

Boots crunching against the ground, Schmitt nervously approached the hydra. He reached a shaking hand out to the beast's flank, pressing his palm against the scaly hide. Clenching his eyes shut, he pushed against the monster. The reptile rolled beneath his touch, but the feared heads did not spring into life.

Schmitt opened his eyes and pushed again. The monster still refused to react. The bandit laughed as he looked at the hideous wounds gouged all over the brute's body. 'It's dead!'

'I told you it was dead,' Kopff scolded him, walking into the chamber. Again his boots crunched across the floor.

'What in the name of Khaine are we walking on?' he swore. He reached down and lifted a dull, greyish piece of what looked like broken pottery into the light. It took a minute for him to decide what the curved, roundish bit of debris was. When he did, Kopff's face was frozen in an expression of abject horror.

Schmitt looked away from his inspection of the dead hydra to find the other bandit still staring in terror at the weird object he held.

'What've you got there, Kopff?' he asked.

Kopff swallowed a knot of fear, looking slowly from the thing in his hand to Schmitt. 'Part... part of... an... eggshell.'

The stench of reptilian musk seemed to swell. The two men looked away from the dead body of the mother hydra, and away from the little circle of daylight. All around them was the unbroken darkness of the mountain. Within that darkness, dozens of cold, hungry eyes watched them, waiting for the light to vanish so that they might crawl out of the shadows to feed.

ABOUT THE AUTHOR

C. L. Werner has written a number of pulp-style horror stories for assorted small press publications, including *Inferno!* magazine. Currently living in the American south-west, he continues to write stories of mayhem and madness set in the Warhammer world.

BOOK ONE OF THE SIGMAR TRILOGY

ISBN 978-1-84416-538-4

Heldenhammer is the first in a ground-breaking new series bringing the history of the Warhammer world to life. This story tells how Sigmar rose to power, culminating in the Battle of Black Fire Pass.

Buy now from *www.blacklibrary.com* or download an extract for free!

Also available in all good bookshops and game stores